The
Fairy Tales of
Hans Christian Andersen

Illustrated by
Edna F. Hart

Printed on acid free ANSI archival quality paper.

ISBN: 978-1-78139-516-5

HANS CHRISTIAN ANDERSEN'S
FAIRY TALES

PREFACE

The Hans Andersen Fairy Tales will be read in schools and homes as long as there are children who love to read. As a story-teller for children the author has no rival in power to enlist the imagination and carry it along natural, healthful lines. The power of his tales to charm and elevate runs like a living thread through whatever he writes. In the two books in which they are here presented they have met the tests and held an undiminishing popularity among the best children's books. They are recognized as standards, and as juvenile writings come to be more carefully standardized, their place in permanent literature will grow wider and more secure. A few children's authors will be ranked among the Immortals, and Hans Andersen is one of them.

Denmark and Finland supplied the natural background for the quaint fancies and growing genius of their gifted son, who was story-teller, playwright, and poet in one. Love of nature, love of country, fellow-feeling with life in everything, and a wonderful gift for investing everything with life wrought together to produce in him a character whose spell is in all his writings. "The Story of My Life" is perhaps the most thrilling of all of them. Recognized in courts of kings and castles of nobles, he recited his little stories with the same simplicity by which he had made them familiar in cottages of the peasantry, and endeared himself alike to all who listened. These attributes, while they do not account for his genius, help us to unravel the charm of it. The simplest of the stories meet Ruskin's requirement for a child's story—they are sweet and sad.

From most writers who have contributed largely to children's literature only a few selected gems are likely to gain permanence. With Andersen the case is different. While there are such gems, the greater value lies in taking these stories as a type of literature and living in it a while, through the power of cumulative reading. It is not too much to say that there is a temper and spirit in Andersen which is all his own—a simple philosophy which continuous reading is sure to impart. For this reason these are good books for a child to own; an occasional re-reading will inspire in him a healthy, normal taste in reading. Many of the stories are of value to read to very young children. They guide an exuberant imagination along natural channels.

The text of the present edition is a reprint of an earlier one which was based upon a sentence-by-sentence comparison of the four or five translations current in Europe and America. It has been widely commended as enjoyable reading, while faithful to the letter and spirit of the Danish original. A slight abridgment has been made in two of the longer stories. The order of the selections adapts the reading to the growing child—the First Series should be sufficiently easy for children of about eight or nine years old.

J. H. STICKNEY

They danced merrily
... around the tree .

THE FIR TREE

AR away in the forest, where the warm sun and the fresh air made a sweet resting place, grew a pretty little fir tree. The situation was all that could be desired; and yet the tree was not happy, it wished so much to be like its tall companions, the pines and firs which grew around it.

The sun shone, and the soft air fluttered its leaves, and the little peasant children passed by, prattling merrily; but the fir tree did not heed them.

Sometimes the children would bring a large basket of raspberries or strawberries, wreathed on straws, and seat themselves near the fir tree, and say, "Is it not a pretty little tree?" which made it feel even more unhappy than before.

And yet all this while the tree grew a notch or joint taller every year, for by the number of joints in the stem of a fir tree we can discover its age.

Still, as it grew, it complained: "Oh! how I wish I were as tall as the other trees; then I would spread out my branches on every side, and my crown would overlook the wide world around. I should have the birds building their nests on my boughs, and when the wind blew, I should bow with stately dignity, like my tall companions."

So discontented was the tree, that it took no pleasure in the warm sunshine, the birds, or the rosy clouds that floated over it morning and evening.

Sometimes in winter, when the snow lay white and glittering on the ground, there was a little hare that would come springing along, and jump right over the little tree's head; then how mortified it would feel.

Two winters passed; and when the third arrived, the tree had grown so tall that the hare was obliged to run round it. Yet it remained unsatisfied and would exclaim: "Oh! to grow, to grow; if I could but keep on growing tall and old! There is nothing else worth caring for in the world."

In the autumn the woodcutters came, as usual, and cut down several of the tallest trees; and the young fir, which was now grown to a good, full height, shuddered as the noble trees fell to the earth with a crash.

After the branches were lopped off, the trunks looked so slender and bare that they could scarcely be recognized. Then they were placed, one upon another, upon wagons and drawn by horses out of the forest. Where could they be going? What would become of them? The young fir tree wished very much to know.

So in the spring, when the swallows and the storks came, it asked: "Do you know where those trees were taken? Did you meet them?"

The swallows knew nothing; but the stork, after a little reflection, nodded his head and said: "Yes, I think I do. As I flew from Egypt, I met several new ships, and they had fine masts that smelt like fir. These must have been the trees; and I assure you they were stately; they sailed right gloriously!"

"Oh, how I wish I were tall enough to go on the sea," said the fir tree. "Tell me what is this sea, and what does it look like?"

"It would take too much time to explain—a great deal too much," said the stork, flying quickly away.

"Rejoice in thy youth," said the sunbeam; "rejoice in thy fresh growth and in the young life that is in thee."

And the wind kissed the tree, and the dew watered it with tears, but the fir tree regarded them not.

Christmas time drew near, and many young trees were cut down, some that were even smaller and younger than the fir tree, who enjoyed neither rest nor peace for longing to leave its forest home. These young trees, which were chosen for their beauty, kept their branches, and they, also, were laid on wagons and drawn by horses far away out of the forest.

"Where are they going?" asked the fir tree. "They are not taller than I am; indeed, one is not so tall. And why do they keep all their branches? Where are they going?"

"We know, we know," sang the sparrows; "we have looked in at the windows of the houses in the town, and we know what is done with them. Oh! you cannot think what honor and glory they receive. They are dressed up in the most splendid manner. We have seen them standing in the middle of a warm room, and adorned with all sorts of beautiful things—honey cakes, gilded apples, playthings, and many hundreds of wax tapers."

"And then," asked the fir tree, trembling in all its branches, "and then what happens?"

"We did not see any more," said the sparrows; "but this was enough for us."

"I wonder whether anything so brilliant will ever happen to me," thought the fir tree. "It would be better even than crossing the sea. I long for it almost with pain. Oh, when will Christmas be here? I am now as tall and well grown as those which were taken away last year. O that I were now laid on the wagon, or standing in the warm room with all that brightness and splendor around me! Something better and more beautiful is to come after, or the trees would not be so decked out. Yes, what follows will be grander and more splendid. What can it be? I am weary with longing. I scarcely know what it is that I feel."

"Rejoice in our love," said the air and the sunlight. "Enjoy thine own bright life in the fresh air."

But the tree would not rejoice, though it grew taller every day, and winter and summer its dark-green foliage might be seen in the forest, while passers-by would say, "What a beautiful tree!"

A short time before the next Christmas the discontented fir tree was the first to fall. As the ax cut sharply through the stem and divided the pith, the tree fell with a groan to the earth, conscious of pain and faintness and forgetting all its dreams of happiness in sorrow at leaving its home in the forest. It knew that it should never again see its dear old companions the trees, nor the little bushes and many-colored flowers that had grown by its side; perhaps not even the birds. Nor was the journey at all pleasant.

The tree first recovered itself while being unpacked in the courtyard of a house, with several other trees; and it heard a man say: "We only want one, and this is the prettiest. This is beautiful!"

Then came two servants in grand livery and carried the fir tree into a large and beautiful apartment. Pictures hung on the walls, and near the tall tile stove stood great china vases with lions on the lids. There were rocking-chairs, silken sofas, and large tables covered with pictures; and there were books, and playthings that had cost a hundred times a hundred dollars—at least so said the children.

Then the fir tree was placed in a large tub full of sand—but green baize hung all round it so that no one could know it was a tub—and it stood on a very handsome carpet. Oh, how the fir tree trembled! What was going to happen to him now? Some young ladies came, and the servants helped them to adorn the tree.

On one branch they hung little bags cut out of colored paper, and each bag was filled with sweetmeats. From other branches hung gilded apples and walnuts, as if they had grown there; and above and all around were hundreds of red, blue, and white tapers, which were fastened upon the branches. Dolls, exactly like real men and women, were placed under the green leaves,—the tree had never seen such things before,—and at the very top was fastened a glittering star made of gold tinsel. Oh, it was very beautiful. "This evening," they all exclaimed, "how bright it will be!"

"O that the evening were come," thought the tree, "and the tapers lighted! Then I shall know what else is going to happen. Will the trees of the forest come to see me? Will the sparrows peep in at the windows, I wonder, as they fly? Shall I grow faster here than in the forest, and shall I keep on all these ornaments during summer and winter?" But guessing was of very little use. His back ached with trying, and this pain is as bad for a slender fir tree as headache is for us.

At last the tapers were lighted, and then what a glistening blaze of splendor the tree presented! It trembled so with joy in all its branches that one of the candles fell among the green leaves and burned some of them. "Help! help!" exclaimed the young ladies; but no harm was done, for they quickly extinguished the fire.

After this the tree tried not to tremble at all, though the fire frightened him, he was so anxious not to hurt any of the beautiful ornaments, even while their brilliancy dazzled him.

And now the folding doors were thrown open, and a troop of children rushed in as if they intended to upset the tree, and were followed more slowly by their elders. For a moment the little ones stood silent with astonishment, and then they shouted for joy till the room rang; and they danced merrily round the tree while one present after another was taken from it.

"What are they doing? What will happen next?" thought the tree. At last the candles burned down to the branches and were put out. Then the children received permission to plunder the tree.

Oh, how they rushed upon it! There was such a riot that the branches cracked, and had it not been fastened with the glistening star to the ceiling, it must have been thrown down.

Then the children danced about with their pretty toys, and no one noticed the tree except the children's maid, who came and peeped among the branches to see if an apple or a fig had been forgotten.

"A story, a story," cried the children, pulling a little fat man towards the tree.

"Now we shall be in the green shade," said the man as he seated himself under it, "and the tree will have the pleasure of hearing, also; but I shall only relate one story. What shall it be? Ivede-Avede or Humpty Dumpty, who fell downstairs, but soon got up again, and at last married a princess?"

"Ivede-Avede," cried some; "Humpty Dumpty," cried others; and there was a famous uproar. But the fir tree remained quite still and thought to himself: "Shall I have anything to do with all this? Ought I to make a noise, too?" but he had already amused them as much as they wished and they paid no attention to him.

Then the old man told them the story of Humpty Dumpty—how he fell downstairs, and was raised up again, and married a princess. And the children clapped their hands and cried, "Tell another, tell another," for they wanted to hear the story of Ivede-Avede; but this time they had only "Humpty Dumpty." After this the fir tree became quite silent and thoughtful. Never had the birds in the forest told such tales as that of Humpty Dumpty, who fell downstairs, and yet married a princess.

"Ah, yes! so it happens in the world," thought the fir tree. He believed it all, because it was related by such a pleasant man.

"Ah, well!" he thought, "who knows? Perhaps I may fall down, too, and marry a princess;" and he looked forward joyfully to the next evening, expecting to be again decked out with lights and playthings, gold and fruit. "To-morrow I will not tremble," thought he; "I will enjoy all my splendor, and I shall hear the story of Humpty Dumpty again, and perhaps of Ivede-Avede." And the tree remained quiet and thoughtful all night.

In the morning the servants and the housemaid came in. "Now," thought the fir tree, "all my splendor is going to begin again." But they dragged him out of the room and upstairs to the garret and threw him on the floor in a dark corner where no daylight shone, and there they left him. "What does this mean?" thought the tree. "What am I to do here?

I can hear nothing in a place like this;" and he leaned against the wall and thought and thought.

And he had time enough to think, for days and nights passed and no one came near him; and when at last somebody did come, it was only to push away some large boxes in a corner. So the tree was completely hidden from sight, as if it had never existed.

Threw him on the floor . . . . . and there they left him .

"It is winter now," thought the tree; "the ground is hard and covered with snow, so that people cannot plant me. I shall be sheltered here, I dare say, until spring comes. How thoughtful and kind everybody is to me! Still, I wish this place were not so dark and so dreadfully lonely, with not even a little hare to look at. How pleasant it was out in the forest while the snow lay on the ground, when the hare would run by, yes, and jump over me, too, although I did not like it then. Oh! it is terribly lonely here."

"Squeak, squeak," said a little mouse, creeping cautiously towards the tree; then came another, and they both sniffed at the fir tree and crept in and out between the branches.

"Oh, it is very cold," said the little mouse. "If it were not we should be very comfortable here, shouldn't we, old fir tree?"

"I am not old," said the fir tree. "There are many who are older than I am."

"Where do you come from?" asked the mice, who were full of curiosity; "and what do you know? Have you seen the most beautiful places in the world, and can you tell us all about them? And have you been in the storeroom, where cheeses lie on the shelf and hams hang from the ceiling? One can run about on tallow candles there; one can go in thin and come out fat."

"I know nothing of that," said the fir tree, "but I know the wood, where the sun shines and the birds sing." And then the tree told the little mice all about its youth. They had never heard such an account in their lives; and after they had listened to it attentively, they said: "What a number of things you have seen! You must have been very happy."

"Happy!" exclaimed the fir tree; and then, as he reflected on what he had been telling them, he said, "Ah, yes! after all, those were happy days." But when he went on and related all about Christmas Eve, and how he had been dressed up with cakes and lights, the mice said, "How happy you must have been, you old fir tree."

"I am not old at all," replied the tree; "I only came from the forest this winter. I am now checked in my growth."

"What splendid stories you can tell," said the little mice. And the next night four other mice came with them to hear what the tree had to tell. The more he talked the more he remembered, and then he thought to himself: "Yes, those were happy days; but they may come again. Humpty Dumpty fell downstairs, and yet he married the princess. Perhaps I may marry a princess, too." And the fir tree thought of the pretty little birch tree that grew in the forest; a real princess, a beautiful princess, she was to him.

"Who is Humpty Dumpty?" asked the little mice. And then the tree related the whole story; he could remember every single word. And the little mice were so delighted with it that they were ready to jump to the top of the tree. The next night a great many more mice made their appearance, and on Sunday two rats came with them; but the rats said it was not a pretty story at all, and the little mice were very sorry, for it made them also think less of it.

"Do you know only that one story?" asked the rats.

"Only that one," replied the fir tree. "I heard it on the happiest evening in my life; but I did not know I was so happy at the time."

"We think it is a very miserable story," said the rats. "Don't you know any story about bacon or tallow in the storeroom?"

"No," replied the tree.

"Many thanks to you, then," replied the rats, and they went their ways.

The little mice also kept away after this, and the tree sighed and said: "It was very pleasant when the merry little mice sat round me and listened while I talked. Now that is all past, too. However, I shall consider myself happy when some one comes to take me out of this place."

But would this ever happen? Yes; one morning people came to clear up the garret; the boxes were packed away, and the tree was pulled out of the corner and thrown roughly on the floor; then the servants dragged it out upon the staircase, where the daylight shone.

"Now life is beginning again," said the tree, rejoicing in the sunshine and fresh air. Then it was carried downstairs and taken into the courtyard so quickly that it forgot to think of itself and could only look about, there was so much to be seen.

The court was close to a garden, where everything looked blooming. Fresh and fragrant roses hung over the little palings. The linden trees were in blossom, while swallows flew here and there, crying, "Twit, twit, twit, my mate is coming"; but it was not the fir tree they meant.

"Now I shall live," cried the tree joyfully, spreading out its branches; but alas! they were all withered and yellow, and it lay in a corner among weeds and nettles. The star of gold paper still stuck in the top of the tree and glittered in the sunshine.

Two of the merry children who had danced round the tree at Christmas and had been so happy were playing in the same courtyard. The youngest saw the gilded star and ran and pulled it off the tree. "Look what is sticking to the ugly old fir tree," said the child, treading on the branches till they crackled under his boots.

And the tree saw all the fresh, bright flowers in the garden and then looked at itself and wished it had remained in the dark corner of the garret. It thought of its fresh youth in the forest, of the merry Christmas evening, and of the little mice who had listened to the story of Humpty Dumpty.

"Past! past!" said the poor tree. "Oh, had I but enjoyed myself while I could have done so! but now it is too late."

Then a lad came and chopped the tree into small pieces, till a large bundle lay in a heap on the ground. The pieces were placed in a fire, and they quickly blazed up brightly, while the tree sighed so deeply that each sigh was like a little pistol shot. Then the children who were at play came and seated themselves in front of the fire, and looked at it and cried, "Pop, pop." But at each "pop," which was a deep sigh, the tree was thinking of a summer day in the forest or of some winter night there when the stars shone brightly, and of Christmas evening, and of Humpty Dumpty,—the only story it had ever heard or knew how to relate,—till at last it was consumed.

The boys still played in the garden, and the youngest wore on his breast the golden star with which the tree had been adorned during the happiest evening of its existence. Now all was past; the tree's life was past and the story also past—for all stories must come to an end at some time or other.

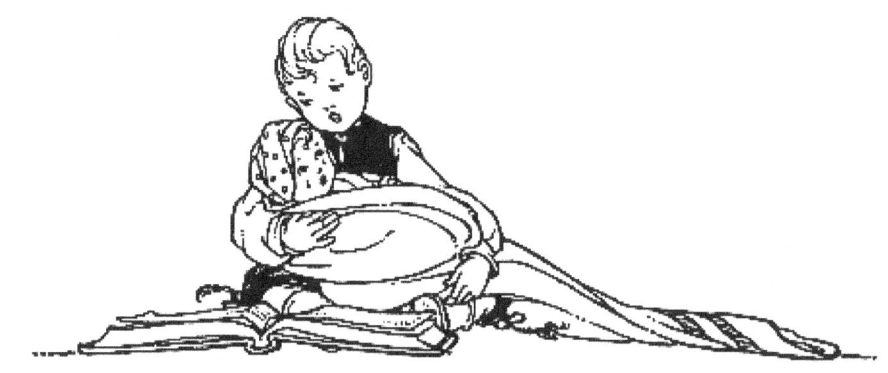

LITTLE TUK

L ITTLE TUK! An odd name, to be sure! However, it was not the little boy's real name. His real name was Carl; but when he was so young that he could not speak plainly, he used to call himself Tuk. It would be hard to say why, for it is not at all like "Carl"; but the name does as well as any, if one only knows it.

Little Tuk was left at home to take care of his sister Gustava, who was much younger than himself; and he had also to learn his lesson. Here were two things to be done at the same time, and they did not at all suit each other. The poor boy sat with his sister in his lap, singing to her all the songs he knew, yet giving, now and then, a glance into his geography, which lay open beside him. By to-morrow morning he must know the names of all the towns in Seeland by heart, and be able to tell about them all that could be told.

His mother came at last, and took little Gustava in her arms. Tuk ran quickly to the window and read and read till he had almost read his eyes out—for it was growing dark, and his mother could not afford to buy candles.

"There goes the old washerwoman down the lane," said the mother, as she looked out of the window. "She can hardly drag herself along, poor thing; and now she has to carry that heavy pail from the pump. Be a good boy, little Tuk, and run across to help the poor creature, will you not?" And little Tuk ran quickly and helped to bear the weight of the pail. But when he came back into the room, it was quite dark. Nothing was said about a candle, and it was of no use to wish for one; he must go to his little trundle-bed, which was made of an old settle.

There he lay, still thinking of the geography lesson, of Seeland, and of all that the master had said. He could not read the book again, as he should by rights have done, for want of a light. So he put the geography-book under his pillow. Somebody had once told him that would help him wonderfully to remember his lesson, but he had never yet found that one could depend upon it.

All in a moment he was on horseback, and on he went, gallop, gallop!

There he lay and thought and thought, till all at once he felt as though some one were gently sealing his mouth and eyes with a kiss. He slept and yet did not sleep, for he seemed to see the old washerwoman's mild, kind eyes fixed upon him, and to hear her say: "It would be a shame, indeed, for you not to know your lesson to-morrow, little Tuk. You helped me; now I will help you, and our Lord will help us both."

All at once the leaves of the book began to rustle under little Tuk's head, and he heard something crawling about under his pillow.

"Cluck, cluck, cluck!" cried a hen, as she crept towards him. (She came from the town of Kjöge.) "I'm a Kjöge hen," she said. And then she told him how many inhabitants the little town contained, and about the battle that had once been fought there, and how it was now hardly worth mentioning, there were so many greater things.

Scratch, scratch! kribbley crabbley! and now a great wooden bird jumped down upon the bed. It was the popinjay from the shooting ground at Præstö. He had reckoned the number of inhabitants in Præstö, and found that there were as many as he had nails in his body. He was a proud bird. "Thorwaldsen lived in one corner of Præstö, close by me. Am I not a pretty bird, a merry popinjay?"

And now little Tuk no longer lay in bed. All in a moment he was on horseback, and on he went, gallop, gallop! A splendid knight, with a bright helmet and waving plume,—a knight of the olden time,—held him on his own horse; and on they rode together, through the wood of the ancient city of Vordingborg, and it was once again a great and busy town. The high towers of the king's castle rose against the sky, and bright lights were seen gleaming through the windows. Within were music and merrymaking. King Waldemar was leading out the noble ladies of his court to dance with him.

Suddenly the morning dawned, the lamps grew pale, the sun rose, the outlines of the buildings faded away, and at last one high tower alone remained to mark the spot where the royal castle had stood. The vast city had shrunk into a poor, mean-looking little town. The schoolboys, coming out of school with their geography-books under their arms, said, "Two thousand inhabitants"; but that was a mere boast, for the town had not nearly so many.

And little Tuk lay in his bed. He knew not whether he had been dreaming or not, but again there was some one close by his side.

"Little Tuk! little Tuk!" cried a voice; it was the voice of a young sailor boy. "I am come to bring you greeting from Korsör. Korsör is a new town, a living town, with steamers and mail coaches. Once people used to call it a low, ugly place, but they do so no longer.

"'I dwell by the seaside,' says Korsör; 'I have broad highroads and pleasure gardens; and I have given birth to a poet, a witty one, too, which is more than all poets are. I once thought of sending a ship all round the world; but I did not do it, though I might as well have done so. I dwell so pleasantly, close by the port; and I am fragrant with perfume, for the loveliest roses bloom round about me, close to my gates.'"

And little Tuk could smell the roses and see them and their fresh green leaves. But in a moment they had vanished; the green leaves spread and thickened—a perfect grove had grown up above the bright waters of the bay, and above the grove rose the two high-pointed towers of a glorious old church. From the side of the grass-grown hill gushed a fountain in rainbow-hued streams, with a merry, musical voice, and close beside it sat a king, wearing a gold crown upon his long dark hair. This was King Hroar of the springs; and hard by was the town of Roskilde (Hroar's Fountain). And up the hill, on a broad highway, went all the kings and queens of Denmark, wearing golden crowns; hand in hand they passed on into the church, and the deep music of the organ mingled with the clear rippling of the fountain. For nearly all the kings and queens of Denmark lie buried in this beautiful church. And little Tuk saw and heard it all.

"Don't forget the towns," said King Hroar.

Then all vanished; though where it went he knew not. It seemed like turning the leaves of a book.

And now there stood before him an old peasant woman from Sorö, the quiet little town where grass grows in the very market place. Her green linen apron was thrown over her head and back, and the apron was very wet, as if it had been raining heavily.

"And so it has," she said. And she told a great many pretty things from Holberg's comedies, and recited ballads about Waldemar and Absalon; for Holberg had founded an academy in her native town.

All at once she cowered down and rocked her head as if she were a frog about to spring. "Koax!" cried she; "it is wet, it is always wet, and it is as still as the grave in Sorö." She had changed into a frog. "Koax!" and again she was an old woman. "One must dress according to the weather," she said.

"It is wet! it is wet! My native town is like a bottle; one goes in at the cork, and by the cork one must come out. In old times we had the finest of fish; now we have fresh, rosy-cheeked boys at the bottom of the bottle. There they learn wisdom—Greek, Greek, and Hebrew! Koax!"

It sounded exactly as if frogs were croaking, or as if some one were walking over the great swamp with heavy boots. So tiresome was her tone, all on the same note, that little Tuk fell fast asleep; and a very good thing it was for him.

But even in sleep there came a dream, or whatever else it may be called. His little sister Gustava, with her blue eyes and flaxen ringlets, was grown into a tall, beautiful girl, who, though she had no wings, could fly; and away they now flew over Seeland—over its green woods and blue waters.

"Hark! Do you hear the cock crow, little Tuk? 'Cock-a-doodle-do!' The fowls are flying hither from Kjöge, and you shall have a farmyard, a great, great poultry yard of your own! You shall never suffer hunger or want. The golden goose, the bird of good omen, shall be yours; you shall become a rich and happy man. Your house shall rise up like King Waldemar's towers and be richly decked with statues like those of Thorwaldsen at Præstö.

"Understand me well; your good name shall be borne round the world, like the ship that was to sail from Korsör, and at Roskilde you shall speak and give counsel wisely and well, little Tuk, like King Hroar; and when at last you shall lie in your peaceful grave you shall sleep as quietly—"

"As if I lay sleeping in Sorö," said Tuk, and he woke. It was a bright morning, and he could not remember his dream, but it was not necessary that he should. One has no need to know what one will live to see.

And now he sprang quickly out of bed and sought his book, that had lain under his pillow. He read his lesson and found that he knew the towns perfectly well.

And the old washerwoman put her head in at the door and said, with a friendly nod: "Thank you, my good child, for yesterday's help. May the Lord fulfill your brightest and most beautiful dreams! I know he will."

Little Tuk had forgotten what he had dreamed, but it did not matter. There was One above who knew it all.

THE UGLY DUCKLING

I T was so beautiful in the country. It was the summer time. The wheat fields were golden, the oats were green, and the hay stood in great stacks in the green meadows. The stork paraded about among them on his long red legs, chattering away in Egyptian, the language he had learned from his lady mother.

All around the meadows and cornfields grew thick woods, and in the midst of the forest was a deep lake. Yes, it was beautiful, it was delightful in the country.

In a sunny spot stood a pleasant old farmhouse circled all about with deep canals; and from the walls down to the water's edge grew great burdocks, so high that under the tallest of them a little child might stand upright. The spot was as wild as if it had been in the very center of the thick wood.

In this snug retreat sat a duck upon her nest, watching for her young brood to hatch; but the pleasure she had felt at first was almost gone; she had begun to think it a wearisome task, for the little ones were so long coming out of their shells, and she seldom had visitors. The other ducks liked much better to swim about in the canals than to climb the slippery banks and sit under the burdock leaves to have a gossip with her. It was a long time to stay so much by herself.

At length, however, one shell cracked, and soon another, and from each came a living creature that lifted its head and cried "Peep, peep."

"Quack, quack!" said the mother; and then they all tried to say it, too, as well as they could, while they looked all about them on every side at the tall green leaves. Their mother allowed them to look about as much as they liked, because green is good for the eyes.

"What a great world it is, to be sure," said the little ones, when they found how much more room they had than when they were in the eggshell.

"Is this all the world, do you imagine?" said the mother. "Wait till you have seen the garden. Far beyond that it stretches down to the pastor's field, though I have never ventured to such a distance. Are you all out?" she continued, rising to look. "No, not all; the largest egg lies there yet, I declare. I wonder how long this business is to last. I'm really beginning to be tired of it;" but for all that she sat down again.

"Well, and how are you to-day?" quacked an old duck who came to pay her a visit.

"There's one egg that takes a deal of hatching. The shell is hard and will not break," said the fond mother, who sat still upon her nest. "But just look at the others. Have I not a pretty family? Are they not the prettiest little ducklings you ever saw? They are the image of their father—the good for naught! He never comes to see me."

"Let me see the egg that will not break," said the old duck. "I've no doubt it's a Guinea fowl's egg. The same thing happened to me once, and a deal of trouble it gave me, for the young ones are afraid of the water. I quacked and clucked, but all to no purpose. Let me take a look at it. Yes, I am right; it's a Guinea fowl, upon my word; so take my advice and leave it where it is. Come to the water and teach the other children to swim."

"I think I will sit a little while longer," said the mother. "I have sat so long, a day or two more won't matter."

"Very well, please yourself," said the old duck, rising; and she went away.

At last the great egg broke, and the latest bird cried "Peep, peep," as he crept forth from the shell. How big and ugly he was! The mother duck stared at him and did not know what to think. "Really," she said, "this is an enormous duckling, and it is not at all like any of the others. I wonder if he will turn out to be a Guinea fowl. Well, we shall see when we get to the water—for into the water he must go, even if I have to push him in myself."

On the next day the weather was delightful. The sun shone brightly on the green burdock leaves, and the mother duck took her whole family down to the water and jumped in with a splash. "Quack, quack!" cried she, and one after another the little ducklings jumped in. The water closed over their heads, but they came up again in an instant and swam about quite prettily, with their legs paddling under them as easily as possible; their legs went of their own accord; and the ugly gray-coat was also in the water, swimming with them.

"Oh," said the mother, "that is not a Guinea fowl. See how well he uses his legs, and how erect he holds himself! He is my own child, and he is not so very ugly after all, if you look at him properly. Quack, quack! come with me now. I will take you into grand society and introduce you to the farmyard, but you must keep close to me or you may be trodden upon; and, above all, beware of the cat."

When they reached the farmyard, there was a wretched riot going on; two families were fighting for an eel's head, which, after all, was carried off by the cat. "See, children, that is the way of the world," said the mother duck, whetting her beak, for she would have liked the eel's head herself. "Come, now, use your legs, and let me see how well you can behave. You must bow your heads prettily to that old duck yonder; she is the highest born of them all and has Spanish blood; therefore she is well off. Don't you see she has a red rag tied to her leg, which is something very grand and a great honor for a duck; it shows that every one is anxious not to lose her, and that she is to be noticed by both man and beast. Come, now, don't turn in your toes; a well-bred duckling spreads his feet wide apart, just like his father and mother, in this way; now bend your necks and say 'Quack!'"

The ducklings did as they were bade, but the other ducks stared, and said, "Look, here comes another brood—as if there were not enough of us already! And bless me, what a queer-looking object one of them is; we don't want him here"; and then one flew out and bit him in the neck.

"Let him alone," said the mother; "he is not doing any harm."

"Yes, but he is so big and ugly. He's a perfect fright," said the spiteful duck, "and therefore he must be turned out. A little biting will do him good."

"The others are very pretty children," said the old duck with the rag on her leg, "all but that one. I wish his mother could smooth him up a bit; he is really ill-favored."

"That is impossible, your grace," replied the mother. "He is not pretty, but he has a very good disposition and swims as well as the others or even better. I think he will grow up pretty, and perhaps be smaller. He has remained too long in the egg, and therefore his figure is not properly formed;" and then she stroked his neck and smoothed the feathers, saying: "It is a drake, and therefore not of so much consequence. I think he will grow up strong and able to take care of himself."

"The other ducklings are graceful enough," said the old duck. "Now make yourself at home, and if you find an eel's head you can bring it to me."

And so they made themselves comfortable; but the poor duckling who had crept out of his shell last of all and looked so ugly was bitten and pushed and made fun of, not only by the ducks but by all the poultry.

Bless me, what a queer-looking object one of them is..

"He is too big," they all said; and the turkey cock, who had been born into the world with spurs and fancied himself really an emperor, puffed himself out like a vessel in full sail and flew at the duckling. He became quite red in the head with passion, so that the poor little thing did not know where to go, and was quite miserable because he was so ugly as to be laughed at by the whole farmyard.

So it went on from day to day; it got worse and worse. The poor duckling was driven about by every one; even his brothers and sisters were unkind to him and would say, "Ah, you ugly creature, I wish the cat would get you" and his mother had been heard to say she wished he had never been born. The ducks pecked him, the chickens beat him, and the girl who fed the poultry pushed him with her feet. So at last he ran away, frightening the little birds in the hedge as he flew over the palings. "They are afraid because I am so ugly," he said. So he flew still farther, until he came out on a large moor inhabited by wild ducks. Here he remained the whole night, feeling very sorrowful.

In the morning, when the wild ducks rose in the air, they stared at their new comrade. "What sort of a duck are you?" they all said, coming round him.

He bowed to them and was as polite as he could be, but he did not reply to their question. "You are exceedingly ugly," said the wild ducks; "but that will not matter if you do not want to marry one of our family."

Poor thing! he had no thoughts of marriage; all he wanted was permission to lie among the rushes and drink some of the water on the moor. After he had been on the moor two days, there came two wild geese, or rather goslings, for they had not been out of the egg long, which accounts for their impertinence. "Listen, friend," said one of them to the duckling; "you are so ugly that we like you very well. Will you go with us and become a bird of passage? Not far from here is another moor, in which there are some wild geese, all of them unmarried. It is a chance for you to get a wife. You may make your fortune, ugly as you are."

"Bang, bang," sounded in the air, and the two wild geese fell dead among the rushes, and the water was tinged with blood. "Bang, bang," echoed far and wide in the distance, and whole flocks of wild geese rose up from the rushes.

The sound continued from every direction, for the sportsmen surrounded the moor, and some were even seated on branches of trees, overlooking the rushes. The blue smoke from the guns rose like clouds over the dark trees, and as it floated away across the water, a number of sporting dogs bounded in among the rushes, which bent beneath them wherever they went. How they terrified the poor duckling! He turned away his head to hide it under his wing, and at the same moment a large, terrible dog passed quite near him. His jaws were open, his tongue hung from his mouth, and his eyes glared fearfully. He thrust his nose close to the duckling, showing his sharp teeth, and then "splash, splash," he went into the water, without touching him.

"Oh," sighed the duckling, "how thankful I am for being so ugly; even a dog will not bite me."

And so he lay quite still, while the shot rattled through the rushes, and gun after gun was fired over him. It was late in the day before all became quiet, but even then the poor young thing did not dare to move. He waited quietly for several hours and then, after looking carefully around him, hastened away from the moor as fast as he could. He ran over field and meadow till a storm arose, and he could hardly struggle against it.

Towards evening he reached a poor little cottage that seemed ready to fall, and only seemed to remain standing because it could not decide on which side to fall first. The storm continued so violent that the duckling could go no farther. He sat down by the cottage, and then he noticed that the door was not quite closed, in consequence of one of the hinges having given way. There was, therefore, a narrow opening near the bottom large enough for him to slip through, which he did very quietly, and got a shelter for the night. Here, in this cottage, lived a woman, a cat, and a hen. The cat, whom his mistress called "My little son," was a great favorite; he could raise his back, and purr, and could even throw out sparks from his fur if it were stroked the wrong way. The hen had very short legs, so she was called "Chickie Short-legs." She laid good eggs, and her mistress loved her as if she had been her own child. In the morning the strange visitor was discovered; the cat began to purr and the hen to cluck.

"What is that noise about?" said the old woman, looking around the room. But her sight was not very good; therefore when she saw the duckling she thought it must be a fat duck that had strayed from home. "Oh, what a prize!" she exclaimed. "I hope it is not a drake, for then I shall have some ducks' eggs. I must wait and see."

So the duckling was allowed to remain on trial for three weeks; but there were no eggs.

Now the cat was the master of the house, and the hen was the mistress; and they always said, "We and the world," for they believed themselves to be half the world, and by far the better half, too. The duckling thought that others might hold a different opinion on the subject, but the hen would not listen to such doubts.

"Can you lay eggs?" she asked. "No." "Then have the goodness to cease talking." "Can you raise your back, or purr, or throw out sparks?" said the cat. "No." "Then you have no right to express an opinion when sensible people are speaking." So the duckling sat in a corner, feeling very low-spirited; but when the sunshine and the fresh air came into the room through the open door, he began to feel such a great longing for a swim that he could not help speaking of it.

"What an absurd idea!" said the hen. "You have nothing else to do; therefore you have foolish fancies. If you could purr or lay eggs, they would pass away."

"But it is so delightful to swim about on the water," said the duckling, "and so refreshing to feel it close over your head while you dive down to the bottom."

"Delightful, indeed! it must be a queer sort of pleasure," said the hen. "Why, you must be crazy! Ask the cat—he is the cleverest animal I know; ask him how he would like to swim about on the water, or to dive under it, for I will not speak of my own opinion. Ask our mistress, the old woman; there is no one in the world more clever than she is. Do you think she would relish swimming and letting the water close over her head?"

"I see you don't understand me," said the duckling.

"We don't understand you? Who can understand you, I wonder? Do you consider yourself more clever than the cat or the old woman?—I will say nothing of myself. Don't imagine such nonsense, child, and thank your good fortune that you have been so well received here. Are you not in a warm room and in society from which you may learn something? But you are a chatterer, and your company is not very agreeable. Believe me, I speak only for your good. I may tell you unpleasant truths, but that is a proof of my friendship. I advise you, therefore, to lay eggs and learn to purr as quickly as possible."

"I believe I must go out into the world again," said the duckling.

"Yes, do," said the hen. So the duckling left the cottage and soon found water on which it could swim and dive, but he was avoided by all other animals because of his ugly appearance.

Autumn came, and the leaves in the forest turned to orange and gold; then, as winter approached, the wind caught them as they fell and whirled them into the cold air. The clouds, heavy with hail and snowflakes, hung low in the sky, and the raven stood among the reeds, crying, "Croak, croak." It made one shiver with cold to look at him. All this was very sad for the poor little duckling.

One evening, just as the sun was setting amid radiant clouds, there came a large flock of beautiful birds out of the bushes. The duckling had never seen any like them before. They were swans; and they curved their graceful necks, while their soft plumage shone with dazzling whiteness. They uttered a singular cry as they spread their glorious wings and flew away from those cold regions to warmer countries across the sea. They mounted higher and higher in the air, and the ugly little duckling had a strange sensation as he watched them. He whirled himself in the water like a wheel, stretched out his neck towards them, and uttered a cry so strange that it frightened even himself. Could he ever forget those beautiful, happy birds! And when at last they were out of his sight, he dived under the water and rose again almost beside himself with excitement. He knew not the names of these birds nor where they had flown, but he felt towards them as he had never felt towards any other bird in the world.

He was not envious of these beautiful creatures; it never occurred to him to wish to be as lovely as they. Poor ugly creature, how gladly he would have lived even with the ducks, had they only treated him kindly and given him encouragement.

The winter grew colder and colder; he was obliged to swim about on the water to keep it from freezing, but every night the space on which he swam became smaller and smaller. At length it froze so hard that the ice in the water crackled as he moved, and the duckling had to paddle with his legs as well as he could, to keep the space from closing up. He became exhausted at last and lay still and helpless, frozen fast in the ice.

Early in the morning a peasant who was passing by saw what had happened. He broke the ice in pieces with his wooden shoe and carried the duckling home to his wife. The warmth revived the poor little creature; but when the children wanted to play with him, the duckling thought they would do him some harm, so he started up in terror, fluttered into the milk pan, and splashed the milk about the room. Then the woman clapped her hands, which frightened him still more. He flew first into the butter cask, then into the meal tub and out again. What a condition he was in! The woman screamed and struck at him with the tongs; the children laughed and screamed and tumbled over each other in their efforts to catch him, but luckily he escaped. The door stood open; the poor creature could just manage to slip out among the bushes and lie down quite exhausted in the newly fallen snow.

It would be very sad were I to relate all the misery and privations which the poor little duckling endured during the hard winter; but when it had passed he found himself lying one morning in a moor, amongst the rushes. He felt the warm sun shining and heard the lark singing and saw that all around was beautiful spring.

Then the young bird felt that his wings were strong, as he flapped them against his sides and rose high into the air. They bore him onwards until, before he well knew how it had happened, he found himself in a large garden. The apple trees were in full blossom, and the fragrant elders bent their long green branches down to the stream, which wound round a smooth lawn. Everything looked beautiful in the freshness of early spring. From a thicket close by came three beautiful white swans, rustling their feathers and swimming lightly over the smooth water. The duckling saw these lovely birds and felt more strangely unhappy than ever.

"I will fly to these royal birds," he exclaimed, "and they will kill me because, ugly as I am, I dare to approach them. But it does not matter; better be killed by them than pecked by the ducks, beaten by the hens, pushed about by the maiden who feeds the poultry, or starved with hunger in the winter."

Then he flew to the water and swam towards the beautiful swans. The moment they espied the stranger they rushed to meet him with outstretched wings.

"Kill me," said the poor bird and he bent his head down to the surface of the water and awaited death.

But what did he see in the clear stream below? His own image—no longer a dark-gray bird, ugly and disagreeable to look at, but a graceful and beautiful swan.

To be born in a duck's nest in a farmyard is of no consequence to a bird if it is hatched from a swan's egg. He now felt glad at having suffered sorrow and trouble, because it enabled him to enjoy so much better all the pleasure and happiness around him; for the great swans swam round the newcomer and stroked his neck with their beaks, as a welcome.

Into the garden presently came some little children and threw bread and cake into the water.

"See," cried the youngest, "there is a new one;" and the rest were delighted, and ran to their father and mother, dancing and clapping their hands and shouting joyously, "There is another swan come; a new one has arrived."

Then they threw more bread and cake into the water and said, "The new one is the most beautiful of all, he is so young and pretty." And the old swans bowed their heads before him.

Then he felt quite ashamed and hid his head under his wing, for he did not know what to do, he was so happy—yet he was not at all proud. He had been persecuted and despised for his ugliness, and now he heard them say he was the most beautiful of all the birds. Even the elder tree bent down its boughs into the water before him, and the sun shone warm and bright. Then he rustled his feathers, curved his slender neck, and cried joyfully, from the depths of his heart, "I never dreamed of such happiness as this while I was the despised ugly duckling."

The new one is the
most beautiful of all . . .

LITTLE IDA'S FLOWERS

"MY POOR flowers are quite faded!" said little Ida. "Only yesterday evening they were so pretty, and now all the leaves are drooping. Why do they do that?" she asked of the student, who sat on the sofa. He was a great favorite with her, because he used to tell her the prettiest of stories and cut out the most amusing things in paper—hearts with little ladies dancing in them, and high castles with doors which one could open and shut. He was a merry student. "Why do the flowers look so wretched to-day?" asked she again, showing him a bouquet of faded flowers.

"Do you not know?" replied the student. "The flowers went to a ball last night, and are tired. That's why they hang their heads."

"What an idea," exclaimed little Ida. "Flowers cannot dance!"

"Of course they can dance! When it is dark, and we are all gone to bed, they jump about as merrily as possible. They have a ball almost every night."

"And can their children go to the ball?" asked Ida.

"Oh, yes," said the student; "daisies and lilies of the valley, that are quite little."

"And when is it that the prettiest flowers dance?"

"Have you not been to the large garden outside the town gate, in front of the castle where the king lives in summer—the garden that is so full of lovely flowers? You surely remember the swans which come swimming up when you give them crumbs of bread? Believe me, they have capital balls there."

"I was out there only yesterday with my mother," said Ida, "but there were no leaves on the trees, and I did not see a single flower. What has become of them? There were so many in the summer."

"They are inside the palace now," replied the student. "As soon as the king and all his court go back to the town, the flowers hasten out of the garden and into the palace, where they have famous times. Oh, if you could but see them! The two most beautiful roses seat themselves on the throne and act king and queen. All the tall red cockscombs stand before them on either side and bow; they are the chamberlains. Then all the pretty flowers come, and there is a great ball. The blue violets represent the naval cadets; they dance with hyacinths and crocuses, who take the part of young ladies. The tulips and the tall tiger lilies are old ladies,—dowagers,—who see to it that the dancing is well done and that all things go on properly."

"But," asked little Ida, "is there no one there to harm the flowers for daring to dance in the king's castle?"

"No one knows anything about it," replied the student. "Once during the night, per-haps, the old steward of the castle does, to be sure, come in with his great bunch of keys to see that all is right; but the moment the flowers hear the clanking of the keys they stand stock-still or hide themselves behind the long silk window curtains. Then the old steward will say, 'Do I not smell flowers here?' but he can't see them."

"That is very funny," exclaimed little Ida, clapping her hands with glee; "but should not I be able to see the flowers?"

"To be sure you can see them," replied the student. "You have only to remember to peep in at the windows the next time you go to the palace. I did so this very day, and saw a long yellow lily lying on the sofa. She was a court lady."

"Do the flowers in the Botanical Garden go to the ball? Can they go all that long dis-tance?"

"Certainly," said the student; "for the flowers can fly if they please. Have you not seen the beautiful red and yellow butterflies that look so much like flowers? They are in fact nothing else. They have flown off their stalks high into the air and flapped their little pet-als just as if they were wings, and thus they came to fly about. As a reward for always behaving well they have leave to fly about in the daytime, too, instead of sitting quietly on their stalks at home, till at last the flower petals have become real wings. That you have seen yourself.

"It may be, though, that the flowers in the Botanical Garden have never been in the king's castle. They may not have heard what frolics take place there every night. But I'll tell you; if, the next time you go to the garden, you whisper to one of the flowers that a great ball is to be given yonder in the castle, the news will spread from flower to flower and they will all fly away. Then should the professor come to his garden there won't be a flower there, and he will not be able to imagine what has become of them."

"But how can one flower tell it to another? for I am sure the flowers cannot speak."

"No; you are right there," returned the student. "They cannot speak, but they can make signs. Have you ever noticed that when the wind blows a little the flowers nod to each other and move all their green leaves? They can make each other understand in this way just as well as we do by talking."

"And does the professor understand their pantomime?" asked Ida.

"Oh, certainly; at least part of it. He came into his garden one morning and saw that a great stinging nettle was making signs with its leaves to a beautiful red carnation. It was saying, 'You are so beautiful, and I love you with all my heart!' But the professor doesn't like that sort of thing, and he rapped the nettle on her leaves, which are her fingers; but she stung him, and since then he has never dared to touch a nettle."

"Ha! ha!" laughed little Ida, "that is very funny."

"How can one put such stuff into a child's head?" said a tiresome councilor, who had come to pay a visit. He did not like the student and always used to scold when he saw him cutting out the droll pasteboard figures, such as a man hanging on a gibbet and holding a heart in his hand to show that he was a stealer of hearts, or an old witch riding on a broomstick and carrying her husband on the end of her nose. The councilor could not bear such jokes, and he would always say, as now: "How can any one put such notions into a child's head? They are only foolish fancies."

But to little Ida all that the student had told her was very entertaining, and she kept thinking it over. She was sure now that her pretty yesterday's flowers hung their heads because they were tired, and that they were tired because they had been to the ball. So she took them to the table where stood her toys. Her doll lay sleeping, but Ida said to her, "You must get up, and be content to sleep to-night in the table drawer, for the poor flowers are ill and must have your bed to sleep in; then perhaps they will be well again by to-morrow."

And she at once took the doll out, though the doll looked vexed at giving up her cradle to the flowers.

Ida laid the flowers in the doll's bed and drew the coverlet quite over them, telling them to lie still while she made some tea for them to drink, in order that they might be well next day. And she drew the curtains about the bed, that the sun might not shine into their eyes.

All the evening she thought of nothing but what the student had told her; and when she went to bed herself, she ran to the window where her mother's tulips and hyacinths stood. She whispered to them, "I know very well that you are going to a ball to-night." The flowers pretended not to understand and did not stir so much as a leaf, but that did not prevent Ida from knowing what she knew.

When she was in bed she lay for a long time thinking how delightful it must be to see the flower dance in the king's castle, and said to herself, "I wonder if my flowers have really been there." Then she fell asleep.

In the night she woke. She had been dreaming of the student and the flowers and the councilor, who told her they were making game of her. All was still in the room, the night lamp was burning on the table, and her father and mother were both asleep.

"I wonder if my flowers are still lying in Sophie's bed," she thought to herself. "How I should like to know!" She raised herself a little and looked towards the door, which stood half open; within lay the flowers and all her playthings. She listened, and it seemed to her that she heard some one playing upon the piano, but quite softly, and more sweetly than she had ever heard before.

"Now all the flowers are certainly dancing," thought she. "Oh, how I should like to see them!" but she dared not get up for fear of waking her father and mother. "If they would only come in here!" But the flowers did not come, and the music went on so prettily that she could restrain herself no longer, and she crept out of her little bed, stole softly to the door, and peeped into the room. Oh, what a pretty sight it was!

On the floor all the flowers danced gracefully....

There was no night lamp in the room, still it was quite bright; the moon shone through the window down upon the floor, and it was almost like daylight. The hyacinths and tulips stood there in two rows. Not one was left on the window, where stood the empty flower pots. On the floor all the flowers danced gracefully, making all the turns, and holding each other by their long green leaves as they twirled around. At the piano sat a large yellow lily, which little Ida remembered to have seen in the summer, for she rec-ollected that the student had said, "How like she is to Miss Laura," and how every one had laughed at the remark. But now she really thought that the lily was very like the young lady. It had exactly her manner of playing—bending its long yellow face, now to one side and now to the other, and nodding its head to mark the time of the beautiful music.

A tall blue crocus now stepped forward, sprang upon the table on which lay Ida's playthings, went straight to the doll's cradle, and drew back the curtains. There lay the sick flowers; but they rose at once, greeted the other flowers, and made a sign that they would like to join in the dance. They did not look at all ill now.

Suddenly a heavy noise was heard, as of something falling from the table. Ida glanced that way and saw that it was the rod she had found on her bed on Shrove Tuesday, and that it seemed to wish to belong to the flowers. It was a pretty rod, for a wax figure that looked exactly like the councilor sat upon the head of it.

The rod began to dance, and the wax figure that was riding on it became long and great, like the councilor himself, and began to exclaim, "How can one put such stuff into a child's head?" It was very funny to see, and little Ida could not help laughing, for the rod kept on dancing, and the councilor had to dance too,—there was no help for it,—whether he remained tall and big or became a little wax figure again. But the other flowers said a good word for him, especially those that had lain in the doll's bed, so that at last the rod left it in peace.

At the same time there was a loud knocking inside the drawer where Sophie, Ida's doll, lay with many other toys. She put out her head and asked in great astonishment: "Is there a ball here? Why has no one told me of it?" She sat down upon the table, expecting some of the flowers to ask her to dance with them; but as they did not, she let herself fall upon the floor so as to make a great noise; and then the flowers all came crowding about to ask if she were hurt, and they were very polite—especially those that had lain in her bed.

She was not at all hurt, and the flowers thanked her for the use of her pretty bed and took her into the middle of the room, where the moon shone, and danced with her, while the other flowers formed a circle around them. So now Sophie was pleased and said they might keep her bed, for she did not mind sleeping in the drawer the least in the world.

But the flowers replied: "We thank you most heartily for your kindness, but we shall not live long enough to need it; we shall be quite dead by to-morrow. But tell little Ida she is to bury us out in the garden near the canary bird's grave; and then we shall wake again next summer and be even more beautiful than we have been this year."

"Oh, no, you must not die," said Sophie, kissing them as she spoke; and then a great company of flowers came dancing in. Ida could not imagine where they could have come from, unless from the king's garden. Two beautiful roses led the way, wearing golden crowns; then followed wallflowers and pinks, who bowed to all present. They brought a band of music with them. Wild hyacinths and little white snowdrops jingled merry bells. It was a most remarkable orchestra. Following these were an immense number of flowers, all dancing—violets, daisies, lilies of the valley, and others which it was a delight to see.

At last all the happy flowers wished one another good night. Little Ida, too, crept back to bed, to dream of all that she had seen.

When she rose next morning she went at once to her little table to see if her flowers were there. She drew aside the curtains of her little bed; yes, there lay the flowers, but they were much more faded to-day than yesterday. Sophie too was in the drawer, but she looked very sleepy.

"Do you remember what you were to say to me?" asked Ida of her.

But Sophie looked quite stupid and had not a word to say.

"You are not kind at all," said Ida; "and yet all the flowers let you dance with them."

Then she chose from her playthings a little pasteboard box with birds painted on it, and in it she laid the dead flowers.

"That shall be your pretty casket," said she; "and when my cousins come to visit me, by and by, they shall help me to bury you in the garden, in order that next summer you may grow again and be still more beautiful."

The two cousins were two merry boys, Gustave and Adolphe. Their father had given them each a new crossbow, which they brought with them to show to Ida. She told them of the poor flowers that were dead and were to be buried in the garden. So the two boys walked in front, with their bows slung across their shoulders, and little Ida followed, carrying the dead flowers in their pretty coffin. A little grave was dug for them in the garden. Ida first kissed the flowers and then laid them in the earth, and Adolphe and Gustave shot with their crossbows over the grave, for they had neither guns nor cannons.

THE STEADFAST TIN SOLDIER

THERE were once five and twenty tin soldiers. They were brothers, for they had all been made out of the same old tin spoon. They all shouldered their bayonets, held themselves upright, and looked straight before them. Their uniforms were very smart-looking—red and blue—and very splendid. The first thing they heard in the world, when the lid was taken off the box in which they lay, was the words "Tin soldiers!" These words were spoken by a little boy, who clapped his hands for joy. The soldiers had been given him because it was his birthday, and now he was putting them out upon the table.

Each was exactly like the rest to a hair, except one who had but one leg. He had been cast last of all, and there had not been quite enough tin to finish him; but he stood as firmly upon his one leg as the others upon their two, and it was he whose fortunes became so remarkable.

On the table where the tin soldiers had been set up were several other toys, but the one that attracted most attention was a pretty little paper castle. Through its tiny windows one could see straight into the hall. In front of the castle stood little trees, clustering round a small mirror which was meant to represent a transparent lake. Swans of wax swam upon its surface, and it reflected back their images.

All this was very pretty, but prettiest of all was a little lady who stood at the castle's open door. She too was cut out of paper, but she wore a frock of the clearest gauze and a narrow blue ribbon over her shoulders, like a scarf, and in the middle of the ribbon was placed a shining tinsel rose. The little lady stretched out both her arms, for she was a dancer, and then she lifted one leg so high that the Soldier quite lost sight of it. He thought that, like himself, she had but one leg.

"That would be just the wife for me," thought he, "if she were not too grand. But she lives in a castle, while I have only a box, and there are five and twenty of us in that. It would be no place for a lady. Still, I must try to make her acquaintance." A snuffbox happened to be upon the table and he lay down at full length behind it, and here he could easily watch the dainty little lady, who still remained standing on one leg without losing her balance.

When the evening came all the other tin soldiers were put away in their box, and the people in the house went to bed. Now the playthings began to play in their turn. They visited, fought battles, and gave balls. The tin soldiers rattled in the box, for they wished to join the rest, but they could not lift the lid. The nutcrackers turned somersaults, and the pencil jumped about in a most amusing way. There was such a din that the canary woke and began to speak—and in verse, too. The only ones who did not move from their places were the Tin Soldier and the Lady Dancer. She stood on tiptoe with out-stretched arms, and he was just as persevering on his one leg; he never once turned away his eyes from her.

Twelve o'clock struck—crash! up sprang the lid of the snuffbox. There was no snuff in it, but a little black goblin. You see it was not a real snuffbox, but a jack-in-the-box.

"Tin Soldier," said the Goblin, "keep thine eyes to thyself. Gaze not at what does not concern thee!"

But the Tin Soldier pretended not to hear.

"Only wait, then, till to-morrow," remarked the Goblin.

Next morning, when the children got up, the Tin Soldier was placed on the window sill, and, whether it was the Goblin or the wind that did it, all at once the window flew open and the Tin Soldier fell head foremost from the third story to the street below. It was a tremendous fall! Over and over he turned in the air, till at last he rested, his cap and bayonet sticking fast between the paving stones, while his one leg stood upright in the air.

Away he sailed
.. down the gutter ..

The maidservant and the little boy came down at once to look for him, but, though they nearly trod upon him, they could not manage to find him. If the Soldier had but once called "Here am I!" they might easily enough have heard him, but he did not think it becoming to cry out for help, being in uniform.

It now began to rain; faster and faster fell the drops, until there was a heavy shower; and when it was over, two street boys came by.

"Look you," said one, "there lies a tin soldier. He must come out and sail in a boat."

So they made a boat out of an old newspaper and put the Tin Soldier in the middle of it, and away he sailed down the gutter, while the boys ran along by his side, clapping their hands.

Goodness! how the waves rocked that paper boat, and how fast the stream ran! The Tin Soldier became quite giddy, the boat veered round so quickly; still he moved not a muscle, but looked straight before him and held his bayonet tightly.

All at once the boat passed into a drain, and it became as dark as his own old home in the box. "Where am I going now?" thought he. "Yes, to be sure, it is all that Goblin's doing. Ah! if the little lady were but sailing with me in the boat, I would not care if it were twice as dark."

Just then a great water rat, that lived under the drain, darted suddenly out.

"Have you a passport?" asked the rat. "Where is your passport?"

But the Tin Soldier kept silence and only held his bayonet with a firmer grasp.

The boat sailed on, but the rat followed. Whew! how he gnashed his teeth and cried to the sticks and straws: "Stop him! stop him! He hasn't paid toll! He hasn't shown his passport!"

But the stream grew stronger and stronger. Already the Tin Soldier could see daylight at the point where the tunnel ended; but at the same time he heard a rushing, roaring noise, at which a bolder man might have trembled. Think! just where the tunnel ended, the drain widened into a great sheet that fell into the mouth of a sewer. It was as perilous a situation for the Soldier as sailing down a mighty waterfall would be for us.

He was now so near it that he could not stop. The boat dashed on, and the Tin Soldier held himself so well that no one might say of him that he so much as winked an eye. Three or four times the boat whirled round and round; it was full of water to the brim and must certainly sink.

The Tin Soldier stood up to his neck in water; deeper and deeper sank the boat, softer and softer grew the paper; and now the water closed over the Soldier's head. He thought of the pretty little dancer whom he should never see again, and in his ears rang the words of the song:

Wild adventure, mortal danger,
Be thy portion, valiant stranger.

The paper boat parted in the middle, and the Soldier was about to sink, when he was swallowed by a great fish.

Oh, how dark it was! darker even than in the drain, and so narrow; but the Tin Soldier retained his courage; there he lay at full length, shouldering his bayonet as before.

To and fro swam the fish, turning and twisting and making the strangest movements, till at last he became perfectly still.

Something like a flash of daylight passed through him, and a voice said, "Tin Soldier!" The fish had been caught, taken to market, sold and bought, and taken to the kitchen, where the cook had cut him with a large knife. She seized the Tin Soldier between her finger and thumb and took him to the room where the family sat, and where all were eager to see the celebrated man who had traveled in the maw of a fish; but the Tin Soldier remained unmoved. He was not at all proud.

They set him upon the table there. But how could so curious a thing happen? The Soldier was in the very same room in which he had been before. He saw the same children, the same toys stood upon the table, and among them the pretty dancing maiden, who still stood upon one leg. She too was steadfast. That touched the Tin Soldier's heart. He could have wept tin tears, but that would not have been proper. He looked at her and she looked at him, but neither spoke a word.

And now one of the little boys took the Tin Soldier and threw him into the stove. He gave no reason for doing so, but no doubt the Goblin in the snuffbox had something to do with it.

The Tin Soldier stood now in a blaze of red light. The heat he felt was terrible, but whether it proceeded from the fire or from the love in his heart, he did not know. He saw that the colors were quite gone from his uniform, but whether that had happened on the journey or had been caused by grief, no one could say. He looked at the little lady, she looked at him, and he felt himself melting; still he stood firm as ever, with his bayonet on his shoulder. Then suddenly the door flew open; the wind caught the Dancer, and she flew straight into the stove to the Tin Soldier, flashed up in a flame, and was gone! The Tin Soldier melted into a lump; and in the ashes the maid found him next day, in the shape of a little tin heart, while of the Dancer nothing remained save the tinsel rose, and that was burned as black as a coal.

LITTLE THUMBELINA

THERE was once a woman who wished very much to have a little child. She went to a fairy and said: "I should so very much like to have a little child. Can you tell me where I can find one?"

"Oh, that can be easily managed," said the fairy. "Here is a barleycorn; it is not exactly of the same sort as those which grow in the farmers' fields, and which the chickens eat. Put it into a flowerpot and see what will happen."

"Thank you," said the woman; and she gave the fairy twelve shillings, which was the price of the barleycorn. Then she went home and planted it, and there grew up a large, handsome flower, somewhat like a tulip in appearance, but with its leaves tightly closed, as if it were still a bud.

"It is a beautiful flower," said the woman, and she kissed the red and golden-colored petals; and as she did so the flower opened, and she could see that it was a real tulip. But within the flower, upon the green velvet stamens, sat a very delicate and graceful little maiden. She was scarcely half as long as a thumb, and they gave her the name of Little Thumb, or Thumbelina, because she was so small.

A walnut shell, elegantly polished, served her for a cradle; her bed was formed of blue violet leaves, with a rose leaf for a counterpane. Here she slept at night, but during the day she amused herself on a table, where the peasant wife had placed a plate full of water.

Round this plate were wreaths of flowers with their stems in the water, and upon it floated a large tulip leaf, which served the little one for a boat. Here she sat and rowed herself from side to side, with two oars made of white horsehair. It was a very pretty sight. Thumbelina could also sing so softly and sweetly that nothing like her singing had ever before been heard.

One night, while she lay in her pretty bed, a large, ugly, wet toad crept through a broken pane of glass in the window and leaped right upon the table where she lay sleeping under her rose-leaf quilt.

"What a pretty little wife this would make for my son," said the toad, and she took up the walnut shell in which Thumbelina lay asleep, and jumped through the window with it, into the garden.

In the swampy margin of a broad stream in the garden lived the toad with her son. He was uglier even than his mother; and when he saw the pretty little maiden in her elegant bed, he could only cry "Croak, croak, croak."

"Don't speak so loud, or she will wake," said the toad, "and then she might run away, for she is as light as swan's-down. We will place her on one of the water-lily leaves out in the stream; it will be like an island to her, she is so light and small, and then she cannot escape; and while she is there we will make haste and prepare the stateroom under the marsh, in which you are to live when you are married."

Far out in the stream grew a number of water lilies with broad green leaves which seemed to float on the top of the water. The largest of these leaves appeared farther off than the rest, and the old toad swam out to it with the walnut shell, in which Thumbelina still lay asleep.

The tiny creature woke very early in the morning and began to cry bitterly when she found where she was, for she could see nothing but water on every side of the large green leaf, and no way of reaching the land.

Meanwhile the old toad was very busy under the marsh, decking her room with rushes and yellow wildflowers, to make it look pretty for her new daughter-in-law. Then she swam out with her ugly son to the leaf on which she had placed poor Thumbelina. She wanted to bring the pretty bed, that she might put it in the bridal chamber to be ready for her. The old toad bowed low to her in the water and said, "Here is my son; he will be your husband, and you will live happily together in the marsh by the stream."

"Croak, croak, croak," was all her son could say for himself. So the toad took up the elegant little bed and swam away with it, leaving Thumbelina all alone on the green leaf, where she sat and wept. She could not bear to think of living with the old toad and having her ugly son for a husband. The little fishes who swam about in the water beneath had seen the toad and heard what she said, so now they lifted their heads above the water to look at the little maiden.

As soon as they caught sight of her they saw she was very pretty, and it vexed them to think that she must go and live with the ugly toads.

"No, it must never be!" So they gathered together in the water, round the green stalk which held the leaf on which the little maiden stood, and gnawed it away at the root with their teeth. Then the leaf floated down the stream, carrying Thumbelina far away out of reach of land.

Thumbelina sailed past many towns, and the little birds in the bushes saw her and sang, "What a lovely little creature." So the leaf swam away with her farther and farther, till it brought her to other lands. A graceful little white butterfly constantly fluttered round her and at last alighted on the leaf. The little maiden pleased him, and she was glad of it, for now the toad could not possibly reach her, and the country through which she sailed was beautiful, and the sun shone upon the water till it glittered like liquid gold. She took off her girdle and tied one end of it round the butterfly, fastening the other end of the ribbon to the leaf, which now glided on much faster than before, taking Thumbelina with it as she stood.

Presently a large cockchafer flew by. The moment he caught sight of her he seized her round her delicate waist with his claws and flew with her into a tree. The green leaf floated away on the brook, and the butterfly flew with it, for he was fastened to it and could not get away.

Oh, how frightened Thumbelina felt when the cockchafer flew with her to the tree! But especially was she sorry for the beautiful white butterfly which she had fastened to the leaf, for if he could not free himself he would die of hunger. But the cockchafer did not trouble himself at all about the matter. He seated himself by her side, on a large green leaf, gave her some honey from the flowers to eat, and told her she was very pretty, though not in the least like a cockchafer.

Glided on much faster than before ....

After a time all the cockchafers who lived in the tree came to pay Thumbelina a visit. They stared at her, and then the young lady cockchafers turned up their feelers and said, "She has only two legs! how ugly that looks." "She has no feelers," said another. "Her waist is quite slim. Pooh! she is like a human being."

"Oh, she is ugly," said all the lady cockchafers. The cockchafer who had run away with her believed all the others when they said she was ugly. He would have nothing more to say to her, and told her she might go where she liked. Then he flew down with her from the tree and placed her on a daisy, and she wept at the thought that she was so ugly that even the cockchafers would have nothing to say to her. And all the while she was really the loveliest creature that one could imagine, and as tender and delicate as a beautiful rose leaf.

During the whole summer poor little Thumbelina lived quite alone in the wide forest. She wove herself a bed with blades of grass and hung it up under a broad leaf, to protect herself from the rain. She sucked the honey from the flowers for food and drank the dew from their leaves every morning.

So passed away the summer and the autumn, and then came the winter—the long, cold winter. All the birds who had sung to her so sweetly had flown away, and the trees and the flowers had withered. The large shamrock under the shelter of which she had lived was now rolled together and shriveled up; nothing remained but a yellow, withered stalk. She felt dreadfully cold, for her clothes were torn, and she was herself so frail and delicate that she was nearly frozen to death. It began to snow, too; and the snowflakes, as they fell upon her, were like a whole shovelful falling upon one of us, for we are tall, but she was only an inch high. She wrapped herself in a dry leaf, but it cracked in the middle and could not keep her warm, and she shivered with cold.

Near the wood in which she had been living was a large cornfield, but the corn had been cut a long time; nothing remained but the bare, dry stubble, standing up out of the frozen ground. It was to her like struggling through a large wood.

Oh! how she shivered with the cold. She came at last to the door of a field mouse, who had a little den under the corn stubble. There dwelt the field mouse in warmth and comfort, with a whole roomful of corn, a kitchen, and a beautiful dining room. Poor Thumbelina stood before the door, just like a little beggar girl, and asked for a small piece of barleycorn, for she had been without a morsel to eat for two days.

"You poor little creature," said the field mouse, for she was really a good old mouse, "come into my warm room and dine with me."

She was pleased with Thumbelina, so she said, "You are quite welcome to stay with me all the winter, if you like; but you must keep my rooms clean and neat, and tell me stories, for I shall like to hear them very much." And Thumbelina did all that the field mouse asked her, and found herself very comfortable.

"We shall have a visitor soon," said the field mouse one day; "my neighbor pays me a visit once a week. He is better off than I am; he has large rooms, and wears a beautiful black velvet coat. If you could only have him for a husband, you would be well provided for indeed. But he is blind, so you must tell him some of your prettiest stories."

Thumbelina did not feel at all interested about this neighbor, for he was a mole. However, he came and paid his visit, dressed in his black velvet coat.

"He is very rich and learned, and his house is twenty times larger than mine," said the field mouse.

He was rich and learned, no doubt, but he always spoke slightingly of the sun and the pretty flowers, because he had never seen them. Thumbelina was obliged to sing to him, "Ladybird, ladybird, fly away home," and many other pretty songs. And the mole fell in love with her because she had so sweet a voice; but he said nothing yet, for he was very prudent and cautious. A short time before, the mole had dug a long passage under the earth, which led from the dwelling of the field mouse to his own, and here she had permission to walk with Thumbelina whenever she liked. But he warned them not to be alarmed at the sight of a dead bird which lay in the passage. It was a perfect bird, with a beak and feathers, and could not have been dead long. It was lying just where the mole had made his passage. The mole took in his mouth a piece of phosphorescent wood, which glittered like fire in the dark. Then he went before them to light them through the long, dark passage. When they came to the spot where the dead bird lay, the mole pushed his broad nose through the ceiling, so that the earth gave way and the daylight shone into the passage.

In the middle of the floor lay a swallow, his beautiful wings pulled close to his sides, his feet and head drawn up under his feathers—the poor bird had evidently died of the cold. It made little Thumbelina very sad to see it, she did so love the little birds; all the summer they had sung and twittered for her so beautifully. But the mole pushed it aside with his crooked legs and said: "He will sing no more now. How miserable it must be to be born a little bird! I am thankful that none of my children will ever be birds, for they can do nothing but cry 'Tweet, tweet,' and must always die of hunger in the winter."

"Yes, you may well say that, as a clever man!" exclaimed the field mouse. "What is the use of his twittering if, when winter comes, he must either starve or be frozen to death? Still, birds are very high bred."

Thumbelina said nothing, but when the two others had turned their backs upon the bird, she stooped down and stroked aside the soft feathers which covered his head, and kissed the closed eyelids. "Perhaps this was the one who sang to me so sweetly in the summer," she said; "and how much pleasure it gave me, you dear, pretty bird."

The mole now stopped up the hole through which the daylight shone, and then accompanied the ladies home. But during the night Thumbelina could not sleep; so she got out of bed and wove a large, beautiful carpet of hay. She carried it to the dead bird and spread it over him, with some down from the flowers which she had found in the field mouse's room. It was as soft as wool, and she spread some of it on each side of the bird, so that he might lie warmly in the cold earth.

"Farewell, pretty little bird," said she, "farewell. Thank you for your delightful singing during the summer, when all the trees were green and the warm sun shone upon us." Then she laid her head on the bird's breast, but she was alarmed, for it seemed as if something inside the bird went "thump, thump." It was the bird's heart; he was not really dead, only benumbed with the cold, and the warmth had restored him to life. In autumn all the swallows fly away into warm countries; but if one happens to linger, the cold seizes it, and it becomes chilled and falls down as if dead. It remains where it fell, and the cold snow covers it.

Thumbelina trembled very much; she was quite frightened, for the bird was large, a great deal larger than herself (she was only an inch high). But she took courage, laid the wool more thickly over the poor swallow, and then took a leaf which she had used for her own counterpane and laid it over his head.

The next night she again stole out to see him. He was alive, but very weak; he could only open his eyes for a moment to look at Thumbelina, who stood by, holding a piece of decayed wood in her hand, for she had no other lantern. "Thank you, pretty little maiden," said the sick swallow; "I have been so nicely warmed that I shall soon regain my strength and be able to fly about again in the warm sunshine."

"Oh," said she, "it is cold out of doors now; it snows and freezes. Stay in your warm bed; I will take care of you."

She brought the swallow some water in a flower leaf, and after he had drunk, he told her that he had wounded one of his wings in a thornbush and could not fly as fast as the others, who were soon far away on their journey to warm countries. At last he had fallen to the earth, and could remember nothing more, nor how he came to be where she had found him.

All winter the swallow remained underground, and Thumbelina nursed him with care and love. She did not tell either the mole or the field mouse anything about it, for they did not like swallows. Very soon the springtime came, and the sun warmed the earth. Then the swallow bade farewell to Thumbelina, and she opened the hole in the ceiling which the mole had made. The sun shone in upon them so beautifully that the swallow asked her if she would go with him. She could sit on his back, he said, and he would fly away with her into the green woods. But she knew it would grieve the field mouse if she left her in that manner, so she said, "No, I cannot."

"Farewell, then, farewell, you good, pretty little maiden," said the swallow, and he flew out into the sunshine.

Thumbelina looked after him, and the tears rose in her eyes. She was very fond of the poor swallow.

"Tweet, tweet," sang the bird, as he flew out into the green woods, and Thumbelina felt very sad. She was not allowed to go out into the warm sunshine. The corn which had been sowed in the field over the house of the field mouse had grown up high into the air and formed a thick wood to Thumbelina, who was only an inch in height.

Nothing must be wanting when you are the wife of the mole . . .

"You are going to be married, little one," said the field mouse. "My neighbor has asked for you. What good fortune for a poor child like you! Now we will prepare your wedding clothes. They must be woolen and linen. Nothing must be wanting when you are the wife of the mole."

Thumbelina had to turn the spindle, and the field mouse hired four spiders, who were to weave day and night. Every evening the mole visited her and was continually speaking of the time when the summer would be over. Then he would keep his wedding day with Thumbelina; but now the heat of the sun was so great that it burned the earth and made it hard, like stone. As soon as the summer was over the wedding should take place. But Thumbelina was not at all pleased, for she did not like the tiresome mole.

Every morning when the sun rose and every evening when it went down she would creep out at the door, and as the wind blew aside the ears of corn so that she could see the blue sky, she thought how beautiful and bright it seemed out there and wished so much to see her dear friend, the swallow, again. But he never returned, for by this time he had flown far away into the lovely green forest.

When autumn arrived Thumbelina had her outfit quite ready, and the field mouse said to her, "In four weeks the wedding must take place."

Then she wept and said she would not marry the disagreeable mole.

"Nonsense," replied the field mouse. "Now don't be obstinate, or I shall bite you with my white teeth. He is a very handsome mole; the queen herself does not wear more beautiful velvets and furs. His kitchens and cellars are quite full. You ought to be very thankful for such good fortune."

So the wedding day was fixed, on which the mole was to take her away to live with him, deep under the earth, and never again to see the warm sun, because *he* did not like it. The poor child was very unhappy at the thought of saying farewell to the beautiful sun, and as the field mouse had given her permission to stand at the door, she went to look at it once more.

"Farewell, bright sun," she cried, stretching out her arm towards it; and then she walked a short distance from the house, for the corn had been cut, and only the dry stubble remained in the fields. "Farewell, farewell," she repeated, twining her arm around a little red flower that grew just by her side. "Greet the little swallow from me, if you should see him again."

"Tweet, tweet," sounded over her head suddenly. She looked up, and there was the swallow himself flying close by. As soon as he spied Thumbelina he was delighted. She told him how unwilling she was to marry the ugly mole, and to live always beneath the earth, nevermore to see the bright sun. And as she told him, she wept.

"Cold winter is coming," said the swallow, "and I am going to fly away into warmer countries. Will you go with me? You can sit on my back and fasten yourself on with your sash. Then we can fly away from the ugly mole and his gloomy rooms—far away, over the mountains, into warmer countries, where the sun shines more brightly than here; where it is always summer, and the flowers bloom in greater beauty. Fly now with me, dear little one; you saved my life when I lay frozen in that dark, dreary passage."

"Yes, I will go with you," said Thumbelina; and she seated herself on the bird's back, with her feet on his outstretched wings, and tied her girdle to one of his strongest feathers.

The swallow rose in the air and flew over forest and over sea—high above the highest mountains, covered with eternal snow. Thumbelina would have been frozen in the cold air, but she crept under the bird's warm feathers, keeping her little head uncovered, so that she might admire the beautiful lands over which they passed. At length they reached the warm countries, where the sun shines brightly and the sky seems so much higher above the earth. Here on the hedges and by the wayside grew purple, green, and white grapes, lemons and oranges hung from trees in the fields, and the air was fragrant with myrtles and orange blossoms. Beautiful children ran along the country lanes, playing with large gay butterflies; and as the swallow flew farther and farther, every place appeared still more lovely.

At last they came to a blue lake, and by the side of it, shaded by trees of the deepest green, stood a palace of dazzling white marble, built in the olden times. Vines clustered round its lofty pillars, and at the top were many swallows' nests, and one of these was the home of the swallow who carried Thumbelina.

"This is my house," said the swallow; "but it would not do for you to live there—you would not be comfortable. You must choose for yourself one of those lovely flowers, and I will put you down upon it, and then you shall have everything that you can wish to make you happy."

"That will be delightful," she said, and clapped her little hands for joy.

A large marble pillar lay on the ground, which, in falling, had been broken into three pieces. Between these pieces grew the most beautiful large white flowers, so the swallow flew down with Thumbelina and placed her on one of the broad leaves. But how surprised she was to see in the middle of the flower a tiny little man, as white and transparent as if he had been made of crystal! He had a gold crown on his head, and delicate wings at his shoulders, and was not much larger than was she herself. He was the angel of the flower, for a tiny man and a tiny woman dwell in every flower, and this was the king of them all.

"Oh, how beautiful he is!" whispered Thumbelina to the swallow.

The little prince was at first quite frightened at the bird, who was like a giant compared to such a delicate little creature as himself; but when he saw Thumbelina he was delighted and thought her the prettiest little maiden he had ever seen. He took the gold crown from his head and placed it on hers, and asked her name and if she would be his wife and queen over all the flowers.

This certainly was a very different sort of husband from the son of the toad, or the mole with his black velvet and fur, so she said Yes to the handsome prince. Then all the flowers opened, and out of each came a little lady or a tiny lord, all so pretty it was quite a pleasure to look at them. Each of them brought Thumbelina a present; but the best gift was a pair of beautiful wings, which had belonged to a large white fly, and they fastened them to Thumbelina's shoulders, so that she might fly from flower to flower.

Then there was much rejoicing, and the little swallow, who sat above them in his nest, was asked to sing a wedding song, which he did as well as he could; but in his heart he felt sad, for he was very fond of Thumbelina and would have liked never to part from her again.

"You must not be called Thumbelina any more," said the spirit of the flowers to her. "It is an ugly name, and you are so very lovely. We will call you Maia."

"Farewell, farewell," said the swallow, with a heavy heart, as he left the warm countries, to fly back into Denmark. There he had a nest over the window of a house in which dwelt the writer of fairy tales. The swallow sang "Tweet, tweet," and from his song came the whole story.

SUNSHINE STORIES

"I AM going to tell a story," said the Wind.

"I beg your pardon," said the Rain, "but now it is my turn. Have you not been howling round the corner this long time, as hard as ever you could?"

"Is this the gratitude you owe me?" said the Wind; "I, who in honor of you turn inside out—yes, even break—all the umbrellas, when the people won't have anything to do with you."

"I will speak myself," said the Sunshine. "Silence!" and the Sunshine said it with such glory and majesty that the weary Wind fell prostrate, and the Rain, beating against him, shook him, as she said:

"We won't stand it! She is always breaking through—is Madame Sunshine. Let us not listen to her; what she has to say is not worth hearing." And still the Sunshine began to talk, and this is what she said:

"A beautiful swan flew over the rolling, tossing waves of the ocean. Every one of its feathers shone like gold; and one feather drifted down to the great merchant vessel that, with sails all set, was sailing away.

"The feather fell upon the light curly hair of a young man, whose business it was to care for the goods in the ship—the supercargo he was called. The feather of the bird of fortune touched his forehead, became a pen in his hand, and brought him such luck that he soon became a wealthy merchant, rich enough to have bought for himself spurs of gold—rich enough to change a golden plate into a nobleman's shield, on which," said the Sunshine, "I shone."

"The swan flew farther, away and away, over the sunny green meadow, where the little shepherd boy, only seven years old, had lain down in the shade of the old tree, the only one there was in sight.

"In its flight the swan kissed one of the leaves of the tree, and falling into the boy's hand, it was changed to three leaves—to ten—to a whole book; yes, and in the book he read about all the wonders of nature, about his native language, about faith and knowledge. At night he laid the book under his pillow, that he might not forget what he had been reading.

"The wonderful book led him also to the schoolroom, and thence everywhere, in search of knowledge. I have read his name among the names of learned men," said the Sunshine.

"The swan flew into the quiet, lonely forest, and rested awhile on the deep, dark lake where the lilies grow, where the wild apples are to be found on the shore, where the cuckoo and the wild pigeon have their homes.

"In the wood was a poor woman gathering firewood—branches and dry sticks that had fallen. She bore them on her back in a bundle, and in her arms she held her little child. She too saw the golden swan, the bird of fortune, as it rose from among the reeds on the shore. What was it that glittered so? A golden egg that was still quite warm. She laid it in her bosom, and the warmth remained. Surely there was life in the egg! She heard the gentle pecking inside the shell, but she thought it was her own heart that was beating.

"At home in her poor cottage she took out the egg. 'Tick! tick!' it said, as if it had been a gold watch, but it was not; it was an egg—a real, living egg.

"The egg cracked and opened, and a dear little baby swan, all feathered as with the purest gold, pushed out its tiny head. Around its neck were four rings, and as this woman had four boys—three at home, and this little one that was with her in the lonely wood—she understood at once that there was one for each boy. Just as she had taken them the little gold bird took flight.

"She kissed each ring, then made each of the children kiss one of the rings, laid it next the child's heart awhile, then put it on his finger. I saw it all," said the Sunshine, "and I saw what happened afterward.

The egg cracked and opened . . .

"One of the boys, while playing by a ditch, took a lump of clay in his hand, then turned and twisted it till it took shape and was like Jason, who went in search of the Golden Fleece and found it.

"The second boy ran out upon the meadow, where stood the flowers—flowers of all imaginable colors. He gathered a handful and squeezed them so tightly that the juice flew into his eyes, and some of it wet the ring upon his hand. It cribbled and crawled in his brain and in his hands, and after many a day and many a year, people in the great city talked of the famous painter that he was.

"The third child held the ring in his teeth, and so tightly that it gave forth sound—the echo of a song in the depth of his heart. Then thoughts and feelings rose in beautiful sounds,—rose like singing swans,—plunged, too, like swans, into the deep, deep sea. He became a great musical composer, a master, of whom every country has the right to say, 'He was mine, for he was the world's.'

"And the fourth little one—yes, he was the 'ugly duck' of the family. They said he had the pip and must eat pepper and butter like a sick chicken, and that was what was given him; but of me he got a warm, sunny kiss," said the Sunshine. "He had ten kisses for one. He was a poet and was first kissed, then buffeted all his life through.

"But he held what no one could take from him—the ring of fortune from Dame Fortune's golden swan. His thoughts took wing and flew up and away like singing butterflies—emblems of an immortal life."

"That was a dreadfully long story," said the Wind.

"And so stupid and tiresome," said the Rain. "Blow upon me, please, that I may revive a little."

And while the Wind blew, the Sunshine said: "The swan of fortune flew over the lovely bay where the fishermen had set their nets. The very poorest one among them was wishing to marry—and marry he did.

"To him the swan brought a piece of amber. Amber draws things toward itself, and this piece drew hearts to the house where the fisherman lived with his bride. Amber is the most wonderful of incense, and there came a soft perfume, as from a holy place, a sweet breath from beautiful nature, that God has made. And the fisherman and his wife were happy and grateful in their peaceful home, content even in their poverty. And so their life became a real Sunshine Story."

"I think we had better stop now," said the Wind. "I am dreadfully bored. The Sunshine has talked long enough."

"I think so, too," said the Rain.

And what do we others who have heard the story say?

We say, "Now the story's done."

THE DARNING-NEEDLE

T HERE was once a Darning-needle who thought herself so fine that she came at last to believe that she was fit for embroidery.

"Mind now that you hold me fast," she said to the Fingers that took her up. "Pray don't lose me. If I should fall on the ground I should certainly be lost, I am so fine."

"That's more than you can tell," said the Fingers, as they grasped her tightly by the waist.

"I come with a train, you see," said the Darning-needle, as she drew her long thread after her; but there was no knot in the thread.

The Fingers pressed the point of the Needle upon an old pair of slippers, in which the upper leather had burst and must be sewed together. The slippers belonged to the cook.

"This is very coarse work!" said the Darning-needle. "I shall never get through alive. There, I'm breaking! I'm breaking!" and break she did. "Did I not say so?" said the Darning-needle. "I'm too delicate for such work as that."

"Now it's quite useless for sewing," said the Fingers; but they still held her all the same, for the cook presently dropped some melted sealing wax upon the needle and then pinned her neckerchief in front with it.

"See, now I'm a breastpin," said the Darning-needle. "I well knew that I should come to honor; when one is something, one always comes to something. Merit is sure to rise." And at this she laughed, only inwardly, of course, for one can never see when a Darning-needle laughs. There she sat now, quite at her ease, and as proud as if she sat in a state carriage and gazed upon all about her.

"May I take the liberty to ask if you are made of gold?" she asked of the pin, her neighbor. "You have a splendid appearance and quite a remarkable head, though it is so little. You should do what you can to grow—of course it is not every one that can have sealing wax dropped upon her."

And the Darning-needle drew herself up so proudly that she fell out of the neckerchief into the sink, which the cook was at that moment rinsing.

"Now I'm going to travel," said the Darning-needle, "if only I don't get lost."

But that was just what happened to her.

"I'm too delicate for this world," she said, as she found herself in the gutter. "But I know who I am, and there is always some little pleasure in that!" It was thus that the Darning-needle kept up her proud bearing and lost none of her good humor. And now all sorts of things swam over her—chips and straws and scraps of old newspapers.

"Only see how they sail along," said the Darning-needle to herself. "They little know what is under them, though it is I, and I sit firmly here. See! there goes a chip! It thinks of nothing in the world but itself—of nothing in the world but a chip! There floats a straw; see how it turns and twirls about. Do think of something besides yourself or you may easily run against a stone. There swims a bit of a newspaper. What's written upon it is forgotten long ago, yet how it spreads itself out and gives itself airs! I sit patiently and quietly here! I know what I am, and I shall remain the same—always."

One day there lay something beside her that glittered splendidly. She thought it must be a diamond, but it was really only a bit of broken glass from a bottle. As it shone so brightly the Darning-needle spoke to it, introducing herself as a breastpin.

"You are a diamond, I suppose," she said.

"Why, yes, something of the sort."

So each believed the other to be some rare and costly trinket; and they began to converse together upon the world, saying how very conceited it was.

"Yes," said the Darning-needle, "I have lived in a young lady's box; and the young lady happened to be a cook. She had five fingers upon each of her hands, and anything more conceited and arrogant than those five fingers, I never saw. And yet they were only there that they might take me out of the box or put me back again."

"Were they of high descent?" asked the Bit of Bottle. "Did they shine?"

"No, indeed," replied the Darning-needle; "but they were none the less haughty. There were five brothers of them—all of the Finger family. And they held themselves so proudly side by side, though they were of quite different heights. The outermost, Thumbling he was called, was short and thick set; he generally stood out of the rank, a little in front of the others; he had only one joint in his back, and could only bow once; but he used to say that if he were cut off from a man, that man would be cut off from military service. Foreman, the second, put himself forward on all occasions, meddled with sweet and sour, pointed to sun and moon, and when the fingers wrote, it was he who pressed the pen. Middleman, the third of the brothers, could look over the others' heads, and gave himself airs for that. Ringman, the fourth, went about with a gold belt about his waist; and little Playman, whom they called Peter Spielman, did nothing at all and was proud of that, I suppose. There was nothing to be heard but boasting, and that is why I took myself away."

"And now we sit here together and shine," said the Bit of Bottle.

At that very moment some water came rushing along the gutter, so that it overflowed and carried the glass diamond along with it.

"So he is off," said the Darning-needle, "and I still remain. I am left here because I am too slender and genteel. But that's my pride, and pride is honorable." And proudly she sat, thinking many thoughts.

"I could almost believe I had been born of a sunbeam, I'm so fine. It seems as if the sunbeams were always trying to seek me under the water. Alas, I'm so delicate that even my own mother cannot find me. If I had my old eye still, which broke off, I think I should cry—but no, I would not; it's not genteel to weep."

One day a couple of street boys were paddling about in the gutter, hunting for old nails, pennies, and such like. It was dirty work, but they seemed to find great pleasure in it.

"Hullo!" cried one of them, as he pricked himself with the Darning-needle; "here's a fellow for you!"

"I'm not a fellow! I'm a young lady!" said the Darning-needle, but no one heard it.

The sealing wax had worn off, and she had become quite black; "but black makes one look slender, and is always becoming." She thought herself finer even than before.

"There goes an eggshell sailing along," said the boys; and they stuck the Darning-needle into the shell.

"A lady in black, and within white walls!" said the Darning-needle; "that is very striking. Now every one can see me. I hope I shall not be seasick, for then I shall break."

But the fear was needless; she was not seasick, neither did she break.

"Nothing is so good to prevent seasickness as to have a steel stomach and to bear in mind that one is something a little more than an ordinary person. My seasickness is all over now. The more genteel and honorable one is, the more one can endure."

Crash went the eggshell, as a wagon rolled over both of them. It was a wonder that she did not break.

"Mercy, what a crushing weight!" said the Darning-needle. "I'm growing seasick, after all. I'm going to break!"

But she was not sick, and she did not break, though the wagon wheels rolled over her. She lay at full length in the road, and there let her lie.

THE LITTLE MATCH GIRL

IT was dreadfully cold; it was snowing fast, and was almost dark, as evening came on—the last evening of the year. In the cold and the darkness, there went along the street a poor little girl, bareheaded and with naked feet. When she left home she had slippers on, it is true; but they were much too large for her feet—slippers that her mother had used till then, and the poor little girl lost them in running across the street when two carriages were passing terribly fast. When she looked for them, one was not to be found, and a boy seized the other and ran away with it, saying he would use it for a cradle some day, when he had children of his own.

So on the little girl went with her bare feet, that were red and blue with cold. In an old apron that she wore were bundles of matches, and she carried a bundle also in her hand. No one had bought so much as a bunch all the long day, and no one had given her even a penny.

Poor little girl! Shivering with cold and hunger she crept along, a perfect picture of misery.

The snowflakes fell on her long flaxen hair, which hung in pretty curls about her throat; but she thought not of her beauty nor of the cold. Lights gleamed in every window, and there came to her the savory smell of roast goose, for it was New Year's Eve. And it was this of which she thought.

In a corner formed by two houses, one of which projected beyond the other, she sat cowering down. She had drawn under her her little feet, but still she grew colder and colder; yet she dared not go home, for she had sold no matches and could not bring a penny of money. Her father would certainly beat her; and, besides, it was cold enough at home, for they had only the house-roof above them, and though the largest holes had been stopped with straw and rags, there were left many through which the cold wind could whistle.

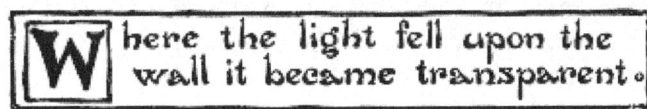

Where the light fell upon the wall it became transparent.

And now her little hands were nearly frozen with cold. Alas! a single match might do her good if she might only draw it from the bundle, rub it against the wall, and warm her fingers by it. So at last she drew one out. Whisht! How it blazed and burned! It gave out a warm, bright flame like a little candle, as she held her hands over it. A wonderful little light it was. It really seemed to the little girl as if she sat before a great iron stove with polished brass feet and brass shovel and tongs. So blessedly it burned that the little maiden stretched out her feet to warm them also. How comfortable she was! But lo! the flame went out, the stove vanished, and nothing remained but the little burned match in her hand.

She rubbed another match against the wall. It burned brightly, and where the light fell upon the wall it became transparent like a veil, so that she could see through it into the room. A snow-white cloth was spread upon the table, on which was a beautiful china dinner-service, while a roast goose, stuffed with apples and prunes, steamed famously and sent forth a most savory smell. And what was more delightful still, and wonderful, the goose jumped from the dish, with knife and fork still in its breast, and waddled along the floor straight to the little girl.

But the match went out then, and nothing was left to her but the thick, damp wall.

She lighted another match. And now she was under a most beautiful Christmas tree, larger and far more prettily trimmed than the one she had seen through the glass doors at the rich merchant's. Hundreds of wax tapers were burning on the green branches, and gay figures, such as she had seen in shop windows, looked down upon her. The child stretched out her hands to them; then the match went out.

Still the lights of the Christmas tree rose higher and higher. She saw them now as stars in heaven, and one of them fell, forming a long trail of fire.

"Now some one is dying," murmured the child softly; for her grandmother, the only person who had loved her, and who was now dead, had told her that whenever a star falls a soul mounts up to God.

She struck yet another match against the wall, and again it was light; and in the brightness there appeared before her the dear old grandmother, bright and radiant, yet sweet and mild, and happy as she had never looked on earth.

"Oh, grandmother," cried the child, "take me with you. I know you will go away when the match burns out. You, too, will vanish, like the warm stove, the splendid New Year's feast, the beautiful Christmas tree." And lest her grandmother should disappear, she rubbed the whole bundle of matches against the wall.

And the matches burned with such a brilliant light that it became brighter than noonday. Her grandmother had never looked so grand and beautiful. She took the little girl in her arms, and both flew together, joyously and gloriously, mounting higher and higher, far above the earth; and for them there was neither hunger, nor cold, nor care—they were with God.

But in the corner, at the dawn of day, sat the poor girl, leaning against the wall, with red cheeks and smiling mouth—frozen to death on the last evening of the old year. Stiff and cold she sat, with the matches, one bundle of which was burned.

"She wanted to warm herself, poor little thing," people said. No one imagined what sweet visions she had had, or how gloriously she had gone with her grandmother to enter upon the joys of a new year.

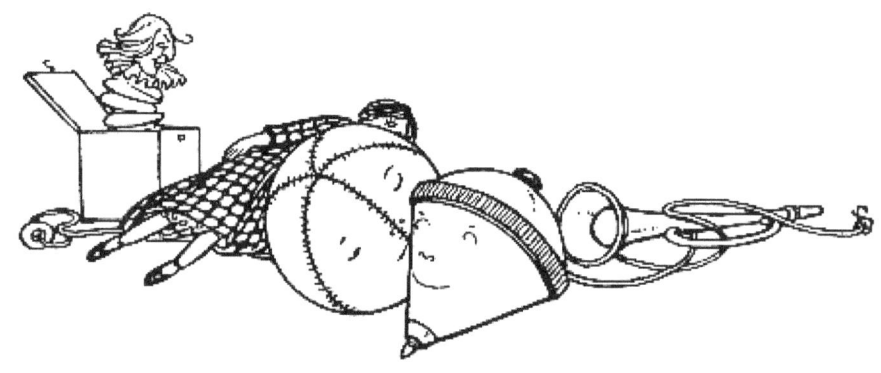

THE LOVING PAIR

A WHIPPING Top and a Ball lay close together in a drawer among other playthings. One day the Top said to the Ball, "Since we are living so much together, why should we not be lovers?"

But the Ball, being made of morocco leather, thought herself a very high-bred lady, and would hear nothing of such a proposal. On the next day the little boy to whom the playthings belonged came to the drawer; he painted the Top red and yellow, and drove a bright brass nail right through the head of it; it looked very smart indeed as it spun around after that.

"Look at me," said he to the Ball. "What do you say to me now; why should we not make a match of it, and become man and wife? We suit each other so well!—you can jump and I can dance. There would not be a happier pair in the whole world!"

"Do you think so?" said the Ball. "Perhaps you do not know that my father and mother were morocco slippers, and that I have a Spanish cork in my body!"

"Yes, but then I am made of mahogany," said the Top; "the Mayor himself turned me. He has a turning lathe of his own, and he took great pleasure in making me."

"Can I trust you in this?" asked the Ball.

"May I never be whipped again, if what I tell you is not true," returned the Top.

"You plead your cause well," said the Ball; "but I am not free to listen to your proposal. I am as good as engaged to a swallow. As often as I fly up into the air, he puts his head out of his nest, and says, 'Will you?' In my heart I have said Yes to him, and that is almost the same as an engagement; but I'll promise never to forget you."

"A deal of good that will do me," said the Top, and they left off speaking to each other.

Next day the Ball was taken out. The Top saw it fly like a bird into the air—so high that it passed quite out of sight. It came back again; but each time that it touched the earth, it sprang higher than before. This must have been either from its longing to mount higher, like the swallow, or because it had the Spanish cork in its body. On the ninth time the little Ball did not return. The boy sought and sought, but all in vain, for it was gone.

"I know very well where she is," sighed the Top. "She is in the swallow's nest, celebrating her wedding."

The more the Top thought of this the more lovely the Ball became to him; that she could not be his bride seemed to make his love for her the greater. She had preferred another rather than himself, but he could not forget her. He twirled round and round, spinning and humming, but always thinking of the Ball, who grew more and more beautiful the more he thought of her. And thus several years passed,—it came to be an old love,—and now the Top was no longer young!

One day he was gilded all over; never in his life had he been half so handsome. He was now a golden top, and bravely he spun, humming all the time. But once he sprang too high—and was gone!

They looked everywhere for him,—even in the cellar,—but he was nowhere to be found. Where was he?

He had jumped into the dustbin, and lay among cabbage stalks, sweepings, dust, and all sorts of rubbish that had fallen from the gutter in the roof.

"Alas! my gay gilding will soon be spoiled here. What sort of trumpery can I have got among?" And then he peeped at a long cabbage stalk which lay much too near him, and at something strange and round, which appeared like an apple, but was not. It was an old Ball that must have lain for years in the gutter, and been soaked through and through with water.

"Thank goodness! at last I see an equal; one of my own sort, with whom I can talk," said the Ball, looking earnestly at the gilded Top. "I am myself made of real morocco, sewed together by a young lady's hands, and within my body is a Spanish cork; though no one would think it now. I was very near marrying the swallow, when by a sad chance I fell into the gutter on the roof. I have lain there five years, and I am now wet through and through. You may think what a wearisome situation it has been for a young lady like me."

The Top made no reply. The more he thought of his old love, and the more he heard, the more sure he became that this was indeed she.

Then came the housemaid to empty the dustbin. "Hullo!" she cried; "why, here's the gilt Top." And so the Top was brought again to the playroom, to be used and honored as before, while nothing was again heard of the Ball.

And the Top never spoke again of his old love—the feeling must have passed away. And it is not strange, when the object of it has lain five years in a gutter, and been drenched through and through, and when one meets her again in a dustbin.

THE LEAPING MATCH

THE Flea, the Grasshopper, and the Frog once wanted to see which of them could jump the highest. They made a festival, and invited the whole world and every one else besides who liked to come and see the grand sight. Three famous jumpers they were, as all should say, when they met together in the room.

"I will give my daughter to him who shall jump highest," said the King; "it would be too bad for you to have the jumping, and for us to offer no prize."

The Flea was the first to come forward. He had most exquisite manners, and bowed to the company on every side; for he was of noble blood, and, besides, was accustomed to the society of man, and that, of course, had been an advantage to him.

Next came the Grasshopper. He was not quite so elegantly formed as the Flea, but he knew perfectly well how to conduct himself, and he wore the green uniform which belonged to him by right of birth. He said, moreover, that he came of a very ancient Egyptian family, and that in the house where he then lived he was much thought of.

The fact was that he had been just brought out of the fields and put in a card-house three stories high, and built on purpose for him, with the colored sides inwards, and doors and windows cut out of the Queen of Hearts. "And I sing so well," said he, "that sixteen parlor-bred crickets, who have chirped from infancy and yet got no one to build them card-houses to live in, have fretted themselves thinner even than before, from sheer vexation on hearing me."

It was thus that the Flea and the Grasshopper made the most of themselves, each thinking himself quite an equal match for the princess.

He made a sideways jump into the lap of the princess.

The Leapfrog said not a word; but people said that perhaps he thought the more; and the housedog who snuffed at him with his nose allowed that he was of good family. The old councilor, who had had three orders given him in vain for keeping quiet, asserted that the Leapfrog was a prophet, for that one could see on his back whether the coming winter was to be severe or mild, which is more than one can see on the back of the man who writes the almanac.

"I say nothing for the present," exclaimed the King; "yet I have my own opinion, for I observe everything."

And now the match began. The Flea jumped so high that no one could see what had become of him; and so they insisted that he had not jumped at all—which was disgraceful after all the fuss he had made.

The Grasshopper jumped only half as high; but he leaped into the King's face, who was disgusted by his rudeness.

The Leapfrog stood for a long time, as if lost in thought; people began to think he would not jump at all.

"I'm afraid he is ill!" said the dog and he went to snuff at him again; when lo! he suddenly made a sideways jump into the lap of the princess, who sat close by on a little golden stool.

"There is nothing higher than my daughter," said the King; "therefore to bound into her lap is the highest jump that can be made. Only one of good understanding would ever have thought of that. Thus the Frog has shown that he has sense. He has brains in his head, that he has."

And so he won the princess.

"I jumped the highest, for all that," said the Flea; "but it's all the same to me. The princess may have the stiff-legged, slimy creature, if she likes. In this world merit seldom meets its reward. Dullness and heaviness win the day. I am too light and airy for a stupid world."

And so the Flea went into foreign service.

The Grasshopper sat without on a green bank and reflected on the world and its ways; and he too said, "Yes, dullness and heaviness win the day; a fine exterior is what people care for nowadays." And then he began to sing in his own peculiar way—and it is from his song that we have taken this little piece of history, which may very possibly be all untrue, although it does stand printed here in black and white.

THE HAPPY FAMILY

THE largest green leaf in this country is certainly the burdock. Put one in front of your waist, and it is just like an apron; or lay it upon your head, and it is almost as good as an umbrella, it is so broad.

Burdock never grows singly; where you find one plant of the kind you may be sure that others grow in its immediate neighborhood. How magnificent they look!

And all this magnificence is food for snails—the great white snails, which grand people in olden times used to have dished up as fricassees, and of which, when they had eaten, they would say, "H'm, how nice!" for they really fancied them delicious. These snails lived on burdock leaves, and that was why burdock was planted.

Now there was an old estate where snails were no longer considered a delicacy. The snails had therefore died out, but the burdock still flourished. In all the alleys and in all the beds it had grown and grown, so that it could no longer be checked; the place had become a perfect forest of burdock.

Here and there stood an apple or plum tree to serve as a kind of token that there had been once a garden, but everything, from one end of the garden to the other, was burdock, and beneath the shade of the burdock lived the last two of the ancient snails.

They did not know themselves how old they were, but they well remembered the time when there were a great many of them, that they had descended from a family that came from foreign lands, and that this forest in which they lived had been planted for them and theirs. They had never been beyond the limits of the garden, but they knew that there was something outside their forest, called the castle, and that there one was boiled, and became black, and was then laid upon a silver dish—though what happened afterward they had never heard, nor could they exactly fancy how it felt to be cooked and laid on a silver dish. It was, no doubt, a fine thing, and exceedingly genteel.

Neither the cockchafer, nor the toad, nor the earthworm, all of whom they questioned on the matter, could give them the least information, for none of them had ever been cooked and served upon silver dishes.

The old white snails were the grandest race in the world; of this they were well aware. The forest had grown for their sake, and the castle or manor house too had been built expressly that in it they might be cooked and served.

Leading now a very quiet and happy life and having no children, they had adopted a little common snail, and had brought it up as their own child. But the little thing would not grow, for he was only a common snail, though his foster mother pretended to see a great improvement in him. She begged the father, since he could not perceive it, to feel the little snail's shell, and to her great joy and his own, he found that his wife was right.

One day it rained very hard. "Listen!" said the Father Snail; "hear what a drumming there is on the burdock leaves—rum-dum-dum, rum-dum-dum!"

"There are drops, too," said the Mother Snail; "they come trickling down the stalks. We shall presently find it very wet here. I'm glad we have such good houses, and that the youngster has his also. There has really been more done for us than for any other creatures. Every one must see that we are superior beings. We have houses from our very birth, and the burdock forest is planted on our account. I should like to know just how far it reaches, and what there is beyond."

"There is nothing better than what we have here," said the Father Snail. "I wish for nothing beyond."

"And yet," said the mother, "I should like to be taken to the castle, and boiled, and laid on a silver dish; that has been the destiny of all our ancestors, and we may be sure it is something quite out of the common way."

"The castle has perhaps fallen to ruin," said the Father Snail, "or it may be overgrown with burdock, so that its inmates are unable to come out. There is no hurry about the matter. You are always in such a desperate hurry, and the youngster there begins to take after you. He's been creeping up that stem yonder these three days. It makes me quite dizzy to look at him."

"But don't scold him," said the mother. "He creeps carefully. We old people have nothing else to live for, and he will be the joy of our old age. Have you thought how we can manage to find a wife for him? Do you not think that farther into the forest there may be others of our own species?"

"I dare say there may be black snails," said the old father, "black snails, without a house at all; and they are vulgar, though they think so much of themselves. But we can employ the black ants, who run about so much—hurrying to and fro as if they had all the business of the world on their hands. They will certainly be able to find a wife for our young gentleman."

"I know the fairest of the fair," said one of the ants; "but I'm afraid it would not do, for she's a queen."

"She's none the worse for that," said both the old snails. "Has she a house?"

"She has a palace," answered the ants; "the most splendid ant castle, with seven hundred galleries."

"Thank you!" said the Mother Snail. "Our boy shall not go to live in an ant hill. If you know of nothing better, we will employ the white gnats, who fly both in rain and sunshine and know all the ins and outs of the whole burdock forest."

"We have found a wife for him," said the gnats. "A hundred paces from here there sits, on a gooseberry bush, a little snail with a house. She is all alone and is old enough to marry. It is only a hundred human steps from here."

"Then let her come to him," said the old couple. "He has a whole forest of burdock, while she has only a bush."

So they went and brought the little maiden snail. It took eight days to perform the journey, but that only showed her high breeding, and that she was of good family.

And then the wedding took place. Six glow-worms gave all the light they could, but in all other respects it was a very quiet affair. The old people could not bear the fatigue of frolic or festivity. The Mother Snail made a very touching little speech. The father was too much overcome to trust himself to say anything.

They gave the young couple the entire burdock forest, saying what they had always said, namely, that it was the finest inheritance in the world, and that if they led an upright and honorable life, and if their family should increase, without doubt both themselves and their children would one day be taken to the manor castle and be boiled black and served as a fricassee in a silver dish.

And after this the old couple crept into their houses and never came out again, but fell asleep. The young pair now ruled in the forest and had a numerous family. But when, as time went on, none of them were ever cooked or served on a silver dish, they concluded that the castle had fallen to ruin and that the world of human beings had died out; and as no one contradicted them, they must have been right.

And the rain continued to fall upon the burdock leaves solely to entertain them with its drumming, and the sun shone to light the forest for their especial benefit, and very happy they were—they and the whole snail family—inexpressibly happy!

THE GREENIES

 ROSE TREE stood in the window. But a little while ago it had been green and fresh, and now it looked sickly—it was in poor health, no doubt. A whole regiment was quartered on it and was eating it up; yet, notwithstanding this seeming greediness, the regiment was a very decent and respectable one. It wore bright-green uniforms. I spoke to one of the "Greenies." He was but three days old, and yet he was already a grandfather. What do you think he said? It is all true—he spoke of himself and of the rest of the regiment. Listen!

"We are the most wonderful creatures in the world. At a very early age we are engaged, and immediately we have the wedding. When the cold weather comes we lay our eggs, but the little ones lie sunny and warm. The wisest of the creatures, the ant,—we have the greatest respect for him!—understands us well. He appreciates us, you may be sure. He does not eat us up at once; he takes our eggs, lays them in the family ant hill on the ground floor—lays them, labeled and numbered, side by side, layer on layer, so that each day a new one may creep out of the egg. Then he puts us in a stable, pinches our hind legs, and milks us till we die. He has given us the prettiest of names—'little milch cow.'

"All creatures who, like the ant, are gifted with common sense call us by this pretty name. It is only human beings who do not. They give us another name, one that we feel to be a great affront—great enough to embitter our whole life. Could you not write a protest against it for us? Could you not rouse these human beings to a sense of the wrong they do us? They look at us so stupidly or, at times, with such envious eyes, just because we eat a rose leaf, while they themselves eat every created thing—whatever grows and is green. And oh, they give us the most humiliating of names! I will not even mention it. Ugh! I feel it to my very stomach. I cannot even pronounce it—at least not when I have my uniform on, and that I always wear.

"I was born on a rose leaf. I and all the regiment live on the rose tree. We live off it, in fact. But then it lives again in us, who belong to the higher order of created beings.

"The human beings do not like us. They pursue and murder us with soapsuds. Oh, it is a horrid drink! I seem to smell it even now. You cannot think how dreadful it is to be washed when one was not made to be washed. Men! you who look at us with your severe, soapsud eyes, think a moment what our place in nature is: we are born upon the roses, we die in roses—our whole life is a rose poem. Do not, I beg you, give us a name which you yourselves think so despicable—the name I cannot bear to pronounce. If you wish to speak of us, call us 'the ants' milch cows—the rose-tree regiment—the little green things.'"

"And I, the man, stood looking at the tree and at the little Greenies (whose name I shall not mention, for I should not like to wound the feelings of the citizens of the rose tree), a large family with eggs and young ones; and I looked at the soapsuds I was going to wash them in, for I too had come with soap and water and murderous intentions. But now I will use it for soap bubbles. Look, how beautiful! Perhaps there lies in each a fairy tale, and the bubble grows large and radiant and looks as if there were a pearl lying inside it.

The bubble swayed and swung. It flew to the door and then burst, but the door opened wide, and there stood Dame Fairytale herself! And now she will tell you better than I can about (I will not say the name) the little green things of the rosebush.

"Plant lice!" said Dame Fairytale. One must call things by their right names. And if one may not do so always, one must at least have the privilege of doing so in a fairy tale.

OLE-LUK-OIE THE DREAM GOD

THERE is nobody in the whole world who knows so many stories as Ole-Luk-Oie, or who can relate them so nicely.

In the evening while the children are seated at the tea table or in their little chairs, very softly he comes up the stairs, for he walks in his socks. He opens the doors without the slightest noise and throws a small quantity of very fine dust in the little ones' eyes (just enough to prevent them from keeping them open), and so they do not see him. Then he creeps behind them and blows softly upon their necks till their heads begin to droop.

But Ole-Luk-Oie does not wish to hurt them. He is very fond of children and only wants them to be quiet that he may tell them pretty stories, and he knows they never are quiet until they are in bed and asleep. Ole-Luk-Oie seats himself upon the bed as soon as they are asleep. He is nicely dressed; his coat is made of silken stuff, it is impossible to say of what color, for it changes from green to red and from red to blue as he turns from side to side. Under each arm he carries an umbrella. One of them, with pictures on the inside, he spreads over good children, and then they dream the most charming stories. But the other umbrella has no pictures, and this he holds over the naughty children, so that they sleep heavily and wake in the morning without having dreamed at all.

Now we shall hear how Ole-Luk-Oie came every night during a whole week to a little boy named Hjalmar, and what it was that he told him. There were seven stories, as there are seven days in the week.

MONDAY

"Now pay attention," said Ole-Luk-Oie in the evening, when Hjalmar was in bed, "and I will decorate the room."

Immediately all the flowers in the flowerpots became large trees with long branches reaching to the ceiling and stretching along the walls, so that the whole room was like a greenhouse. All the branches were loaded with flowers, each flower as beautiful and as fragrant as a rose, and had any one tasted them he would have found them sweeter even than jam. The fruit glittered like gold, and there were cakes so full of plums that they were nearly bursting. It was incomparably beautiful.

At the same time sounded dismal moans from the table drawer in which lay Hjalmar's schoolbooks.

"What can that be now?" said Ole-Luk-Oie, going to the table and pulling out the drawer.

It was a slate, in such distress because of a wrong figure in a sum that it had almost broken itself to pieces. The pencil pulled and tugged at its string as if it were a little dog that wanted to help but could not.

And then came a moan from Hjalmar's copy book. Oh, it was quite terrible to hear! On each leaf stood a row of capital letters, every one having a small letter by its side. This formed a copy. Under these were other letters, which Hjalmar had written; they fancied they looked like the copy, but they were mistaken, for they were leaning on one side as if they intended to fall over the pencil lines.

"See, this is the way you should hold yourselves," said the copy. "Look here, you should slope thus, with a graceful curve."

"Oh, we are very willing to do so," said Hjalmar's letters, "but we cannot, we are so wretchedly made."

"You must be scratched out, then," said Ole-Luk-Oie.

"Oh, no!" they cried, and then they stood up so gracefully that it was quite a pleasure to look at them.

"Now we must give up our stories, and exercise these letters," said Ole-Luk-Oie. "One, two—one, two—" So he drilled them till they stood up gracefully and looked as beautiful as a copy could look. But after Ole-Luk-Oie was gone, and Hjalmar looked at them in the morning, they were as wretched and awkward as ever.

TUESDAY

As soon as Hjalmar was in bed Ole-Luk-Oie touched with his little magic wand all the furniture in the room, which immediately began to chatter. And each article talked only of itself.

Over the chest of drawers hung a large picture in a gilt frame, representing a landscape, with fine old trees, flowers in the grass, and a broad stream which flowed through the wood past several castles far out into the wild ocean.

Ole-Luk-Oie touched the picture with his magic wand, and immediately the birds began to sing, the branches of the trees rustled, and the clouds moved across the sky, casting their shadows on the landscape beneath them.

Then Ole-Luk-Oie lifted little Hjalmar up to the frame and placed his feet in the picture, on the high grass, and there he stood with the sun shining down upon him through the branches of the trees. He ran to the water and seated himself in a little boat which lay there, and which was painted red and white.

The sails glittered like silver, and six swans, each with a golden circlet round its neck and a bright, blue star on its forehead, drew the boat past the green wood, where the trees talked of robbers and witches, and the flowers of beautiful little elves and fairies whose histories the butterflies had related to them.

Brilliant fish with scales like silver and gold swam after the boat, sometimes making a spring and splashing the water round them; while birds, red and blue, small and great, flew after him in two long lines. The gnats danced round them, and the cockchafers cried "Buzz, buzz." They all wanted to follow Hjalmar, and all had some story to tell him. It was a most delightful sail.

On the balconies stood princesses.

Sometimes the forests were thick and dark, sometimes like a beautiful garden gay with sunshine and flowers; he passed great palaces of glass and of marble, and on the balconies stood princesses, whose faces were those of little girls whom Hjalmar knew well and had often played with. One of the little girls held out her hand, in which was a heart made of sugar, more beautiful than any confectioner ever sold. As Hjalmar sailed by he caught hold of one side of the sugar heart and held it fast, and the princess held fast too, so that it broke in two pieces. Hjalmar had one piece and the princess the other, but Hjalmar's was the larger.

At each castle stood little princes acting as sentinels. They presented arms and had golden swords and made it rain plums and tin soldiers, so that they must have been real princes.

Hjalmar continued to sail, sometimes through woods, sometimes as it were through large halls, and then by large cities. At last he came to the town where his nurse lived, who had carried him in her arms when he was a very little boy and had always been kind to him. She nodded and beckoned to him and then sang the little verses she had herself composed and sent to him:

How many, many hours I think on thee,
My own dear Hjalmar, still my pride and joy!
How have I hung delighted over thee,
Kissing thy rosy cheeks, my darling boy!

Thy first low accents it was mine to hear,
To-day my farewell words to thee shall fly.
Oh, may the Lord thy shield be ever near
And fit thee for a mansion in the sky!

And all the birds sang the same tune, the flowers danced on their stems, and the old trees nodded as if Ole-Luk-Oie had been telling them stories, as well.

WEDNESDAY

How the rain did pour down! Hjalmar could hear it in his sleep, and when Ole-Luk-Oie opened the window the water flowed quite up to the window sill. It had the appearance of a large lake outside, and a beautiful ship lay close to the house.

"Wilt thou sail with me to-night, little Hjalmar?" said Ole-Luk-Oie. "Then we shall see foreign countries, and thou shalt return here in the morning."

All in a moment there stood Hjalmar, in his best clothes, on the deck of the noble ship, and immediately the weather became fine.

They sailed through the streets, round by the church, while on every side rolled the wide, great sea.

They sailed till the land disappeared, and then they saw a flock of storks who had left their own country and were traveling to warmer climates. The storks flew one behind another and had already been a long, long time on the wing.

One of them seemed so tired that his wings could scarcely carry him. He was soon left very far behind. At length he sank lower and lower, with outstretched wings, flapping them in vain, till his feet touched the rigging of the ship, and he slid from the sails to the deck and stood before them. Then a sailor boy caught him and put him in the henhouse with the fowls, the ducks, and the turkeys, while the poor stork stood quite bewildered among them.

"Just look at that fellow," said the chickens.

Then the turkey cock puffed himself out as large as he could and inquired who he was, and the ducks waddled backwards, crying, "Quack, quack!"

The stork told them all about warm Africa—of the pyramids and of the ostrich, which, like a wild horse, runs across the desert. But the ducks did not understand what he said, and quacked amongst themselves, "We are all of the same opinion; namely, that he is stupid."

"Yes, to be sure, he is stupid," said the turkey cock, and gobbled.

Then the stork remained quite silent and thought of his home in Africa.

"Those are handsome thin legs of yours," said the turkey cock. "What do they cost a yard?"

"Quack, quack, quack," grinned the ducks; but the stork pretended not to hear.

"You may as well laugh," said the turkey, "for that remark was rather witty, but perhaps it was above you. Ah, ah, is he not clever? He will be a great amusement to us while he remains here." And then he gobbled, and the ducks quacked: "Gobble, gobble"; "Quack, quack!"

What a terrible uproar they made while they were having such fun among themselves!

Then Hjalmar went to the henhouse and, opening the door, called to the stork. He hopped out on the deck. He had rested himself now, and he looked happy and seemed as if he nodded to Hjalmar as if to thank him. Then he spread his wings and flew away to warmer countries, while the hens clucked, the ducks quacked, and the turkey cock's head turned quite scarlet.

"To-morrow you shall be made into soup," said Hjalmar to the fowls; and then he awoke and found himself lying in his little bed.

It was a wonderful journey which Ole-Luk-Oie had made him take this night.

THURSDAY

"What do you think I have here?" said the Dream Man. "Do not be frightened, and you shall see a little mouse." And then he held out his hand, in which lay a lovely little creature. "It has come to invite you to a wedding. Two little mice are going to be married to-night. They live under the floor of your mother's storeroom, and that must be a fine dwelling place."

"But how can I get through the little mouse-hole in the floor?" asked the little boy.

"Leave me to manage that," said the Dream Man. "I will soon make you small enough." And then he touched the boy with his magic wand, upon which he became smaller and smaller until at last he was no longer than a little finger. "Now you can borrow the dress of your tin soldier. I think it will just fit you. It looks well to wear a uniform when you go into company."

"Yes, certainly," said the boy, and in a moment he was dressed as neatly as the neatest of all tin soldiers.

"Will you be so good as to seat yourself in your mamma's thimble," said the little mouse, "that I may have the pleasure of drawing you to the wedding?"

"Will you really take so much trouble, young lady?" said he. And so in this way he rode to the mouse's wedding.

First they went under the floor, and then through a long passage which was scarcely high enough to allow the thimble to drive under, and the whole passage was lit up with the light of rotten wood.

"Does it not smell delicious?" asked the mouse, as she drew him along. "The wall and the floor have been smeared with bacon rind; nothing could be nicer."

Very soon they arrived at the bridal hall. On the right stood all the little lady mice, whispering and giggling as if they were making game of each other. To the left were the gentlemen mice, stroking their whiskers with their forepaws. And in the center of the hall could be seen the bridal pair, standing side by side in a hollow cheese rind and kissing each other while all eyes were upon them.

More and more friends kept coming, till the mice were in danger of treading each other to death; for the bridal pair now stood in the doorway, and none could pass in or out.

The room had been rubbed over with bacon rind like the passage, which was all the refreshment offered to the guests. But for dessert a pea was passed around, on which a mouse had bitten the first letters of the names of the betrothed pair. This was something quite uncommon. All the mice said it was a very beautiful wedding, and that they had been very agreeably entertained.

After this Hjalmar returned home. He had certainly been in grand society, but he had been obliged to creep under a room and to make himself small enough to wear the uniform of a tin soldier.

FRIDAY

"It is incredible how many old people there are who would be glad to have me at night," said Ole-Luk-Oie, "especially those who have done something wrong.

"'Good old Ole,' say they to me, 'we cannot close our eyes, and we lie awake the whole night and see all our evil deeds sitting on our beds like little imps and sprinkling us with scalding water. Will you come and drive them away, that we may have a good night's rest?' and then they sigh so deeply and say: 'We would gladly pay you for it. Good night, Ole-Luk, the money lies in the window.' But I never do anything for gold."

"What shall we do to-night?" asked Hjalmar.

"I do not know whether you would care to go to another wedding," replied Ole-Luk-Oie, "although it is quite a different affair from the one we saw last night. Your sister's large doll, that is dressed like a man and is called Herman, intends to marry the doll Bertha. It is also the dolls' birthday, and they will receive many presents."

"Yes, I know that already," said Hjalmar; "my sister always allows her dolls to keep their birthdays or to have a wedding when they require new clothes. That has happened already a hundred times, I am quite sure."

"Yes, so it may; but to-night is the hundred-and-first wedding, and when that has taken place it must be the last; therefore this is to be extremely beautiful. Only look."

Hjalmar looked at the table, and there stood the little cardboard dolls' house, with lights in all the windows, and drawn up before it were the tin soldiers, presenting arms.

The bridal pair were seated on the floor, leaning against the leg of the table, looking very thoughtful and with good reason. Then Ole-Luk-Oie, dressed up in grandmother's black gown, married them.

As soon as the ceremony was concluded all the furniture in the room joined in singing a beautiful song which had been composed by the lead pencil, and which went to the melody of a military tattoo:

"Waft, gentle breeze, our kind farewell
To the tiny house where the bride folks dwell.
 With their skin of kid leather fitting so well,
They are straight and upright as a tailor's ell.
Hurrah! hurrah! for beau and belle.
Let echo repeat our kind farewell."

And now came the presents; but the bridal pair had nothing to eat, for love was to be their food.

"Shall we go to a country house, or travel?" asked the bridegroom.

They consulted the swallow, who had traveled so far, and the old hen in the yard, who had brought up five broods of chickens.

And the swallow talked to them of warm countries where the grapes hang in large clusters on the vines and the air is soft and mild, and about the mountains glowing with colors more beautiful than we can think of.

"But they have no red cabbage such as we have," said the hen. "I was once in the country with my chickens for a whole summer. There was a large sand pit in which we could walk about and scratch as we liked. Then we got into a garden in which grew red cabbage. Oh, how nice it was! I cannot think of anything more delicious."

"But one cabbage stalk is exactly like another," said the swallow; "and here we often have bad weather."

"Yes, but we are accustomed to it," said the hen.

"But it is so cold here, and freezes sometimes."

"Cold weather is good for cabbages," said the hen; "besides, we do have it warm here sometimes. Four years ago we had a summer that lasted more than five weeks, and it was so hot one could scarcely breathe. And then in this country we have no poisonous animals, and we are free from robbers. He must be a blockhead, who does not consider our country the finest of all lands. He ought not to be allowed to live here." And then the hen wept very much and said: "I have also traveled. I once went twelve miles in a coop, and it was not pleasant traveling at all."

"The hen is a sensible woman," said the doll Bertha. "I don't care for traveling over mountains, just to go up and come down again. No, let us go to the sand pit in front of the gate and then take a walk in the cabbage garden."

And so they settled it.

SATURDAY

"Am I to hear any more stories?" asked little Hjalmar, as soon as Ole-Luk-Oie had sent him to sleep.

"We shall have no time this evening," said he, spreading out his prettiest umbrella over the child. "Look at these Chinese people." And then the whole umbrella appeared like a large china bowl, with blue trees and pointed bridges upon which stood little Chinamen nodding their heads.

"We must make all the world beautiful for to-morrow morning," said Ole-Luk-Oie, "for it will be a holiday; it is Sunday. I must now go to the church steeple and see if the little sprites who live there have polished the bells so that they may sound sweetly; then I must go into the fields and see if the wind has blown the dust from the grass and the leaves; and the most difficult task of all which I have to do is to take down all the stars and brighten them up. I have to number them first before I put them in my apron, and also to number the places from which I take them, so that they may go back into the right holes, or else they would not remain and we should have a number of falling stars, for they would all tumble down one after another."

"Hark ye, Mr. Luk-Oie!" said an old portrait which hung on the wall of Hjalmar's bed-room. "Do you know me? I am Hjalmar's great-grandfather. I thank you for telling the boy stories, but you must not confuse his ideas. The stars cannot be taken down from the sky and polished; they are spheres like our earth, which is a good thing for them."

"Thank you, old great-grandfather," said Ole-Luk-Oie. "I thank you. You may be the head of the family, as no doubt you are, and very old, but I am older still. I am an ancient heathen. The old Romans and Greeks named me the Dream God. I have visited the no-blest houses,—yes, and I continue to do so,—still I know how to conduct myself both to high and low, and now you may tell the stories yourself"; and so Ole-Luk-Oie walked off, taking his umbrellas with him.

"Well, well, one is never to give an opinion, I suppose," grumbled the portrait. And it woke Hjalmar.

SUNDAY

"Good evening," said Ole-Luk-Oie.

Hjalmar nodded, and then sprang out of bed and turned his great-grandfather's por-trait to the wall so that it might not interrupt them as it had done yesterday. "Now," said he, "you must tell me some stories about five green peas that lived in one pod, or of the chickseed that courted the chickweed, or of the Darning-needle who acted so proudly because she fancied herself an embroidery needle."

"You may have too much of a good thing," said Ole-Luk-Oie. "You know that I like best to show you something, so I will show you my brother. He is also called Ole-Luk-Oie, but he never visits any one but once, and when he does come he takes him away on his horse and tells him stories as they ride along.

"He knows only two stories. One of these is so wonderfully beautiful that no one in the world can imagine anything at all like it, but the other it would be impossible to de-scribe."

Then Ole-Luk-Oie lifted Hjalmar up to the window. "There, now you can see my brother, the other Ole-Luk-Oie; he is also called Death. You see he is not so bad as they represent him in picture books. There he is a skeleton, but here his coat is embroidered with silver, and he wears the splendid uniform of a hussar, and a mantle of black velvet flies behind him over the horse. Look, how he gallops along."

Hjalmar saw that as this Ole-Luk-Oie rode on he lifted up old and young and carried them away on his horse. Some he seated in front of him and some behind, but always inquired first, "How stands the record book?"

"Good," they all answered.

"Yes, but let me see for myself," he replied, and they were obliged to give him the books. Then all those who had "Very good" or "Exceedingly good" came in front of the horse and heard the beautiful story, while those who had "Middling" or "Fairly good" in their books were obliged to sit behind. They cried and wanted to jump down from the horse, but they could not get free, for they seemed fastened to the seat.

"Why, Death is a most splendid Luk-Oie," said Hjalmar. "I am not in the least afraid of him."

"You need have no fear of him," said Ole-Luk-Oie; "but take care and keep a good conduct book."

"Now I call that very instructive," murmured the great-grandfather's portrait. "It is useful sometimes to express an opinion." So he was quite satisfied.

These are some of the doings and sayings of Ole-Luk-Oie. I hope he may visit you himself this evening and relate some more.

THE MONEY BOX

I N a nursery where a number of toys lay scattered about, a money box stood on the top of a very high wardrobe. It was made of clay in the shape of a pig and had been bought of the potter. In the back of the pig was a slit, and this slit had been enlarged with a knife so that dollars, or even crown pieces, might slip through— and indeed there were two in the box, besides a number of pence. The money-pig was stuffed so full that it could no longer rattle, which is the highest state of perfectness to which a money-pig can attain.

There he stood upon the cupboard, high and lofty, looking down upon everything else in the room. He knew very well that he had enough inside himself to buy up all the other toys, and this gave him a very good opinion of his own value.

The rest thought of this fact also, although they did not express it, there were so many other things to talk about. A large doll, still handsome (though rather old, for her neck had been mended) lay inside one of the drawers, which was partly open. She called out to the others, "Let us have a game at being men and women; that is something worth playing at."

Upon this there was a great uproar; even the engravings which hung in frames on the wall turned round in their excitement and showed that they had a wrong side to them, although they had not the least intention of exposing themselves in this way or of object- ing to the game.

It was late at night, but as the moon shone through the windows, they had light at a cheap rate. And as the game was now to begin, all were invited to take part in it, even the children's wagon, which certainly belonged among the coarser playthings. "Each has its own value," said the wagon; "we cannot all be noblemen; there must be some to do the work."

The money-pig was the only one who received a written invitation. He stood so high that they were afraid he would not accept a verbal message. But in his reply he said if he had to take a part he must enjoy the sport from his own home; they were to arrange for him to do so. And so they did.

The little toy theater was therefore put up in such a way that the money-pig could look directly into it. Some wanted to begin with a comedy and afterwards to have a tea party and a discussion for mental improvement, but they began with the latter first.

The rocking-horse spoke of training and races; the wagon, of railways and steam pow- er—for these subjects belonged to each of their professions, and it was right they should talk of them. The clock talked politics—"Tick, tick." He professed to know what was the time of the day, but there was a whisper that he did not go correctly. The bamboo cane stood by, looking stiff and proud (he was vain of his brass ferrule and silver top), and on the sofa lay two worked cushions, pretty but stupid.

When the play at the little theater began, the rest sat and looked on; they were re- quested to applaud and stamp, or crack, whenever they felt gratified with what they saw. The riding whip said he never cracked for old people, only for the young—those who were not yet married. "I crack for everybody," said the nutcracker.

"Yes, and a fine noise you make," thought the audience as the play went on.

It was not worth much, but it was very well played, and all the actors turned their painted sides to the audience, for they were made to be seen only on one side. The acting was wonderful, excepting that sometimes the actors came out beyond the lamps, because the wires were a little too long.

The doll whose neck had been mended was so excited that the place in her neck burst, and the money-pig declared he must do something for one of the players as they had all pleased him so much. So he made up his mind to mention one of them in his will as the one to be buried with him in the family vault, whenever that event should happen.

They enjoyed the comedy so much that they gave up all thoughts of the tea party and only carried out their idea of intellectual amusement, which they called playing at men and women. And there was nothing wrong about it, for it was only play. All the while each one thought most of himself or of what the money-pig could be thinking. The money-pig's thoughts were on (as he supposed) a very far-distant time—of making his will, and of his burial, and of when it might all come to pass.

Certainly sooner than he expected; for all at once down he came from the top of the press, fell on the floor, and was broken to pieces. Then all the pennies hopped and danced about in the most amusing manner. The little ones twirled round like tops, and the large ones rolled away as far as they could, especially the one great silver crown piece, who had often wanted to go out into the world. And he had his wish as well as all the rest of the money. The pieces of the money-pig were thrown into the dustbin, and the next day there stood a new money-pig on the cupboard, but it had not a farthing inside it yet, and therefore, like the old one, could not rattle.

This was the beginning with him, and with us it shall be the end of our story.

ELDER-TREE MOTHER

THERE was once a little boy who had taken cold by going out and getting his feet wet. No one could think how he had managed to do so, for the weather was quite dry. His mother undressed him and put him to bed, and then she brought in the teapot to make him a good cup of elder tea, which is so warming.

At the same time the friendly old man who lived all alone at the top of the house came in at the door. He had neither wife nor child, but he was very fond of children and knew so many fairy tales and stories that it was a pleasure to hear him talk. "Now, if you drink your tea," said the mother, "very likely you will have a story in the meantime."

"ut how did the little fellow get his feet wet?" asked he ...

"Yes, if I could think of a new one to tell," said the old man. "But how did the little fellow get his feet wet?" asked he.

"Ah," said the mother, "that is what we cannot make out."

"Will you tell me a story?" asked the boy.

"Yes, if you can tell me exactly how deep the gutter is in the little street through which you go to school."

"Just halfway up to my knee," said the boy, promptly; "that is, if I stand in the deepest part."

"It is easy to see how we got our feet wet," said the old man. "Well, now I suppose I ought to tell a story, but really I don't know any more."

"You can make up one, I know," said the boy. "Mother says that you can turn everything you look at into a story, and everything, even, that you touch."

"Ah, but those tales and stories are worth nothing. The real ones come of themselves; they knock at my forehead and say, 'Here we are!'"

"Won't there be a knock soon?" asked the boy. And his mother laughed as she put elder flowers in the teapot and poured boiling water over them. "Oh, do tell me a story."

"Yes, if a story comes of itself, but tales and stories are very grand; they only come when it pleases them. Stop," he cried all at once, "here we have it; look! there is a story in the teapot now."

The little boy looked at the teapot and saw the lid raise itself gradually and long branches stretch out, even from the spout, in all directions till they became larger and larger, and there appeared a great elder tree covered with flowers white and fresh. It spread itself even to the bed and pushed the curtains aside, and oh, how fragrant the blossoms were!

In the midst of the tree sat a pleasant-looking old woman in a very strange dress. The dress was green, like the leaves of the elder tree, and was decorated with large white elder blossoms. It was not easy to tell whether the border was made of some kind of stuff or of real flowers.

"What is that woman's name?" asked the boy.

"The Romans and Greeks called her a dryad," said the old man, "but we do not understand that name; we have a better one for her in the quarter of the town where the sailors live. They call her Elder-flower Mother, and you must pay attention to her now, and listen while you look at the beautiful tree.

"Just such a large, blooming tree as this stands outside in the corner of a poor little yard, and under this tree, one bright sunny afternoon, sat two old people, a sailor and his wife. They had great-grandchildren, and would soon celebrate the golden wedding, which is the fiftieth anniversary of the wedding day in many countries, and the Elder Mother sat in the tree and looked as pleased as she does now.

"'I know when the golden wedding is to be,' said she, but they did not hear her; they were talking of olden times. 'Do you remember,' said the old sailor, 'when we were quite little and used to run about and play in the very same yard where we are now sitting, and how we planted little twigs in one corner and made a garden?'

"'Yes,' said the old woman, 'I remember it quite well; and how we watered the twigs, and one of them was a sprig of elder that took root and put forth green shoots, until in time it became the great tree under which we old people are now seated.'

"'To be sure,' he replied, 'and in that corner yonder stands the water butt in which I used to swim my boat that I had cut out all myself; and it sailed well too. But since then I have learned a very different kind of sailing.'

"'Yes, but before that we went to school,' said she, 'and then we were prepared for confirmation. How we both cried on that day! But in the afternoon we went hand in hand up to the round tower and saw the view over Copenhagen and across the water; then we went to Fredericksburg, where the king and queen were sailing in their beautiful boat on the canals.'

"'But I had to sail on a very different voyage elsewhere and be away from home for years on long voyages,' said the old sailor.

"'Ah yes, and I used to cry about you,' said she, 'for I thought you must be lying drowned at the bottom of the sea, with the waves sweeping over you. And many a time have I got up in the night to see if the weathercock had turned; it turned often enough, but you came not. How well I remember one day the rain was pouring down from the skies, and the man came to the house where I was in service to take away the dust. I went down to him with the dust box and stood for a moment at the door,—what shocking weather it was!—and while I stood there the postman came up and brought me a letter from you.

"'How that letter had traveled about! I tore it open and read it. I laughed and wept at the same time, I was so happy. It said that you were in warm countries where the coffee berries grew, and what a beautiful country it was, and described many other wonderful things. And so I stood reading by the dustbin, with the rain pouring down, when all at once somebody came and clasped me round the waist.'

"'Yes, and you gave him such a box on the ears that they tingled,' said the old man.

"'I did not know that it was you,' she replied; 'but you had arrived as quickly as your letter, and you looked so handsome, and, indeed, so you are still. You had a large yellow silk handkerchief in your pocket and a shiny hat on your head. You looked quite fine. And all the time what weather it was, and how dismal the street looked!'

"'And then do you remember,' said he, 'when we were married, and our first boy came, and then Marie, and Niels, and Peter, and Hans Christian?'

"'Indeed I do,' she replied; 'and they are all grown up respectable men and women, whom every one likes.'

"'And now their children have little ones,' said the old sailor. 'There are great-grandchildren for us, strong and healthy too. Was it not about this time of year that we were married?'

"'Yes, and to-day is the golden-wedding day,' said Elder-tree Mother, popping her head out just between the two old people; and they thought it was a neighbor nodding to them. Then they looked at each other and clasped their hands together. Presently came their children and grand*-children, who knew very well that it was the golden-wedding day. They had already wished them joy on that very morning, but the old people had forgotten it, although they remembered so well all that had happened many years before. And the elder tree smelled sweet, and the setting sun shone upon the faces of the old people till they looked quite ruddy. And the youngest of their grandchildren danced round them joyfully, and said they were going to have a feast in the evening, and there were to be hot potatoes. Then the Elder Mother nodded in the tree and cried 'Hurrah!' with all the rest."

"But that is not a story," said the little boy who had been listening.

"Not till you understand it," said the old man. "But let us ask the Elder Mother to explain it."

"It was not exactly a story," said the Elder Mother, "but the story is coming now, and it is a true one. For out of truth the most wonderful stories grow, just as my beautiful elder bush has sprung out of the teapot." And then she took the little boy out of bed and laid him on her bosom, and the blooming branches of elder closed over them so that they sat, as it were, in a leafy bower, and the bower flew with them through the air in the most delightful manner.

Then the Elder Mother all at once changed to a beautiful young maiden, but her dress was still of the same green stuff, ornamented with a border of white elder blossoms such as the Elder Mother had worn. In her bosom she wore a real elder flower, and a wreath of the same was entwined in her golden ringlets. Her large blue eyes were very beautiful to look at. She was of the same age as the boy, and they kissed each other and felt very happy.

They left the arbor together, hand in hand, and found themselves in a beautiful flower garden which belonged to their home. On the green lawn their father's stick was tied up. There was life in this stick for the little ones, for no sooner did they place themselves upon it than the white knob changed into a pretty neighing head with a black, flowing mane, and four long, slender legs sprung forth. The creature was strong and spirited, and galloped with them round the grassplot.

"Hurrah! now we will ride many miles away," said the boy; "we'll ride to the nobleman's estate, where we went last year."

Then they rode round the grassplot again, and the little maiden, who, we know, was Elder-tree Mother, kept crying out: "Now we are in the country. Do you see the farm-house, with a great baking oven standing out from the wall by the road-side like a gigantic egg? There is an elder spreading its branches over it, and a cock is marching about and scratching for the chickens. See how he struts!

"Now we are near the church. There it stands on the hill, shaded by the great oak trees, one of which is half dead. See, here we are at the blacksmith's forge. How the fire burns! And the half-clad men are striking the hot iron with the hammer, so that the sparks fly about. Now then, away to the nobleman's beautiful estate!" And the boy saw all that the little girl spoke of as she sat behind him on the stick, for it passed before him although they were only galloping round the grassplot. Then they played together in a side walk and raked up the earth to make a little garden. Then she took elder flowers out of her hair and planted them, and they grew just like those which he had heard the old people talking about, and which they had planted in their young days. They walked about hand in hand too, just as the old people had done when they were children, but they did not go up the round tower nor to Fredericksburg garden. No; but the little girl seized the boy round the waist, and they rode all over the whole country (sometimes it was spring, then summer; then autumn and winter followed), while thousands of images were pre-sented to the boy's eyes and heart, and the little girl constantly sang to him, "You must never forget all this." And through their whole flight the elder tree sent forth the sweetest fragrance.

They passed roses and fresh beech trees, but the perfume of the elder tree was strong-er than all, for its flowers hung round the little maiden's heart, against which the boy so often leaned his head during their flight.

"It is beautiful here in the spring," said the maiden, as they stood in a grove of beech trees covered with fresh green leaves, while at their feet the sweet-scented thyme and blushing anemone lay spread amid the green grass in delicate bloom. "O that it were al-ways spring in the fragrant beech groves!"

"Here it is delightful in summer," said the maiden, as they passed old knights' castles telling of days gone by and saw the high walls and pointed gables mirrored in the rivers beneath, where swans were sailing about and peeping into the cool green avenues. In the fields the corn waved to and fro like the sea. Red and yellow flowers grew amongst the ruins, and the hedges were covered with wild hops and blooming convolvulus. In the evening the moon rose round and full, and the haystacks in the meadows filled the air with their sweet scent. These were scenes never to be forgotten.

"It is lovely here also in autumn," said the little maiden, and then the scene changed again. The sky appeared higher and more beautifully blue, while the forest glowed with colors of red, green, and gold. The hounds were off to the chase, and large flocks of wild birds flew screaming over the Huns' graves, where the blackberry bushes twined round the old ruins. The dark blue sea was dotted with white sails, and in the barns sat old women, maidens, and children picking hops into a large tub. The young ones sang songs, and the old ones told fairy tales of wizards and witches. There could be nothing more pleasant than all this.

"Again," said the maiden, "it is beautiful here in winter." Then in a moment all the trees were covered with hoarfrost, so that they looked like white coral. The snow crackled beneath the feet as if every one had on new boots, and one shooting star after another fell from the sky. In warm rooms there could be seen the Christmas trees, decked out with presents and lighted up amid festivities and joy. In the country farmhouses could be heard the sound of a violin, and there were games for apples, so that even the poorest child could say, "It is beautiful in winter."

And beautiful indeed were all the scenes which the maiden showed to the little boy, and always around them floated the fragrance of the elder blossom, and ever above them waved the red flag with the white cross, under which the old seaman had sailed. The boy—who had become a youth, and who had gone as a sailor out into the wide world and sailed to warm countries where the coffee grew, and to whom the little girl had given an elder blossom from her bosom for a keepsake, when she took leave of him—placed the flower in his hymn book; and when he opened it in foreign lands he always turned to the spot where this flower of remembrance lay, and the more he looked at it the fresher it appeared. He could, as it were, breathe the homelike fragrance of the woods, and see the little girl looking at him from between the petals of the flower with her clear blue eyes, and hear her whispering, "It is beautiful here at home in spring and summer, in autumn and in winter," while hundreds of these home scenes passed through his memory.

Many years had passed, and he was now an old man, seated with his old wife under an elder tree in full blossom. They were holding each other's hands, just as the great-grandfather and grandmother had done, and spoke, as they did, of olden times and of the golden wedding. The little maiden with the blue eyes and with the elder blossoms in her hair sat in the tree and nodded to them and said, "To-day is the golden wedding."

And then she took two flowers out of her wreath and kissed them, and they shone first like silver and then like gold, and as she placed them on the heads of the old people, each flower became a golden crown. And there they sat like a king and queen under the sweet-scented tree, which still looked like an elder bush. Then he related to his old wife the story of the Elder-tree Mother, just as he had heard it told when he was a little boy,

As she placed them on the heads of the old people, each flower became a golden crown

and they both fancied it very much like their own story, especially in parts which they liked the best.

"Well, and so it is," said the little maiden in the tree. "Some call me Elder Mother, others a dryad, but my real name is Memory. It is I who sit in the tree as it grows and grows, and I can think of the past and relate many things. Let me see if you have still preserved the flower."

Then the old man opened his hymn book, and there lay the elder flower, as fresh as if it had only just been placed there, and Memory nodded. And the two old people with the golden crowns on their heads sat in the red glow of the evening sunlight and closed their eyes, and—and—the story was ended.

The little boy lay in his bed and did not quite know whether he had been dreaming or listening to a story. The teapot stood on the table, but no elder bush grew out of it, and the old man who had really told the tale was on the threshold and just going out at the door.

"How beautiful it was," said the little boy. "Mother, I have been to warm countries."

"I can quite believe it," said his mother. "When any one drinks two full cups of elder-flower tea, he may well get into warm countries"; and then she covered him up, that he should not take cold. "You have slept well while I have been disputing with the old man as to whether it was a real story or a fairy legend."

"And where is the Elder-tree Mother?" asked the boy.

"She is in the teapot," said the mother, "and there she may stay."

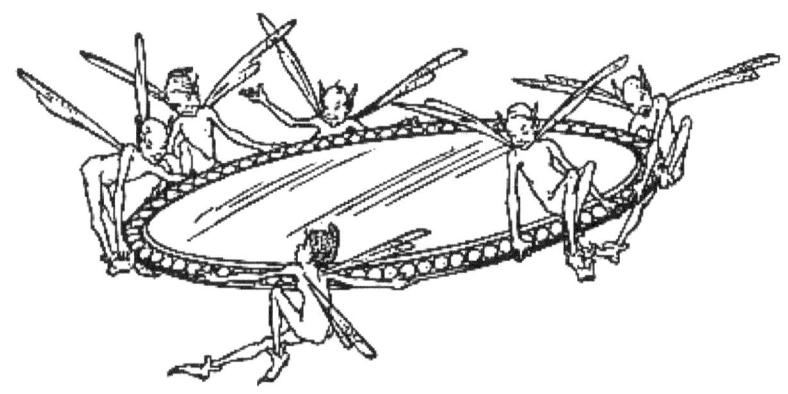

THE SNOW QUEEN

STORY THE FIRST

WHICH DESCRIBES A LOOKING-GLASS AND ITS BROKEN FRAGMENTS

YOU must attend to the beginning of this story, for when we get to the end we shall know more than we now do about a very wicked hobgoblin; he was one of the most mischievous of all sprites, for he was a real demon.

One day when he was in a merry mood he made a looking-glass which had the power of making everything good or beautiful that was reflected in it shrink almost to nothing, while everything that was worthless and bad was magnified so as to look ten times worse than it really was.

The most lovely landscapes appeared like boiled spinach, and all the people became hideous and looked as if they stood on their heads and had no bodies. Their countenances were so distorted that no one could recognize them, and even one freckle on the face appeared to spread over the whole of the nose and mouth. The demon said this was very amusing. When a good or holy thought passed through the mind of any one a wrinkle was seen in the mirror, and then how the demon laughed at his cunning invention.

All who went to the demon's school—for he kept a school—talked everywhere of the wonders they had seen, and declared that people could now, for the first time, see what the world and its inhabitants were really like. They carried the glass about everywhere, till at last there was not a land nor a people who had not been looked at through this distorted mirror.

They wanted even to fly with it up to heaven to see the angels, but the higher they flew the more slippery the glass became, and they could scarcely hold it. At last it slipped from their hands, fell to the earth, and was broken into millions of pieces.

But now the looking-glass caused more unhappiness than ever, for some of the fragments were not so large as a grain of sand, and they flew about the world into every country. And when one of these tiny atoms flew into a person's eye it stuck there, unknown to himself, and from that moment he viewed everything the wrong way, and could see only the worst side of what he looked at, for even the smallest fragment retained the same power which had belonged to the whole mirror.

Some few persons even got a splinter of the looking-glass in their hearts, and this was terrible, for their hearts became cold and hard like a lump of ice. A few of the pieces were so large that they could be used as windowpanes; it would have been a sad thing indeed to look at our friends through them. Other pieces were made into spectacles, and this was dreadful, for those who wore them could see nothing either rightly or justly. At all this the wicked demon laughed till his sides shook, to see the mischief he had done. There are still a number of these little fragments of glass floating about in the air, and now you shall hear what happened with one of them.

SECOND STORY

A LITTLE BOY AND A LITTLE GIRL

In a large town full of houses and people there is not room for everybody to have even a little garden. Most people are obliged to content themselves with a few flowers in flowerpots.

In one of these large towns lived two poor children who had a garden somewhat larger and better than a few flowerpots. They were not brother and sister, but they loved each other almost as much as if they had been. Their parents lived opposite each other in two garrets where the roofs of neighboring houses nearly joined each other, and the water pipe ran between them. In each roof was a little window, so that any one could step across the gutter from one window to the other.

The parents of each of these children had a large wooden box in which they cultivated kitchen vegetables for their own use, and in each box was a little rosebush which grew luxuriantly.

After a while the parents decided to place these two boxes across the water pipe, so that they reached from one window to the other and looked like two banks of flowers. Sweet peas drooped over the boxes, and the rosebushes shot forth long branches, which were trained about the windows and clustered together almost like a triumphal arch of leaves and flowers.

The boxes were very high, and the children knew they must not climb upon them without permission; but they often had leave to step out and sit upon their little stools under the rosebushes or play quietly together.

In winter all this pleasure came to an end, for the windows were sometimes quite frozen over. But they would warm copper pennies on the stove and hold the warm pennies against the frozen pane; then there would soon be a little round hole through which they could peep, and the soft, bright eyes of the little boy and girl would sparkle through the hole at each window as they looked at each other. Their names were Kay and Gerda. In summer they could be together with one jump from the window, but in winter they had to go up and down the long staircase and out through the snow before they could meet.

"See! there are the white bees swarming," said Kay's old grandmother one day when it was snowing.

"Have they a queen bee?" asked the little boy, for he knew that the real bees always had a queen.

"To be sure they have," said the grandmother. "She is flying there where the swarm is thickest. She is the largest of them all and never remains on the earth, but flies up to the dark clouds. Often at midnight she flies through the streets of the town and breathes with her frosty breath upon the windows; then the ice freezes on the panes into wonderful forms that look like flowers and castles."

"Yes, I have seen them," said both the children; and they knew it must be true.

"Can the Snow Queen come in here?" asked the little girl.

"Only let her come," said the boy. "I'll put her on the warm stove, and then she'll melt."

The grandmother smoothed his hair and told him more stories.

That same evening when little Kay was at home, half undressed, he climbed upon a chair by the window and peeped out through the little round hole. A few flakes of snow were falling, and one of them, rather larger than the rest, alighted on the edge of one of the flower boxes. Strange to say, this snowflake grew larger and larger till at last it took the form of a woman dressed in garments of white gauze, which looked like millions of starry snowflakes linked together. She was fair and beautiful, but made of ice—glittering, dazzling ice. Still, she was alive, and her eyes sparkled like bright stars, though there was neither peace nor rest in them. She nodded toward the window and waved her hand. The little boy was frightened and sprang from the chair, and at the same moment it seemed as if a large bird flew by the window.

On the following day there was a clear frost, and very soon came the spring. The sun shone; the young green leaves burst forth; the swallows built their nests; windows were opened, and the children sat once more in the garden on the roof, high above all the other rooms.

The children sat once more in the garden on the roof . . .

How beautifully the roses blossomed this summer! The little girl had learned a hymn in which roses were spoken of. She thought of their own roses, and she sang the hymn to the little boy, and he sang, too:

"Roses bloom and fade away;
The Christ-child shall abide alway.
Blessed are we his face to see
And ever little children be."

Then the little ones held each other by the hand, and kissed the roses, and looked at the bright sunshine, and spoke to it as if the Christ-child were really there. Those were glorious summer days. How beautiful and fresh it was out among the rosebushes, which seemed as if they would never leave off blooming.

One day Kay and Gerda sat looking at a book of pictures of animals and birds. Just then, as the clock in the church tower struck twelve, Kay said, "Oh, something has struck my heart!" and soon after, "There is certainly something in my eye."

The little girl put her arm round his neck and looked into his eye, but she could see nothing.

"I believe it is gone," he said. But it was not gone; it was one of those bits of the looking-glass,—that magic mirror of which we have spoken,—the ugly glass which made everything great and good appear small and ugly, while all that was wicked and bad became more visible, and every little fault could be plainly seen. Poor little Kay had also received a small splinter in his heart, which very quickly turned to a lump of ice. He felt no more pain, but the glass was there still. "Why do you cry?" said he at last. "It makes you look ugly. There is nothing the matter with me now. Oh, fie!" he cried suddenly; "that rose is worm-eaten, and this one is quite crooked. After all, they are ugly roses, just like the box in which they stand." And then he kicked the boxes with his foot and pulled off the two roses.

"Why, Kay, what are you doing?" cried the little girl; and then when he saw how grieved she was he tore off another rose and jumped through his own window, away from sweet little Gerda.

When afterward she brought out the picture book he said, "It is only fit for babies in long clothes," and when grandmother told stories he would interrupt her with "but"; or sometimes when he could manage it he would get behind her chair, put on a pair of spectacles, and imitate her very cleverly to make the people laugh. By and by he began to mimic the speech and gait of persons in the street. All that was peculiar or disagreeable in a person he would imitate directly, and people said, "That boy will be very clever; he has a remarkable genius." But it was the piece of glass in his eye and the coldness in his heart that made him act like this. He would even tease little Gerda, who loved him with all her heart.

His games too were quite different; they were not so childlike. One winter's day, when it snowed, he brought out a burning glass, then, holding out the skirt of his blue coat, let the snowflakes fall upon it.

"Look in this glass, Gerda," said he, and she saw how every flake of snow was magnified and looked like a beautiful flower or a glittering star.

"Is it not clever," said Kay, "and much more interesting than looking at real flowers? There is not a single fault in it. The snowflakes are quite perfect till they begin to melt."

Soon after, Kay made his appearance in large, thick gloves and with his sledge at his back. He called upstairs to Gerda, "I've got leave to go into the great square, where the other boys play and ride." And away he went.

In the great square the boldest among the boys would often tie their sledges to the wagons of the country people and so get a ride. This was capital. But while they were all amusing themselves, and Kay with them, a great sledge came by; it was painted white, and in it sat some one wrapped in a rough white fur and wearing a white cap. The sledge drove twice round the square, and Kay fastened his own little sledge to it, so that when it went away he went with it. It went faster and faster right through the next street, and the person who drove turned round and nodded pleasantly to Kay as if they were well acquainted with each other; but whenever Kay wished to loosen his little sledge the driver turned and nodded as if to signify that he was to stay, so Kay sat still, and they drove out through the town gate.

Then the snow began to fall so heavily that the little boy could not see a hand's breadth before him, but still they drove on. He suddenly loosened the cord so that the large sledge might go on without him, but it was of no use; his little carriage held fast, and away they went like the wind. Then he called out loudly, but nobody heard him, while the snow beat upon him, and the sledge flew onward. Every now and then it gave a jump, as if they were going over hedges and ditches. The boy was frightened and tried to say a prayer, but he could remember nothing but the multiplication table.

The snowflakes became larger and larger, till they appeared like great white birds. All at once they sprang on one side, the great sledge stopped, and the person who had driven it rose up. The fur and the cap, which were made entirely of snow, fell off, and he saw a lady, tall and white; it was the Snow Queen.

"We have driven well," said she; "but why do you tremble so? Here, creep into my warm fur." Then she seated him beside her in the sledge, and as she wrapped the fur about him, he felt as if he were sinking into a snowdrift.

"Are you still cold?" she asked, as she kissed him on the forehead. The kiss was colder than ice; it went quite through to his heart, which was almost a lump of ice already. He felt as if he were going to die, but only for a moment—he soon seemed quite well and did not notice the cold all around him.

"My sledge! Don't forget my sledge," was his first thought, and then he looked and saw that it was bound fast to one of the white birds which flew behind him. The Snow Queen kissed little Kay again, and by this time he had forgotten little Gerda, his grandmother, and all at home.

"Now you must have no more kisses," she said, "or I should kiss you to death."

Kay looked at her. She was so beautiful, he could not imagine a more lovely face; she did not now seem to be made of ice as when he had seen her through his window and she had nodded to him.

In his eyes she was perfect, and he did not feel at all afraid. He told her he could do mental arithmetic as far as fractions, and that he knew the number of square miles and the number of inhabitants in the country. She smiled, and it occurred to him that she thought he did not yet know so very much.

He looked around the vast expanse as she flew higher and higher with him upon a black cloud, while the storm blew and howled as if it were singing songs of olden time. They flew over woods and lakes, over sea and land; below them roared the wild wind; wolves howled, and the snow crackled; over them flew the black, screaming crows, and above all shone the moon, clear and bright—and so Kay passed through the long, long winter's night, and by day he slept at the feet of the Snow Queen.

THIRD STORY

THE ENCHANTED FLOWER GARDEN

But how fared little Gerda in Kay's absence?

What had become of him no one knew, nor could any one give the slightest information, excepting the boys, who said that he had tied his sledge to another very large one, which had driven through the street and out at the town gate. No one knew where it went. Many tears were shed for him, and little Gerda wept bitterly for a long time. She said she knew he must be dead, that he was drowned in the river which flowed close by the school. The long winter days were very dreary. But at last spring came with warm sunshine.

"Kay is dead and gone," said little Gerda.

"I don't believe it," said the sunshine.

"He is dead and gone," she said to the sparrows.

"We don't believe it," they replied, and at last little Gerda began to doubt it herself.

"I will put on my new red shoes," she said one morning, "those that Kay has never seen, and then I will go down to the river and ask for him."

It was quite early when she kissed her old grandmother, who was still asleep; then she put on her red shoes and went, quite alone, out of the town gate, toward the river.

"Is it true that you have taken my little playmate away from me?" she said to the river. "I will give you my red shoes if you will give him back to me."

And it seemed as if the waves nodded to her in a strange manner. Then she took off her red shoes, which she liked better than anything else, and threw them both into the river, but they fell near the bank, and the little waves carried them back to land just as if the river would not take from her what she loved best, because it could not give her back little Kay.

But she thought the shoes had not been thrown out far enough. Then she crept into a boat that lay among the reeds, and threw the shoes again from the farther end of the boat into the water; but it was not fastened, and her movement sent it gliding away from the land. When she saw this she hastened to reach the end of the boat, but before she could do so it was more than a yard from the bank and drifting away faster than ever.

Little Gerda was very much frightened. She began to cry, but no one heard her except the sparrows, and they could not carry her to land, but they flew along by the shore and sang as if to comfort her: "Here we are! Here we are!"

The boat floated with the stream, and little Gerda sat quite still with only her stockings on her feet; the red shoes floated after her, but she could not reach them because the boat kept so much in advance.

There came a very old
woman out of the house

The banks on either side of the river were very pretty. There were beautiful flowers, old trees, sloping fields in which cows and sheep were grazing, but not a human being to be seen.

"Perhaps the river will carry me to little Kay," thought Gerda, and then she became more cheerful, and raised her head and looked at the beautiful green banks; and so the boat sailed on for hours. At length she came to a large cherry orchard, in which stood a small house with strange red and blue windows. It had also a thatched roof, and outside were two wooden soldiers that presented arms to her as she sailed past. Gerda called out to them, for she thought they were alive; but of course they did not answer, and as the boat drifted nearer to the shore she saw what they really were.

Then Gerda called still louder, and there came a very old woman out of the house, leaning on a crutch. She wore a large hat to shade her from the sun, and on it were painted all sorts of pretty flowers.

"You poor little child," said the old woman, "how did you manage to come this long, long distance into the wide world on such a rapid, rolling stream?" And then the old woman walked into the water, seized the boat with her crutch, drew it to land, and lifted little Gerda out. And Gerda was glad to feel herself again on dry ground, although she was rather afraid of the strange old woman.

"Come and tell me who you are," said she, "and how you came here."

Then Gerda told her everything, while the old woman shook her head and said, "Hem-hem"; and when Gerda had finished she asked the old woman if she had not seen little Kay. She told her he had not passed that way, but he very likely would come. She told Gerda not to be sorrowful, but to taste the cherries and look at the flowers; they were better than any picture book, for each of them could tell a story. Then she took Gerda by the hand, and led her into the little house, and closed the door. The windows were very high, and as the panes were red, blue, and yellow, the daylight shone through them in all sorts of singular colors. On the table stood some beautiful cherries, and Gerda had permission to eat as many as she would. While she was eating them the old woman combed out her long flaxen ringlets with a golden comb, and the glossy curls hung down on each side of the little round, pleasant face, which looked fresh and blooming as a rose.

"I have long been wishing for a dear little maiden like you," said the old woman, "and now you must stay with me and see how happily we shall live together." And while she went on combing little Gerda's hair the child thought less and less about her adopted brother Kay, for the old woman was an enchantress, although she was not a wicked witch; she conjured only a little for her own amusement, and, now, because she wanted to keep Gerda. Therefore she went into the garden and stretched out her crutch toward all the rose trees, beautiful though they were, and they immediately sank into the dark earth, so that no one could tell where they had once stood. The old woman was afraid that if little Gerda saw roses, she would think of those at home and then remember little Kay and run away.

Then she took Gerda into the flower garden. How fragrant and beautiful it was! Every flower that could be thought of, for every season of the year, was here in full bloom; no picture book could have more beautiful colors. Gerda jumped for joy, and played till the sun went down behind the tall cherry trees; then she slept in an elegant bed, with red silk pillows embroidered with colored violets, and she dreamed as pleasantly as a queen on her wedding day.

The next day, and for many days after, Gerda played with the flowers in the warm sunshine. She knew every flower, and yet, although there were so many of them, it seemed as if one were missing, but what it was she could not tell. One day, however, as she sat looking at the old woman's hat with the painted flowers on it, she saw that the prettiest of them all was a rose. The old woman had forgotten to take it from her hat when she made all the roses sink into the earth. But it is difficult to keep the thoughts together in everything, and one little mistake upsets all our arrangements.

"What! are there no roses here?" cried Gerda, and she ran out into the garden and examined all the beds, and searched and searched. There was not one to be found. Then she sat down and wept, and her tears fell just on the place where one of the rose trees had sunk down. The warm tears moistened the earth, and the rose tree sprouted up at once, as blooming as when it had sunk; and Gerda embraced it, and kissed the roses, and thought of the beautiful roses at home, and, with them, of little Kay.

"Oh, how I have been detained!" said the little maiden. "I wanted to seek for little Kay. Do you know where he is?" she asked the roses; "do you think he is dead?"

And the roses answered: "No, he is not dead. We have been in the ground, where all the dead lie, but Kay is not there."

"Thank you," said little Gerda, and then she went to the other flowers and looked into their little cups and asked, "Do you know where little Kay is?" But each flower as it stood in the sunshine dreamed only of its own little fairy tale or history. Not one knew anything of Kay. Gerda heard many stories from the flowers, as she asked them one after another about him.

And then she ran to the other end of the garden. The door was fastened, but she pressed against the rusty latch, and it gave way. The door sprang open, and little Gerda ran out with bare feet into the wide world. She looked back three times, but no one seemed to be following her. At last she could run no longer, so she sat down to rest on a great stone, and when she looked around she saw that the summer was over and autumn very far advanced. She had known nothing of this in the beautiful garden where the sun shone and the flowers grew all the year round.

"Oh, how I have wasted my time!" said little Gerda. "It is autumn; I must not rest any longer," and she rose to go on. But her little feet were wounded and sore, and everything around her looked cold and bleak. The long willow leaves were quite yellow, the dewdrops fell like water, leaf after leaf dropped from the trees; the sloe thorn alone still bore fruit, but the sloes were sour and set the teeth on edge. Oh, how dark and weary the whole world appeared!

FOURTH STORY

THE PRINCE AND PRINCESS

Gerda was obliged to rest again, and just opposite the place where she sat she saw a great crow come hopping toward her across the snow. He stood looking at her for some time, and then he wagged his head and said, "Caw, caw, good day, good day." He pronounced the words as plainly as he could, because he meant to be kind to the little girl, and then he asked her where she was going all alone in the wide world.

The word "alone" Gerda understood very well and felt how much it expressed. So she told the crow the whole story of her life and adventures and asked him if he had seen little Kay.

The crow nodded his head very gravely and said, "Perhaps I have—it may be."

"No! Do you really think you have?" cried little Gerda, and she kissed the crow and hugged him almost to death, with joy.

"Gently, gently," said the crow. "I believe I know. I think it may be little Kay; but he has certainly forgotten you by this time, for the princess."

"Does he live with a princess?" asked Gerda.

"Yes, listen," replied the crow; "but it is so difficult to speak your language. If you understand the crows' language, then I can explain it better. Do you?"

"No, I have never learned it," said Gerda, "but my grandmother understands it, and used to speak it to me. I wish I had learned it."

"It does not matter," answered the crow. "I will explain as well as I can, although it will be very badly done"; and he told her what he had heard.

"In this kingdom where we now are," said he, "there lives a princess who is so wonderfully clever that she has read all the newspapers in the world—and forgotten them too, although she is so clever.

"A short time ago, as she was sitting on her throne, which people say is not such an agreeable seat as is often supposed, she began to sing a song which commences with these words:

Why should I not be married?

'Why not, indeed?' said she, and so she determined to marry if she could find a husband who knew what to say when he was spoken to, and not one who could only look grand, for that was so tiresome. She assembled all her court ladies at the beat of the drum, and when they heard of her intentions they were very much pleased.

"'We are so glad to hear of it,' said they. 'We were talking about it ourselves the other day.'

"You may believe that every word I tell you is true," said the crow, "for I have a tame sweetheart who hops freely about the palace, and she told me all this."

Of course his sweetheart was a crow, for "birds of a feather flock together," and one crow always chooses another crow.

"Newspapers were published immediately with a border of hearts and the initials of the princess among them. They gave notice that every young man who was handsome was free to visit the castle and speak with the princess, and those who could reply loud enough to be heard when spoken to were to make themselves quite at home at the palace, and the one who spoke best would be chosen as a husband for the princess.

"Yes, yes, you may believe me. It is all as true as I sit here," said the crow.

"The people came in crowds. There was a great deal of crushing and running about, but no one succeeded either on the first or the second day. They could all speak very well while they were outside in the streets, but when they entered the palace gates and saw the guards in silver uniforms and the footmen in their golden livery on the staircase and the great halls lighted up, they became quite confused. And when they stood before the throne on which the princess sat they could do nothing but repeat the last words she had said, and she had no particular wish to hear her own words over again. It was just as if they had all taken something to make them sleepy while they were in the palace, for they did not recover themselves nor speak till they got back again into the street. There was a long procession of them, reaching from the town gate to the palace.

"I went myself to see them," said the crow. "They were hungry and thirsty, for at the palace they did not even get a glass of water. Some of the wisest had taken a few slices of bread and butter with them, but they did not share it with their neighbors; they thought if the others went in to the princess looking hungry, there would be a better chance for themselves."

"But Kay! tell me about little Kay!" said Gerda. "Was he among the crowd?"

"Stop a bit; we are just coming to him. It was on the third day that there came marching cheerfully along to the palace a little personage without horses or carriage, his eyes sparkling like yours. He had beautiful long hair, but his clothes were very poor."

"That was Kay," said Gerda, joyfully. "Oh, then I have found him!" and she clapped her hands.

"He had a little knapsack on his back," added the crow.

"No, it must have been his sledge," said Gerda, "for he went away with it."

"It may have been so," said the crow; "I did not look at it very closely. But I know from my tame sweetheart that he passed through the palace gates, saw the guards in their silver uniform and the servants in their liveries of gold on the stairs, but was not in the least embarrassed.

"'It must be very tiresome to stand on the stairs,' he said. 'I prefer to go in.'

"The rooms were blazing with light; councilors and ambassadors walked about with bare feet, carrying golden vessels; it was enough to make any one feel serious. His boots creaked loudly as he walked, and yet he was not at all uneasy."

"It must be Kay," said Gerda; "I know he had new boots on. I heard them creak in grandmother's room."

"They really did creak," said the crow, "yet he went boldly up to the princess herself, who was sitting on a pearl as large as a spinning wheel. And all the ladies of the court were present with their maids and all the cavaliers with their servants, and each of the maids had another maid to wait upon her, and the cavaliers' servants had their own servants as well as each a page. They all stood in circles round the princess, and the nearer they stood to the door the prouder they looked. The servants' pages, who always wore slippers, could hardly be looked at, they held themselves up so proudly by the door."

"It must be quite awful," said little Gerda; "but did Kay win the princess?"

"If I had not been a crow," said he, "I would have married her myself, although I am engaged. He spoke as well as I do when I speak the crows' language. I heard this from my tame sweetheart. He was quite free and agreeable and said he had not come to woo the princess, but to hear her wisdom. And he was as pleased with her as she was with him."

"Oh, certainly that was Kay," said Gerda; "he was so clever; he could work mental arithmetic and fractions. Oh, will you take me to the palace?"

"It is very easy to ask that," replied the crow, "but how are we to manage it? However, I will speak about it to my tame sweetheart and ask her advice, for, I must tell you, it will be very difficult to gain permission for a little girl like you to enter the palace."

"Oh, yes, but I shall gain permission easily," said Gerda, "for when Kay hears that I am here he will come out and fetch me in immediately."

"Wait for me here by the palings," said the crow, wagging his head as he flew away.

It was late in the evening before the crow returned. "Caw, caw!" he said; "she sends you greeting, and here is a little roll which she took from the kitchen for you. There is plenty of bread there, and she thinks you must be hungry. It is not possible for you to enter the palace by the front entrance. The guards in silver uniform and the servants in gold livery would not allow it. But do not cry; we will manage to get you in. My sweetheart knows a little back staircase that leads to the sleeping apartments, and she knows where to find the key."

Then they went into the garden, through the great avenue, where the leaves were falling one after another, and they could see the lights in the palace being put out in the same manner. And the crow led little Gerda to a back door which stood ajar. Oh! how her heart beat with anxiety and longing; it was as if she were going to do something wrong, and yet she only wanted to know where little Kay was.

"It must be he," she thought, "with those clear eyes and that long hair."

She could fancy she saw him smiling at her as he used to at home when they sat among the roses. He would certainly be glad to see her, and to hear what a long distance she had come for his sake, and to know how sorry they had all been at home because he did not come back. Oh, what joy and yet what fear she felt!

They were now on the stairs, and in a small closet at the top a lamp was burning. In the middle of the floor stood the tame crow, turning her head from side to side and gazing at Gerda, who curtsied as her grandmother had taught her to do.

"My betrothed has spoken so very highly of you, my little lady," said the tame crow. "Your story is very touching. If you will take the lamp, I will walk before you. We will go straight along this way; then we shall meet no one."

"I feel as if somebody were behind us," said Gerda, as something rushed by her like a shadow on the wall; and then it seemed to her that horses with flying manes and thin legs, hunters, ladies and gentlemen on horseback, glided by her like shadows.

"They are only dreams," said the crow; "they are coming to carry the thoughts of the great people out hunting. All the better, for if their thoughts are out hunting, we shall be able to look at them in their beds more safely. I hope that when you rise to honor and favor you will show a grateful heart."

"You may be quite sure of that," said the crow from the forest.

They now came into the first hall, the walls of which were hung with rose-colored satin embroidered with artificial flowers. Here the dreams again flitted by them, but so quickly that Gerda could not distinguish the royal persons. Each hall appeared more splendid than the last. It was enough to bewilder one. At length they reached a bedroom. The ceiling was like a great palm tree, with glass leaves of the most costly crystal, and over the center of the floor two beds, each resembling a lily, hung from a stem of gold. One, in which the princess lay, was white; the other was red. And in this Gerda had to seek for little Kay.

She pushed one of the red leaves aside and saw a little brown neck. Oh, that must be Kay! She called his name loudly and held the lamp over him. The dreams rushed back into the room on horseback. He woke and turned his head round—it was not little Kay! The prince was only like him; still he was young and pretty. Out of her white-lily bed peeped the princess, and asked what was the matter. Little Gerda wept and told her story, and all that the crows had done to help her.

"You poor child," said the prince and princess; then they praised the crows, and said they were not angry with them for what they had done, but that it must not happen again, and that this time they should be rewarded.

The prince and princess themselves helped her into the coach.

"Would you like to have your freedom?" asked the princess, "or would you prefer to be raised to the position of court crows, with all that is left in the kitchen for yourselves?"

Then both the crows bowed and begged to have a fixed appointment; for they thought of their old age, and it would be so comfortable, they said, to feel that they had made provision for it.

And then the prince got out of his bed and gave it up to Gerda—he could not do more—and she lay down. She folded her little hands and thought, "How good everybody is to me, both men and animals"; then she closed her eyes and fell into a sweet sleep. All the dreams came flying back again to her, looking like angels now, and one of them drew a little sledge, on which sat Kay, who nodded to her. But all this was only a dream. It vanished as soon as she awoke.

The following day she was dressed from head to foot in silk and velvet and invited to stay at the palace for a few days and enjoy herself; but she only begged for a pair of boots and a little carriage and a horse to draw it, so that she might go out into the wide world to seek for Kay.

And she obtained not only boots but a muff, and was neatly dressed; and when she was ready to go, there at the door she found a coach made of pure gold with the coat of arms of the prince and princess shining upon it like a star, and the coachman, footman, and outriders all wearing golden crowns upon their heads. The prince and princess themselves helped her into the coach and wished her success.

The forest crow, who was now married, accompanied her for the first three miles; he sat by Gerda's side, as he could not bear riding backwards. The tame crow stood in the doorway flapping her wings. She could not go with them, because she had been suffering from headache ever since the new appointment, no doubt from overeating. The coach was well stored with sweet cakes, and under the seat were fruit and gingerbread nuts.

"Farewell, farewell," cried the prince and princess, and little Gerda wept, and the crow wept; and then, after a few miles, the crow also said farewell, and this parting was even more sad. However he flew to a tree and stood flapping his black wings as long as he could see the coach, which glittered like a sunbeam.

FIFTH STORY

THE LITTLE ROBBER GIRL

The coach drove on through a thick forest, where it lighted up the way like a torch and dazzled the eyes of some robbers, who could not bear to let it pass them unmolested.

"It is gold! it is gold!" cried they, rushing forward and seizing the horses. Then they struck dead the little jockeys, the coachman, and the footman, and pulled little Gerda out of the carriage.

"She is plump and pretty. She has been fed with the kernels of nuts," said the old robber woman, who had a long beard, and eyebrows that hung over her eyes. "She is as good as a fatted lamb; how nice she will taste!" and as she said this she drew forth a shining knife, that glittered horribly. "Oh!" screamed the old woman at the same moment, for her own daughter, who held her back, had bitten her in the ear. "You naughty girl," said the mother, and now she had not time to kill Gerda.

"She shall play with me," said the little robber girl. "She shall give me her muff and her pretty dress, and sleep with me in my bed." And then she bit her mother again, and all the robbers laughed.

"I will have a ride in the coach," said the little robber girl, and she would have her own way, for she was self-willed and obstinate.

She and Gerda seated themselves in the coach and drove away over stumps and stones, into the depths of the forest. The little robber girl was about the same size as Gerda, but stronger; she had broader shoulders and a darker skin; her eyes were quite black, and she had a mournful look. She clasped little Gerda round the waist and said:

"They shall not kill you as long as you don't make me vexed with you. I suppose you are a princess."

"No," said Gerda; and then she told her all her history and how fond she was of little Kay.

The robber girl looked earnestly at her, nodded her head slightly, and said, "They shan't kill you even if I do get angry with you, for I will do it myself." And then she wiped Gerda's eyes and put her own hands into the beautiful muff, which was so soft and warm.

The coach stopped in the courtyard of a robber's castle, the walls of which were full of cracks from top to bottom. Ravens and crows flew in and out of the holes and crevices, while great bulldogs, each of which looked as if it could swallow a man, were jumping about; but they were not allowed to bark.

In the large old smoky hall a bright fire was burning on the stone floor. There was no chimney, so the smoke went up to the ceiling and found a way out for itself. Soup was boiling in a large cauldron, and hares and rabbits were roasting on the spit.

"You shall sleep with me and all my little animals to-night," said the robber girl after they had had something to eat and drink. So she took Gerda to a corner of the hall where some straw and carpets were laid down. Above them, on laths and perches, were more than a hundred pigeons that all seemed to be asleep, although they moved slightly when the two little girls came near them. "These all belong to me," said the robber girl, and she seized the nearest to her, held it by the feet, and shook it till it flapped its wings. "Kiss it," cried she, flapping it in Gerda's face.

"There sit the wood pigeons," continued she, pointing to a number of laths and a cage which had been fixed into the walls, near one of the openings. "Both rascals would fly away directly, if they were not closely locked up. And here is my old sweetheart 'Ba,'" and she dragged out a reindeer by the horn; he wore a bright copper ring round his neck and was tethered to the spot. "We are obliged to hold him tight too, else he would run away from us also. I tickle his neck every evening with my sharp knife, which frightens him very much." And the robber girl drew a long knife from a chink in the wall and let it slide gently over the reindeer's neck. The poor animal began to kick, and the little robber girl laughed and pulled down Gerda into bed with her.

"Will you have that knife with you while you are asleep?" asked Gerda, looking at it in great fright.

"I always sleep with the knife by me," said the robber girl. "No one knows what may happen. But now tell me again all about little Kay, and why you went out into the world."

Then Gerda repeated her story over again, while the wood pigeons in the cage over her cooed, and the other pigeons slept. The little robber girl put one arm across Gerda's neck, and held the knife in the other, and was soon fast asleep and snoring. But Gerda could not close her eyes at all; she knew not whether she was to live or to die. The robbers sat round the fire, singing and drinking. It was a terrible sight for a little girl to witness.

Then the wood pigeons said: "Coo, coo, we have seen little Kay. A white fowl carried his sledge, and he sat in the carriage of the Snow Queen, which drove through the wood while we were lying in our nest. She blew upon us, and all the young ones died, excepting us two. Coo, coo."

"What are you saying up there?" cried Gerda. "Where was the Snow Queen going? Do you know anything about it?"

"She was most likely traveling to Lapland, where there is always snow and ice. Ask the reindeer that is fastened up there with a rope."

"Yes, there is always snow and ice," said the reindeer, "and it is a glorious place; you can leap and run about freely on the sparkling icy plains. The Snow Queen has her summer tent there, but her strong castle is at the North Pole, on an island called Spitzbergen."

"O Kay, little Kay!" sighed Gerda.

"Lie still," said the robber girl, "or you shall feel my knife."

In the morning Gerda told her all that the wood pigeons had said, and the little robber girl looked quite serious, and nodded her head and said: "That is all talk, that is all talk. Do you know where Lapland is?" she asked the reindeer.

"Who should know better than I do?" said the animal, while his eyes sparkled. "I was born and brought up there and used to run about the snow-covered plains."

"Now listen," said the robber girl; "all our men are gone away; only mother is here, and here she will stay; but at noon she always drinks out of a great bottle, and afterwards sleeps for a little while; and then I'll do something for you." She jumped out of bed, clasped her mother round the neck, and pulled her by the beard, crying, "My own little nanny goat, good morning!" And her mother pinched her nose till it was quite red; yet she did it all for love.

When the mother had gone to sleep the little robber maiden went to the reindeer and said: "I should like very much to tickle your neck a few times more with my knife, for it makes you look so funny, but never mind—I will untie your cord and set you free, so that you may run away to Lapland; but you must make good use of your legs and carry this little maiden to the castle of the Snow Queen, where her playfellow is. You have heard what she told me, for she spoke loud enough, and you were listening."

The reindeer jumped for joy, and the little robber girl lifted Gerda on his back and had the forethought to tie her on and even to give her her own little cushion to sit upon.

"Here are your fur boots for you," said she, "for it will be very cold; but I must keep the muff, it is so pretty. However, you shall not be frozen for the want of it; here are my mother's large warm mittens; they will reach up to your elbows. Let me put them on. There, now your hands look just like my mother's."

But Gerda wept for joy.

"I don't like to see you fret," said the little robber girl. "You ought to look quite happy now. And here are two loaves and a ham, so that you need not starve."

These were fastened upon the reindeer, and then the little robber maiden opened the door, coaxed in all the great dogs, cut the string with which the reindeer was fastened, with her sharp knife, and said, "Now run, but mind you take good care of the little girl." And Gerda stretched out her hand, with the great mitten on it, toward the little robber girl and said "Farewell," and away flew the reindeer over stumps and stones, through the great forest, over marshes and plains, as quickly as he could. The wolves howled and the ravens screamed, while up in the sky quivered red lights like flames of fire. "There are my old northern lights," said the reindeer; "see how they flash!" And he ran on day and night still faster and faster, but the loaves and the ham were all eaten by the time they reached Lapland.

SIXTH STORY

THE LAPLAND WOMAN AND THE FINLAND WOMAN

They stopped at a little hut; it was very mean looking. The roof sloped nearly down to the ground, and the door was so low that the family had to creep in on their hands and knees when they went in and out. There was no one at home but an old Lapland woman who was dressing fish by the light of a train-oil lamp.

The reindeer told her all about Gerda's story after having first told his own, which seemed to him the most important. But Gerda was so pinched with the cold that she could not speak.

"Oh, you poor things," said the Lapland woman, "you have a long way to go yet. You must travel more than a hundred miles farther, to Finland. The Snow Queen lives there now, and she burns Bengal lights every evening. I will write a few words on a dried stock-fish, for I have no paper, and you can take it from me to the Finland woman who lives there. She can give you better information than I can."

So when Gerda was warmed and had taken something to eat and drink, the woman wrote a few words on the dried fish and told Gerda to take great care of it. Then she tied her again on the back of the reindeer, and he sprang high into the air and set off at full speed. Flash, flash, went the beautiful blue northern lights the whole night long.

And at length they reached Finland and knocked at the chimney of the Finland woman's hut, for it had no door above the ground. They crept in, but it was so terribly hot inside that the woman wore scarcely any clothes. She was small and very dirty looking. She loosened little Gerda's dress and took off the fur boots and the mittens, or Gerda would have been unable to bear the heat; and then she placed a piece of ice on the reindeer's head and read what was written on the dried fish. After she had read it three times she knew it by heart, so she popped the fish into the soup saucepan, as she knew it was good to eat, and she never wasted anything.

The reindeer told his own story first and then little Gerda's, and the Finlander twinkled with her clever eyes, but said nothing.

"You are so clever," said the reindeer; "I know you can tie all the winds of the world with a piece of twine. If a sailor unties one knot, he has a fair wind; when he unties the second, it blows hard; but if the third and fourth are loosened, then comes a storm which will root up whole forests. Cannot you give this little maiden something which will make her as strong as twelve men, to overcome the Snow Queen?"

"The power of twelve men!" said the Finland woman. "That would be of very little use." But she went to a shelf and took down and unrolled a large skin on which were inscribed wonderful characters, and she read till the perspiration ran down from her forehead.

But the reindeer begged so hard for little Gerda, and Gerda looked at the Finland woman with such tender, tearful eyes, that her own eyes began to twinkle again. She drew the reindeer into a corner and whispered to him while she laid a fresh piece of ice on his head: "Little Kay is really with the Snow Queen, but he finds everything there so much to his taste and his liking that he believes it is the finest place in the world; and this is because he has a piece of broken glass in his heart and a little splinter of glass in his eye. These must be taken out, or he will never be a human being again, and the Snow Queen will retain her power over him."

"But can you not give little Gerda something to help her to conquer this power?"

"I can give her no greater power than she has already," said the woman; "don't you see how strong that is? how men and animals are obliged to serve her, and how well she has gotten through the world, barefooted as she is? She cannot receive any power from me greater than she now has, which consists in her own purity and innocence of heart. If she cannot herself obtain access to the Snow Queen and remove the glass fragments from little Kay, we can do nothing to help her. Two miles from here the Snow Queen's garden begins. You can carry the little girl so far, and set her down by the large bush which stands in the snow, covered with red berries. Do not stay gossiping, but come back here as quickly as you can." Then the Finland woman lifted little Gerda upon the reindeer, and he ran away with her as quickly as he could.

"Oh, I have forgotten my boots and my mittens," cried little Gerda, as soon as she felt the cutting cold; but the reindeer dared not stop, so he ran on till he reached the bush with the red berries. Here he set Gerda down, and he kissed her, and the great bright tears trickled over the animal's cheeks; then he left her and ran back as fast as he could.

There stood poor Gerda, without shoes, without gloves, in the midst of cold, dreary, ice-bound Finland. She ran forward as quickly as she could, when a whole regiment of snowflakes came round her. They did not, however, fall from the sky, which was quite clear and glittered with the northern lights. The snowflakes ran along the ground, and the nearer they came to her the larger they appeared. Gerda remembered how large and beautiful they looked through the burning glass. But these were really larger and much more terrible, for they were alive and were the guards of the Snow Queen and had the strangest shapes. Some were like great porcupines, others like twisted serpents with their heads stretching out, and some few were like little fat bears with their hair bristled; but all were dazzlingly white, and all were living snowflakes.

Little Gerda repeated the Lord's Prayer, and the cold was so great that she could see her own breath come out of her mouth like steam, as she uttered the words. The steam appeared to increase as she continued her prayer, till it took the shape of little angels, who grew larger the moment they touched the earth. They all wore helmets on their heads and carried spears and shields. Their number continued to increase more and more, and by the time Gerda had finished her prayers a whole legion stood round her. They thrust their spears into the terrible snowflakes so that they shivered into a hundred pieces, and little Gerda could go forward with courage and safety. The angels stroked her hands and feet, so that she felt the cold less as she hastened on to the Snow Queen's castle.

But now we must see what Kay is doing. In truth he thought not of little Gerda, and least of all that she could be standing at the front of the palace.

SEVENTH STORY

OF THE PALACE OF THE SNOW QUEEN AND
WHAT HAPPENED THERE AT LAST

The walls of the palace were formed of drifted snow, and the windows and doors of cutting winds. There were more than a hundred rooms in it, all as if they had been formed of snow blown together. The largest of them extended for several miles. They were all lighted up by the vivid light of the aurora, and were so large and empty, so icy cold and glittering!

There were no amusements here; not even a little bear's ball, when the storm might have been the music, and the bears could have danced on their hind legs and shown their good manners. There were no pleasant games of snapdragon, or touch, nor even a gossip over the tea table for the young-lady foxes. Empty, vast, and cold were the halls of the Snow Queen.

The flickering flames of the northern lights could be plainly seen, whether they rose high or low in the heavens, from every part of the castle. In the midst of this empty, endless hall of snow was a frozen lake, broken on its surface into a thousand forms; each piece resembled another, because each was in itself perfect as a work of art, and in the center of this lake sat the Snow Queen when she was at home. She called the lake "The Mirror of Reason," and said that it was the best, and indeed the only one, in the world.

Little Kay was quite blue with cold,—indeed, almost black,—but he did not feel it; for the Snow Queen had kissed away the icy shiverings, and his heart was already a lump of ice. He dragged some sharp, flat pieces of ice to and fro and placed them together in all kinds of positions, as if he wished to make something out of them—just as we try to form various figures with little tablets of wood, which we call a "Chinese puzzle." Kay's figures were very artistic; it was the icy game of reason at which he played, and in his eyes the figures were very remarkable and of the highest importance; this opinion was owing to the splinter of glass still sticking in his eye. He composed many complete figures, forming different words, but there was one word he never could manage to form, although he wished it very much. It was the word "Eternity."

The Snow Queen had said to him, "When you can find out this, you shall be your own master, and I will give you the whole world and a new pair of skates." But he could not accomplish it.

In the center of the lake
° ° sat the Snow Queen ° °

"Now I must hasten away to warmer countries," said the Snow Queen. "I will go and look into the black craters of the tops of the burning mountains, Etna and Vesuvius, as they are called. I shall make them look white, which will be good for them and for the lemons and the grapes." And away flew the Snow Queen, leaving little Kay quite alone in the great hall which was so many miles in length. He sat and looked at his pieces of ice and was thinking so deeply and sat so still that any one might have supposed he was frozen.

Just at this moment it happened that little Gerda came through the great door of the castle. Cutting winds were raging around her, but she offered up a prayer, and the winds sank down as if they were going to sleep. On she went till she came to the large, empty hall and caught sight of Kay. She knew him directly; she flew to him and threw her arms around his neck and held him fast while she exclaimed, "Kay, dear little Kay, I have found you at last!"

But he sat quite still, stiff and cold.

Then little Gerda wept hot tears, which fell on his breast, and penetrated into his heart, and thawed the lump of ice, and washed away the little piece of glass which had stuck there. Then he looked at her, and she sang:

"Roses bloom and fade away,
But we the Christ-child see alway."

Then Kay burst into tears. He wept so that the splinter of glass swam out of his eye. Then he recognized Gerda and said joyfully, "Gerda, dear little Gerda, where have you been all this time, and where have I been?" And he looked all around him and said, "How cold it is, and how large and empty it all looks," and he clung to Gerda, and she laughed and wept for joy.

It was so pleasing to see them that even the pieces of ice danced, and when they were tired and went to lie down they formed themselves into the letters of the word which the Snow Queen had said he must find out before he could be his own master and have the whole world and a pair of new skates.

Gerda kissed his cheeks, and they became blooming; and she kissed his eyes till they shone like her own; she kissed his hands and feet, and he became quite healthy and cheerful. The Snow Queen might come home now when she pleased, for there stood his certainty of freedom, in the word she wanted, written in shining letters of ice.

Then they took each other by the hand and went forth from the great palace of ice. They spoke of the grandmother and of the roses on the roof, and as they went on the winds were at rest, and the sun burst forth. When they arrived at the bush with red berries, there stood the reindeer waiting for them, and he had brought another young reindeer with him, whose udders were full, and the children drank her warm milk and kissed her on the mouth.

They carried Kay and Gerda first to the Finland woman, where they warmed themselves thoroughly in the hot room and had directions about their journey home. Next they went to the Lapland woman, who had made some new clothes for them and put their sleighs in order. Both the reindeer ran by their side and followed them as far as the boundaries of the country, where the first green leaves were budding. And here they took leave of the two reindeer and the Lapland woman, and all said farewell.

Then birds began to twitter, and the forest too was full of green young leaves, and out of it came a beautiful horse, which Gerda remembered, for it was one which had drawn the golden coach. A young girl was riding upon it, with a shining red cap on her head and pistols in her belt. It was the little robber maiden, who had got tired of staying at home; she was going first to the north, and if that did not suit her, she meant to try some other part of the world. She knew Gerda directly, and Gerda remembered her; it was a joyful meeting.

"You are a fine fellow to go gadding about in this way," said she to little Kay. "I should like to know whether you deserve that any one should go to the end of the world to find you."

But Gerda patted her cheeks and asked after the prince and princess.

"They are gone to foreign countries," said the robber girl.

"And the crow?" asked Gerda.

"Oh, the crow is dead," she replied. "His tame sweetheart is now a widow and wears a bit of black worsted round her leg. She mourns very pitifully, but it is all stuff. But now tell me how you managed to get him back."

Then Gerda and Kay told her all about it.

"Snip, snap, snurre! it's all right at last," said the robber girl.

She took both their hands and promised that if ever she should pass through the town, she would call and pay them a visit. And then she rode away into the wide world.

But Gerda and Kay went hand in hand toward home, and as they advanced, spring appeared more lovely with its green verdure and its beautiful flowers. Very soon they recognized the large town where they lived, and the tall steeples of the churches in which the sweet bells were ringing a merry peal, as they entered it and found their way to their grandmother's door.

They went upstairs into the little room, where all looked just as it used to do. The old clock was going "Tick, tick," and the hands pointed to the time of day, but as they passed through the door into the room they perceived that they were both grown up and become a man and woman. The roses out on the roof were in full bloom and peeped in at the window, and there stood the little chairs on which they had sat when children, and Kay and Gerda seated themselves each on their own chair and held each other by the hand, while the cold, empty grandeur of the Snow Queen's palace vanished from their memories like a painful dream.

The grandmother sat in God's bright sunshine, and she read aloud from the Bible, "Except ye become as little children, ye shall in no wise enter into the kingdom of God." And Kay and Gerda looked into each other's eyes and all at once understood the words of the old song:

Roses bloom and fade away,
But we the Christ-child see alway.

And they both sat there, grown up, yet children at heart, and it was summer—warm, beautiful summer.

THE ROSES AND THE SPARROWS

IT really appeared as if something very important were going on by the duck pond, but this was not the case.

A few minutes before, all the ducks had been resting on the water or standing on their heads—for that they can do—and then they all swam in a bustle to the shore. The traces of their feet could be seen on the wet earth, and far and wide could be heard their quacking. The water, so lately clear and bright as a mirror, was in quite a commotion.

But a moment before, every tree and bush near the old farmhouse—and even the house itself with the holes in the roof and the swallows' nests and, above all, the beautiful rosebush covered with roses—had been clearly reflected in the water. The rosebush on the wall hung over the water, which resembled a picture only that everything appeared upside down, but when the water was set in motion all vanished, and the picture disappeared.

Two feathers, dropped by the fluttering ducks, floated to and fro on the water. All at once they took a start as if the wind were coming, but it did not come, so they were obliged to lie still, as the water became again quiet and at rest. The roses could once more behold their own reflections. They were very beautiful, but they knew it not, for no one had told them. The sun shone between the delicate leaves, and the sweet fragrance spread itself, carrying happiness everywhere.

"How beautiful is our existence!" said one of the roses. "I feel as if I should like to kiss the sun, it is so bright and warm. I should like to kiss the roses too, our images in the water, and the pretty birds there in their nests. There are some birds too in the nest above us; they stretch out their heads and cry 'Tweet, tweet,' very faintly. They have no feathers yet, such as their father and mother have. Both above us and below us we have good neighbors. How beautiful is our life!"

The young birds above and the young ones below were the same; they were sparrows, and their nest was reflected in the water. Their parents were sparrows also, and they had taken possession of an empty swallow's nest of the year before, occupying it now as if it were their own.

"Are those ducks' children that are swimming about? asked the young sparrows, as they spied the feathers on the water.

"If you must ask questions, pray ask sensible ones," said the mother. "Can you not see that these are feathers, the living stuff for clothes, which I wear and which you will wear soon, only ours are much finer? I should like, however, to have them up here in the nest, they would make it so warm. I am rather curious to know why the ducks were so alarmed just now. It could not be from fear of us, certainly, though I did say 'tweet' rather loudly. The thick-headed roses really ought to know, but they are very ignorant; they only look at one another and smell. I am heartily tired of such neighbors."

"Listen to the sweet little birds above us," said the roses; "they are trying to sing. They cannot manage it yet, but it will be done in time. What a pleasure it will be, and how nice to have such lively neighbors!"

Suddenly two horses came prancing along to drink at the water. A peasant boy rode on one of them; he had a broad-brimmed black hat on, but had taken off the most of his clothes, that he might ride into the deepest part of the pond; he whistled like a bird, and while passing the rosebush he plucked a rose and placed it in his hat and then rode on thinking himself very fine. The other roses looked at their sister and asked each other where she could be going, but they did not know.

"I should like for once to go out into the world," said one, "although it is very lovely here in our home of green leaves. The sun shines warmly by day, and in the night we can see that heaven is more beautiful still, as it sparkles through the holes in the sky."

She meant the stars, for she knew no better.

"We make the house very lively," said the mother sparrow, "and people say that a swallow's nest brings luck, therefore they are pleased to see us; but as to our neighbors, a rosebush on the wall produces damp. It will most likely be removed, and perhaps corn will grow here instead of it. Roses are good for nothing but to be looked at and smelt, or perhaps one may chance to be stuck in a hat. I have heard from my mother that they fall off every year. The farmer's wife preserves them by laying them in salt, and then they receive a French name which I neither can nor will pronounce; then they are sprinkled on the fire to produce a pleasant smell. Such you see is their life. They are only formed to please the eye and the nose. Now you know all about them."

As the evening approached, the gnats played about in the warm air beneath the rosy clouds, and the nightingale came and sang to the roses that *the beautiful* was like sunshine to the world, and that *the beautiful* lives forever. The roses thought that the nightingale was singing of herself, which any one indeed could easily suppose; they never imagined that her song could refer to them. But it was a joy to them, and they wondered to themselves whether all the little sparrows in the nest would become nightingales.

"We understood that bird's song very well," said the young sparrows, "but one word was not clear. What is *the beautiful?*"

"Oh, nothing of any consequence," replied the mother sparrow. "It is something relating to appearances over yonder at the nobleman's house. The pigeons have a house of their own, and every day they have corn and peas spread for them. I have dined there with them sometimes, and so shall you by and by, for I believe the old maxim—'Tell me what company you keep, and I will tell you what you are.' Well, over at the noble house there are two birds with green throats and crests on their heads. They can spread out their tails like large wheels, and they reflect so many beautiful colors that it dazzles the eyes to look at them. These birds are called peacocks, and they belong to *the beautiful;* but if only a few of their feathers were plucked off, they would not appear better than we do. I would myself have plucked some out had they not been so large."

"I will pluck them," squeaked the youngest sparrow, who had as yet no feathers of his own.

In the cottage dwelt two young married people, who loved each other very much and were industrious and active so that everything looked neat and pretty around them. Early on Sunday mornings the young wife came out, gathered a handful of the most beautiful roses, and put them in a glass of water, which she placed on a side table.

"I see now that it is Sunday," said the husband, as he kissed his little wife. Then they sat down and read in their hymn books, holding each other's hands, while the sun shone down upon the young couple and upon the fresh roses in the glass.

"This sight is really too wearisome," said the mother sparrow, who from her nest could look into the room; and she flew away.

The same thing occurred the next Sunday; and indeed every Sunday fresh roses were gathered and placed in a glass, but the rose tree continued to bloom in all its beauty. After a while the young sparrows were fledged and wanted to fly, but the mother would not allow it, and so they were obliged to remain in the nest for the present, while she flew away alone. It so happened that some boys had fastened a snare made of horsehair to the branch of a tree, and before she was aware, her leg became entangled in the horsehair so tightly as almost to cut it through. What pain and terror she felt! The boys ran up quickly and seized her, not in a very gentle manner.

"It is only a sparrow," they said. However they did not let her fly, but took her home with them, and every time she cried they tapped her on the beak.

In the farmyard they met an old man who knew how to make soap for shaving and washing, in cakes or in balls. When he saw the sparrow which the boys had brought home and which they said they did not know what to do with, he said, "Shall we make it beautiful?"

A cold shudder passed over the sparrow when she heard this. The old man then took a shell containing a quantity of glittering gold leaf from a box full of beautiful colors and told the youngsters to fetch the white of an egg, with which he besmeared the sparrow all over and then laid the gold leaf upon it, so that the mother sparrow was now gilded from head to tail. She thought not of her appearance, but trembled in every limb. Then the soap maker tore a little piece out of the red lining of his jacket, cut notches in it, so that it looked like a cock'scomb, and stuck it on the bird's head.

"Now you shall see gold-jacket fly," said the old man, and he released the sparrow, which flew away in deadly terror with the sunlight shining upon her. How she did glitter! All the sparrows, and even a crow, who is a knowing old boy, were startled at the sight, yet they all followed it to discover what foreign bird it could be. Driven by anguish and terror, she flew homeward almost ready to sink to the earth for want of strength. The flock of birds that were following increased and some even tried to peck her.

"Look at him! look at him!" they all cried. "Look at him! look at him!" cried the young ones as their mother approached the nest, for they did not know her. "That must be a young peacock, for he glitters in all colors. It quite hurts one's eyes to look at him, as mother told us; 'tweet,' this is *the beautiful*." And then they pecked the bird with their little beaks so that she was quite unable to get into the nest and was too much exhausted even to say "tweet," much less "I am your mother." So the other birds fell upon the sparrow and pulled out feather after feather till she sank bleeding into the rosebush.

"You poor creature," said the roses, "be at rest. We will hide you; lean your little head against us."

The sparrow spread out her wings once more, then drew them in close about her and lay dead among the roses, her fresh and lovely neighbors.

"Tweet," sounded from the nest; "where can our mother be staying? It is quite unaccountable. Can this be a trick of hers to show us that we are now to take care of ourselves? She has left us the house as an inheritance, but as it cannot belong to us all when we have families, who is to have it?"

"It won't do for you all to stay with me when I increase my household with a wife and children," remarked the youngest.

"I shall have more wives and children than you," said the second.

"But I am the eldest," cried a third.

Then they all became angry, beat each other with their wings, pecked with their beaks, till one after another bounced out of the nest. There they lay in a rage, holding their heads on one side and twinkling the eye that looked upward. This was their way of looking sulky.

They could all fly a little, and by practice they soon learned to do so much better. At length they agreed upon a sign by which they might be able to recognize each other in case they should meet in the world after they had separated. This sign was to be the cry of "tweet, tweet," and a scratching on the ground three times with the left foot.

The youngster who was left behind in the nest spread himself out as broad as ever he could; he was the householder now. But his glory did not last long, for during that night red flames of fire burst through the windows of the cottage, seized the thatched roof, and blazed up frightfully. The whole house was burned, and the sparrow perished with it, while the young couple fortunately escaped with their lives.

When the sun rose again, and all nature looked refreshed as after a quiet sleep, nothing remained of the cottage but a few blackened, charred beams leaning against the chimney, that now was the only master of the place. Thick smoke still rose from the ruins, but outside on the wall the rosebush remained unhurt, blooming and fresh as ever, while each flower and each spray was mirrored in the clear water beneath.

"How beautifully the roses are blooming on the walls of that ruined cottage," said a passer-by. "A more lovely picture could scarcely be imagined. I must have it."

And the speaker took out of his pocket a little book full of white leaves of paper (for he was an artist), and with a pencil he made a sketch of the smoking ruins, the blackened rafters, and the chimney that overhung them and which seemed more and more to totter; and quite in the foreground stood the large, blooming rosebush, which added beauty to the picture; indeed, it was for the sake of the roses that the sketch had been made. Later in the day two of the sparrows who had been born there came by.

"Where is the house?" they asked. "Where is the nest? Tweet, tweet; all is burned down, and our strong brother with it. That is all he got by keeping the nest. The roses have escaped famously; they look as well as ever, with their rosy cheeks; they do not trouble themselves about their neighbors' misfortunes. I won't speak to them. And really, in my opinion, the place looks very ugly"; so they flew away.

On a fine, bright, sunny day in autumn, so bright that any one might have supposed it was still the middle of summer, a number of pigeons were hopping about in the nicely kept courtyard of the nobleman's house, in front of the great steps. Some were black, others white, and some of various colors, and their plumage glittered in the sunshine. An old mother pigeon said to her young ones, "Place yourselves in groups! place yourselves in groups! it has a much better appearance."

"What are those little gray creatures which are running about behind us?" asked an old pigeon with red and green round her eyes. "Little gray ones, little gray ones," she cried.

"They are sparrows—good little creatures enough. We have always had the character of being very good-natured, so we allow them to pick up some corn with us; they do not interrupt our conversation, and they draw back their left foot so prettily."

Sure enough, so they did, three times each, and with the left foot too, and said "tweet," by which we recognize them as the sparrows that were brought up in the nest on the house that was burned down.

"The food here is very good," said the sparrows; while the pigeons strutted round each other, puffed out their throats, and formed their own opinions on what they observed.

"Do you see the pouter pigeon?" asked one pigeon of another. "Do you see how he swallows the peas? He takes too much and always chooses the best of everything. Coo-oo, coo-oo. How the ugly, spiteful creature erects his crest." And all their eyes sparkled with malice. "Place yourselves in groups, place yourselves in groups. Little gray coats, little gray coats. Coo-oo, coo-oo."

So they went on, and it will be the same a thousand years hence.

The sparrows feasted bravely and listened attentively; they even stood in ranks like the pigeons, but it did not suit them. So having satisfied their hunger, they left the pigeons passing their own opinions upon them to each other and slipped through the garden railings. The door of a room in the house, leading into the garden, stood open, and one of them, feeling brave after his good dinner, hopped upon the threshold crying, "Tweet, I can venture so far."

"Tweet," said another, "I can venture that, and a great deal more," and into the room he hopped.

The first followed, and, seeing no one there, the third became courageous and flew right across the room, saying: "Venture everything, or do not venture at all. This is a wonderful place—a man's nest, I suppose; and look! what can this be?"

Just in front of the sparrows stood the ruins of the burned cottage; roses were blooming over it, and their reflection appeared in the water beneath, and the black, charred beams rested against the tottering chimney. How could it be? How came the cottage and the roses in a room in the nobleman's house? And then the sparrows tried to fly over the roses and the chimney, but they only struck themselves against a flat wall. It was a picture—a large, beautiful picture which the artist had painted from the little sketch he had made.

"Tweet," said the sparrows, "it is really nothing, after all; it only looks like reality. Tweet, I suppose that is *the beautiful.* Can you understand it? I cannot."

Then some persons entered the room and the sparrows flew away. Days and years passed. The pigeons had often "coo-oo-d"—we must not say quarreled, though perhaps they did, the naughty things! The sparrows had suffered from cold in the winter and lived gloriously in summer. They were all betrothed, or married, or whatever you like to call it. They had little ones, and each considered its own brood the wisest and the prettiest.

One flew in this direction and another in that, and when they met they recognized each other by saying "tweet" and three times drawing back the left foot. The eldest remained single; she had no nest nor young ones. Her great wish was to see a large town, so she flew to Copenhagen.

Close by the castle, and by the canal, in which swam many ships laden with apples and pottery, there was to be seen a great house. The windows were broader below than at the top, and when the sparrows peeped through they saw a room that looked to them like a tulip with beautiful colors of every shade. Within the tulip were white figures of human beings, made of marble—some few of plaster, but this is the same thing to a sparrow. Upon the roof stood a metal chariot and horses, and the goddess of victory, also of metal, was seated in the chariot driving the horses.

It was Thorwaldsen's museum. "How it shines and glitters," said the maiden sparrow. "This must be *the beautiful*,—tweet,—only this is larger than a peacock." She remembered what her mother had told them in her childhood, that the peacock was one of the greatest examples of *the beautiful*. She flew down into the courtyard, where everything also was very grand. The walls were painted to represent palm branches, and in the midst of the court stood a large, blooming rose tree, spreading its young, sweet, rose-covered branches over a grave. Thither the maiden sparrow flew, for she saw many others of her own kind.

"Tweet," said she, drawing back her foot three times. She had, during the years that had passed, often made the usual greeting to the sparrows she met, but without receiving any acknowledgment; for friends who are once separated do not meet every day. This manner of greeting was become a habit to her, and to-day two old sparrows and a young one returned the greeting.

"Tweet," they replied and drew back the left foot three times. They were two old sparrows out of the nest, and a young one belonging to the family. "Ah, good day; how do you do? To think of our meeting here! This is a very grand place, but there is not much to eat; this is *the beautiful*. Tweet!"

A great many people now came out of the side rooms, in which the marble statues stood, and approached the grave where rested the remains of the great master who carved them. As they stood round Thorwaldsen's grave, each face had a reflected glory, and some few gathered up the fallen rose leaves to preserve them. They had all come from afar; one from mighty England, others from Germany and France. One very handsome lady plucked a rose and concealed it in her bosom. Then the sparrows thought that the roses ruled in this place, and that the whole house had been built for them—which seemed really too much honor; but as all the people showed their love for the roses, the sparrows thought they would not remain behindhand in paying their respects.

"Tweet," they said, and swept the ground with their tails, and glanced with one eye at the roses. They had not looked at them very long, however, before they felt convinced that they were old acquaintances, and so they actually were. The artist who had sketched the rosebush and the ruins of the cottage had since then received permission to transplant the bush and had given it to the architect, for more beautiful roses had never been seen. The architect had planted it on the grave of Thorwaldsen, where it continued to bloom, the image of *the beautiful*, scattering its fragrant, rosy leaves to be gathered and carried away into distant lands in memory of the spot on which they fell.

"Have you obtained a situation in town?" then asked the sparrows of the roses.

The roses nodded. They recognized their little brown neighbors and were rejoiced to see them again.

"It is very delightful," said the roses, "to live here and to blossom, to meet old friends, and to see cheerful faces every day. It is as if each day were a holiday."

"Tweet," said the sparrows to each other. "Yes, these really are our old neighbors. We remember their origin near the pond. Tweet! how they have risen, to be sure. Some people seem to get on while they are asleep. Ah! there's a withered leaf. I can see it quite plainly."

And they pecked at the leaf till it fell, but the rosebush continued fresher and greener than ever. The roses bloomed in the sunshine on Thorwaldsen's grave and thus became linked with his immortal name.

THE OLD HOUSE

A VERY old house once stood in a street with several others that were quite new and clean. One could read the date of its erection, which had been carved on one of the beams and surrounded by scrolls formed of tulips and hop tendrils; by this date it could be seen that the old house was nearly three hundred years old. Entire verses too were written over the windows in old-fashioned letters, and grotesque faces, curiously carved, grinned at you from under the cornices. One story projected a long way over the other, and under the roof ran a leaden gutter with a dragon's head at the end. The rain was intended to pour out at the dragon's mouth, but it ran out of his body instead, for there was a hole in the gutter.

All the other houses in the street were new and well built, with large windowpanes and smooth walls. Any one might see they had nothing to do with the old house. Perhaps they thought: "How long will that heap of rubbish remain here, to be a disgrace to the whole street? The parapet projects so far forward that no one can see out of our windows what is going on in that direction. The stairs are as broad as the staircase of a castle and as steep as if they led to a church tower. The iron railing looks like the gate of a cemetery, and there are brass knobs upon it. It is really too ridiculous."

Opposite to the old house were more nice new houses, which had just the same opinion as their neighbors.

At the window of one of them sat a little boy with fresh, rosy cheeks and clear, sparkling eyes, who was very fond of the old house in sunshine or in moonlight. He would sit and look at the wall, from which the plaster had in some places fallen off, and fancy all sorts of scenes which had been in former times—how the street must have looked when the houses had all gable roofs, open staircases, and gutters with dragons at the spout. He could even see soldiers walking about with halberds. Certainly it was a very good house to look at for amusement.

An old man lived in it who wore knee breeches, a coat with large brass buttons, and a wig which any one could see was a real one. Every morning there came an old man to clean the rooms and to wait upon him, otherwise the old man in the knee breeches would have been quite alone in the house. Sometimes he came to one of the windows and looked out; then the little boy nodded to him, and the old man nodded back again, till they became acquainted, and were friends, although they had never spoken to each other; but that was of no consequence.

The little boy one day heard his parents say, "The old man is very well off, but he must be terribly lonely." So the next Sunday morning the little boy wrapped something in a paper, and took it to the door of the old house, and said to the attendant who waited upon the old man: "Will you please to give this from me to the gentleman who lives here? I have two tin soldiers, and this is one of them, and he shall have it, because I know he is terribly lonely."

The old attendant nodded and looked very much pleased, and then he carried the tin soldier into the house.

Afterwards he was sent over to ask the little boy if he would not like to pay a visit himself. His parents gave him permission, and so it was that he gained admission to the old house.

The brass knobs on the railings shone more brightly than ever, as if they had been polished on account of his visit; and on the doors were carved trumpeters standing in tulips, and it seemed as if they were blowing with all their might, their cheeks were so puffed out: "Tanta-ra-ra, the little boy is coming. Tanta-ra-ra, the little boy is coming."

Then the door opened. All round the hall hung old portraits of knights in armor and ladies in silk gowns; and the armor rattled, and the silk dresses rustled. Then came a staircase which went up a long way, and then came down a little way and led to a balcony which was in a very ruinous state. There were large holes and long cracks, out of which grew grass and leaves; indeed the whole balcony, the courtyard, and the walls were so overgrown with green that they looked like a garden.

In the balcony stood flowerpots on which were heads having asses' ears, but the flowers in them grew just as they pleased. In one pot, pinks were growing all over the sides,—at least the green leaves were,—shooting forth stalk and stem and saying as plainly as they could speak, "The air has fanned me, the sun has kissed me, and I am promised a little flower for next Sunday—really for next Sunday!"

Then they entered a room in which the walls were covered with leather, and the leather had golden flowers stamped upon it.

"Gilding wears out with time and bad weather,
But leather endures; there's nothing like leather,"

said the walls. Chairs handsomely carved, with elbows on each side and with very high backs, stood in the room; and as they creaked they seemed to say: "Sit down. Oh dear! how I am creaking; I shall certainly have the gout like the old cupboard. Gout in my back, ugh!"

And then the little boy entered the room where the old man sat.

"Thank you for the tin soldier, my little friend," said the old man, "and thank you also for coming to see me."

"Thanks, thanks"—or "Creak, creak"—said all the furniture.

There was so much furniture that the pieces stood in each other's way to get a sight of the little boy. On the wall near the center of the room hung the picture of a beautiful lady, young and gay, dressed in the fashion of the olden times, with powdered hair and a full, stiff skirt. She said neither "thanks" nor "creak," but she looked down upon the little boy with her mild eyes, and he said to the old man,

"Where did you get that picture?"

"From the shop opposite," he replied. "Many portraits hang there. No one seems to know any of them or to trouble himself about them. The persons they represent have been dead and buried long since. But I knew this lady many years ago, and she has been dead nearly half a century."

"Thank you for the tin soldier, my little friend," said the old man

Under a glass beneath the picture hung a nosegay of withered flowers, which were, no doubt, half a century old too, at least they appeared so.

And the pendulum of the old clock went to and fro, and the hands turned round, and as time passed on everything in the room grew older, but no one seemed to notice it.

"They say at home," said the little boy, "that you are very lonely."

"Oh," replied the old man, "I have pleasant thoughts of all that is past recalled by memory, and now you too are come to visit me, and that is very pleasant."

Then he took from the bookcase a book full of pictures representing long processions of wonderful coaches such as are never seen at the present time, soldiers like the knave of clubs, and citizens with waving banners. The tailors had a flag with a pair of scissors supported by two lions, and on the shoemakers' flag there were not boots but an eagle with two heads, for the shoemakers must have everything arranged so that they can say, "This is a pair." What a picture book it was! And then the old man went into another room to fetch apples and nuts. It was very pleasant, certainly, to be in that old house.

"I cannot endure it," said the tin soldier, who stood on a shelf; "it is so lonely and dull here. I have been accustomed to live in a family, and I cannot get used to this life. I cannot bear it. The whole day is long enough, but the evening is longer. It is not here as it was in your house opposite, when your father and mother talked so cheerfully together, while you and all the dear children made such a delightful noise. Do you think he gets any kisses? Do you think he ever has friendly looks or a Christmas tree? He will have nothing now but the grave. Oh! I cannot bear it."

"You must not look on the sorrowful side so much," said the little boy. "I think everything in this house is beautiful, and all the old, pleasant thoughts come back here to pay visits."

"Ah, but I never see any, and I don't know them," said the tin soldier; "and I cannot bear it."

"You must bear it," said the little boy. Then the old man came back with a pleasant face, and brought with him beautiful preserved fruits as well as apples and nuts, and the little boy thought no more of the tin soldier.

How happy and delighted the little boy was! And after he returned home, and while days and weeks passed, a great deal of nodding took place from one house to the other, and then the little boy went to pay another visit. The carved trumpeters blew: "Tanta-ra-ra, there is the little boy. Tanta-ra-ra." The swords and armor on the old knights' pictures rattled, the silk dresses rustled, the leather repeated its rhyme, and the old chairs that had the gout in their backs cried "Creak"; it was all exactly like the first time, for in that house one day and one hour were just like another.

"I cannot bear it any longer," said the tin soldier; "I have wept tears of tin, it is so melancholy here. Let me go to the wars and lose an arm or a leg; that would be some change. I cannot bear it. Now I know what it is to have visits from one's old recollections and all they bring with them. I have had visits from mine, and you may believe me it is not altogether pleasant. I was very nearly jumping from the shelf. I saw you all in your house opposite, as if you were really present.

"It was Sunday morning, and you children stood round the table, singing the hymn that you sing every morning. You were standing quietly with your hands folded, and your father and mother were looking just as serious, when the door opened, and your little sister Maria, who is not two years old, was brought into the room. You know she always dances when she hears music and singing of any sort, so she began to dance immediately, although she ought not to have done so; but she could not get into the right time because the tune was so slow, so she stood first on one foot and then on the other and bent her head very low, but it would not suit the music. You all stood looking grave, although it was very difficult to do so, but I laughed so to myself that I fell down from the table and got a bruise, which is still there. I know it was not right to laugh. So all this, and everything else that I have seen, keeps running in my head, and these must be the old recollections that bring so many thoughts with them. Tell me whether you still sing on Sundays, and tell me about your little sister Maria, and how my old comrade is, the other tin soldier. Ah, really he must be very happy. I cannot endure this life."

"You are given away," said the little boy; "you must stay. Don't you see that?" Then the old man came in with a box containing many curious things to show him. Rouge-pots, scent-boxes, and old cards so large and so richly gilded that none are ever seen like them in these days. And there were smaller boxes to look at, and the piano was opened, and inside the lid were painted landscapes. But when the old man played, the piano sounded quite out of tune. Then he looked at the picture he had bought at the broker's, and his eyes sparkled brightly as he nodded at it and said, "Ah, she could sing that tune."

"I will go to the wars! I will go to the wars!" cried the tin soldier as loud as he could, and threw himself down on the floor. Where could he have fallen? The old man searched, and the little boy searched, but he was gone and could not be found. "I shall find him again," said the old man. But he did not find him; the tin soldier had fallen through a crack between the boards and lay there now as in an open grave.

The day went by, and the little boy returned home; the week passed, and many more weeks. It was winter, and the windows were quite frozen, so that the little boy was obliged to breathe on the panes and rub a hole to peep through at the old house. Snow-drifts were lying in all the scrolls and on the inscriptions, and the steps were covered with snow as if no one were at home. And indeed nobody was at home, for the old man was dead.

In the evening the old man was to be taken to the country to be buried there in his own grave; so they carried him away. No one followed him, for all his friends were dead, and the little boy kissed his hand to his old friend as he saw him borne away.

A few days after, there was an auction at the old house, and from his window the little boy saw the people carrying away the pictures of old knights and ladies, the flowerpots with the long ears, the old chairs, and the cupboards. Some were taken one way, some another. *Her* portrait, which had been bought at the picture dealer's, went back again to his shop, and there it remained, for no one seemed to know her or to care for the old picture.

In the spring they began to pull the house itself down; people called it complete rubbish. From the street could be seen the room in which the walls were covered with leather, ragged and torn, and the green in the balcony hung straggling over the beams; they pulled it down quickly, for it looked ready to fall, and at last it was cleared away altogether. "What a good riddance," said the neighbors' houses.

Afterward a fine new house was built, farther back from the road. It had lofty windows and smooth walls, but in front, on the spot where the old house really stood, a little garden was planted, and wild vines grew up over the neighboring walls. In front of the garden were large iron railings and a great gate which looked very stately. People used to stop and peep through the railings. The sparrows assembled in dozens upon the wild vines and chattered all together as loud as they could, but not about the old house. None of them could remember it, for many years had passed by; so many, indeed, that the little boy was now a man, and a really good man too, and his parents were very proud of him. He had just married and had come with his young wife to reside in the new house with the garden in front of it, and now he stood there by her side while she planted a field flower that she thought very pretty. She was planting it herself with her little hands and pressing down the earth with her fingers. "Oh, dear, what was that?" she exclaimed as something pricked her. Out of the soft earth something was sticking up.

It was—only think!—it was really the tin soldier, the very same which had been lost up in the old man's room and had been hidden among old wood and rubbish for a long time till it sank into the earth, where it must have been for many years. And the young wife wiped the soldier, first with a green leaf and then with her fine pocket handkerchief, that smelt of a beautiful perfume. And the tin soldier felt as if he were recovering from a fainting fit.

"Let me see him," said the young man, and then he smiled and shook his head and said, "It can scarcely be the same, but it reminds me of something that happened to one of my tin soldiers when I was a little boy." And then he told his wife about the old house and the old man and of the tin soldier which he had sent across because he thought the old man was lonely. And he related the story so clearly that tears came into the eyes of the young wife for the old house and the old man.

"It is very likely that this is really the same soldier," said she, "and I will take care of him and always remember what you have told me; but some day you must show me the old man's grave."

"I don't know where it is," he replied; "no one knows. All his friends are dead. No one took care of him or tended his grave, and I was only a little boy."

"Oh, how dreadfully lonely he must have been," said she.

"Yes, terribly lonely," cried the tin soldier; "still it is delightful not to be forgotten."

"Delightful indeed!" cried a voice quite near to them. No one but the tin soldier saw that it came from a rag of the leather which hung in tatters. It had lost all its gilding and looked like wet earth, but it had an opinion, and it spoke it thus:

"Gilding wears out with time and bad weather,
But leather endures; there's nothing like leather."

But the tin soldier did not believe any such thing.

THE CONCEITED APPLE BRANCH

IT WAS the month of May. The wind still blew cold, but from bush and tree, field and flower, came the welcome sound, "Spring is come."

Wild flowers in profusion covered the hedges. Under the little apple tree Spring seemed busy, and he told his tale from one of the branches, which hung fresh and blooming and covered with delicate pink blossoms that were just ready to open.

The branch well knew how beautiful it was; this knowledge exists as much in the leaf as in the blood. I was therefore not surprised when a nobleman's carriage, in which sat the young countess, stopped in the road just by. The apple branch, she said, was a most lovely object, an emblem of spring in its most charming aspect. The branch was broken off for her, and she held it in her delicate hand and sheltered it with her silk parasol.

Then they drove to the castle, in which were lofty halls and splendid drawing-rooms. Pure white curtains fluttered before the open windows, and beautiful flowers stood in transparent vases. In one of them, which looked as if it had been cut out of newly fallen snow, the apple branch was placed among some fresh light twigs of beech. It was a charming sight. And the branch became proud, which was very much like human nature.

People of every description entered the room, and according to their position in society so dared they to express their admiration. Some few said nothing, others expressed too much, and the apple branch very soon got to understand that there was as much difference in the characters of human beings as in those of plants and flowers. Some are all for pomp and parade, others have a great deal to do to maintain their own importance, while the rest might be spared without much loss to society. So thought the apple branch as he stood before the open window, from which he could see out over gardens and fields, where there were flowers and plants enough for him to think and reflect upon—some rich and beautiful, some poor and humble indeed.

"Poor despised herbs," said the apple branch; "there is really a difference between them and such as I am. How unhappy they must be if they can feel as those in my position do! There is a difference indeed, and so there ought to be, or we should all be equals."

And the apple branch looked with a sort of pity upon them, especially on a certain little flower that is found in fields and in ditches. No one bound these flowers together in a nosegay, they were too common,—they were even known to grow between the paving stones, shooting up everywhere like bad weeds,—and they bore the very ugly name of "dog flowers," or "dandelions."

"Poor despised plants," said the apple bough, "it is not your fault that you are so ugly and that you have such an ugly name, but it is with plants as with men—there must be a difference."

"A difference!" cried the sunbeam as he kissed the blooming apple branch and then kissed the yellow dandelion out in the fields. All were brothers, and the sunbeam kissed them—the poor flowers as well as the rich.

The apple bough had never thought of the boundless love of God which extends over all the works of creation, over everything which lives and moves and has its being in Him. He had never thought of the good and beautiful which are so often hidden, but can never remain forgotten by Him, not only among the lower creation, but also among men. The sunbeam, the ray of light, knew better.

"You do not see very far nor very clearly," he said to the apple branch. "Which is the despised plant you so specially pity?"

"The dandelion," he replied. "No one ever places it in a nosegay; it is trodden under foot, there are so many of them; and when they run to seed they have flowers like wool, which fly away in little pieces over the roads and cling to the dresses of the people; they are only weeds—but of course there must be weeds. Oh, I am really very thankful that I was not made like one of these flowers."

There came presently across the fields a whole group of children, the youngest of whom was so small that he had to be carried by the others; and when he was seated on the grass, among the yellow flowers, he laughed aloud with joy, kicked out his little legs, rolled about, plucked the yellow flowers and kissed them in childlike innocence.

The elder children broke off the flowers with long stems, bent the stalks one round the other to form links, and made first a chain for the neck, then one to go across the shoulders and hang down to the waist, and at last a wreath to wear about the head; so that they looked quite splendid in their garlands of green stems and golden flowers. But the eldest among them gathered carefully the faded flowers, on the stem of which were grouped together the seeds, in the form of a white, feathery coronal.

These loose, airy wool-flowers are very beautiful, and look like fine, snowy feathers or down. The children held them to their mouths and tried to blow away the whole coronal with one puff of the breath. They had been told by their grandmothers that whoever did so would be sure to have new clothes before the end of the year. The despised flower was by this raised to the position of a prophet, or foreteller of events.

"Do you see," said the sunbeam, "do you see the beauty of these flowers? Do you see their powers of giving pleasure?"

"Yes, to children," said the apple bough.

By and by an old woman came into the field and, with a blunt knife without a handle, began to dig round the roots of some of the dandelion plants and pull them up. With some she intended to make tea for herself, but the rest she was going to sell to the chemist and obtain money.

"But beauty is of higher value than all this," said the apple-tree branch; "only the chosen ones can be admitted into the realms of the beautiful. There is a difference between plants, just as there is a difference between men."

Then the sunbeam spoke of the boundless love of God as seen in creation and over all that lives, and of the equal distribution of His gifts, both in time and in eternity.

"That is your opinion," said the apple bough.

Then some people came into the room and among them the young countess—the lady who had placed the apple bough in the transparent vase, so pleasantly beneath the rays of sunlight. She carried in her hand something that seemed like a flower. The object was hidden by two or three great leaves which covered it like a shield so that no draft or gust of wind could injure it, and it was carried more carefully than the apple branch had ever been.

Very cautiously the large leaves were removed, and there appeared the feathery seed crown of the despised yellow dandelion. This was what the lady had so carefully plucked and carried home so safely covered, so that not one of the delicate feathery arrows of which its mistlike shape was so lightly formed should flutter away. She now drew it forth quite uninjured and wondered at its beautiful form, its airy lightness and singular construction so soon to be blown away by the wind.

"See," she exclaimed, "how wonderfully God has made this little flower. I will paint it in a picture with the apple branch. Every one admires the beauty of the apple bough, but this humble flower has been endowed by Heaven with another kind of loveliness, and although they differ in appearance both are children of the realms of beauty."

Then the sunbeam kissed both the lowly flower and the blooming apple branch, upon whose leaves appeared a rosy blush.

PREFACE TO THE SECOND SERIES

THE present volume is the second of the selected stories from Hans Andersen. Together the books include what, out of a larger number, are the best for children's use. The story-telling activity of this inimitable genius covered a period of more than forty years. Besides these shorter juvenile tales, there are a few which deserve to survive. "The Ice Maiden" is a standard, if not a classic, and "The Sandhills of Jutland" was pronounced by Ruskin the most perfect story that he knew.

It adds a charm to the little stories of these two volumes to know that the genial author traveled widely for a man of his time and everywhere was urged to tell the tales himself. This he did with equal charm in the kitchens of the humble and in the courts and palaces of nobles.

As was said in the preface to the first volume, wherever there are children to read, the stories of Hans Christian Andersen will be read and loved.

They wanted to see
the paper burn . . . .

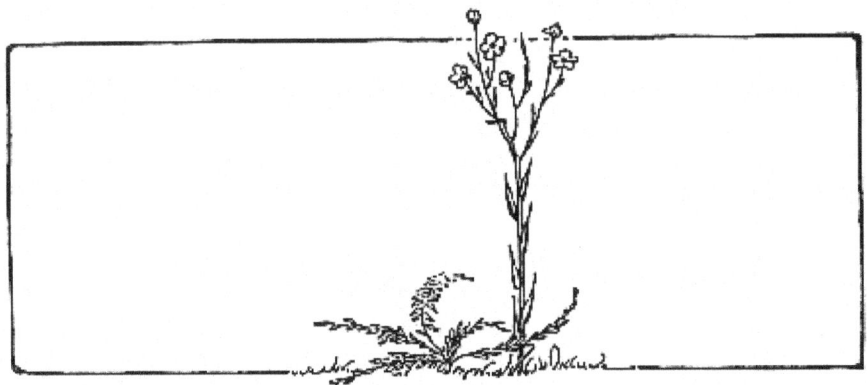

THE FLAX

THE flax was in full bloom; it had pretty little blue flowers, as delicate as the wings of a moth. The sun shone on it and the showers watered it; and this was as good for the flax as it is for little children to be washed and then kissed by their mothers. They look much prettier for it, and so did the flax.

"People say that I look exceedingly well," said the flax, "and that I am so fine and long that I shall make a beautiful piece of linen. How fortunate I am! It makes me so happy to know that something can be made of me. How the sunshine cheers me, and how sweet and refreshing is the rain! My happiness overpowers me; no one in the world can feel happier than I."

"Ah, yes, no doubt," said the fern, "but you do not know the world yet as well as I do, for my sticks are knotty"; and then it sang quite mournfully:

"Snip, snap, snurre,
Basse lurre.
The song is ended."

"No, it is not ended," said the flax. "To-morrow the sun will shine or the rain descend. I feel that I am growing. I feel that I am in full blossom. I am the happiest of all creatures, for I may some day come to something."

Well, one day some people came, who took hold of the flax and pulled it up by the roots, which was very painful. Then it was laid in water, as if it were to be drowned, and after that placed near a fire, as if it were to be roasted. All this was very shocking.

"We cannot expect to be happy always," said the flax. "By experiencing evil as well as good we become wise." And certainly there was plenty of evil in store for the flax. It was steeped, and roasted, and broken, and combed; indeed, it scarcely knew what was done to it. At last it was put on the spinning wheel. "Whir, whir," went the wheel, so quickly that the flax could not collect its thoughts.

"Well, I have been very happy," it thought in the midst of its pain, "and must be contented with the past." And contented it remained, till it was put on the loom and became a beautiful piece of white linen. All the flax, even to the last stalk, was used in making this one piece.

"Well, this is quite wonderful," said the flax. "I could not have believed that I should be so favored by fortune. The fern was not wrong when it sang,

'Snip, snap, snurre,
Basse lurre.'

But the song is not ended yet, I am sure; it is only just beginning. How wonderful it is that, after all I have suffered, I am made something of at last! I am the luckiest person in the world—so strong and fine. And how white and long I am! This is far better than being a mere plant and bearing flowers. Then I had no attention, nor any water unless it rained; now I am watched and cared for. Every morning the maid turns me over, and I have a shower bath from the watering-pot every evening. Yes, and the clergyman's wife noticed me and said I was the best piece of linen in the whole parish. I cannot be happier than I am now."

After some time the linen was taken into the house, and there cut with the scissors and torn into pieces and then pricked with needles. This certainly was not pleasant, but at last it was made into twelve garments of the kind that everybody wears. "See now, then," said the flax, "I have become something of importance. This was my destiny; it is quite a blessing. Now I shall be of some use in the world, as every one ought to be; it is the only way to be happy. I am now divided into twelve pieces, and yet the whole dozen is all one and the same. It is most extraordinary good fortune."

Years passed away, and at last the linen was so worn it could scarcely hold together. "It must end very soon," said the pieces to each other. "We would gladly have held together a little longer, but it is useless to expect impossibilities." And at length they fell into rags and tatters and thought it was all over with them, for they were torn to shreds and steeped in water and made into a pulp and dried, and they knew not what besides, till all at once they found themselves beautiful white paper. "Well, now, this is a surprise—a glorious surprise too," said the paper. "Now I am finer than ever, and who can tell what fine things I may have written upon me? This is wonderful luck!" And so it was, for the most beautiful stories and poetry were written upon it, and only once was there a blot, which was remarkable good fortune. Then people heard the stories and poetry read, and it made them wiser and better; for all that was written had a good and sensible meaning, and a great blessing was contained in it.

"I never imagined anything like this when I was only a little blue flower growing in the fields," said the paper. "How could I know that I should ever be the means of bringing knowledge and joy to men? I cannot understand it myself, and yet it is really so. Heaven knows that I have done nothing myself but what I was obliged to do with my weak powers for my own preservation; and yet I have been promoted from one joy and honor to another. Each time I think that the song is ended, and then something higher and better begins for me. I suppose now I shall be sent out to journey about the world, so that people may read me. It cannot be otherwise, for I have more splendid thoughts written upon me than I had pretty flowers in olden times. I am happier than ever."

But the paper did not go on its travels. It was sent to the printer, and all the words written upon it were set up in type to make a book,—or rather many hundreds of books,—for many more persons could derive pleasure and profit from a printed book than from the written paper; and if the paper had been sent about the world, it would have been worn out before it had half finished its journey.

"Yes, this is certainly the wisest plan," said the written paper; "I really did not think of this. I shall remain at home and be held in honor like some old grandfather, as I really am to all these new books. They will do some good. I could not have wandered about as they can, yet he who wrote all this has looked at me as every word flowed from his pen upon my surface. I am the most honored of all."

Then the paper was tied in a bundle with other papers and thrown into a tub that stood in the washhouse.

"After work, it is well to rest," said the paper, "and a very good opportunity to collect one's thoughts. Now I am able, for the first time, to learn what is in me; and to know one's self is true progress. What will be done with me now, I wonder? No doubt I shall still go forward. I have always progressed hitherto, I know quite well."

Now it happened one day that all the paper in the tub was taken out and laid on the hearth to be burned. People said it could not be sold at the shop, to wrap up butter and sugar, because it had been written upon. The children in the house stood round the hearth to watch the blaze, for paper always flamed up so prettily, and afterwards, among the ashes, there were so many red sparks to be seen running one after the other, here and there, as quick as the wind. They called it seeing the children come out of school, and the last spark, they said, was the schoolmaster. They would often think the last spark had come, and one would cry, "There goes the schoolmaster," but the next moment another spark would appear, bright and beautiful. How they wanted to know where all the sparks went to! Perhaps they will find out some day.

The whole bundle of paper had been placed on the fire and was soon burning. "Ugh!" cried the paper as it burst into a bright flame; "ugh!" It was certainly not very pleasant to be burned. But when the whole was wrapped in flames, the sparks mounted up into the air, higher than the flax had ever been able to raise its little blue flowers, and they glistened as the white linen never could have glistened. All the written letters became quite red in a moment, and all the words and thoughts turned to fire.

"Now I am mounting straight up to the sun," said a voice in the flames; and it was as if a thousand voices echoed the words as the flames darted up through the chimney and went out at the top. Then a number of tiny beings, as many as the flowers on the flax had been, and invisible to mortal eyes, floated above the children. They were even lighter and more delicate than the blue flowers from which they were born; and as the flames died out and nothing remained of the paper but black ashes, these little beings danced upon it, and wherever they touched it, bright red sparks appeared.

"The children are all out of school, and the schoolmaster was the last of all," said the children. It was good fun, and they sang over the dead ashes:

"Snip, snap, snurre,
Basse lurre.
The song is ended."
But the little invisible beings said, "The song is never ended; the most beautiful is yet to come."

But the children could neither hear nor understand this; nor should they, for children must not know everything.

_____

THE DAISY

NOW listen. Out in the country, close by the roadside, stood a pleasant house; you have seen one like it, no doubt, very often. In front lay a little fenced-in garden, full of blooming flowers. Near the hedge, in the soft green grass, grew a little daisy. The sun shone as brightly and warmly upon her as upon the large and beautiful garden flowers, so the daisy grew from hour to hour. Every morning she unfolded her little white petals, like shining rays round the little golden sun in the center of the flower. She never seemed to think that she was unseen down in the grass or that she was only a poor, insignificant flower. She felt too happy to care for that. Merrily she turned toward the warm sun, looked up to the blue sky, and listened to the lark singing high in the air.

One day the little flower was as joyful as if it had been a great holiday, although it was only Monday. All the children were at school, and while they sat on their benches learning their lessons, she, on her little stem, learned also from the warm sun and from everything around her how good God is, and it made her happy to hear the lark express-ing in his song her own glad feelings. The daisy admired the happy bird who could warble so sweetly and fly so high, and she was not at all sorrowful because she could not do the same.

"I can see and hear," thought she; "the sun shines upon me, and the wind kisses me; what else do I need to make me happy?"

Within the garden grew a number of aristocratic flowers; the less scent they had the more they flaunted. The peonies considered it a grand thing to be so large, and puffed themselves out to be larger than the roses. The tulips knew that they were marked with beautiful colors, and held themselves bolt upright so that they might be seen more plain-ly.

They did not notice the little daisy outside, but she looked at them and thought: "How rich and beautiful they are! No wonder the pretty bird flies down to visit them. How glad I am that I grow so near them, that I may admire their beauty!"

Just at this moment the lark flew down, crying "Tweet," but he did not go to the tall peonies and tulips; he hopped into the grass near the lowly daisy. She trembled for joy and hardly knew what to think. The little bird hopped round the daisy, singing, "Oh, what sweet, soft grass, and what a lovely little flower, with gold in its heart and silver on its dress!" For the yellow center in the daisy looked like gold, and the leaves around were glittering white, like silver.

How happy the little daisy felt, no one can describe. The bird kissed her with his beak, sang to her, and then flew up again into the blue air above. It was at least a quarter of an hour before the daisy could recover herself. Half ashamed, yet happy in herself, she glanced at the other flowers; they must have seen the honor she had received, and would understand her delight and pleasure.

But the tulips looked prouder than ever; indeed, they were evidently quite vexed about it. The peonies were disgusted, and could they have spoken, the poor little daisy would no doubt have received a good scolding. She could see they were all out of temper, and it made her very sorry.

At this moment there came into the garden a girl with a large, glittering knife in her hand. She went straight to the tulips and cut off several of them.

"O dear," sighed the daisy, "how shocking! It is all over with them now." The girl car-ried the tulips away, and the daisy felt very glad to grow outside in the grass and to be only a poor little flower. When the sun set, she folded up her leaves and went to sleep. She dreamed the whole night long of the warm sun and the pretty little bird.

The next morning, when she joyfully stretched out her white leaves once more to the warm air and the light, she recognized the voice of the bird, but his song sounded mournful and sad.

Alas! he had good reason to be sad: he had been caught and made a prisoner in a cage that hung close by the open window. He sang of the happy time when he could fly in the air, joyous and free; of the young green corn in the fields, from which he would spring higher and higher to sing his glorious song—but now he was a prisoner in a cage.

The little daisy wished very much to help him. But what could she do? In her anxiety she forgot all the beautiful things around her, the warm sunshine, and her own pretty, shining, white leaves. Alas! she could think of nothing but the captive bird and her own inability to help him.

Two boys came out of the garden; one of them carried a sharp knife in his hand, like the one with which the girl had cut the tulips. They went straight to the little daisy, who could not think what they were going to do.

"We can cut out a nice piece of turf for the lark here," said one of the boys; and he began to cut a square piece round the daisy, so that she stood just in the center.

So the daisy remained, and was put with the turf in the lark's cage.

"Pull up the flower," said the other boy; and the daisy trembled with fear, for to pluck her up would destroy her life and she wished so much to live and to be taken to the captive lark in his cage.

"No, let it stay where it is," said the boy, "it looks so pretty." So the daisy remained, and was put with the turf in the lark's cage. The poor bird was complaining loudly about his lost freedom, beating his wings against the iron bars of his prison. The little daisy could make no sign and utter no word to console him, as she would gladly have done. The whole morning passed in this manner.

"There is no water here," said the captive lark; "they have all gone out and have forgotten to give me a drop to drink. My throat is hot and dry; I feel as if I had fire and ice within me, and the air is so heavy. Alas! I must die. I must bid farewell to the warm sunshine, the fresh green, and all the beautiful things which God has created." And then he thrust his beak into the cool turf to refresh himself a little with the fresh grass, and, as he did so, his eye fell upon the daisy. The bird nodded to her and kissed her with his beak and said: "You also will wither here, you poor little flower! They have given you to me, with the little patch of green grass on which you grow, in exchange for the whole world which was mine out there. Each little blade of grass is to me as a great tree, and each of your white leaves a flower. Alas! you only show me how much I have lost."

"Oh, if I could only comfort him!" thought the daisy, but she could not move a leaf. The perfume from her leaves was stronger than is usual in these flowers, and the bird noticed it, and though he was fainting with thirst, and in his pain pulled up the green blades of grass, he did not touch the flower.

The evening came, and yet no one had come to bring the bird a drop of water. Then he stretched out his pretty wings and shook convulsively; he could only sing "Tweet, tweet," in a weak, mournful tone. His little head bent down toward the flower; the bird's heart was broken with want and pining. Then the flower could not fold her leaves as she had done the evening before when she went to sleep, but, sick and sorrowful, drooped toward the earth.

Not till morning did the boys come, and when they found the bird dead, they wept many and bitter tears. They dug a pretty grave for him and adorned it with leaves of flowers. The bird's lifeless body was placed in a smart red box and was buried with great honor.

Poor bird! while he was alive and could sing, they forgot him and allowed him to sit in his cage and suffer want, but now that he was dead, they mourned for him with many tears and buried him in royal state.

But the turf with the daisy on it was thrown out into the dusty road. No one thought of the little flower that had felt more for the poor bird than had any one else and that would have been so glad to help and comfort him if she had been able.

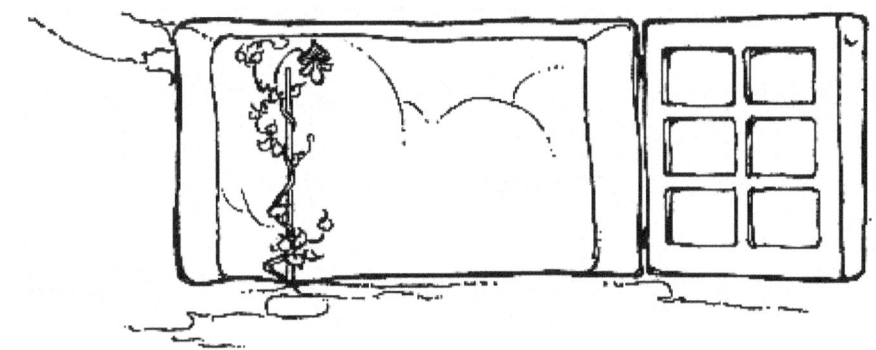

THE PEA BLOSSOM

THERE were once five peas in one shell; they were green, and the shell was green, and so they believed that the whole world must be green also, which was a very natural conclusion.

The shell grew, and the peas grew; and as they grew they arranged themselves all in a row. The sun shone without and warmed the shell, and the rain made it clear and transparent; it looked mild and agreeable in broad daylight and dark at night, just as it should. And the peas, as they sat there, grew bigger and bigger, and more thoughtful as they mused, for they felt there must be something for them to do.

"Are we to sit here forever?" asked one. "Shall we not become hard, waiting here so long? It seems to me there must be something outside; I feel sure of it."

Weeks passed by; the peas became yellow, and the shell became yellow.

"All the world is turning yellow, I suppose," said they—and perhaps they were right.

Suddenly they felt a pull at the shell. It was torn off and held in human hands; then it was slipped into the pocket of a jacket, together with other full pods.

"Now we shall soon be let out," said one, and that was just what they all wanted.

"I should like to know which of us will travel farthest," said the smallest of the five; "and we shall soon see."

"What is to happen will happen," said the largest pea.

"Crack!" went the shell, and the five peas rolled out into the bright sunshine. There they lay in a child's hand. A little boy was holding them tightly. He said they were fine peas for his pea-shooter, and immediately he put one in and shot it out.

"Now I am flying out into the wide world," said the pea. "Catch me if you can." And he was gone in a moment.

"I intend to fly straight to the sun," said the second. "That is a shell that will suit me exactly, for it lets itself be seen." And away he went.

"We will go to sleep wherever we find ourselves," said the next two; "we shall still be rolling onwards." And they did fall to the floor and roll about, but they got into the pea-shooter for all that. "We will go farthest of any," said they.

"What is to happen will happen," exclaimed the last one, as he was shot out of the pea-shooter. Up he flew against an old board under a garret window and fell into a little crevice which was almost filled with moss and soft earth. The moss closed itself about him, and there he lay—a captive indeed, but not unnoticed by God.

"What is to happen will happen," said he to himself.

Within the little garret lived a poor woman, who went out to clean stoves, chop wood into small pieces, and do other hard work, for she was both strong and industrious. Yet she remained always poor, and at home in the garret lay her only daughter, not quite grown up and very delicate and weak. For a whole year she had kept her bed, and it seemed as if she could neither die nor get well.

"She is going to her little sister," said the woman. "I had only the two children, and it was not an easy thing to support them; but the good God provided for one of them by taking her home to himself. The other was left to me, but I suppose they are not to be separated, and my sick girl will soon go to her sister in heaven."

All day long the sick girl lay quietly and patiently, while her mother went out to earn money.

Spring came, and early one morning the sun shone through the little window and threw his rays mildly and pleasantly over the floor of the room. Just as the mother was going to her work, the sick girl fixed her gaze on the lowest pane of the window. "Mother," she exclaimed, "what can that little green thing be that peeps in at the window? It is moving in the wind."

The mother stepped to the window and half opened it. "Oh!" she said, "there is actually a little pea that has taken root and is putting out its green leaves. How could it have got into this crack? Well, now, here is a little garden for you to amuse yourself with." So the bed of the sick girl was drawn nearer to the window, that she might see the budding plant; and the mother went forth to her work.

"Mother, I believe I shall get well," said the sick child in the evening. "The sun has shone in here so bright and warm to-day, and the little pea is growing so fast, that I feel better, too, and think I shall get up and go out into the warm sunshine again."

"God grant it!" said the mother, but she did not believe it would be so. She took a little stick and propped up the green plant which had given her daughter such pleasure, so that it might not be broken by the winds. She tied the piece of string to the window-sill and to the upper part of the frame, so that the pea tendrils might have something to twine round. And the plant shot up so fast that one could almost see it grow from day to day.

"A flower is really coming," said the mother one morning. At last she was beginning to let herself hope that her little sick daughter might indeed recover. She remembered that for some time the child had spoken more cheerfully, and that during the last few days she had raised herself in bed in the morning to look with sparkling eyes at her little garden which contained but a single pea plant.

A week later the invalid sat up by the open window a whole hour, feeling quite happy in the warm sunshine, while outside grew the little plant, and on it a pink pea blossom in full bloom. The little maiden bent down and gently kissed the delicate leaves. This day was like a festival to her.

"Our heavenly Father himself has planted that pea and made it grow and flourish, to bring joy to you and hope to me, my blessed child," said the happy mother, and she smiled at the flower as if it had been an angel from God.

But what became of the other peas? Why, the one who flew out into the wide world and said, "Catch me if you can," fell into a gutter on the roof of a house and ended his travels in the crop of a pigeon. The two lazy ones were carried quite as far and were of some use, for they also were eaten by pigeons; but the fourth, who wanted to reach the sun, fell into a sink and lay there in the dirty water for days and weeks, till he had swelled to a great size.

"I am getting beautifully fat," said the pea; "I expect I shall burst at last; no pea could do more than that, I think. I am the most remarkable of all the five that were in the shell." And the sink agreed with the pea.

On it a pink pea blossom in full bloom.

But the young girl, with sparkling eyes and the rosy hue of health upon her cheeks, stood at the open garret window and, folding her thin hands over the pea blossom, thanked God for what He had done.

THE STORKS

O N the last house in the village there lay a stork's nest. The mother stork sat in it with her four little ones, who were stretching out their heads with their pointed black bills that had not yet turned red. At a little distance, on the top of the roof, stood the father stork, bolt upright and as stiff as could be. That he might not appear quite idle while standing sentry, he had drawn one leg up under him, as is the manner of storks. One might have taken him to be carved in marble, so still did he stand.

"It must look very grand for my wife to have a sentinel to guard her nest," he thought. "They can't know that I am her husband and will, of course, conclude that I am commanded to stand here by her nest. It looks aristocratic!"

Below, in the street, a crowd of children were playing. When they chanced to catch sight of the storks, one of the boldest of the boys began to sing the old song about the stork. The others soon joined him, but each sang the words that he happened to have heard. This is one of the ways:

"Stork, stork, fly away;
Stand not on one leg to-day.
Thy dear wife sits in the nest,
To lull the little ones to rest.

"There's a halter for one,
There's a stake for another,
For the third there's a gun,
And a spit for his brother!"

"Only listen," said the young storks, "to what the boys are singing. Do you hear them say we're to be hanged and shot?"

"Don't listen to what they say; if you don't mind, it won't hurt you," said the mother.

But the boys went on singing, and pointed mockingly at the sentinel stork. Only one boy, whom they called Peter, said it was a shame to make game of animals, and he would not join in the singing at all.

The mother stork tried to comfort her young ones. "Don't mind them," she said; "see how quiet your father stands on one leg there."

"But we are afraid," said the little ones, drawing back their beaks into the nest.

The children assembled again on the next day, and no sooner did they see the storks than they again began their song:

"The first will be hanged,
The second be hit."

"Tell us, are we to be hanged and burned?" asked the young storks.

"No, no; certainly not," replied the mother. "You are to learn to fly, and then we shall pay a visit to the frogs. They will bow to us in the water and sing 'Croak! croak!' and we shall eat them up, and that will be a great treat."

"And then what?" questioned the young storks.

"Oh, then all the storks in the land will assemble, and the autumn sports will begin; only then one must be able to fly well, for that is very important. Whoever does not fly as he should will be pierced to death by the general's beak, so mind that you learn well, when the drill begins."

"Yes, but then, after that, we shall be killed, as the boys say. Hark! they are singing it again."

"Attend to me and not to them," said the mother stork. "After the great review we shall fly away to warm countries, far from here, over hills and forests. To Egypt we shall fly, where are the three-cornered houses of stone, one point of which reaches to the clouds; they are called pyramids and are older than a stork can imagine. In that same land there is a river which overflows its banks and turns the whole country into mire. We shall go into the mire and eat frogs."

"Oh! oh!" exclaimed all the youngsters.

"Yes, it is indeed a delightful place. We need do nothing all day long but eat; and while we are feasting there so comfortably, in this country there is not a green leaf left on the trees. It is so cold here that the very clouds freeze in lumps or fall down in little white rags." It was hail and snow that she meant, but she did not know how to say it better.

"And will the naughty boys freeze in lumps?" asked the young storks.

"No, they will not freeze in lumps, but they will come near it, and they will sit moping and cowering in gloomy rooms while you are flying about in foreign lands, amid bright flowers and warm sunshine."

Some time passed, and the nestlings had grown so large and strong that they could stand upright in the nest and look all about them. Every day the father stork came with delicious frogs, nice little snakes, and other such dainties that storks delight in. How funny it was to see the clever feats he performed to amuse them! He would lay his head right round upon his tail; and sometimes he would clatter with his beak, as if it were a little rattle; or he would tell them stories, all relating to swamps and fens.

"Come, children," said the mother stork one day, "now you must learn to fly." And all the four young storks had to go out on the ridge of the roof. How they did totter and stagger about! They tried to balance themselves with their wings, but came very near falling to the ground.

"Look at me!" said the mother. "This is the way to hold your head. And thus you must place your feet. Left! right! left! right! that's what will help you on in the world."

Then she flew a little way, and the young ones took a clumsy little leap. Bump! plump! down they fell, for their bodies were still too heavy for them.

"I will not fly," said one of the young storks, as he crept back to the nest. "I don't care about going to warm countries."

"Do you want to stay here and freeze when the winter comes? Will you wait till the boys come to hang, to burn, or to roast you? Well, then, I'll call them."

"Oh, no!" cried the timid stork, hopping back to the roof with the rest.

By the third day they actually began to fly a little. Then they had no doubt that they could soar or hover in the air, upborne by their wings. And this they attempted to do, but down they fell, flapping their wings as fast as they could.

Again the boys came to the street, singing their song, "Storks, storks, fly home and rest."

"Shall we fly down and peck them?" asked the young ones.

"No, leave them alone. Attend to me; that's far more important. One—two—three! now we fly round to the right. One—two—three! now to the left, round the chimney. There! that was very good. That last flap with your wings and the kick with your feet were so graceful and proper that to-morrow you shall fly with me to the marsh. Several of the nicest stork families will be there with their children. Let me see that mine are the best bred of all. Carry your heads high and mind you strut about proudly, for that looks well and helps to make one respected."

"But shall we not take revenge upon the naughty boys?" asked the young storks.

"No, no; let them scream away, as much as they please. You are to fly up to the clouds and away to the land of the pyramids, while they are freezing and can neither see a green leaf nor taste a sweet apple."

"But we will revenge ourselves," they whispered one to another. And then the training began again.

Among all the children down in the street the one that seemed most bent upon singing the song that made game of the storks was the boy who had begun it, and he was a little fellow hardly more than six years old. The young storks, to be sure, thought he was at least a hundred, for he was much bigger than their parents, and, besides, what did they know about the ages of either children or grown men? Their whole vengeance was to be aimed at this one boy. It was always he who began the song and persisted in mocking them. The young storks were very angry, and as they grew larger they also grew less patient under insult, and their mother was at last obliged to promise them that they might be revenged—but not until the day of their departure.

"We must first see how you carry yourselves at the great review. If you do so badly that the general runs his beak through you, then the boys will be in the right—at least in one way. We must wait and see!"

"Yes, you shall see!" cried all the young storks; and they took the greatest pains, practicing every day, until they flew so evenly and so lightly that it was a pleasure to see them.

The autumn now set in; all the storks began to assemble, in order to start for the warm countries and leave winter behind them. And such exercises as there were! Young fledglings were set to fly over forests and villages, to see if they were equal to the long journey that was before them. So well did our young storks acquit themselves, that, as a proof of the satisfaction they had given, the mark they got was, "Remarkably well," with a present of a frog and a snake, which they lost no time in eating.

"Now," said they, "we will be revenged."

"Yes, certainly," said their mother; "and I have thought of a way that will surely be the fairest. I know a pond where all the little human children lie till the stork comes to take them to their parents. There lie the pretty little babies, dreaming more sweetly than they ever dream afterwards. All the parents are wishing for one of these little ones, and the children all want a sister or a brother. Now we'll fly to the pond and bring back a baby for every child who did not sing the naughty song that made game of the storks."

"But the very naughty boy who was the first to begin the song," cried the young storks, "what shall we do with him?"

"There is a little dead child in the pond—one that has dreamed itself to death. We will bring that for him. Then he will cry because we have brought a little dead brother to him.

"But that good boy,—you have not forgotten him!—the one who said it was a shame to mock at the animals; for him we will bring both a brother and a sister. And because his name is Peter, all of you shall be called Peter, too."

All was done as the mother had said; the storks were named Peter, and so they are called to this day.

THE WILD SWANS

FAR away, in the land to which the swallows fly when it is winter, dwelt a king who had eleven sons, and one daughter, named Eliza.

The eleven brothers were princes, and each went to school with a star on his breast and a sword by his side. They wrote with diamond pencils on golden slates and learned their lessons so quickly and read so easily that every one knew they were princes. Their sister Eliza sat on a little stool of plate-glass and had a book full of pictures, which had cost as much as half a kingdom.

Happy, indeed, were these children; but they were not long to remain so, for their father, the king, married a queen who did not love the children, and who proved to be a wicked sorceress.

The queen began to show her unkindness the very first day. While the great festivities were taking place in the palace, the children played at receiving company; but the queen, instead of sending them the cakes and apples that were left from the feast, as was customary, gave them some sand in a teacup and told them to pretend it was something good. The next week she sent the little Eliza into the country to a peasant and his wife. Then she told the king so many untrue things about the young princes that he gave himself no more trouble about them.

"Go out into the world and look after yourselves," said the queen. "Fly like great birds without a voice." But she could not make it so bad for them as she would have liked, for they were turned into eleven beautiful wild swans.

With a strange cry, they flew through the windows of the palace, over the park, to the forest beyond. It was yet early morning when they passed the peasant's cottage where their sister lay asleep in her room. They hovered over the roof, twisting their long necks and flapping their wings, but no one heard them or saw them, so they at last flew away, high up in the clouds, and over the wide world they sped till they came to a thick, dark wood, which stretched far away to the seashore.

Poor little Eliza was alone in the peasant's room playing with a green leaf, for she had no other playthings. She pierced a hole in the leaf, and when she looked through it at the sun she seemed to see her brothers' clear eyes, and when the warm sun shone on her cheeks she thought of all the kisses they had given her.

One day passed just like another. Sometimes the winds rustled through the leaves of the rosebush and whispered to the roses, "Who can be more beautiful than you?" And the roses would shake their heads and say, "Eliza is." And when the old woman sat at the cottage door on Sunday and read her hymn book, the wind would flutter the leaves and say to the book, "Who can be more pious than you?" And then the hymn book would answer, "Eliza." And the roses and the hymn book told the truth.

When she was fifteen she returned home, but because she was so beautiful the witch-queen became full of spite and hatred toward her. Willingly would she have turned her into a swan like her brothers, but she did not dare to do so for fear of the king.

Early one morning the queen went into the bathroom; it was built of marble and had soft cushions trimmed with the most beautiful tapestry. She took three toads with her, and kissed them, saying to the first, "When Eliza comes to bathe seat yourself upon her head, that she may become as stupid as you are." To the second toad she said, "Place yourself on her forehead, that she may become as ugly as you are, and that her friends may not know her." "Rest on her heart," she whispered to the third; "then she will have evil inclinations and suffer because of them." So she put the toads into the clear water, which at once turned green. She next called Eliza and helped her undress and get into the bath.

As Eliza dipped her head under the water one of the toads sat on her hair, a second on her forehead, and a third on her breast. But she did not seem to notice them, and when she rose from the water there were three red poppies floating upon it. Had not the creatures been venomous or had they not been kissed by the witch, they would have become red roses. At all events they became flowers, because they had rested on Eliza's head and on her heart. She was too good and too innocent for sorcery to have any power over her.

When the wicked queen saw this, she rubbed Eliza's face with walnut juice, so that she was quite brown; then she tangled her beautiful hair and smeared it with disgusting ointment until it was quite impossible to recognize her.

The king was shocked, and declared she was not his daughter. No one but the watchdog and the swallows knew her, and they were only poor animals and could say nothing. Then poor Eliza wept and thought of her eleven brothers who were far away. Sorrowfully she stole from the palace and walked the whole day over fields and moors, till she came to the great forest. She knew not in what direction to go, but she was so unhappy and longed so for her brothers, who, like herself, had been driven out into the world, that she was determined to seek them.

She had been in the wood only a short time when night came on and she quite lost the path; so she laid herself down on the soft moss, offered up her evening prayer, and leaned her head against the stump of a tree. All nature was silent, and the soft, mild air fanned her forehead. The light of hundreds of glowworms shone amidst the grass and the moss like green fire, and if she touched a twig with her hand, ever so lightly, the brilliant insects fell down around her like shooting stars.

All night long she dreamed of her brothers. She thought they were all children again, playing together. She saw them writing with their diamond pencils on golden slates, while she looked at the beautiful picture book which had cost half a kingdom. They were not writing lines and letters, as they used to do, but descriptions of the noble deeds they had performed and of all that they had discovered and seen. In the picture book, too, everything was living. The birds sang, and the people came out of the book and spoke to Eliza and her brothers; but as the leaves were turned over they darted back again to their places, that all might be in order.

When she awoke, the sun was high in the heavens. She could not see it, for the lofty trees spread their branches thickly overhead, but its gleams here and there shone through the leaves like a gauzy golden mist. There was a sweet fragrance from the fresh verdure, and the birds came near and almost perched on her shoulders. She heard water rippling from a number of springs, all flowing into a lake with golden sands. Bushes grew thickly round the lake, and at one spot, where an opening had been made by a deer, Eliza went down to the water.

The lake was so clear that had not the wind rustled the branches of the trees and the bushes so that they moved, they would have seemed painted in the depths of the lake; for every leaf, whether in the shade or in the sunshine, was reflected in the water.

When Eliza saw her own face she was quite terrified at finding it so brown and ugly, but after she had wet her little hand and rubbed her eyes and forehead, the white skin gleamed forth once more; and when she had undressed and dipped herself in the fresh water, a more beautiful king's daughter could not have been found anywhere in the wide world.

As soon as she had dressed herself again and braided her long hair, she went to the bubbling spring and drank some water out of the hollow of her hand. Then she wandered far into the forest, not knowing whither she went. She thought of her brothers and of her father and mother and felt sure that God would not forsake her. It is God who makes the wild apples grow in the wood to satisfy the hungry, and He now showed her one of these trees, which was so loaded with fruit that the boughs bent beneath the weight. Here she ate her noonday meal, and then placing props under the boughs, she went into the gloomiest depths of the forest.

It was so still that she could hear the sound of her own footsteps, as well as the rustling of every withered leaf which she crushed under her feet. Not a bird was to be seen, not a sunbeam could penetrate the large, dark boughs of the trees. The lofty trunks stood so close together that when she looked before her it seemed as if she were enclosed within trelliswork. Here was such solitude as she had never known before!

The night was very dark. Not a glowworm was glittering in the moss. Sorrowfully Eliza laid herself down to sleep. After a while it seemed to her as if the branches of the trees parted over her head and the mild eyes of angels looked down upon her from heaven.

In the morning, when she awoke, she knew not whether this had really been so or whether she had dreamed it. She continued her wandering, but she had not gone far when she met an old woman who had berries in her basket and who gave her a few to eat. Eliza asked her if she had not seen eleven princes riding through the forest.

"No," replied the old woman, "but I saw yesterday eleven swans with gold crowns on their heads, swimming in the river close by." Then she led Eliza a little distance to a sloping bank, at the foot of which ran a little river. The trees on its banks stretched their long leafy branches across the water toward each other, and where they did not meet naturally the roots had torn themselves away from the ground, so that the branches might mingle their foliage as they hung over the water.

Eliza bade the old woman farewell and walked by the flowing river till she reached the shore of the open sea. And there, before her eyes, lay the glorious ocean, but not a sail appeared on its surface; not even a boat could be seen. How was she to go farther? She noticed how the countless pebbles on the shore had been smoothed and rounded by the action of the water. Glass, iron, stones, everything that lay there mingled together, had been shaped by the same power until they were as smooth as her own delicate hand.

"The water rolls on without weariness," she said, "till all that is hard becomes smooth; so will I be unwearied in my task. Thanks for your lesson, bright rolling waves; my heart tells me you will one day lead me to my dear brothers."

Eliza asked her if she had not seen eleven princes riding through the forest.

On the foam-covered seaweeds lay eleven white swan feathers, which she gathered and carried with her. Drops of water lay upon them; whether they were dewdrops or tears no one could say. It was lonely on the seashore, but she did not know it, for the ever-moving sea showed more changes in a few hours than the most varying lake could produce in a whole year. When a black, heavy cloud arose, it was as if the sea said, "I can look dark and angry too"; and then the wind blew, and the waves turned to white foam as they rolled. When the wind slept and the clouds glowed with the red sunset, the sea looked like a rose leaf. Sometimes it became green and sometimes white. But, however quietly it lay, the waves were always restless on the shore and rose and fell like the breast of a sleeping child.

When the sun was about to set, Eliza saw eleven white swans, with golden crowns on their heads, flying toward the land, one behind the other, like a long white ribbon. She went down the slope from the shore and hid herself behind the bushes. The swans alighted quite close to her, flapping their great white wings. As soon as the sun had disappeared under the water, the feathers of the swans fell off and eleven beautiful princes, Eliza's brothers, stood near her.

She uttered a loud cry, for, although they were very much changed, she knew them immediately. She sprang into their arms and called them each by name. Very happy the princes were to see their little sister again; they knew her, although she had grown so tall and beautiful. They laughed and wept and told each other how cruelly they had been treated by their stepmother.

"We brothers," said the eldest, "fly about as wild swans while the sun is in the sky, but as soon as it sinks behind the hills we recover our human shape. Therefore we must always be near a resting place before sunset; for if we were flying toward the clouds when we recovered our human form, we should sink deep into the sea.

"We do not dwell here, but in a land just as fair that lies far across the ocean; the way is long, and there is no island upon which we can pass the night—nothing but a little rock rising out of the sea, upon which, even crowded together, we can scarcely stand with safety. If the sea is rough, the foam dashes over us; yet we thank God for this rock. We have passed whole nights upon it, or we should never have reached our beloved fatherland, for our flight across the sea occupies two of the longest days in the year.

"We have permission to visit our home once every year and to remain eleven days. Then we fly across the forest to look once more at the palace where our father dwells and where we were born, and at the church beneath whose shade our mother lies buried. The very trees and bushes here seem related to us. The wild horses leap over the plains as we have seen them in our childhood. The charcoal burners sing the old songs to which we have danced as children. This is our fatherland, to which we are drawn by loving ties; and here we have found you, our dear little sister. Two days longer we can remain here, and then we must fly away to a beautiful land which is not our home. How can we take you with us? We have neither ship nor boat."

"How can I break this spell?" asked the sister. And they talked about it nearly the whole night, slumbering only a few hours.

Eliza was awakened by the rustling of the wings of swans soaring above her. Her brothers were again changed to swans. They flew in circles, wider and wider, till they were far away; but one of them, the youngest, remained behind and laid his head in his sister's lap, while she stroked his wings. They remained together the whole day.

Towards evening the rest came back, and as the sun went down they resumed their natural forms. "To-morrow," said one, "we shall fly away, not to return again till a whole year has passed. But we cannot leave you here. Have you courage to go with us? My arm is strong enough to carry you through the wood, and will not all our wings be strong enough to bear you over the sea?"

"Yes, take me with you," said Eliza. They spent the whole night in weaving a large, strong net of the pliant willow and rushes. On this Eliza laid herself down to sleep, and when the sun rose and her brothers again became wild swans, they took up the net with their beaks, and flew up to the clouds with their dear sister, who still slept. When the sunbeams fell on her face, one of the swans soared over her head so that his broad wings might shade her.

They were far from the land when Eliza awoke. She thought she must still be dreaming, it seemed so strange to feel herself being carried high in the air over the sea. By her side lay a branch full of beautiful ripe berries and a bundle of sweet-tasting roots; the youngest of her brothers had gathered them and placed them there. She smiled her thanks to him; she knew it was the same one that was hovering over her to shade her with his wings. They were now so high that a large ship beneath them looked like a white sea gull skimming the waves. A great cloud floating behind them appeared like a vast mountain, and upon it Eliza saw her own shadow and those of the eleven swans, like gigantic flying things. Altogether it formed a more beautiful picture than she had ever before seen; but as the sun rose higher and the clouds were left behind, the picture vanished.

Onward the whole day they flew through the air like winged arrows, yet more slowly than usual, for they had their sister to carry. The weather grew threatening, and Eliza watched the sinking sun with great anxiety, for the little rock in the ocean was not yet in sight. It seemed to her as if the swans were exerting themselves to the utmost. Alas! she was the cause of their not advancing more quickly. When the sun set they would change to men, fall into the sea, and be drowned.

Then she offered a prayer from her inmost heart, but still no rock appeared. Dark clouds came nearer, the gusts of wind told of the coming storm, while from a thick, heavy mass of clouds the lightning burst forth, flash after flash. The sun had reached the edge of the sea, when the swans darted down so swiftly that Eliza's heart trembled; she believed they were falling, but they again soared onward.

Presently, and by this time the sun was half hidden by the waves, she caught sight of the rock just below them. It did not look larger than a seal's head thrust out of the water. The sun sank so rapidly that at the moment their feet touched the rock it shone only like a star, and at last disappeared like the dying spark in a piece of burnt paper. Her brothers stood close around her with arms linked together, for there was not the smallest space to spare. The sea dashed against the rock and covered them with spray. The heavens were lighted up with continual flashes, and thunder rolled from the clouds. But the sister and brothers stood holding each other's hands, and singing hymns.

In the early dawn the air became calm and still, and at sunrise the swans flew away from the rock, bearing their sister with them. The sea was still rough, and from their great height the white foam on the dark-green waves looked like millions of swans swimming on the water. As the sun rose higher, Eliza saw before her, floating in the air, a range of mountains with shining masses of ice on their summits. In the center rose a castle that seemed a mile long, with rows of columns rising one above another, while around it palm trees waved and flowers as large as mill wheels bloomed. She asked if this was the land to which they were hastening. The swans shook their heads, for what she beheld were the beautiful, ever-changing cloud-palaces of the Fata Morgana, into which no mortal can enter.

Eliza was still gazing at the scene, when mountains, forests, and castles melted away, and twenty stately churches rose in their stead, with high towers and pointed Gothic windows. She even fancied she could hear the tones of the organ, but it was the music of the murmuring sea. As they drew nearer to the churches, these too were changed and became a fleet of ships, which seemed to be sailing beneath her; but when she looked again she saw only a sea mist gliding over the ocean.

One scene melted into another, until at last she saw the real land to which they were bound, with its blue mountains, its cedar forests, and its cities and palaces. Long before the sun went down she was sitting on a rock in front of a large cave, the floor of which was overgrown with delicate green creeping plants, like an embroidered carpet.

"Now we shall expect to hear what you dream of to-night," said the youngest brother, as he showed his sister her bedroom.

"Heaven grant that I may dream how to release you!" she replied. And this thought took such hold upon her mind that she prayed earnestly to God for help, and even in her sleep she continued to pray. Then it seemed to her that she was flying high in the air toward the cloudy palace of the Fata Morgana, and that a fairy came out to meet her, radiant and beautiful, yet much like the old woman who had given her berries in the wood, and who had told her of the swans with golden crowns on their heads.

"Your brothers can be released," said she, "if you only have courage and perseverance. Water is softer than your own delicate hands, and yet it polishes and shapes stones. But it feels no pain such as your fingers will feel; it has no soul and cannot suffer such agony and torment as you will have to endure. Do you see the stinging nettle which I hold in my hand? Quantities of the same sort grow round the cave in which you sleep, but only these, and those that grow on the graves of a churchyard, will be of any use to you. These you must gather, even while they burn blisters on your hands. Break them to pieces with your hands and feet, and they will become flax, from which you must spin and weave eleven coats with long sleeves; if these are then thrown over the eleven swans, the spell will be broken. But remember well, that from the moment you commence your task until it is finished, even though it occupy years of your life, you must not speak. The first word you utter will pierce the hearts of your brothers like a deadly dagger. Their lives hang upon your tongue. Remember all that I have told you."

And as she finished speaking, she touched Eliza's hand lightly with the nettle, and a pain as of burning fire awoke her.

It was broad daylight, and near her lay a nettle like the one she had seen in her dream. She fell on her knees and offered thanks to God. Then she went forth from the cave to begin work with her delicate hands. She groped in amongst the ugly nettles, which burned great blisters on her hands and arms, but she determined to bear the pain gladly if she could only release her dear brothers. So she bruised the nettles with her bare feet and spun the flax.

At sunset her brothers returned, and were much frightened when she did not speak. They believed her to be under the spell of some new sorcery, but when they saw her hands they understood what she was doing in their behalf. The youngest brother wept, and where his tears touched her the pain ceased and the burning blisters vanished. Eliza kept to her work all night, for she could not rest till she had released her brothers. During the whole of the following day, while her brothers were absent, she sat in solitude, but never before had the time flown so quickly.

One coat was already finished and she had begun the second, when she heard a huntsman's horn and was struck with fear. As the sound came nearer and nearer, she also heard dogs barking, and fled with terror into the cave. She hastily bound together the nettles she had gathered, and sat upon them. In a moment there came bounding toward her out of the ravine a great dog, and then another and another; they ran back and forth barking furiously, until in a few minutes all the huntsmen stood before the cave. The handsomest of them was the king of the country, who, when he saw the beautiful maiden, advanced toward her, saying, "How did you come here, my sweet child?"

Eliza shook her head. She dared not speak, for it would cost her brothers their deliverance and their lives. And she hid her hands under her apron, so that the king might not see how she was suffering.

"Come with me," he said; "here you cannot remain. If you are as good as you are beautiful, I will dress you in silk and velvet, I will place a golden crown on your head, and you shall rule and make your home in my richest castle." Then he lifted her onto his horse. She wept and wrung her hands, but the king said: "I wish only your happiness. A time will come when you will thank me for this."

He galloped away over the mountains, holding her before him on his horse, and the hunters followed behind them. As the sun went down they approached a fair, royal city, with churches and cupolas. On arriving at the castle, the king led her into marble halls, where large fountains played and where the walls and the ceilings were covered with rich paintings. But she had no eyes for all these glorious sights; she could only mourn and weep. Patiently she allowed the women to array her in royal robes, to weave pearls in her hair, and to draw soft gloves over her blistered fingers. As she stood arrayed in her rich dress, she looked so dazzlingly beautiful that the court bowed low in her presence.

Then the king declared his intention of making her his bride, but the archbishop shook his head and whispered that the fair young maiden was only a witch, who had blinded the king's eyes and ensnared his heart. The king would not listen to him, however, and ordered the music to sound, the daintiest dishes to be served, and the loveliest maidens to dance before them.

Afterwards he led her through fragrant gardens and lofty halls, but not a smile appeared on her lips or sparkled in her eyes. She looked the very picture of grief. Then the king opened the door of a little chamber in which she was to sleep. It was adorned with rich green tapestry and resembled the cave in which he had found her. On the floor lay the bundle of flax which she had spun from the nettles, and under the ceiling hung the coat she had made. These things had been brought away from the cave as curiosities, by one of the huntsmen.

"Here you can dream yourself back again in the old home in the cave," said the king; "here is the work with which you employed yourself. It will amuse you now, in the midst of all this splendor, to think of that time."

When Eliza saw all these things which lay so near her heart, a smile played around her mouth, and the crimson blood rushed to her cheeks. The thought of her brothers and their release made her so joyful that she kissed the king's hand. Then he pressed her to his heart.

Very soon the joyous church bells announced the marriage feast; the beautiful dumb girl of the woods was to be made queen of the country. A single word would cost her brothers their lives, but she loved the kind, handsome king, who did everything to make her happy, more and more each day; she loved him with her whole heart, and her eyes beamed with the love she dared not speak. Oh! if she could only confide in him and tell him of her grief. But dumb she must remain till her task was finished.

Therefore at night she crept away into her little chamber which had been decked out to look like the cave and quickly wove one coat after another. But when she began the seventh, she found she had no more flax. She knew that the nettles she wanted to use grew in the churchyard and that she must pluck them herself. How should she get out there? "Oh, what is the pain in my fingers to the torment which my heart endures?" thought she. "I must venture; I shall not be denied help from heaven."

Then with a trembling heart, as if she were about to perform a wicked deed, Eliza crept into the garden in the broad moonlight, and passed through the narrow walks and the deserted streets till she reached the churchyard. She prayed silently, gathered the burning nettles, and carried them home with her to the castle.

One person only had seen her, and that was the archbishop—he was awake while others slept. Now he felt sure that his suspicions were correct; all was not right with the queen; she was a witch and had bewitched the king and all the people. Secretly he told the king what he had seen and what he feared, and as the hard words came from his tongue, the carved images of the saints shook their heads as if they would say, "It is not so; Eliza is innocent."

But the archbishop interpreted it in another way; he believed that they witnessed against her and were shaking their heads at her wickedness. Two tears rolled down the king's cheeks. He went home with doubt in his heart, and at night pretended to sleep. But no real sleep came to his eyes, for every night he saw Eliza get up and disappear from her chamber. Day by day his brow became darker, and Eliza saw it, and although she did not understand the reason, it alarmed her and made her heart tremble for her brothers. Her hot tears glittered like pearls on the regal velvet and diamonds, while all who saw her were wishing they could be queen.

In the meantime she had almost finished her task; only one of her brothers' coats was wanting, but she had no flax left and not a single nettle. Once more only, and for the last time, must she venture to the churchyard and pluck a few handfuls. She went, and the king and the archbishop followed her. The king turned away his head and said, "The people must condemn her." Quickly she was condemned to suffer death by fire.

Away from the gorgeous regal halls she was led to a dark, dreary cell, where the wind whistled through the iron bars. Instead of the velvet and silk dresses, they gave her the ten coats which she had woven, to cover her, and the bundle of nettles for a pillow. But they could have given her nothing that would have pleased her more. She continued her task with joy and prayed for help, while the street boys sang jeering songs about her and not a soul comforted her with a kind word.

Toward evening she heard at the grating the flutter of a swan's wing; it was her youngest brother. He had found his sister, and she sobbed for joy, although she knew that probably this was the last night she had to live. Still, she had hope, for her task was almost finished and her brothers were come.

Then the archbishop arrived, to be with her during her last hours as he had promised the king. She shook her head and begged him, by looks and gestures, not to stay; for in this night she knew she must finish her task, otherwise all her pain and tears and sleepless nights would have been suffered in vain. The archbishop withdrew, uttering bitter words against her, but she knew that she was innocent and diligently continued her work.

Little mice ran about the floor, dragging the nettles to her feet, to help as much as they could; and a thrush, sitting outside the grating of the window, sang to her the whole night long as sweetly as possible, to keep up her spirits.

It was still twilight, and at least an hour before sunrise, when the eleven brothers stood at the castle gate and demanded to be brought before the king. They were told it could not be; it was yet night; the king slept and could not be disturbed. They threatened, they entreated, until the guard appeared, and even the king himself, inquiring what all the noise meant. At this moment the sun rose, and the eleven brothers were seen no more, but eleven wild swans flew away over the castle.

Now all the people came streaming forth from the gates of the city to see the witch burned. An old horse drew the cart on which she sat. They had dressed her in a garment of coarse sackcloth. Her lovely hair hung loose on her shoulders, her cheeks were deadly pale, her lips moved silently while her fingers still worked at the green flax. Even on the way to death she would not give up her task. The ten finished coats lay at her feet; she was working hard at the eleventh, while the mob jeered her and said: "See the witch; how she mutters! She has no hymn book in her hand; she sits there with her ugly sorcery. Let us tear it into a thousand pieces."

They pressed toward her, and doubtless would have destroyed the coats had not, at that moment, eleven wild swans flown over her and alighted on the cart. They flapped their large wings, and the crowd drew back in alarm.

"It is a sign from Heaven that she is innocent," whispered many of them; but they did not venture to say it aloud.

As the executioner seized her by the hand to lift her out of the cart, she hastily threw the eleven coats over the eleven swans, and they immediately became eleven handsome princes; but the youngest had a swan's wing instead of an arm, for she had not been able to finish the last sleeve of the coat.

"Now I may speak," she exclaimed. "I am innocent."

Even on the way to death she would not give up her task.

Then the people, who saw what had happened, bowed to her as before a saint; but she sank unconscious in her brothers' arms, overcome with suspense, anguish, and pain.

"Yes, she is innocent," said the eldest brother, and related all that had taken place. While he spoke, there rose in the air a fragrance as from millions of roses. Every piece of fagot in the pile made to burn her had taken root, and threw out branches until the whole appeared like a thick hedge, large and high, covered with roses; while above all bloomed a white, shining flower that glittered like a star. This flower the king plucked, and when he placed it in Eliza's bosom she awoke from her swoon with peace and happiness in her heart. Then all the church bells rang of themselves, and the birds came in great flocks. And a marriage procession, such as no king had ever before seen, returned to the castle.

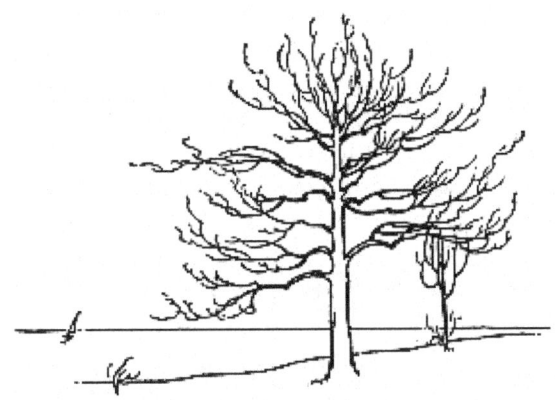

THE LAST DREAM OF THE OLD OAK

I N THE forest, high up on the steep shore and not far from the open seacoast, stood a very old oak tree. It was just three hundred and sixty-five years old, but that long time was to the tree as the same number of days might be to us. We wake by day and sleep by night, and then we have our dreams. It is different with the tree; it is obliged to keep awake through three seasons of the year and does not get any sleep till winter comes. Winter is its time for rest—its night after the long day of spring, summer, and autumn.

During many a warm summer, the Ephemeras, which are flies that exist for only a day, had fluttered about the old oak, enjoyed life, and felt happy. And if, for a moment, one of the tiny creatures rested on the large, fresh leaves, the tree would always say: "Poor little creature! your whole life consists of but a single day. How very short! It must be quite melancholy."

"Melancholy! what do you mean?" the little creature would always reply. "Why do you say that? Everything around me is so wonderfully bright and warm and beautiful that it makes me joyous."

"But only for one day, and then it is all over."

"Over!" repeated the fly; "what is the meaning of 'all over'? Are you 'all over' too?"

"No, I shall very likely live for thousands of your days, and my day is whole seasons long; indeed, it is so long that you could never reckon it up."

"No? then I don't understand you. You may have thousands of my days, but I have thousands of moments in which I can be merry and happy. Does all the beauty of the world cease when you die?"

"No," replied the tree; "it will certainly last much longer, infinitely longer than I can think of."

"Well, then," said the little fly, "we have the same time to live, only we reckon differently." And the little creature danced and floated in the air, rejoicing in its delicate wings of gauze and velvet, rejoicing in the balmy breezes laden with the fragrance from the clover fields and wild roses, elder blossoms and honeysuckle, and from the garden hedges of wild thyme, primroses, and mint. The perfume of all these was so strong that it almost intoxicated the little fly. The long and beautiful day had been so full of joy and sweet delights, that, when the sun sank, the fly felt tired of all its happiness and enjoyment. Its wings could sustain it no longer, and gently and slowly it glided down to the soft, waving blades of grass, nodded its little head as well as it could, and slept peacefully and sweetly. The fly was dead.

"Poor little Ephemera!" said the oak; "what a short life!" And so on every summer day the dance was repeated, the same questions were asked and the same answers given, and there was the same peaceful falling asleep at sunset. This continued through many generations of Ephemeras, and all of them felt merry and happy.

The oak remained awake through the morning of spring, the noon of summer, and the evening of autumn; its time of rest, its night, drew near—its winter was coming. Here fell a leaf and there fell a leaf. Already the storms were singing: "Good night, good night. We will rock you and lull you. Go to sleep, go to sleep. We will sing you to sleep, and shake you to sleep, and it will do your old twigs good; they will even crackle with pleasure. Sleep sweetly, sleep sweetly, it is your three hundred and sixty-fifth night. You are still very young in the world. Sleep sweetly; the clouds will drop snow upon you, which will be your coverlid, warm and sheltering to your feet. Sweet sleep to you, and pleasant dreams."

And there stood the oak, stripped of all its leaves, left to rest during the whole of a long winter, and to dream many dreams of events that had happened, just as men dream.

The great tree had once been small; indeed, in its cradle it had been an acorn. According to human reckoning, it was now in the fourth century of its existence. It was the largest and best tree in the forest. Its summit towered above all the other trees and could be seen far out at sea, so that it served as a landmark to the sailors. It had no idea how many eyes looked eagerly for it. In its topmost branches the wood pigeon built her nest, and the cuckoo sang his well-known song, the familiar notes echoing among the boughs; and in autumn, when the leaves looked like beaten copper plates, the birds of passage came and rested on the branches before beginning their flight across the sea.

But now that it was winter, the tree stood leafless, so that every one could see how crooked and bent were the branches that sprang forth from the trunk. Crows and rooks came by turns and sat on them, and talked of the hard times that were beginning, and how difficult it was in winter to obtain a living.

It was just at the holy Christmas time that the tree dreamed a dream. The tree had doubtless a feeling that the festive time had arrived, and in its dream fancied it heard the bells of the churches ringing. And yet it seemed to be a beautiful summer's day, mild and warm. The tree's mighty summit was crowned with spreading, fresh green foliage; the sunbeams played among its leaves and branches, and the air was full of fragrance from herb and blossom; painted butterflies chased each other; the summer flies danced around it as if the world had been created merely that they might dance and be merry. All that had happened to the tree during all the years of its life seemed to pass before it as if in a festive pageant.

It saw the knights of olden times and noble ladies ride through the wood on their gallant steeds, with plumes waving in their hats and with falcons on their wrists, while the hunting horn sounded and the dogs barked. It saw hostile warriors, in colored dress and glittering armor, with spear and halberd, pitching their tents and again taking them down; the watchfires blazed, and men sang and slept under the hospitable shelter of the tree. It saw lovers meet in quiet happiness near it in the moonshine, and carve the initials of their names in the grayish-green bark of its trunk

Once, but long years had passed since then, guitars and Æolian harps had been hung on its boughs by merry travelers; now they seemed to hang there again, and their marvelous notes sounded again. The wood pigeons cooed as if to express the feelings of the tree, and the cuckoo called out to tell it how many summer days it had yet to live.

Then it appeared to it that new life was thrilling through every fiber of root and stem and leaf, rising even to its highest branches. The tree felt itself stretching and spreading out, while through the root beneath the earth ran the warm vigor of life. As it grew higher and still higher and its strength increased, the topmost boughs became broader and fuller; and in proportion to its growth its self-satisfaction increased, and there came a joyous longing to grow higher and higher—to reach even to the warm, bright sun itself.

It saw lovers meet in quiet happiness near it in the moonshine • • •

Already had its topmost branches pierced the clouds, which floated beneath them like troops of birds of passage or large white swans; every leaf seemed gifted with sight, as if it possessed eyes to see. The stars became visible in broad daylight, large and sparkling, like clear and gentle eyes. They brought to the tree's memory the light that it had seen in the eyes of a child and in the eyes of lovers who had once met beneath the branches of the old oak.

These were wonderful and happy moments for the old oak, full of peace and joy; and yet amidst all this happiness, the tree felt a yearning desire that all the other trees, bushes, herbs, and flowers beneath it might also be able to rise higher, to see all this splendor and experience the same happiness. The grand, majestic oak could not be quite happy in its enjoyment until all the rest, both great and small, could share it. And this feeling of yearning trembled through every branch, through every leaf, as warmly and fervently as through a human heart.

The summit of the tree waved to and fro and bent downwards, as if in its silent longing it sought something. Then there came to it the fragrance of thyme and the more powerful scent of honeysuckle and violets, and the tree fancied it heard the note of the cuckoo.

At length its longing was satisfied. Up through the clouds came the green summits of the forest trees, and the oak watched them rising higher and higher. Bush and herb shot upward, and some even tore themselves up by the roots to rise more quickly. The quickest of all was the birch tree. Like a lightning flash the slender stem shot upwards in a zigzag line, the branches spreading round it like green gauze and banners. Every native of the wood, even to the brown and feathery rushes, grew with the rest, while the birds ascended with the melody of song. On a blade of grass that fluttered in the air like a long green ribbon sat a grasshopper cleaning its wings with its legs. May beetles hummed, bees murmured, birds sang—each in its own way; the air was filled with the sounds of song and gladness.

"But where is the little blue flower that grows by the water, and the purple bellflower, and the daisy?" asked the oak. "I want them all."

"Here we are; here we are," came the reply in words and in song.

"But the beautiful thyme of last summer, where is that? And where are the lilies of the valley which last year covered the earth with their bloom, and the wild apple tree with its fragrant blossoms, and all the glory of the wood, which has flourished year after year? And where is even what may have but just been born?"

"We are here; we are here," sounded voices high up in the air, as if they had flown there beforehand.

"Why, this is beautiful, too beautiful to be believed," cried the oak in a joyful tone. "I have them all here, both great and small; not one has been forgotten. Can such happiness be imagined? It seems almost impossible."

"In heaven with the Eternal God it can be imagined, for all things are possible," sounded the reply through the air.

And the old tree, as it still grew upwards and onwards, felt that its roots were loosening themselves from the earth.

"It is right so; it is best," said the tree. "No fetters hold me now. I can fly up to the very highest point in light and glory. And all I love are with me, both small and great. All—all are here."

Such was the dream of the old oak at the holy Christmas time. And while it dreamed, a mighty storm came rushing over land and sea. The sea rolled in great billows toward the shore. A cracking and crushing was heard in the tree. Its roots were torn from the ground, just at the moment when in its dream it was being loosened from the earth. It fell; its three hundred and sixty-five years were ended like the single day of the Ephemera.

On the morning of Christmas Day, when the sun rose, the storm had ceased. From all the churches sounded the festive bells, and from every hearth, even of the smallest hut, rose the smoke into the blue sky, like the smoke from the festive thank-offerings on the Druids' altars. The sea gradually became calm, and on board a great ship that had withstood the tempest during the night, all the flags were displayed as a token of joy and festivity.

"The tree is down! the old oak—our landmark on the coast!" exclaimed the sailors. "It must have fallen in the storm of last night. Who can replace it? Alas! no one." This was the old tree's funeral oration, brief but well said.

There it lay stretched on the snow-covered shore, and over it sounded the notes of a song from the ship—a song of Christmas joy, of the redemption of the soul of man, and of eternal life through Christ.

Sing aloud on this happy morn,
All is fulfilled, for Christ is born;
With songs of joy let us loudly sing,
"Hallelujahs to Christ our King."

Thus sounded the Christmas carol, and every one on board the ship felt his thoughts elevated through the song and the prayer, even as the old tree had felt lifted up in its last beautiful dream on that Christmas morn.

THE PORTUGUESE DUCK

A DUCK once arrived from Portugal. There were some who said she came from Spain, but that is almost the same thing. At all events, she was called the Portuguese duck, and she laid eggs, was killed and cooked, and that was the end of her.

The ducklings which crept forth from her eggs were also called Portuguese ducks, and about that there may be some question. But of all the family only one remained in the duck yard, which may be called a farmyard, since the chickens were admitted to it and the cock strutted about in a very hostile manner.

"He annoys me with his loud crowing," said the Portuguese duck, "but still, he's a handsome bird, there's no denying that, even if he is not a duck. He ought to moderate his voice, like those little birds who are singing in the lime trees over there in our neighbor's garden—but that is an art only acquired in polite society. How sweetly they sing there; it is quite a pleasure to listen to them! I call it Portuguese singing. If I only had such a little singing bird, I'd be as kind and good to him as a mother, for it's in my Portuguese nature."

While she was speaking, one of the little singing birds came tumbling head over heels from the roof into the yard. The cat was after him, but he had escaped from her with a broken wing and so came fluttering into the yard. "That's just like the cat; she's a villain," said the Portuguese duck. "I remember her ways when I had children of my own. How can such a creature be allowed to live and wander about upon the roofs? I don't think they allow such things in Portugal."

She pitied the little singing bird, and so did all the other ducks, who were not Portuguese.

"Poor little creature!" they said, one after another, as they came up. "We can't sing, certainly; but we have a sounding board, or something of the kind, within us, though we don't talk about it."

"But I can talk," said the Portuguese duck. "I'll do something for the little fellow; it's my duty." So she stepped into the watering trough and beat her wings upon the water so strongly that the little bird was nearly drowned. But the duck meant it kindly. "That is a good deed," she said; "I hope the others will take example from it."

"Tweet, tweet!" said the little bird. One of his wings was broken and he found it difficult to shake himself, but he quite understood that the bath was meant kindly, so he said, "You are very kind-hearted, madam." But he did not wish for a second bath.

"I have never thought about my heart," replied the Portuguese duck; "but I know that I love all my fellow creatures, except the cat, and nobody can expect me to love her, for she ate up two of my ducklings. But pray make yourself at home; it is easy to make oneself comfortable. I myself am from a foreign country, as you may see by my bearing and my feathery dress. My husband is a native of these parts; he's not of my race, but I am not proud on that account. If any one here can understand you, I may say positively that I am that person."

"She's quite full of *portulak*," said a little common duck, who was witty. All the common ducks considered the word "portulak" a good joke, for it sounded like "Portugal." They nudged each other and said, "Quack! that was witty!"

Then the other ducks began to notice the newcomer. "The Portuguese has certainly a great flow of language," they said to the little bird. "For our part, we don't care to fill our beaks with such long words, but we sympathize with you quite as much. If we don't do anything else, we can walk about with you everywhere; that is the best we can do."

"You have a lovely voice," said one of the eldest ducks; "it must be a great satisfaction to you to be able to give as much pleasure as you do. I am certainly no judge of your singing, so I keep my beak shut, which is better than talking nonsense as others do."

"Don't plague him so," interrupted the Portuguese duck; "he requires rest and nursing. My little singing bird, do you wish me to prepare another bath for you?"

"Oh, no! no! pray let me be dry," implored the little bird.

"The water cure is the only remedy for me when I am not well," said the Portuguese. "Amusement, too, is very beneficial. The fowls from the neighborhood will soon be here to pay you a visit. There are two Cochin-Chinese among them; they wear feathers on their legs and are well educated. They have been brought from a great distance, and consequently I treat them with greater respect than I do the others."

Then the fowls arrived, and the cock was polite enough to keep from being rude. "You are a real songster," he said, "and you do as much with your little voice as it is possible to do; but more noise and shrillness is necessary if one wishes others to know who he is."

The two Chinese were quite enchanted with the appearance of the singing bird. His feathers had been much ruffled by his bath, so that he seemed to them quite like a tiny Chinese fowl. "He's charming," they said to each other, and began a conversation with him in whispers, using the most aristocratic Chinese dialect.

"We are of the same race as yourself," they said. "The ducks, even the Portuguese, are all aquatic birds, as you must have noticed. You do not know us yet—very few, even of the fowls, know us or give themselves the trouble to make our acquaintance, though we were born to occupy a higher position in society than most of them. But that does not disturb us; we quietly go our way among them. Their ideas are certainly not ours, for we look at the bright side of things and only speak of what is good, although that is sometimes difficult to find where none exists. Except ourselves and the cock, there is not one in the yard who can be called talented or polite. It cannot be said even of the ducks, and we warn you, little bird, not to trust that one yonder, with the short tail feathers, for she is cunning. Then the curiously marked one, with the crooked stripes on her wings, is a mischief-maker and never lets any one have the last word, though she is always in the wrong. The fat duck yonder speaks evil of every one, and that is against our principles; if we have nothing good to tell, we close our beaks. The Portuguese is the only one who has had any education and with whom we can associate, but she is passionate and talks too much about Portugal."

"I wonder what those two Chinese are whispering about," whispered one duck to another. "They are always doing it, and it annoys me. We never speak to them."

Now the drake came up, and he thought the little singing bird was a sparrow. "Well, I don't understand the difference," he said; "it appears to me all the same. He's only a plaything, and if people will have playthings, why let them, I say."

"Don't take any notice of what he says," whispered the Portuguese; "he is very well in matters of business, and with him business is first. Now I shall lie down and have a little rest. It is a duty we owe to ourselves, so that we shall be nice and fat when we come to be embalmed with sage and onions and apples."

So she laid herself down in the sun and winked with one eye. She had a very comfortable place and felt so at ease that she fell asleep. The little singing bird busied himself for some time with his broken wing, and at last he too lay down, quite close to his protectress. The sun shone warm and bright, and he found it a very good place. But the fowls of the neighborhood were all awake, and, to tell the truth, they had paid a visit to the duck yard solely to find food for themselves. The Chinese were the first to leave, and the other fowls soon followed them.

The witty little duck said of the Portuguese that "the old lady" was getting to be quite a "doting ducky." All the other ducks laughed at this. "'Doting ducky,'" they whispered; "oh, that's too witty!" Then they repeated the joke about "portulak" and declared it was most amusing. After that they all lay down to have a nap.

They had been lying asleep for quite a while, when suddenly something was thrown into the yard for them to eat. It came down with such a bang that the whole company started up and clapped their wings. The Portuguese awoke, too, and rushed over to the other side of the yard. In doing this she trod upon the little singing bird.

"Tweet," he cried; "you trod very hard upon me, madam."

"Well, then, why do you lie in my way?" she retorted. "You must not be so touchy. I have nerves of my own, but I do not cry 'Tweet.'"

"Don't be angry," said the little bird; "the 'Tweet' slipped out of my beak before I knew it."

The Portuguese did not listen to him, but began eating as fast as she could, and made a good meal. When she had finished she lay down again, and the little bird, who wished to be amiable, began to sing:

"Chirp and twitter,
The dewdrops glitter,
In the hours of sunny spring;
I'll sing my best,
Till I go to rest,
With my head behind my wing."

"Now I want rest after my dinner," said the Portuguese. "You must conform to the rules of the place while you are here. I want to sleep now."

The little bird was quite taken aback, for he meant it kindly. When madam awoke afterwards, there he stood before her with a little corn he had found, and laid it at her feet; but as she had not slept well, she was naturally in a bad temper. "Give that to a chicken," she said, "and don't be always standing in my way."

"Why are you angry with me?" replied the little singing bird; "what have I done?"

"Done!" repeated the Portuguese duck; "your mode of expressing yourself is not very polite. I must call your attention to that fact."

"There was sunshine here yesterday," said the little bird, "but to-day it is cloudy and the air is heavy."

"You know very little about the weather, I fancy," she retorted; "the day is not over yet. Don't stand there looking so stupid."

"But you are looking at me just as the wicked eyes looked when I fell into the yard yesterday."

"Impertinent creature!" exclaimed the Portuguese duck. "Would you compare me with the cat—that beast of prey? There's not a drop of malicious blood in me. I've taken your part, and now I'll teach you better manners." So saying, she made a bite at the little singing-bird's head, and he fell to the ground dead. "Now whatever is the meaning of this?" she said. "Could he not bear even such a little peck as I gave him? Then, certainly, he was not made for this world. I've been like a mother to him, I know that, for I've a good heart."

Then the cock from the neighboring yard stuck his head in and crowed with steam-engine power.

"You'll kill me with your crowing," she cried. "It's all your fault. He's lost his life, and I'm very near losing mine."

"There's not much of him lying there," observed the cock.

"Speak of him with respect," said the Portuguese duck, "for he had manners and education, and he could sing. He was affectionate and gentle, and those are as rare qualities in animals as in those who call themselves human beings."

Then all the ducks came crowding round the little dead bird. Ducks have strong passions, whether they feel envy or pity. There was nothing to envy here, so they all showed a great deal of pity. So also did the two Chinese. "We shall never again have such a singing bird among us; he was almost a Chinese," they whispered, and then they wept with such a noisy, clucking sound that all the other fowls clucked too. But the ducks went about with redder eyes afterwards. "We have hearts of our own," they said; "nobody can deny that."

"Hearts!" repeated the Portuguese. "Indeed you have—almost as tender as the ducks in Portugal."

"Let us think of getting something to satisfy our hunger," said the drake; "that's the most important business. If one of our toys is broken, why, we have plenty more."

THE SNOW MAN

"IT IS so delightfully cold that it makes my whole body crackle," said the Snow Man. "This is just the kind of wind to blow life into one. How that great red thing up there is staring at me!" He meant the sun, which was just setting. "It shall not make me wink. I shall manage to keep the pieces."

He had two triangular pieces of tile in his head instead of eyes, and his mouth, being made of an old broken rake, was therefore furnished with teeth. He had been brought into existence amid the joyous shouts of boys, the jingling of sleigh bells, and the slashing of whips.

The sun went down, and the full moon rose, large, round, and clear, shining in the deep blue.

"There it comes again, from the other side," said the Snow Man, who supposed the sun was showing itself once more. "Ah, I have cured it of staring. Now it may hang up there and shine, so that I may see myself. If I only knew how to manage to move away from this place—I should so like to move! If I could, I would slide along yonder on the ice, as I have seen the boys do; but I don't understand how. I don't even know how to run."

"Away, away!" barked the old yard dog. He was quite hoarse and could not pronounce "Bow-wow" properly. He had once been an indoor dog and lain by the fire, and he had been hoarse ever since. "The sun will make you run some day. I saw it, last winter, make your predecessor run, and his predecessor before him. Away, away! They all have to go."

"I don't understand you, comrade," said the Snow Man. "Is that thing up yonder to teach me to run? I saw it running itself, a little while ago, and now it has come creeping up from the other side."

"You know nothing at all," replied the yard dog. "But then, you've only lately been patched up. What you see yonder is the moon, and what you saw before was the sun. It will come again to-morrow and most likely teach you to run down into the ditch by the well, for I think the weather is going to change. I can feel such pricks and stabs in my left leg that I am sure there is going to be a change."

"I don't understand him," said the Snow Man to himself, "but I have a feeling that he is talking of something very disagreeable. The thing that stared so hard just now, which he calls the sun, is not my friend; I can feel that too."

"Away, away!" barked the yard dog, and then he turned round three times and crept into his kennel to sleep.

There really was a change in the weather. Toward morning a thick fog covered the whole country and a keen wind arose, so that the cold seemed to freeze one's bones. But when the sun rose, a splendid sight was to be seen. Trees and bushes were covered with hoarfrost and looked like a forest of white coral, while on every twig glittered frozen dewdrops. The many delicate forms, concealed in summer by luxuriant foliage, were now clearly defined and looked like glittering lacework. A white radiance glistened from every twig. The birches, waving in the wind, looked as full of life as in summer and as wondrously beautiful. Where the sun shone, everything glittered and sparkled as if diamond dust had been strewn about; and the snowy carpet of the earth seemed covered with diamonds from which gleamed countless lights, whiter even than the snow itself.

"This is really beautiful," said a girl who had come into the garden with a young friend; and they both stood still near the Snow Man, contemplating the glittering scene. "Summer cannot show a more beautiful sight," she exclaimed, while her eyes sparkled.

"And we can't have such a fellow as this in the summer-time," replied the young man, pointing to the Snow Man. "He is capital."

The girl laughed and nodded at the Snow Man, then tripped away over the snow with her friend. The snow creaked and crackled beneath her feet, as if she had been treading on starch.

"Who are those two?" asked the Snow Man of the yard dog. "You have been here longer than I; do you know them?"

"Of course I know them," replied the yard dog; "the girl has stroked my back many times, and the young man has often given me a bone of meat. I never bite those two."

"But what are they?" asked the Snow Man.

"They are lovers," he replied. "They will go and live in the same kennel, by and by, and gnaw at the same bone. Away, away!"

"Are they the same kind of beings as you and I?" asked the Snow Man.

"Well, they belong to the master," retorted the yard dog. "Certainly people know very little who were only born yesterday. I can see that in you. I have age and experience. I know every one here in the house, and I know there was once a time when I did not lie out here in the cold, fastened to a chain. Away, away!"

"The cold is delightful," said the Snow Man. "But do tell me, tell me; only you must not clank your chain so, for it jars within me when you do that."

"Away, away!" barked the yard dog. "I'll tell you: they said I was a pretty little fellow, once; then I used to lie in a velvet-covered chair, up at the master's house, and sit in the mistress's lap; they used to kiss my nose, and wipe my paws with an embroidered hand-kerchief, and I was called 'Ami, dear Ami, sweet Ami.' But after a while I grew too big for them, and they sent me away to the housekeeper's room; so I came to live on the lower story. You can look into the room from where you stand, and see where I was once master—for I was, indeed, master to the housekeeper. It was a much smaller room than those upstairs, but I was more comfortable, for I was not continually being taken hold of and pulled about by the children, as I had been. I received quite as good food and even better. I had my own cushion, and there was a stove—it is the finest thing in the world at this season of the year. I used to go under the stove and lie down. Ah, I still dream of that stove. Away, away!"

"Does a stove look beautiful?" asked the Snow Man. "Is it at all like me?"

"It is just the opposite of you," said the dog. "It's as black as a crow and has a long neck and a brass knob; it eats firewood, and that makes fire spurt out of its mouth. One has to keep on one side or under it, to be comfortable. You can see it through the window from where you stand."

Then the Snow Man looked, and saw a bright polished thing with a brass knob, and fire gleaming from the lower part of it. The sight of this gave the Snow Man a strange sensation; it was very odd, he knew not what it meant, and he could not account for it. But there are people who are not men of snow who understand what the feeling is. "And why did you leave her?" asked the Snow Man, for it seemed to him that the stove must be of the female sex. "How could you give up such a comfortable place?"

"I was obliged to," replied the yard dog. "They turned me out of doors and chained me up here. I had bitten the youngest of my master's sons in the leg, because he kicked away the bone I was gnawing. 'Bone for bone,' I thought. But they were very angry, and since that time I have been fastened to a chain and have lost my voice. Don't you hear how hoarse I am? Away, away! I can't talk like other dogs any more. Away, away! That was the end of it all."

But the Snow Man was no longer listening. He was looking into the housekeeper's room on the lower story, where the stove, which was about the same size as the Snow Man himself, stood on its four iron legs. "What a strange crackling I feel within me," he said. "Shall I ever get in there? It is an innocent wish, and innocent wishes are sure to be fulfilled. I must go in there and lean against her, even if I have to break the window."

"You must never go in there," said the yard dog, "for if you approach the stove, you will melt away, away."

"I might as well go," said the Snow Man, "for I think I am breaking up as it is."

During the whole day the Snow Man stood looking in through the window, and in the twilight hour the room became still more inviting, for from the stove came a gentle glow, not like the sun or the moon; it was only the kind of radiance that can come from a stove when it has been well fed. When the door of the stove was opened, the flames darted out of its mouth,—as is customary with all stoves,—and the light of the flames fell with a ruddy gleam directly on the face and breast of the Snow Man. "I can endure it no longer," said he. "How beautiful it looks when it stretches out its tongue!"

The night was long, but it did not appear so to the Snow Man, who stood there enjoying his own reflections and crackling with the cold. In the morning the window-panes of the housekeeper's room were covered with ice. They were the most beautiful ice flowers any Snow Man could desire, but they concealed the stove. These window-panes would not thaw, and he could see nothing of the stove, which he pictured to himself as if it had been a beautiful human being. The snow crackled and the wind whistled around him; it was just the kind of frosty weather a Snow Man ought to enjoy thoroughly. But he did not enjoy it. How, indeed, could he enjoy anything when he was so stove-sick?

"That is a terrible disease for a Snow Man to have," said the yard dog. "I have suffered from it myself, but I got over it. Away, away!" he barked, and then added, "The weather is going to change."

The weather did change. It began to thaw, and as the warmth increased, the Snow Man decreased. He said nothing and made no complaint, which is a sure sign.

One morning he broke and sank down altogether; and behold! where he had stood, something that looked like a broomstick remained sticking up in the ground. It was the pole round which the boys had built him.

"Ah, now I understand why he had such a great longing for the stove," said the yard dog. "Why, there's the shovel that is used for cleaning out the stove, fastened to the pole. The Snow Man had a stove scraper in his body; that was what moved him so. But it is all over now. Away, away!"

And soon the winter passed. "Away, away!" barked the hoarse yard dog, but the girls in the house sang:

"Come from your fragrant home, green thyme;
Stretch your soft branches, willow tree;
The months are bringing the sweet spring-time,
When the lark in the sky sings joyfully.
Come, gentle sun, while the cuckoo sings,
And I'll mock his note in my wanderings."

And nobody thought any more of the Snow Man.

THE FARMYARD COCK AND THE WEATHERCOCK

THERE were once two cocks; one of them stood on a dunghill, the other on the roof. Both were conceited, but the question is, Which of the two was the more useful?

A wooden partition divided the poultry yard from another yard, in which lay a heap of manure sheltering a cucumber bed. In this bed grew a large cucumber, which was fully aware that it was a plant that should be reared in a hot-bed.

"It is the privilege of birth," said the Cucumber to itself. "All cannot be born cucumbers; there must be other kinds as well. The fowls, the ducks, and the cattle in the next yard are all different creatures, and there is the yard cock—I can look up to him when he is on the wooden partition. He is certainly of much greater importance than the weathercock, who is so highly placed, and who can't even creak, much less crow—besides, he has neither hens nor chickens, and thinks only of himself, and perspires verdigris. But the yard cock is something like a cock. His gait is like a dance, and his crowing is music, and wherever he goes it is instantly known. What a trumpeter he is! If he would only come in here! Even if he were to eat me up, stalk and all, it would be a pleasant death." So said the Cucumber.

During the night the weather became very bad; hens, chickens, and even the cock himself sought shelter. The wind blew down with a crash the partition between the two yards, and the tiles came tumbling from the roof, but the weathercock stood firm. He did not even turn round; in fact, he could not, although he was fresh and newly cast. He had been born full grown and did not at all resemble the birds, such as the sparrows and swallows, that fly beneath the vault of heaven. He despised them and looked upon them as little twittering birds that were made only to sing. The pigeons, he admitted, were large and shone in the sun like mother-of-pearl. They somewhat resembled weathercocks, but were fat and stupid and thought only of stuffing themselves with food. "Besides," said the weathercock, "they are very tiresome things to converse with."

The birds of passage often paid a visit to the weathercock and told him tales of foreign lands, of large flocks passing through the air, and of encounters with robbers and birds of prey. These were very interesting when heard for the first time, but the weathercock knew the birds always repeated themselves, and that made it tedious to listen.

"They are tedious, and so is every one else," said he; "there is no one fit to associate with. One and all of them are wearisome and stupid. The whole world is worth nothing—it is made up of stupidity."

The weathercock was what is called "lofty," and that quality alone would have made him interesting in the eyes of the Cucumber, had she known it. But she had eyes only for the yard cock, who had actually made his appearance in her yard; for the violence of the storm had passed, but the wind had blown down the wooden palings.

"What do you think of that for crowing?" asked the yard cock of his hens and chickens. It was rather rough, and wanted elegance, but they did not say so, as they stepped upon the dunghill while the cock strutted about as if he had been a knight. "Garden plant," he cried to the Cucumber. She heard the words with deep feeling, for they showed that he understood who she was, and she forgot that he was pecking at her and eating her up—a happy death!

Then the hens came running up, and the chickens followed, for where one runs the rest run also. They clucked and chirped and looked at the cock and were proud that they belonged to him. "Cock-a-doodle-doo!" crowed he; "the chickens in the poultry yard will grow to be large fowls if I make my voice heard in the world."

And the hens and chickens clucked and chirped, and the cock told them a great piece of news. "A cock can lay an egg," he said. "And what do you think is in that egg? In that egg lies a basilisk. No one can endure the sight of a basilisk. Men know my power, and now you know what I am capable of, also, and what a renowned bird I am." And with this the yard cock flapped his wings, erected his comb, and crowed again, till all the hens and chickens trembled; but they were proud that one of their race should be of such renown in the world. They clucked and they chirped so that the weathercock heard it; he had heard it all, but had not stirred.

"It's all stupid stuff," said a voice within the weathercock. "The yard cock does not lay eggs any more than I do, and I am too lazy. I could lay a wind egg if I liked, but the world is not worth a wind egg. And now I don't intend to sit here any longer."

With that, the weathercock broke off and fell into the yard. He did not kill the yard cock, although the hens said he intended to do so.

And what does the moral say? "Better to crow than to be vainglorious and break down at last."

THE RED SHOES

THERE was once a pretty, delicate little girl, who was so poor that she had to go barefoot in summer and wear coarse wooden shoes in winter, which made her little instep quite red.

In the center of the village there lived an old shoemaker's wife. One day this good woman made, as well as she could, a little pair of shoes out of some strips of old red cloth. The shoes were clumsy enough, to be sure, but they fitted the little girl tolerably well, and anyway the woman's intention was kind. The little girl's name was Karen.

On the very day that Karen received the shoes, her mother was to be buried. They were not at all suitable for mourning, but she had no others, so she put them on her little bare feet and followed the poor plain coffin to its last resting place.

Just at that time a large, old-fashioned carriage happened to pass by, and the old lady who sat in it saw the little girl and pitied her.

"Give me the little girl," she said to the clergyman, "and I will take care of her."

Karen supposed that all this happened because of the red shoes, but the old lady thought them frightful and ordered them to be burned. Karen was then dressed in neat, well-fitting clothes and taught to read and sew. People told her she was pretty, but the mirror said, "You are much more than pretty—you are beautiful."

It happened not long afterwards that the queen and her little daughter, the princess, traveled through the land. All the people, Karen among the rest, flocked toward the palace and crowded around it, while the little princess, dressed in white, stood at the window for every one to see. She wore neither a train nor a golden crown, but on her feet were beautiful red morocco shoes, which, it must be admitted, were prettier than those the shoemaker's wife had given to little Karen. Surely nothing in the world could be compared to those red shoes.

Now that Karen was old enough to be confirmed, she of course had to have a new frock and new shoes. The rich shoemaker in the town took the measure of her little feet in his own house, in a room where stood great glass cases filled with all sorts of fine shoes and elegant, shining boots. It was a pretty sight, but the old lady could not see well and naturally did not take so much pleasure in it as Karen. Among the shoes were a pair of red ones, just like those worn by the little princess. Oh, how gay they were! The shoemaker said they had been made for the child of a count, but had not fitted well.

"Are they of polished leather, that they shine so?" asked the old lady.

"Yes, indeed, they do shine," replied Karen. And since they fitted her, they were bought. But the old lady had no idea that they were red, or she would never in the world have allowed Karen to go to confirmation in them, as she now did. Every one, of course, looked at Karen's shoes; and when she walked up the nave to the chancel it seemed to her that even the antique figures on the monuments, the portraits of clergymen and their wives, with their stiff ruffs and long black robes, were fixing their eyes on her red shoes. Even when the bishop laid his hand upon her head and spoke of her covenant with God and how she must now begin to be a full-grown Christian, and when the organ pealed forth solemnly and the children's fresh, sweet voices joined with those of the choir—still Karen thought of nothing but her shoes.

In the afternoon, when the old lady heard every one speak of the red shoes, she said it was very shocking and improper and that, in the future, when Karen went to church it must always be in black shoes, even if they were old.

The next Sunday was Karen's first Communion day. She looked at her black shoes, and then at her red ones, then again at the black and at the red—and the red ones were put on.

The sun shone very brightly, and Karen and the old lady walked to church through the cornfields, for the road was very dusty.

At the door of the church stood an old soldier, who leaned upon a crutch and had a marvelously long beard that was not white but red. He bowed almost to the ground and asked the old lady if he might dust her shoes. Karen, in her turn, put out her little foot.

"Oh, look, what smart little dancing pumps!" said the old soldier. "Mind you do not let them slip off when you dance," and he passed his hands over them. The old lady gave the soldier a half-penny and went with Karen into the church.

As before, every one saw Karen's red shoes, and all the carved figures too bent their gaze upon them. When Karen knelt at the chancel she thought only of the shoes; they floated before her eyes, and she forgot to say her prayer or sing her psalm.

At last all the people left the church, and the old lady got into her carriage. As Karen lifted her foot to step in, the old soldier said, "See what pretty dancing shoes!" And Karen, in spite of herself, made a few dancing steps. When she had once begun, her feet went on of themselves; it was as though the shoes had received power over her. She danced round the church corner,—she could not help it,—and the coachman had to run behind and catch her to put her into the carriage. Still her feet went on dancing, so, that she trod upon the good lady's toes. It was not until the shoes were taken from her feet that she had rest.

The shoes were put away in a closet, but Karen could not resist going to look at them every now and then.

Soon after this the old lady lay ill in bed, and it was said that she could not recover. She had to be nursed and waited on, and this, of course, was no one's duty so much as it was Karen's, as Karen herself well knew. But there happened to be a great ball in the town, and Karen was invited. She looked at the old lady, who was very ill, and she looked at the red shoes. She put them on, for she thought there could not be any sin in that, and of course there was not—but she went next to the ball and began to dance.

Strange to say, when she wanted to move to the right the shoes bore her to the left; and when she wished to dance up the room the shoes persisted in going down the room. Down the stairs they carried her at last, into the street, and out through the town gate. On and on she danced, for dance she must, straight out into the gloomy wood. Up among the trees something glistened. She thought it was the round, red moon, for she saw a face; but no, it was the old soldier with the red beard, who sat and nodded, saying, "See what pretty dancing shoes!"

She was dreadfully frightened and tried to throw away the red shoes, but they clung fast and she could not unclasp them. They seemed to have grown fast to her feet. So dance she must, and dance she did, over field and meadow, in rain and in sunshine, by night and by day—and by night it was by far more dreadful.

She danced out into the open churchyard, but the dead there did not dance; they were at rest and had much better things to do. She would have liked to sit down on the poor man's grave, where the bitter tansy grew, but for her there was no rest.

She danced past
the open church door ○ · ○

She danced past the open church door, and there she saw an angel in long white robes and with wings that reached from his shoulders to the earth. His look was stern and grave, and in his hand he held a broad, glittering sword.

"Thou shalt dance," he said, "in thy red shoes, till thou art pale and cold, and till thy body is wasted like a skeleton. Thou shalt dance from door to door, and wherever proud, haughty children dwell thou shalt knock, that, hearing thee, they may take warning. Dance thou shalt—dance on!"

"Mercy!" cried Karen; but she did not hear the answer of the angel, for the shoes carried her past the door and on into the fields.

One morning she danced past a well-known door. Within was the sound of a psalm, and presently a coffin strewn with flowers was borne out. She knew that her friend, the old lady, was dead, and in her heart she felt that she was abandoned by all on earth and condemned by God's angel in heaven.

Still on she danced—for she could not stop—through thorns and briers, while her feet bled. Finally, she danced to a lonely little house where she knew that the executioner dwelt, and she tapped at the window, saying, "Come out, come out! I cannot come in, for I must dance."

The man said, "Do you know who I am and what I do?"

"Yes," said Karen; "but do not strike off my head, for then I could not live to repent of my sin. Strike off my feet, that I may be rid of my red shoes."

Then she confessed her sin, and the executioner struck off the red shoes, which danced away over the fields and into the deep wood. To Karen it seemed that the feet had gone with the shoes, for she had almost lost the power of walking.

"Now I have suffered enough for the red shoes," she said; "I will go to the church, that people may see me." But no sooner had she hobbled to the church door than the shoes danced before her and frightened her back.

All that week she endured the keenest sorrow and shed many bitter tears. When Sunday came, she said: "I am sure I must have suffered and striven enough by this time. I am quite as good, I dare say, as many who are holding their heads high in the church." So she took courage and went again. But before she reached the churchyard gate the red shoes were dancing there, and she turned back again in terror, more deeply sorrowful than ever for her sin.

She then went to the pastor's house and begged as a favor to be taken into the family's service, promising to be diligent and faithful. She did not want wages, she said, only a home with good people. The clergyman's wife pitied her and granted her request, and she proved industrious and very thoughtful.

Earnestly she listened when at evening the preacher read aloud the Holy Scriptures. All the children came to love her, but when they spoke of beauty and finery, she would shake her head and turn away.

On Sunday, when they all went to church, they asked her if she would not go, too, but she looked sad and bade them go without her. Then she went to her own little room, and as she sat with the psalm book in her hand, reading its pages with a gentle, pious mind, the wind brought to her the notes of the organ. She raised her tearful eyes and said, "O God, do thou help me!"

Then the sun shone brightly, and before her stood the white angel that she had seen at the church door. He no longer bore the glittering sword, but in his hand was a beautiful branch of roses. He touched the ceiling with it, and the ceiling rose, and at each place where the branch touched it there shone a star. He touched the walls, and they widened so that Karen could see the organ that was being played at the church. She saw, too, the old pictures and statues on the walls, and the congregation sitting in the seats and singing psalms, for the church itself had come to the poor girl in her narrow room, or she in her chamber had come to it. She sat in the seat with the rest of the clergyman's household, and when the psalm was ended, they nodded and said, "Thou didst well to come, Karen!"

"This is mercy," said she. "It is the grace of God."

The organ pealed, and the chorus of children's voices mingled sweetly with it. The bright sunshine shed its warm light, through the windows, over the pew in which Karen sat. Her heart was so filled with sunshine, peace, and joy that it broke, and her soul was borne by a sunbeam up to God, where there was nobody to ask about the red shoes.

THE LITTLE MERMAID

FAR out in the ocean, where the water is as blue as the prettiest cornflower and as clear as crystal, it is very, very deep; so deep, indeed, that no cable could sound it, and many church steeples, piled one upon another, would not reach from the ground beneath to the surface of the water above. There dwell the Sea King and his subjects.

We must not imagine that there is nothing at the bottom of the sea but bare yellow sand. No, indeed, for on this sand grow the strangest flowers and plants, the leaves and stems of which are so pliant that the slightest agitation of the water causes them to stir as if they had life. Fishes, both large and small, glide between the branches as birds fly among the trees here upon land.

In the deepest spot of all stands the castle of the Sea King. Its walls are built of coral, and the long Gothic windows are of the clearest amber. The roof is formed of shells that open and close as the water flows over them. Their appearance is very beautiful, for in each lies a glittering pearl which would be fit for the diadem of a queen.

The Sea King had been a widower for many years, and his aged mother kept house for him. She was a very sensible woman, but exceedingly proud of her high birth, and on that account wore twelve oysters on her tail, while others of high rank were only allowed to wear six.

She was, however, deserving of very great praise, especially for her care of the little sea princesses, her six granddaughters. They were beautiful children, but the youngest was the prettiest of them all. Her skin was as clear and delicate as a rose leaf, and her eyes as blue as the deepest sea; but, like all the others, she had no feet and her body ended in a fish's tail. All day long they played in the great halls of the castle or among the living flowers that grew out of the walls. The large amber windows were open, and the fish swam in, just as the swallows fly into our houses when we open the windows; only the fishes swam up to the princesses, ate out of their hands, and allowed themselves to be stroked.

Outside the castle there was a beautiful garden, in which grew bright-red and dark-blue flowers, and blossoms like flames of fire; the fruit glittered like gold, and the leaves and stems waved to and fro continually. The earth itself was the finest sand, but blue as the flame of burning sulphur. Over everything lay a peculiar blue radiance, as if the blue sky were everywhere, above and below, instead of the dark depths of the sea. In calm weather the sun could be seen, looking like a reddish-purple flower with light streaming from the calyx.

Each of the young princesses had a little plot of ground in the garden, where she might dig and plant as she pleased. One arranged her flower bed in the form of a whale; another preferred to make hers like the figure of a little mermaid; while the youngest child made hers round, like the sun, and in it grew flowers as red as his rays at sunset.

She was a strange child, quiet and thoughtful. While her sisters showed delight at the wonderful things which they obtained from the wrecks of vessels, she cared only for her pretty flowers, red like the sun, and a beautiful marble statue. It was the representation of a handsome boy, carved out of pure white stone, which had fallen to the bottom of the sea from a wreck.

She planted by the statue a rose-colored weeping willow. It grew rapidly and soon hung its fresh branches over the statue, almost down to the blue sands. The shadows had the color of violet and waved to and fro like the branches, so that it seemed as if the crown of the tree and the root were at play, trying to kiss each other.

Nothing gave her so much pleasure as to hear about the world above the sea. She made her old grandmother tell her all she knew of the ships and of the towns, the people and the animals. To her it seemed most wonderful and beautiful to hear that the flowers of the land had fragrance, while those below the sea had none; that the trees of the forest were green; and that the fishes among the trees could sing so sweetly that it was a pleasure to listen to them. Her grandmother called the birds fishes, or the little mermaid would not have understood what was meant, for she had never seen birds.

"When you have reached your fifteenth year," said the grandmother, "you will have permission to rise up out of the sea and sit on the rocks in the moonlight, while the great ships go sailing by. Then you will see both forests and towns."

In the following year, one of the sisters would be fifteen, but as each was a year younger than the other, the youngest would have to wait five years before her turn came to rise up from the bottom of the ocean to see the earth as we do. However, each promised to tell the others what she saw on her first visit and what she thought was most beautiful. Their grandmother could not tell them enough—there were so many things about which they wanted to know.

None of them longed so much for her turn to come as the youngest—she who had the longest time to wait and who was so quiet and thoughtful. Many nights she stood by the open window, looking up through the dark blue water and watching the fish as they splashed about with their fins and tails. She could see the moon and stars shining faintly, but through the water they looked larger than they do to our eyes. When something like a black cloud passed between her and them, she knew that it was either a whale swimming over her head, or a ship full of human beings who never imagined that a pretty little mermaid was standing beneath them, holding out her white hands towards the keel of their ship.

At length the eldest was fifteen and was allowed to rise to the surface of the ocean.

When she returned she had hundreds of things to talk about. But the finest thing, she said, was to lie on a sand bank in the quiet moonlit sea, near the shore, gazing at the lights of the near-by town, that twinkled like hundreds of stars, and listening to the sounds of music, the noise of carriages, the voices of human beings, and the merry pealing of the bells in the church steeples. Because she could not go near all these wonderful things, she longed for them all the more.

Oh, how eagerly did the youngest sister listen to all these descriptions! And afterwards, when she stood at the open window looking up through the dark-blue water, she thought of the great city, with all its bustle and noise, and even fancied she could hear the sound of the church bells down in the depths of the sea.

In another year the second sister received permission to rise to the surface of the water and to swim about where she pleased. She rose just as the sun was setting, and this, she said, was the most beautiful sight of all. The whole sky looked like gold, and violet and rose-colored clouds, which she could not describe, drifted across it. And more swiftly than the clouds, flew a large flock of wild swans toward the setting sun, like a long white veil across the sea. She also swam towards the sun, but it sank into the waves, and the rosy tints faded from the clouds and from the sea.

The third sister's turn followed, and she was the boldest of them all, for she swam up a broad river that emptied into the sea. On the banks she saw green hills covered with beautiful vines, and palaces and castles peeping out from amid the proud trees of the forest. She heard birds singing and felt the rays of the sun so strongly that she was obliged often to dive under the water to cool her burning face. In a narrow creek she found a large group of little human children, almost naked, sporting about in the water. She wanted to play with them, but they fled in a great fright; and then a little black animal—it was a dog, but she did not know it, for she had never seen one before—came to the water and barked at her so furiously that she became frightened and rushed back to the open sea. But she said she should never forget the beautiful forest, the green hills, and the pretty children who could swim in the water although they had no tails.

The fourth sister was more timid. She remained in the midst of the sea, but said it was quite as beautiful there as nearer the land. She could see many miles around her, and the sky above looked like a bell of glass. She had seen the ships, but at such a great distance that they looked like sea gulls. The dolphins sported in the waves, and the great whales spouted water from their nostrils till it seemed as if a hundred fountains were playing in every direction.

The fifth sister's birthday occurred in the winter, so when her turn came she saw what the others had not seen the first time they went up. The sea looked quite green, and large icebergs were floating about, each like a pearl, she said, but larger and loftier than the churches built by men. They were of the most singular shapes and glittered like diamonds. She had seated herself on one of the largest and let the wind play with her long hair. She noticed that all the ships sailed past very rapidly, steering as far away as they could, as if they were afraid of the iceberg. Towards evening, as the sun went down, dark clouds covered the sky, the thunder rolled, and the flashes of lightning glowed red on the icebergs as they were tossed about by the heaving sea. On all the ships the sails were reefed with fear and trembling, while she sat on the floating iceberg, calmly watching the lightning as it darted its forked flashes into the sea.

Each of the sisters, when first she had permission to rise to the surface, was delighted with the new and beautiful sights. Now that they were grown-up girls and could go when they pleased, they had become quite indifferent about it. They soon wished themselves back again, and after a month had passed they said it was much more beautiful down below and pleasanter to be at home.

Yet often, in the evening hours, the five sisters would twine their arms about each other and rise to the surface together. Their voices were more charming than that of any human being, and before the approach of a storm, when they feared that a ship might be lost, they swam before the vessel, singing enchanting songs of the delights to be found in the depths of the sea and begging the voyagers not to fear if they sank to the bottom. But the sailors could not understand the song and thought it was the sighing of the storm.

These things were never beautiful to them, for if the ship sank, the men were drowned and their dead bodies alone reached the palace of the Sea King.

When the sisters rose, arm in arm, through the water, their youngest sister would stand quite alone, looking after them, ready to cry—only, since mermaids have no tears, she suffered more acutely.

"Oh, were I but fifteen years old!" said she. "I know that I shall love the world up there, and all the people who live in it."

At last she reached her fifteenth year.

"Well, now you are grown up," said the old dowager, her grandmother. "Come, and let me adorn you like your sisters." And she placed in her hair a wreath of white lilies, of which every flower leaf was half a pearl. Then the old lady ordered eight great oysters to attach themselves to the tail of the princess to show her high rank.

"But they hurt me so," said the little mermaid.

"Yes, I know; pride must suffer pain," replied the old lady.

Oh, how gladly she would have shaken off all this grandeur and laid aside the heavy wreath! The red flowers in her own garden would have suited her much better. But she could not change herself, so she said farewell and rose as lightly as a bubble to the surface of the water.

The sun had just set when she raised her head above the waves. The clouds were tinted with crimson and gold, and through the glimmering twilight beamed the evening star in all its beauty. The sea was calm, and the air mild and fresh. A large ship with three masts lay becalmed on the water; only one sail was set, for not a breeze stirred, and the sailors sat idle on deck or amidst the rigging. There was music and song on board, and as darkness came on, a hundred colored lanterns were lighted, as if the flags of all nations waved in the air.

The little mermaid swam close to the cabin windows, and now and then, as the waves lifted her up, she could look in through glass window-panes and see a number of gayly dressed people.

Among them, and the most beautiful of all, was a young prince with large, black eyes. He was sixteen years of age, and his birthday was being celebrated with great display. The sailors were dancing on deck, and when the prince came out of the cabin, more than a hundred rockets rose in the air, making it as bright as day. The little mermaid was so startled that she dived under water, and when she again stretched out her head, it looked as if all the stars of heaven were falling around her.

She had never seen such fireworks before. Great suns spurted fire about, splendid fireflies flew into the blue air, and everything was reflected in the clear, calm sea beneath. The ship itself was so brightly illuminated that all the people, and even the smallest rope, could be distinctly seen. How handsome the young prince looked, as he pressed the hands of all his guests and smiled at them, while the music resounded through the clear night air!

It was very late, yet the little mermaid could not take her eyes from the ship or from the beautiful prince. The colored lanterns had been extinguished, no more rockets rose in the air, and the cannon had ceased firing; but the sea became restless, and a moaning, grumbling sound could be heard beneath the waves. Still the little mermaid remained by the cabin window, rocking up and down on the water, so that she could look within. After a while the sails were quickly set, and the ship went on her way. But soon the waves rose higher, heavy clouds darkened the sky, and lightning appeared in the distance. A dreadful storm was approaching. Once more the sails were furled, and the great ship pursued her flying course over the raging sea. The waves rose mountain high, as if they would overtop the mast, but the ship dived like a swan between them, then rose again on their lofty, foaming crests. To the little mermaid this was pleasant sport; but not so to the sailors. At length the ship groaned and creaked; the thick planks gave way under the lashing of the sea, as the waves broke over the deck; the mainmast snapped asunder like a reed, and as the ship lay over on her side, the water rushed in.

The little mermaid now perceived that the crew were in danger; even she was obliged to be careful, to avoid the beams and planks of the wreck which lay scattered on the water. At one moment it was pitch dark so that she could not see a single object, but when a flash of lightning came it revealed the whole scene; she could see every one who had been on board except the prince. When the ship parted, she had seen him sink into the deep waves, and she was glad, for she thought he would now be with her. Then she remembered that human beings could not live in the water, so that when he got down to her father's palace he would certainly be quite dead.

No, he must not die! So she swam about among the beams and planks which strewed the surface of the sea, forgetting that they could crush her to pieces. Diving deep under the dark waters, rising and falling with the waves, she at length managed to reach the young prince, who was fast losing the power to swim in that stormy sea. His limbs were failing him, his beautiful eyes were closed, and he would have died had not the little mermaid come to his assistance. She held his head above the water and let the waves carry them where they would.

In the morning the storm had ceased, but of the ship not a single fragment could be seen. The sun came up red and shining out of the water, and its beams brought back the hue of health to the prince's cheeks, but his eyes remained closed. The mermaid kissed his high, smooth forehead and stroked back his wet hair. He seemed to her like the marble statue in her little garden, so she kissed him again and wished that he might live.

Presently they came in sight of land, and she saw lofty blue mountains on which the white snow rested as if a flock of swans were lying upon them. Beautiful green forests were near the shore, and close by stood a large building, whether a church or a convent she could not tell. Orange and citron trees grew in the garden, and before the door stood lofty palms. The sea here formed a little bay, in which the water lay quiet and still, but very deep. She swam with the handsome prince to the beach, which was covered with fine white sand, and there she laid him in the warm sunshine, taking care to raise his head higher than his body. Then bells sounded in the large white building, and some young girls came into the garden. The little mermaid swam out farther from the shore and hid herself among some high rocks that rose out of the water. Covering her head and neck with the foam of the sea, she watched there to see what would become of the poor prince.

It was not long before she saw a young girl approach the spot where the prince lay. She seemed frightened at first, but only for a moment; then she brought a number of people, and the mermaid saw that the prince came to life again and smiled upon those who stood about him. But to her he sent no smile; he knew not that she had saved him. This made her very sorrowful, and when he was led away into the great building, she dived down into the water and returned to her father's castle.

She had always been silent and thoughtful, and now she was more so than ever. Her sisters asked her what she had seen during her first visit to the surface of the water, but she could tell them nothing. Many an evening and morning did she rise to the place where she had left the prince. She saw the fruits in the garden ripen and watched them gathered; she watched the snow on the mountain tops melt away; but never did she see the prince, and therefore she always returned home more sorrowful than before.

It was her only comfort to sit in her own little garden and fling her arm around the beautiful marble statue, which was like the prince. She gave up tending her flowers, and they grew in wild confusion over the paths, twining their long leaves and stems round the branches of the trees so that the whole place became dark and gloomy.

At length she could bear it no longer and told one of her sisters all about it. Then the others heard the secret, and very soon it became known to several mermaids, one of whom had an intimate friend who happened to know about the prince. She had also seen the festival on board ship, and she told them where the prince came from and where his palace stood.

"Come, little sister," said the other princesses. Then they entwined their arms and rose together to the surface of the water, near the spot where they knew the prince's palace stood. It was built of bright-yellow, shining stone and had long flights of marble steps, one of which reached quite down to the sea. Splendid gilded cupolas rose over the roof, and between the pillars that surrounded the whole building stood lifelike statues of marble. Through the clear crystal of the lofty windows could be seen noble rooms, with cost-costly silk curtains and hangings of tapestry and walls covered with beautiful paintings. In the center of the largest salon a fountain threw its sparkling jets high up into the glass cupola of the ceiling, through which the sun shone in upon the water and upon the beautiful plants that grew in the basin of the fountain.

Now that the little mermaid knew where the prince lived, she spent many an evening and many a night on the water near the palace. She would swim much nearer the shore than any of the others had ventured, and once she went up the narrow channel under the marble balcony, which threw a broad shadow on the water. Here she sat and watched the young prince, who thought himself alone in the bright moonlight.

She often saw him evenings, sailing in a beautiful boat on which music sounded and flags waved. She peeped out from among the green rushes, and if the wind caught her long silvery-white veil, those who saw it believed it to be a swan, spreading out its wings.

Many a night, too, when the fishermen set their nets by the light of their torches, she heard them relate many good things about the young prince. And this made her glad that she had saved his life when he was tossed about half dead on the waves. She remembered how his head had rested on her bosom and how heartily she had kissed him, but he knew nothing of all this and could not even dream of her.

She grew more and more to like human beings and wished more and more to be able to wander about with those whose world seemed to be so much larger than her own. They could fly over the sea in ships and mount the high hills which were far above the clouds; and the lands they possessed, their woods and their fields, stretched far away beyond the reach of her sight. There was so much that she wished to know! but her sisters were unable to answer all her questions. She then went to her old grandmother, who knew all about the upper world, which she rightly called "the lands above the sea."

"If human beings are not drowned," asked the little mermaid, "can they live forever? Do they never die, as we do here in the sea?"

"Yes," replied the old lady, "they must also die, and their term of life is even shorter than ours. We sometimes live for three hundred years, but when we cease to exist here, we become only foam on the surface of the water and have not even a grave among those we love. We have not immortal souls, we shall never live again; like the green seaweed when once it has been cut off, we can never flourish more. Human beings, on the contrary, have souls which live forever, even after the body has been turned to dust. They rise up through the clear, pure air, beyond the glittering stars. As we rise out of the water and behold all the land of the earth, so do they rise to unknown and glorious regions which we shall never see."

"Why have not we immortal souls?" asked the little mermaid, mournfully. "I would gladly give all the hundreds of years that I have to live, to be a human being only for one day and to have the hope of knowing the happiness of that glorious world above the stars."

"You must not think that," said the old woman. "We believe that we are much happier and much better off than human beings."

"So I shall die," said the little mermaid, "and as the foam of the sea I shall be driven about, never again to hear the music of the waves or to see the pretty flowers or the red sun? Is there anything I can do to win an immortal soul?"

"No," said the old woman; "unless a man should love you so much that you were more to him than his father or his mother, and if all his thoughts and all his love were fixed upon you, and the priest placed his right hand in yours, and he promised to be true to you here and hereafter—then his soul would glide into your body, and you would obtain a share in the future happiness of mankind. He would give to you a soul and retain his own as well; but this can never happen. Your fish's tail, which among us is considered so beautiful, on earth is thought to be quite ugly. They do not know any better, and they think it necessary, in order to be handsome, to have two stout props, which they call legs."

Then the little mermaid sighed and looked sorrowfully at her fish's tail. "Let us be happy," said the old lady, "and dart and spring about during the three hundred years that we have to live, which is really quite long enough. After that we can rest ourselves all the better. This evening we are going to have a court ball."

It was one of those splendid sights which we can never see on earth. The walls and the ceiling of the large ballroom were of thick but transparent crystal. Many hundreds of colossal shells,—some of a deep red, others of a grass green,—with blue fire in them, stood in rows on each side. These lighted up the whole salon, and shone through the walls so that the sea was also illuminated. Innumerable fishes, great and small, swam past the crystal walls; on some of them the scales glowed with a purple brilliance, and on others shone like silver and gold. Through the halls flowed a broad stream, and in it danced the mermen and the mermaids to the music of their own sweet singing.

No one on earth has such lovely voices as they, but the little mermaid sang more sweetly than all. The whole court applauded her with hands and tails, and for a moment her heart felt quite gay, for she knew she had the sweetest voice either on earth or in the sea. But soon she thought again of the world above her; she could not forget the charming prince, nor her sorrow that she had not an immortal soul like his. She crept away silently out of her father's palace, and while everything within was gladness and song, she sat in her own little garden, sorrowful and alone. Then she heard the bugle sounding through the water and thought: "He is certainly sailing above, he in whom my wishes center and in whose hands I should like to place the happiness of my life. I will venture all for him and to win an immortal soul. While my sisters are dancing in my father's palace I will go to the sea witch, of whom I have always been so much afraid; she can give me counsel and help."

Then the little mermaid went out from her garden and took the road to the foaming whirlpools, behind which the sorceress lived. She had never been that way before. Neither flowers nor grass grew there; nothing but bare, gray, sandy ground stretched out to the whirlpool, where the water, like foaming mill wheels, seized everything that came within its reach and cast it into the fathomless deep. Through the midst of these crushing whirlpools the little mermaid was obliged to pass before she could reach the dominions of the sea witch. Then, for a long distance, the road lay across a stretch of warm, bubbling mire, called by the witch her turf moor.

Beyond this was the witch's house, which stood in the center of a strange forest, where all the trees and flowers were polypi, half animals and half plants. They looked like serpents with a hundred heads, growing out of the ground. The branches were long, slimy arms, with fingers like flexible worms, moving limb after limb from the root to the top. All that could be reached in the sea they seized upon and held fast, so that it never escaped from their clutches.

The little mermaid was so alarmed at what she saw that she stood still and her heart beat with fear. She came very near turning back, but she thought of the prince and of the human soul for which she longed, and her courage returned. She fastened her long, flowing hair round her head, so that the polypi should not lay hold of it. She crossed her hands on her bosom, and then darted forward as a fish shoots through the water, between the supple arms and fingers of the ugly polypi, which were stretched out on each side of her. She saw that they all held in their grasp something they had seized with their numerous little arms, which were as strong as iron bands. Tightly grasped in their clinging arms were white skeletons of human beings who had perished at sea and had sunk down into the deep waters; skeletons of land animals; and oars, rudders, and chests, of ships. There was even a little mermaid whom they had caught and strangled, and this seemed the most shocking of all to the little princess.

She now came to a space of marshy ground in the wood, where large, fat water snakes were rolling in the mire and showing their ugly, drab-colored bodies. In the midst of this spot stood a house, built of the bones of shipwrecked human beings. There sat the sea witch, allowing a toad to eat from her mouth just as people sometimes feed a canary with pieces of sugar. She called the ugly water snakes her little chickens and allowed them to crawl all over her bosom.

"I know what you want," said the sea witch. "It is very stupid of you, but you shall have your way, though it will bring you to sorrow, my pretty princess. You want to get rid of your fish's tail and to have two supports instead, like human beings on earth, so that the young prince may fall in love with you and so that you may have an immortal soul." And then the witch laughed so loud and so disgustingly that the toad and the snakes fell to the ground and lay there wriggling.

"You are but just in time," said the witch, "for after sunrise to-morrow I should not be able to help you till the end of another year. I will prepare a draft for you, with which you must swim to land to-morrow before sunrise; seat yourself there and drink it. Your tail will then disappear, and shrink up into what men call legs.

"You will feel great pain, as if a sword were passing through you. But all who see you will say that you are the prettiest little human being they ever saw. You will still have the same floating gracefulness of movement, and no dancer will ever tread so lightly. Every step you take, however, will be as if you were treading upon sharp knives and as if the blood must flow. If you will bear all this, I will help you."

"Yes, I will," said the little princess in a trembling voice, as she thought of the prince and the immortal soul.

"But think again," said the witch, "for when once your shape has become like a human being, you can no more be a mermaid. You will never return through the water to your sisters or to your father's palace again. And if you do not win the love of the prince, so that he is willing to forget his father and mother for your sake and to love you with his whole soul and allow the priest to join your hands that you may be man and wife, then you will never have an immortal soul. The first morning after he marries another, your heart will break and you will become foam on the crest of the waves."

"I will do it," said the little mermaid, and she became pale as death.

"But I must be paid, also," said the witch, "and it is not a trifle that I ask. You have the sweetest voice of any who dwell here in the depths of the sea, and you believe that you will be able to charm the prince with it. But this voice you must give to me. The best thing you possess will I have as the price of my costly draft, which must be mixed with my own blood so that it may be as sharp as a two-edged sword."

"But if you take away my voice," said the little mermaid, "what is left for me?"

"Your beautiful form, your graceful walk, and your expressive eyes. Surely with these you can enchain a man's heart. Well, have you lost your courage? Put out your little tongue, that I may cut it off as my payment; then you shall have the powerful draft."

"It shall be," said the little mermaid.

Then the witch placed her caldron on the fire, to prepare the magic draft.

"Cleanliness is a good thing," said she, scouring the vessel with snakes which she had tied together in a large knot. Then she pricked herself in the breast and let the black blood drop into the caldron. The steam that rose twisted itself into such horrible shapes that no one could look at them without fear. Every moment the witch threw a new ingredient into the vessel, and when it began to boil, the sound was like the weeping of a crocodile. When at last the magic draft was ready, it looked like the clearest water.

"There it is for you," said the witch. Then she cut off the mermaid's tongue, so that she would never again speak or sing. "If the polypi should seize you as you return through the wood," said the witch, "throw over them a few drops of the potion, and their fingers will be torn into a thousand pieces." But the little mermaid had no occasion to do this, for the polypi sprang back in terror when they caught sight of the glittering draft, which shone in her hand like a twinkling star.

So she passed quickly through the wood and the marsh and between the rushing whirlpools. She saw that in her father's palace the torches in the ballroom were extinguished and that all within were asleep. But she did not venture to go in to them, for now that she was dumb and going to leave them forever she felt as if her heart would break. She stole into the garden, took a flower from the flower bed of each of her sisters, kissed her hand towards the palace a thousand times, and then rose up through the dark-blue waters.

The sun had not risen when she came in sight of the prince's palace and approached the beautiful marble steps, but the moon shone clear and bright. Then the little mermaid drank the magic draft, and it seemed as if a two-edged sword went through her delicate body. She fell into a swoon and lay like one dead. When the sun rose and shone over the sea, she recovered and felt a sharp pain, but before her stood the handsome young prince.

He fixed his coal-black eyes upon her so earnestly that she cast down her own and then became aware that her fish's tail was gone and that she had as pretty a pair of white legs and tiny feet as any little maiden could have. But she had no clothes, so she wrapped herself in her long, thick hair. The prince asked her who she was and whence she came. She looked at him mildly and sorrowfully with her deep blue eyes, but could not speak. He took her by the hand and led her to the palace.

Every step she took was as the witch had said it would be; she felt as if she were treading upon the points of needles or sharp knives. She bore it willingly, however, and moved at the prince's side as lightly as a bubble, so that he and all who saw her wondered at her graceful, swaying movements. She was very soon arrayed in costly robes of silk and muslin and was the most beautiful creature in the palace; but she was dumb and could neither speak nor sing.

Beautiful female slaves, dressed in silk and gold, stepped forward and sang before the prince and his royal parents. One sang better than all the others, and the prince clapped his hands and smiled at her. This was a great sorrow to the little mermaid, for she knew how much more sweetly she herself once could sing, and she thought, "Oh, if he could only know that I have given away my voice forever, to be with him!"

The slaves next performed some pretty fairy-like dances, to the sound of beautiful music. Then the little mermaid raised her lovely white arms, stood on the tips of her toes, glided over the floor, and danced as no one yet had been able to dance. At each moment her beauty was more revealed, and her expressive eyes appealed more directly to the heart than the songs of the slaves. Every one was enchanted, especially the prince, who called her his little foundling. She danced again quite readily, to please him, though each time her foot touched the floor it seemed as if she trod on sharp knives.

Before her stood the handsome young prince ° °

The prince said she should remain with him always, and she was given permission to sleep at his door, on a velvet cushion. He had a page's dress made for her, that she might accompany him on horseback. They rode together through the sweet-scented woods, where the green boughs touched their shoulders, and the little birds sang among the fresh leaves. She climbed with him to the tops of high mountains, and although her tender feet bled so that even her steps were marked, she only smiled, and followed him till they could see the clouds beneath them like a flock of birds flying to distant lands. While at the prince's palace, and when all the household were asleep, she would go and sit on the broad marble steps, for it eased her burning feet to bathe them in the cold sea water. It was then that she thought of all those below in the deep.

Once during the night her sisters came up arm in arm, singing sorrowfully as they floated on the water. She beckoned to them, and they recognized her and told her how she had grieved them; after that, they came to the same place every night. Once she saw in the distance her old grandmother, who had not been to the surface of the sea for many years, and the old Sea King, her father, with his crown on his head. They stretched out their hands towards her, but did not venture so near the land as her sisters had.

As the days passed she loved the prince more dearly, and he loved her as one would love a little child. The thought never came to him to make her his wife. Yet unless he married her, she could not receive an immortal soul, and on the morning after his marriage with another, she would dissolve into the foam of the sea.

"Do you not love me the best of them all?" the eyes of the little mermaid seemed to say when he took her in his arms and kissed her fair forehead.

"Yes, you are dear to me," said the prince, "for you have the best heart and you are the most devoted to me. You are like a young maiden whom I once saw, but whom I shall never meet again. I was in a ship that was wrecked, and the waves cast me ashore near a holy temple where several young maidens performed the service. The youngest of them found me on the shore and saved my life. I saw her but twice, and she is the only one in the world whom I could love. But you are like her, and you have almost driven her image from my mind. She belongs to the holy temple, and good fortune has sent you to me in her stead. We will never part.

"Ah, he knows not that it was I who saved his life," thought the little mermaid. "I carried him over the sea to the wood where the temple stands; I sat beneath the foam and watched till the human beings came to help him. I saw the pretty maiden that he loves better than he loves me." The mermaid sighed deeply, but she could not weep. "He says the maiden belongs to the holy temple, therefore she will never return to the world—they will meet no more. I am by his side and see him every day. I will take care of him, and love him, and give up my life for his sake."

Very soon it was said that the prince was to marry and that the beautiful daughter of a neighboring king would be his wife, for a fine ship was being fitted out. Although the prince gave out that he intended merely to pay a visit to the king, it was generally supposed that he went to court the princess. A great company were to go with him. The little mermaid smiled and shook her head. She knew the prince's thoughts better than any of the others.

"I must travel," he had said to her; "I must see this beautiful princess. My parents desire it, but they will not oblige me to bring her home as my bride. I cannot love her, because she is not like the beautiful maiden in the temple, whom you resemble. If I were forced to choose a bride, I would choose you, my dumb foundling, with those expressive eyes." Then he kissed her rosy mouth, played with her long, waving hair, and laid his head on her heart, while she dreamed of human happiness and an immortal soul.

"You are not afraid of the sea, my dumb child, are you?" he said, as they stood on the deck of the noble ship which was to carry them to the country of the neighboring king. Then he told her of storm and of calm, of strange fishes in the deep beneath them, and of what the divers had seen there. She smiled at his descriptions, for she knew better than any one what wonders were at the bottom of the sea.

In the moonlight night, when all on board were asleep except the man at the helm, she sat on deck, gazing down through the clear water. She thought she could distinguish her father's castle, and upon it her aged grandmother, with the silver crown on her head, looking through the rushing tide at the keel of the vessel. Then her sisters came up on the waves and gazed at her mournfully, wringing their white hands. She beckoned to them, and smiled, and wanted to tell them how happy and well off she was. But the cabin boy approached, and when her sisters dived down, he thought what he saw was only the foam of the sea.

The next morning the ship sailed into the harbor of a beautiful town belonging to the king whom the prince was going to visit. The church bells were ringing, and from the high towers sounded a flourish of trumpets. Soldiers, with flying colors and glittering bayonets, lined the roads through which they passed. Every day was a festival, balls and entertainments following one another. But the princess had not yet appeared. People said that she had been brought up and educated in a religious house, where she was learning every royal virtue.

At last she came. Then the little mermaid, who was anxious to see whether she was really beautiful, was obliged to admit that she had never seen a more perfect vision of beauty. Her skin was delicately fair, and beneath her long, dark eyelashes her laughing blue eyes shone with truth and purity.

"It was you," said the prince, "who saved my life when I lay as if dead on the beach," and he folded his blushing bride in his arms.

"Oh, I am too happy!" said he to the little mermaid; "my fondest hopes are now fulfilled. You will rejoice at my happiness, for your devotion to me is great and sincere."

The little mermaid kissed his hand and felt as if her heart were already broken. His wedding morning would bring death to her, and she would change into the foam of the sea.

All the church bells rang, and the heralds rode through the town proclaiming the betrothal. Perfumed oil was burned in costly silver lamps on every altar. The priests waved the censers, while the bride and the bridegroom joined their hands and received the blessing of the bishop. The little mermaid, dressed in silk and gold, held up the bride's train; but her ears heard nothing of the festive music, and her eyes saw not the holy ceremony. She thought of the night of death which was coming to her, and of all she had lost in the world.

On the same evening the bride and bridegroom went on board the ship. Cannons were roaring, flags waving, and in the center of the ship a costly tent of purple and gold had been erected. It contained elegant sleeping couches for the bridal pair during the night. The ship, under a favorable wind, with swelling sails, glided away smoothly and lightly over the calm sea.

When it grew dark, a number of colored lamps were lighted and the sailors danced merrily on the deck. The little mermaid could not help thinking of her first rising out of the sea, when she had seen similar joyful festivities, so she too joined in the dance, poised herself in the air as a swallow when he pursues his prey, and all present cheered her wonderingly. She had never danced so gracefully before. Her tender feet felt as if cut with sharp knives, but she cared not for the pain; a sharper pang had pierced her heart.

She knew this was the last evening she should ever see the prince for whom she had forsaken her kindred and her home. She had given up her beautiful voice and suffered unheard-of pain daily for him, while he knew nothing of it. This was the last evening that she should breathe the same air with him or gaze on the starry sky and the deep sea. An eternal night, without a thought or a dream, awaited her. She had no soul, and now could never win one.

All was joy and gaiety on the ship until long after midnight. She smiled and danced with the rest, while the thought of death was in her heart. The prince kissed his beautiful bride and she played with his raven hair till they went arm in arm to rest in the sumptuous tent. Then all became still on board the ship, and only the pilot, who stood at the helm, was awake. The little mermaid leaned her white arms on the edge of the vessel and looked towards the east for the first blush of morning—for that first ray of the dawn which was to be her death. She saw her sisters rising out of the flood. They were as pale as she, but their beautiful hair no longer waved in the wind; it had been cut off.

"We have given our hair to the witch," said they, "to obtain help for you, that you may not die to-night. She has given us a knife; see, it is very sharp. Before the sun rises you must plunge it into the heart of the prince. When the warm blood falls upon your feet they will grow together again into a fish's tail, and you will once more be a mermaid and can return to us to live out your three hundred years before you are changed into the salt sea foam. Haste, then; either he or you must die before sunrise. Our old grandmother mourns so for you that her white hair is falling, as ours fell under the witch's scissors. Kill the prince, and come back. Hasten! Do you not see the first red streaks in the sky? In a few minutes the sun will rise, and you must die."

Then they sighed deeply and mournfully, and sank beneath the waves.

The little mermaid drew back the crimson curtain of the tent and beheld the fair bride, whose head was resting on the prince's breast. She bent down and kissed his noble brow, then looked at the sky, on which the rosy dawn grew brighter and brighter. She glanced at the sharp knife and again fixed her eyes on the prince, who whispered the name of his bride in his dreams.

She was in his thoughts, and the knife trembled in the hand of the little mermaid—but she flung it far from her into the waves. The water turned red where it fell, and the drops that spurted up looked like blood. She cast one more lingering, half-fainting glance at the prince, then threw herself from the ship into the sea and felt her body dissolving into foam.

The sun rose above the waves, and his warm rays fell on the cold foam of the little mermaid, who did not feel as if she were dying. She saw the bright sun, and hundreds of transparent, beautiful creatures floating around her—she could see through them the white sails of the ships and the red clouds in the sky. Their speech was melodious, but could not be heard by mortal ears—just as their bodies could not be seen by mortal eyes. The little mermaid perceived that she had a body like theirs and that she continued to rise higher and higher out of the foam. "Where am I?" asked she, and her voice sounded ethereal, like the voices of those who were with her. No earthly music could imitate it.

"Among the daughters of the air," answered one of them. "A mermaid has not an immortal soul, nor can she obtain one unless she wins the love of a human being. On the will of another hangs her eternal destiny. But the daughters of the air, although they do not possess an immortal soul, can, by their good deeds, procure one for themselves. We fly to warm countries and cool the sultry air that destroys mankind with the pestilence. We carry the perfume of the flowers to spread health and restoration.

"After we have striven for three hundred years to do all the good in our power, we receive an immortal soul and take part in the happiness of mankind. You, poor little mermaid, have tried with your whole heart to do as we are doing. You have suffered and endured, and raised yourself to the spirit world by your good deeds, and now, by striving for three hundred years in the same way, you may obtain an immortal soul."

The little mermaid lifted her glorified eyes toward the sun and, for the first time, felt them filling with tears.

On the ship in which she had left the prince there were life and noise, and she saw him and his beautiful bride searching for her. Sorrowfully they gazed at the pearly foam, as if they knew she had thrown herself into the waves. Unseen she kissed the forehead of the bride and fanned the prince, and then mounted with the other children of the air to a rosy cloud that floated above.

"After three hundred years, thus shall we float into the kingdom of heaven," said she. "And we may even get there sooner," whispered one of her companions. "Unseen we can enter the houses of men where there are children, and for every day on which we find a good child that is the joy of his parents and deserves their love, our time of probation is shortened. The child does not know, when we fly through the room, that we smile with joy at his good conduct—for we can count one year less of our three hundred years. But when we see a naughty or a wicked child we shed tears of sorrow, and for every tear a day is added to our time of trial."

BUCKWHEAT

I F YOU should chance, after a tempest, to cross a field where buckwheat is growing, you may observe that it looks black and singed, as if a flame of fire had passed over it. And should you ask the reason, a farmer will tell you, "The lightning did that."

But how is it that the lightning did it?

I will tell you what the sparrow told me, and the sparrow heard it from an aged willow which stood—and still stands for that matter—close to the field of buckwheat.

This willow is tall and venerable, though old and crippled. Its trunk is split clear through the middle, and grass and blackberry tendrils creep out through the cleft. The tree bends forward, and its branches droop like long, green hair.

In the fields around the willow grew rye, wheat, and oats—beautiful oats that, when ripe, looked like little yellow canary birds sitting on a branch. The harvest had been blessed, and the fuller the ears of grain the lower they bowed their heads in reverent humility.

There was also a field of buckwheat lying just in front of the old willow. The buckwheat did not bow its head, like the rest of the grain, but stood erect in stiff-necked pride.

"I am quite as rich as the oats," it said; "and, moreover, I am much more sightly. My flowers are as pretty as apple blossoms. It is a treat to look at me and my companions. Old willow, do you know anything more beautiful than we?"

The willow nodded his head, as much as to say, "Indeed I do!" But the buckwheat was so puffed with pride that it only said: "The stupid tree! He is so old that grass is growing out of his body."

Now there came on a dreadful storm, and the flowers of the field folded their leaves or bent their heads as it passed over them. The buckwheat flower alone stood erect in all its pride.

"Bow your heads, as we do," called the flowers.

"There is no need for me to do that," answered the buckwheat.

"Bow your head as we do," said the grain. "The angel of storms comes flying hither. He has wings that reach from the clouds to the earth; he will smite you before you have time to beg for mercy."

"But I do not choose to bow down," said the buckwheat.

"Close your flowers and fold your leaves," said the old willow. "Do not look at the lightning when the cloud breaks. Even human beings dare not do that, for in the midst of the lightning one may look straight into God's heaven. The sight strikes human beings blind, so dazzling is it. What would not happen to us, mere plants of the field, who are so much humbler, if we should dare do so?"

"So much humbler! Indeed! If there is a chance, I shall look right into God's heaven." And in its pride and haughtiness it did so. The flashes of lightning were so awful that it seemed as if the whole world were in flames.

When the tempest was over, both the grain and the flowers, greatly refreshed by the rain, again stood erect in the pure, quiet air. But the buckwheat had been burned as black as a cinder by the lightning and stood in the field like a dead, useless weed.

The old willow waved his branches to and fro in the wind, and large drops of water fell from his green leaves, as if he were shedding tears. The sparrows asked: "Why are you weeping when all around seems blest? Do you not smell the sweet perfume of flowers and bushes? The sun shines, and the clouds have passed from the sky. Why do you weep, old tree?"

Then the willow told them of the buckwheat's stubborn pride and of the punishment which followed.

I, who tell this tale, heard it from the sparrows. They told it to me one evening when I had asked them for a story.

WHAT HAPPENED TO THE THISTLE

ROUND a lordly old mansion was a beautiful, well-kept garden, full of all kinds of rare trees and flowers. Guests always expressed their delight and admiration at the sight of its wonders. The people from far and near used to come on Sundays and holidays and ask permission to see it. Even whole schools made excursions for the sole purpose of seeing its beauties.

Near the fence that separated the garden from the meadow stood an immense thistle. It was an uncommonly large and fine thistle, with several branches spreading out just above the root, and altogether was so strong and full as to make it well worthy of the name "thistle bush."

No one ever noticed it, save the old donkey that pulled the milk cart for the dairy-maids. He stood grazing in the meadow hard by and stretched his old neck to reach the thistle, saying: "You are beautiful! I should like to eat you!" But the tether was too short to allow him to reach the thistle, so he did not eat it.

There were guests at the Hall, fine, aristocratic relatives from town, and among them a young lady who had come from a long distance—all the way from Scotland. She was of old and noble family and rich in gold and lands—a bride well worth the winning, thought more than one young man to himself; yes, and their mothers thought so, too!

The young people amused themselves on the lawn, playing croquet and flitting about among the flowers, each young girl gathering a flower to put in the buttonhole of some one of the gentlemen.

The young Scotch lady looked about for a flower, but none of them seemed to please her, until, happening to glance over the fence, she espied the fine, large thistle bush, full of bluish-red, sturdy-looking flowers. She smiled as she saw it, and begged the son of the house to get one of them for her.

"That is Scotland's flower," she said; "it grows and blossoms in our coat of arms. Get that one yonder for me, please."

And he gathered the finest of the thistle flowers, though he pricked his fingers as much in doing so as if it had been growing on a wild rosebush.

She took the flower and put it in his buttonhole, which made him feel greatly honored. Each of the other young men would gladly have given up his graceful garden flower if he might have worn the one given by the delicate hands of the Scotch girl. As keenly as the son of the house felt the honor conferred upon him, the thistle felt even more highly honored. It seemed to feel dew and sunshine going through it.

"It seems I am of more consequence than I thought," it said to itself. "I ought by rights to stand inside and not outside the fence. One gets strangely placed in this world, but now I have at least one of my flowers over the fence—and not only there, but in a buttonhole!"

To each one of its buds as it opened, the thistle bush told this great event. And not many days had passed before it heard—not from the people who passed, nor yet from the twittering of little birds, but from the air, which gives out, far and wide, the sounds that it has treasured up from the shadiest walks of the beautiful garden and from the most secluded rooms at the Hall, where doors and windows are left open—that the young man who received the thistle flower from the hands of the Scottish maiden had received her heart and hand as well.

"That is my doing!" said the thistle, thinking of the flower she had given to the buttonhole. And every new flower that came was told of this wonderful event.

"Surely I shall now be taken and planted in the garden," thought the thistle. "Perhaps I shall be put into a flowerpot, for that is by far the most honorable position." It thought of this so long that it ended by saying to itself with the firm conviction of truth, "I shall be planted in a flowerpot!"

It promised every little bud that came that it also should be placed in a pot and perhaps have a place in a buttonhole—that being the highest position one could aspire to. But none of them got into a flowerpot, and still less into a gentleman's buttonhole.

They lived on light and air, and drank sunshine in the day and dew at night. They received visits from bee and hornet, who came to look for the honey in the flower, and who took the honey and left the flower.

"The good-for-nothing fellows," said the thistle bush. "I would pierce them if I could!"

The flowers drooped and faded, but new ones always came.

"You come as if you had been sent," said the thistle bush to them. "I am expecting every moment to be taken over the fence."

A couple of harmless daisies and a huge, thin plant of canary grass listened to this with the deepest respect, believing all they heard. The old donkey, that had to pull the milk cart, cast longing looks toward the blooming thistle and tried to reach it, but his tether was too short. And the thistle bush thought and thought, so much and so long, of the Scotch thistle—to whom it believed itself related—that at last it fancied it had come from Scotland and that its parents had grown into the Scottish arms.

It was a great thought, but a great thistle may well have great thoughts.

"Sometimes one is of noble race even if one does not know it," said the nettle growing close by—it had a kind of presentiment that it might be turned into muslin, if properly treated.

The summer passed, and the autumn passed; the leaves fell from the trees; the flowers came with stronger colors and less perfume; the gardener's lad sang on the other side of the fence:

"Up the hill and down the hill,
That's the way of the world still."

The young pine trees in the wood began to feel a longing for Christmas, though Christmas was still a long way off.

"Here I am still," said the thistle. "It seems that I am quite forgotten, and yet it was I who made the match. They were engaged, and now they are married—the wedding was a week ago. I do not make a single step forward, for I cannot."

Some weeks passed. The thistle had its last, solitary flower, which was large and full and growing down near the root. The wind blew coldly over it, the color faded, and all its glory disappeared, leaving only the cup of the flower, now grown to be as large as the flower of an artichoke and glistening like a silvered sunflower.

The young couple, who were now man and wife, came along the garden path, and as they passed near the fence, the bride, glancing over it, said, "Why, there stands the large thistle! it has no flowers now."

"Yes, there is still the ghost of the last one," said her husband, pointing to the silvery remains of the last flower—a flower in itself.

"How beautiful it is!" she said. "We must have one carved in the frame of our picture."

And once more the young man had to get over the fence, to break off the silvery cup of the thistle flower. It pricked his fingers for his pains, because he had called it a ghost. And then it was brought into the garden, and to the Hall, and into the drawing room. There stood a large picture—the portraits of the two, and in the bridegroom's buttonhole was painted a thistle. They talked of it and of the flower cup they had brought in with them—the last silver-shimmering thistle flower, that was to be reproduced in the carving of the frame.

The air took all their words and scattered them about, far and wide.

"What strange things happen to one!" said the thistle bush. "My first-born went to live in a buttonhole, my last-born in a frame! I wonder what is to become of me."

The old donkey, standing by the roadside, cast loving glances at the thistle and said, "Come to me, my sweetheart, for I cannot go to you; my tether is too short!"

But the thistle bush made no answer. It grew more and more thoughtful, and it thought as far ahead as Christmas, till its budding thoughts opened into flower.

"When one's children are safely housed, a mother is quite content to stay beyond the fence."

"That is true," said the sunshine; "and you will be well placed, never fear."

"In a flowerpot or in a frame?" asked the thistle.

"In a story," answered the sunshine. And here is the story!

THE PEN AND THE INKSTAND

IN A POET'S room, where his inkstand stood on the table, the remark was once made: "It is wonderful what can be brought out of an inkstand. What will come next? It is indeed wonderful."

"Yes, certainly," said the inkstand to the pen and to the other articles that stood on the table; "that's what I always say. It is wonderful and extraordinary what a number of things come out of me. It's quite incredible, and I really never know what is coming next when that man dips his pen into me. One drop out of me is enough for half a page of paper—and what cannot half a page contain?

"From me all the works of the poet are produced—all those imaginary characters whom people fancy they have known or met, and all the deep feeling, the humor, and the vivid pictures of nature. I myself don't understand how it is, for I am not acquainted with nature, but it is certainly in me. From me have gone forth to the world those wonderful descriptions of charming maidens, and of brave knights on prancing steeds; of the halt and the blind—and I know not what more, for I assure you I never think of these things."

"There you are right," said the pen, "for you don't think at all. If you did, you would see that you can only provide the means. You give the fluid, that I may place upon the paper what dwells in me and what I wish to bring to light. It is the pen that writes. No man doubts that; and indeed most people understand as much about poetry as an old inkstand."

"You have had very little experience," replied the inkstand. "You have hardly been in service a week and are already half worn out. Do you imagine you are a poet? You are only a servant, and before you came I had many like you, some of the goose family and others of English manufacture. I know a quill pen as well as I know a steel one. I have had both sorts in my service, and I shall have many more as long as *he* comes—the man who performs the mechanical part—and writes down what he obtains from me. I should like to know what will be the next thing he gets out of me."

"Inkpot!" retorted the pen, contemptuously.

Late in the evening the poet returned home from a concert, where he had been quite enchanted by the admirable performance of a famous violin player.

The player had produced from his instrument a richness of tone that sometimes sounded like tinkling water drops or rolling pearls, sometimes like the birds twittering in chorus, and then again, rising and swelling like the wind through the fir trees. The poet felt as if his own heart were weeping, but in tones of melody, like the sound of a woman's voice. These sounds seemed to come not only from the strings but from every part of the instrument. It was a wonderful performance and a difficult piece, and yet the bow seemed to glide across the strings so easily that one would think any one could do it. The violin and the bow seemed independent of their master who guided them. It was as if soul and spirit had been breathed into the instrument. And the audience forgot the performer in the beautiful sounds he produced.

Not so the poet; he remembered him and wrote down his thoughts on the subject: "How foolish it would be for the violin and the bow to boast of their performance, and yet we men often commit that folly. The poet, the artist, the man of science in his laboratory, the general—we all do it, and yet we are only the instruments which the Almighty uses. To Him alone the honor is due. We have nothing in ourselves of which we should be proud." Yes, this is what the poet wrote. He wrote it in the form of a parable and called it "The Master and the Instruments."

"That is what you get, madam," said the pen to the inkstand when the two were alone again. "Did you hear him read aloud what I had written down?"

"Yes, what I gave you to write," retorted the inkstand. "That was a cut at you, because of your conceit. To think that you could not understand that you were being quizzed! I gave you a cut from within me. Surely I must know my own satire."

"Ink pitcher!" cried the pen.

"Writing stick!" retorted the inkstand. And each of them felt satisfied that he had given a good answer. It is pleasing to be convinced that you have settled a matter by your reply; it is something to make you sleep well. And they both slept well over it.

But the poet did not sleep. Thoughts rose within him, like the tones of the violin, falling like pearls or rushing like the strong wind through the forest. He understood his own heart in these thoughts; they were as a ray from the mind of the Great Master of all minds.

"To Him be all the honor."

THE TEAPOT

THERE was once a proud teapot; it was proud of being porcelain, proud of its long spout, proud of its broad handle. It had something before and behind,—the spout before and the handle behind,—and that was what it talked about. But it did not talk of its lid, which was cracked and riveted; these were defects, and one does not talk of one's defects, for there are plenty of others to do that. The cups, the cream pot, and the sugar bowl, the whole tea service, would think much oftener of the lid's imperfections—and talk about them—than of the sound handle and the remarkable spout. The teapot knew it.

"I know you," it said within itself. "I know, too, my imperfection, and I am well aware that in that very thing is seen my humility, my modesty. Imperfections we all have, but we also have compensations. The cups have a handle, the sugar bowl a lid; I have both, and one thing besides, in front, which they can never have. I have a spout, and that makes me the queen of the tea table. I spread abroad a blessing on thirsting mankind, for in me the Chinese leaves are brewed in the boiling, tasteless water."

All this said the teapot in its fresh young life. It stood on the table that was spread for tea; it was lifted by a very delicate hand, but the delicate hand was awkward. The teapot fell, the spout snapped off, and the handle snapped off. The lid was no worse to speak of; the worst had been spoken of that.

The teapot lay in a swoon on the floor, while the boiling water ran out of it. It was a horrid shame, but the worst was that everybody jeered at it; they jeered at the teapot and not at the awkward hand.

"I never shall forget that experience," said the teapot, when it afterward talked of its life. "I was called an invalid, and placed in a corner, and the next day was given to a woman who begged for victuals. I fell into poverty, and stood dumb both outside and in. But then, just as I was, began my better life. One can be one thing and still become quite another.

"Earth was placed in me. For a teapot, this is the same as being buried, but in the earth was placed a flower bulb. Who placed it there, who gave it, I know not; but given it was, and it became a compensation for the Chinese leaves and the boiling water, a compensation for the broken handle and spout.

"And the bulb lay in the earth, the bulb lay in me; it became my heart, my living heart, such as I had never before possessed. There was life in me, power and might. The heart pulsed, and the bulb put forth sprouts; it was the springing up of thoughts and feelings which burst forth into flower.

"I saw it, I bore it, I forgot myself in its delight. Blessed is it to forget oneself in another. The flower gave me no thanks; it did not think of me. It was admired and praised, and I was glad at that. How happy it must have been! One day I heard some one say that the flower deserved a better pot. I was thumped hard on my back, which was a great affliction, and the flower was put into a better pot. I was thrown out into the yard, where I lie as an old potsherd. But I have the memory, and that I can never lose."

SOUP FROM A SAUSAGE SKEWER

E HAD such an excellent dinner yesterday," said an old lady-mouse to another who had not been present at the feast. "I sat number twenty-one below the mouse-king, which was not a bad place. Shall I tell you what we had? Everything was excellent—moldy bread, tallow candle, and sausage.

"Then, when we had finished that course, the same came on all over again; it was as good as two feasts. We were very sociable, and there was as much joking and fun as if we had been all of one family circle. Nothing was left but the sausage skewers, and this formed a subject of conversation till at last some one used the expression, 'Soup from sausage sticks'; or, as the people in the neighboring country call it, 'Soup from a sausage skewer.'

"Every one had heard the expression, but no one had ever tasted the soup, much less prepared it. A capital toast was drunk to the inventor of the soup, and some one said he ought to be made a relieving officer to the poor. Was not that witty?

"Then the old mouse-king rose and promised that the young lady-mouse who should learn how best to prepare this much-admired and savory soup should be his queen, and a year and a day should be allowed for the purpose."

"That was not at all a bad proposal," said the other mouse; "but how is the soup made?"

"Ah, that is more than I can tell you. All the young lady-mice were asking the same question. They wish very much to be the queen, but they do not want to take the trouble to go out into the world to learn how to make soup, which it is absolutely necessary to do first.

"It is not every one who would care to leave her family or her happy corner by the fireside at home, even to be made queen. It is not always easy in foreign lands to find bacon and cheese rind every day, and, after all, it is not pleasant to endure hunger and perhaps be eaten alive by the cat."

Probably some such thoughts as these discouraged the majority from going out into the world to collect the required information. Only four mice gave notice that they were ready to set out on the journey.

They were young and sprightly, but poor. Each of them wished to visit one of the four divisions of the world, to see which of them would be most favored by fortune. Each took a sausage skewer as a traveler's staff and to remind her of the object of her journey.

They left home early in May, and none of them returned till the first of May in the following year, and then only three of them. Nothing was seen or heard of the fourth, although the day of decision was close at hand. "Ah, yes, there is always some trouble mingled with the greatest pleasure," said the mouse-king. But he gave orders that all the mice within a circle of many miles should be invited at once.

They were to assemble in the kitchen, and the three travelers were to stand in a row before them, and a sausage skewer covered with crape was to stand in the place of the missing mouse. No one dared express an opinion until the king spoke and desired one of them to proceed with her story. And now we shall hear what she said.

WHAT THE FIRST LITTLE MOUSE SAW AND HEARD ON HER TRAVELS

"When I first went out into the world," said the little mouse, "I fancied, as so many of my age do, that I already knew everything—but it was not so. It takes years to acquire great knowledge.

"I went at once to sea, in a ship bound for the north. I had been told that the ship's cook must know how to prepare every dish at sea, and it is easy enough to do that with plenty of sides of bacon, and large tubs of salt meat and musty flour. There I found plenty of delicate food but no opportunity to learn how to make soup from a sausage skewer.

"We sailed on for many days and nights; the ship rocked fearfully, and we did not escape without a wetting. As soon as we arrived at the port to which the ship was bound, I left it and went on shore at a place far towards the north. It is a wonderful thing to leave your own little corner at home, to hide yourself in a ship where there are sure to be some nice snug corners for shelter, then suddenly to find yourself thousands of miles away in a foreign land.

"I saw large, pathless forests of pine and birch trees, which smelt so strong that I sneezed and thought of sausage. There were great lakes also, which looked as black as ink at a distance but were quite clear when I came close to them. Large swans were floating upon them, and I thought at first they were only foam, they lay so still; but when I saw them walk and fly, I knew directly what they were. They belonged to the goose species. One could see that by their walk, for no one can successfully disguise his family descent.

"I kept with my own kind and associated with the forest and field mice, who, however, knew very little—especially about what I wanted to know and what had actually made me travel abroad.

"The idea that soup could be made from a sausage skewer was so startling to them that it was repeated from one to another through the whole forest. They declared that the problem would never be solved—that the thing was an impossibility. How little I thought that in this place, on the very first night, I should be initiated into the manner of its preparation!

"It was the height of summer, which the mice told me was the reason that the forest smelt so strong, and that the herbs were so fragrant, and that the lakes with the white, swimming swans were so dark and yet so clear.

"On the margin of the wood, near several houses, a pole as large as the mainmast of a ship had been erected, and from the summit hung wreaths of flowers and fluttering ribbons. It was the Maypole. Lads and lasses danced round it and tried to outdo the violins of the musicians with their singing. They were as gay as ever at sunset and in the moonlight, but I took no part in the merrymaking. What has a little mouse to do with a Maypole dance? I sat in the soft moss and held my sausage skewer tight. The moon shone particularly bright on one spot where stood a tree covered with very fine moss. I may almost venture to say that it was as fine and soft as the fur of the mouse-king, but it was green, which is a color very agreeable to the eye.

"All at once I saw the most charming little people marching towards me. They did not reach higher than my knee, although they looked like human beings but were better proportioned. They called themselves elves, and wore clothes that were very delicate and fine, for they were made of the leaves of flowers, trimmed with the wings of flies and gnats. The effect was by no means bad.

"They seemed to be seeking something—I knew not what, till at last one of them espied me. They came towards me, and the foremost pointed to my sausage skewer, saying: 'There, that is just what we want. See, it is pointed at the top; is it not capital?' The longer he looked at my pilgrim's staff the more delighted he became.

"'I will lend it to you,' said I, 'but not to keep.'

"'Oh, no, we won't keep it!' they all cried. Then they seized the skewer, which I gave up to them, and dancing with it to the tree covered with delicate moss, set it up in the middle of the green. They wanted a Maypole, and the one they now had seemed made especially for them. This they decorated so beautifully that it was quite dazzling to look at. Little spiders spun golden threads around it, and it was hung with fluttering veils and flags, as delicately white as snow glittering in the moonlight. Then they took colors from the butterfly's wing, sprinkling them over the white drapery until it gleamed as if covered with flowers and diamonds, and I could no longer recognize my sausage skewer. Such a Maypole as this has never been seen in all the world.

"Then came a great company of real elves. Nothing could be finer than their clothes. They invited me to be present at the feast, but I was to keep at a certain distance because I was too large for them. Then began music that sounded like a thousand glass bells, and was so full and strong that I thought it must be the song of the swans. I fancied also that I heard the voices of the cuckoo and the blackbird, and it seemed at last as if the whole forest sent forth glorious melodies—the voices of children, the tinkling of bells, and the songs of the birds. And all this wonderful melody came from the elfin Maypole. My sausage peg was a complete peal of bells. I could scarcely believe that so much could have been produced from it, till I remembered into what hands it had fallen. I was so much affected that I wept tears such as a little mouse can weep, but they were tears of joy.

"The night was far too short for me; there are no long nights there in summer, as we often have in this part of the world. When the morning dawned and the gentle breeze rippled the glassy mirror of the forest lake, all the delicate veils and flags fluttered away into thin air. The waving garlands of the spider's web, the hanging bridges and galleries, or whatever else they may be called, vanished away as if they had never been. Six elves brought me back my sausage skewer and at the same time asked me to make any request, which they would grant if it lay in their power. So I begged them, if they could, to tell me how to make soup from a sausage skewer.

"'How do we make it?' asked the chief of the elves, with a smile. 'Why, you have just seen us. You scarcely knew your sausage skewer again, I am sure.'

"'They think themselves very wise,' thought I to myself. Then I told them all about it, and why I had traveled so far, and also what promise had been made at home to the one who should discover the method of preparing this soup.

"'What good will it do the mouse-king or our whole mighty kingdom,' I asked, 'for me to have seen all these beautiful things? I cannot shake the sausage peg and say, "Look, here is the skewer, and now the soup will come." That would only produce a dish to be served when people were keeping a fast.'

"Then the elf dipped his finger into the cup of a violet and said, 'Look, I will anoint your pilgrim's staff, so that when you return to your home and enter the king's castle, you have only to touch the king with your staff and violets will spring forth, even in the coldest winter time. I think I have given you something worth carrying home, and a little more than something.'"

Before the little mouse explained what this something more was, she stretched her staff toward the king, and as it touched him the most beautiful bunch of violets sprang forth and filled the place with their perfume. The smell was so powerful that the mouse-king ordered the mice who stood nearest the chimney to thrust their tails into the fire that there might be a smell of burning, for the perfume of the violets was overpowering and not the sort of scent that every one liked.

"But what was the something more, of which you spoke just now?" asked the mouse-king.

"Why," answered the little mouse, "I think it is what they call 'effect.'" Thereupon she turned the staff round, and behold, not a single flower was to be seen on it! She now held only the naked skewer, and lifted it up as a conductor lifts his baton at a concert.

"Violets, the elf told me," continued the mouse, "are for the sight, the smell, and the touch; so we have only to produce the effect of hearing and tasting." Then, as the little mouse beat time with her staff, there came sounds of music; not such music as was heard in the forest, at the elfin feast, but such as is often heard in the kitchen—the sounds of boiling and roasting. It came quite suddenly, like wind rushing through the chimneys, and it seemed as if every pot and kettle were boiling over.

The fire shovel clattered down on the brass fender, and then, quite as suddenly, all was still,—nothing could be heard but the light, vapory song of the teakettle, which was quite wonderful to hear, for no one could rightly distinguish whether the kettle was just beginning to boil or just going to stop. And the little pot steamed, and the great pot simmered, but without any regard for each other; indeed, there seemed no sense in the pots at all. As the little mouse waved her baton still more wildly, the pots foamed and threw up bubbles and boiled over, while again the wind roared and whistled through the chimney, and at last there was such a terrible hubbub that the little mouse let her stick fall.

"That is a strange sort of soup," said the mouse-king. "Shall we not now hear about the preparation?"

"That is all," answered the little mouse, with a bow.

"That all!" said the mouse-king; "then we shall be glad to hear what information the next may have to give us."

WHAT THE SECOND MOUSE HAD TO TELL

"I was born in the library, at a castle," said the second mouse. "Very few members of our family ever had the good fortune to get into the dining room, much less into the storeroom. To-day and while on my journey are the only times I have ever seen a kitchen. We were often obliged to suffer hunger in the library, but we gained a great deal of knowledge. The rumor reached us of the royal prize offered to those who should be able to make soup from a sausage skewer.

"Then my old grandmother sought out a manuscript,—which she herself could not read, to be sure, but she had heard it read,—and in it were written these words, 'Those who are poets can make soup of sausage skewers.' She asked me if I was a poet. I told her I felt myself quite innocent of any such pretensions. Then she said I must go out and make myself a poet. I asked again what I should be required to do, for it seemed to me quite as difficult as to find out how to make soup of a sausage skewer. My grandmother had heard a great deal of reading in her day, and she told me that three principal qualifications were necessary—understanding, imagination, and feeling. 'If you can manage to acquire these three, you will be a poet, and the sausage-skewer soup will seem quite simple to you.'

"So I went forth into the world and turned my steps toward the west, that I might become a poet. Understanding is the most important matter of all. I was sure of that, for the other two qualifications are not thought much of; so I went first to seek understanding. Where was I to find it?

"'Go to the ant and learn wisdom,' said the great Jewish king. I learned this from living in a library. So I went straight on till I came to the first great ant hill. There I set myself to watch, that I might become wise. The ants are a very respectable people; they are wisdom itself. All they do is like the working of a sum in arithmetic, which comes right. 'To work, and to lay eggs,' say they, 'and to provide for posterity, is to live out your time properly.' This they truly do. They are divided into clean and dirty ants, and their rank is indicated by a number. The ant-queen is number ONE. Her opinion is the only correct one on everything, and she seems to have in her the wisdom of the whole world. This was just what I wished to acquire. She said a great deal that was no doubt very clever—yet it sounded like nonsense to me. She said the ant hill was the loftiest thing in the world, although close to the mound stood a tall tree which no one could deny was loftier, much loftier. Yet she made no mention of the tree.

"One evening an ant lost herself on this tree. She had crept up the stem, not nearly to the top but higher than any ant had ever ventured, and when at last she returned home she said that she had found something in her travels much higher than the ant hill. The rest of the ants considered this an insult to the whole community, and condemned her to wear a muzzle and live in perpetual solitude.

"A short time afterwards another ant got on the tree and made the same journey and the same discovery. But she spoke of it cautiously and indefinitely, and as she was one of the superior ants and very much respected, they believed her. And when she died they erected an egg-shell as a monument to her memory, for they cultivated a great respect for science.

"I saw," said the little mouse, "that the ants were always running to and fro with their burdens on their backs. Once I saw one of them, who had dropped her load, try very hard to raise it again, but she did not succeed. Two others came up and tried with all their strength to help her, till they nearly dropped their own burdens. Then they were obliged to stop a moment, for every one must think of himself first. The ant-queen remarked that their conduct that day showed that they possessed kind hearts and good understanding. 'These two qualities,' she continued, 'place us ants in the highest degree above all other reasonable beings. Understanding must therefore stand out prominently among us, and my wisdom is greatest.' So saying, she raised herself on her two hind legs, that no one else might be mistaken for her. I could not, therefore, have made a mistake, so I ate her up. We are to go to the ants to learn wisdom, and I had secured the queen.

"I now turned and went nearer to the lofty tree already mentioned, which was an oak. It had a tall trunk, with a wide-spreading top, and was very old. I knew that a living being dwelt here, a dryad, as she is called, who is born with the tree and dies with it. I had heard this in the library, and here was just such a tree and in it an oak maiden. She uttered a terrible scream when she caught sight of me so near to her. Like women, she was very much afraid of mice, and she had more real cause for fear than they have, for I might have gnawed through the tree on which her life depended.

"I spoke to her in a friendly manner and begged her to take courage. At last she took me up in her delicate hand, and I told me what had brought me out into the world. She told me that perhaps on that very evening she would be able to obtain for me one of the two treasures for which I was seeking. She told me that Phantæsus, the genius of the imagination, was her very dear friend; that he was as beautiful as the god of love; that he rested many an hour with her under the leafy boughs of the tree, which then rustled and waved more than ever. He called her his dryad, she said, and the tree his tree, for the grand old oak with its gnarled trunk was just to his taste. The root, which spread deep into the earth, and the top, which rose high in the fresh air, knew the value of the drifting snow, the keen wind, and the warm sunshine, as it ought to be known. 'Yes,' continued the dryad, 'the birds sing up above in the branches and talk to each other about the beautiful fields they have visited in foreign lands. On one of the withered boughs a stork has built his nest—it is beautifully arranged, and, besides, it is pleasant to hear a little about the land of the pyramids. All this pleases Phantæsus, but it is not enough for him. I am obliged to relate to him of my life in the woods and to go back to my childhood, when I was little and the tree so small and delicate that a stinging nettle could overshadow it, and I have to tell everything that has happened since then until now, when the tree is so large and strong. Sit you down now under the green bindwood and pay attention. When Phantæsus comes I will find an opportunity to lay hold of his wing and to pull out one of the little feathers. That feather you shall have. A better was never given to any poet, and it will be quite enough for you.'

"And when Phantæsus came the feather was plucked," said the little mouse, "and I seized and put it in water and kept it there till it was quite soft. It was very heavy and indigestible, but I managed to nibble it up at last. It is not so easy to nibble oneself into a poet, there are so many things to get through. Now, however, I had two of them, understanding and imagination, and through these I knew that the third was to be found in the library.

"A great man has said and written that there are novels whose sole and only use appears to be to attempt to relieve mankind of overflowing tears—a kind of sponge, in fact, for sucking up feelings and emotions. I remembered a few of these books. They had always appeared tempting to the appetite, for they had been much read and were so greasy that they must have absorbed no end of emotions in themselves.

"I retraced my steps to the library and literally devoured a whole novel—that is, properly speaking, the interior, or soft part of it. The crust, or binding, I left. When I had digested not only this, but a second, I felt a stirring within me. I then ate a small piece of a third romance and felt myself a poet. I said it to myself and told others the same. I had headache and backache and I cannot tell what aches besides. I thought over all the stories that may be said to be connected with sausage pegs; and all that has ever been written about skewers, and sticks, and staves, and splinters came to my thoughts—the ant-queen must have had a wonderfully clear understanding. I remembered the man who placed in his mouth a white stick, by which he could make himself and the stick invisible. I thought of sticks as hobbyhorses, staves of music or rime, of breaking a stick over a man's back, and of Heaven knows how many more phrases of the same sort, relating to sticks, staves, and skewers. All my thoughts ran on skewers, sticks of wood, and staves. As I am at last a poet and have worked terribly hard to make myself one, I can of course make poetry on anything. I shall therefore be able to wait upon you every day in the week with a poetical history of a skewer. And that is my soup."

"In that case," said the mouse-king, "we will hear what the third mouse has to say."

"Squeak, squeak," cried a little mouse at the kitchen door. It was the fourth, and not the third, of the four who were contending for the prize, the one whom the rest supposed to be dead. She shot in like an arrow and overturned the sausage peg that had been covered with crape. She had been running day and night, for although she had traveled in a baggage train, by railway, yet she had arrived almost too late. She pressed forward, looking very much ruffled.

She had lost her sausage skewer but not her voice, and she began to speak at once, as if they waited only for her and would hear her only—as if nothing else in the world were of the least consequence. She spoke out so clearly and plainly, and she had come in so suddenly, that no one had time to stop her or to say a word while she was speaking. This is what she said.

WHAT THE FOURTH MOUSE, WHO SPOKE BEFORE THE THIRD, HAD TO TELL

"I started off at once to the largest town," said she, "but the name of it has escaped me. I have a very bad memory for names. I was carried from the railway, with some goods on which duties had not been paid, to the jail, and on arriving I made my escape, running into the house of the keeper. He was speaking of his prisoners, especially of one who had uttered thoughtless words. These words had given rise to other words, and at length they were written down and registered. 'The whole affair is like making soup of sausage skewers,' said he, 'but the soup may cost him his neck.'

"Now this raised in me an interest for the prisoner," continued the little mouse, "and I watched my opportunity and slipped into his apartment, for there is a mousehole to be found behind every closed door.

"The prisoner, who had a great beard and large, sparkling eyes, looked pale. There was a lamp burning, but the walls were so black that they only looked the blacker for it. The prisoner scratched pictures and verses with white chalk on the black walls, but I did not read the verses. I think he found his confinement wearisome, so that I was a welcome guest. He enticed me with bread crumbs, with whistling, and with gentle words, and seemed so friendly towards me that by degrees I gained confidence in him and we became friends. He divided his bread and water with me and gave me cheese and sausage, and I began to love him. Altogether, I must own that it was a very pleasant intimacy. He let me run about on his hand, on his arm, into his sleeve, and even into his beard. He called me his little friend, and I forgot for what I had come out into the world; forgot my sausage skewer, which I had laid in a crack in the floor, where it is still lying. I wished to stay with him always, for I knew that if I went away, the poor prisoner would have no one to be his friend, which is a sad thing.

"I stayed, but he did not. He spoke to me so mournfully for the last time, gave me double as much bread and cheese as usual, and kissed his hand to me. Then he went away and never came back. I know nothing more of his history.

"The jailer took possession of me now. He said something about soup from a sausage skewer, but I could not trust him. He took me in his hand, certainly, but it was to place me in a cage like a treadmill. Oh, how dreadful it was! I had to run round and round without getting any farther, and only to make everybody laugh.

"The jailer's granddaughter was a charming little thing. She had merry eyes, curly hair like the brightest gold, and such a smiling mouth.

"'You poor little mouse,' said she one day, as she peeped into my cage, 'I will set you free.' She then drew forth the iron fastening, and I sprang out on the window-sill, and from thence to the roof. Free! free! that was all I could think of, and not of the object of my journey.

"It grew dark, and as night was coming on I found a lodging in an old tower, where dwelt a watchman and an owl. I had no confidence in either of them, least of all in the owl, which is like a cat and has a great failing, for she eats mice. One may, however, be mistaken sometimes, and I was now, for this was a respectable and well-educated old owl, who knew more than the watchman and even as much as I did myself. The young owls made a great fuss about everything, but the only rough words she would say to them were, 'You had better go and try to make some soup from sausage skewers.' She was very indulgent and loving to her own children. Her conduct gave me such confidence in her that from the crack where I sat I called out 'Squeak.'

"This confidence pleased her so much that she assured me she would take me under her own protection and that not a creature should do me harm. The fact was, she wickedly meant to keep me in reserve for her own eating in the winter, when food would be scarce. Yet she was a very clever lady-owl. She explained to me that the watchman could only hoot with the horn that hung loose at his side and that he was so terribly proud of it that he imagined himself an owl in the tower, wanted to do great things, but only succeeded in small—soup from a sausage skewer.

"Then I begged the owl to give me the recipe for this soup. 'Soup from a sausage skewer,' said she, 'is only a proverb amongst mankind and may be understood in many ways. Each believes his own way the best, and, after all, the proverb signifies nothing.' 'Nothing!' I exclaimed. I was quite struck. Truth is not always agreeable, but truth is above everything else, as the old owl said. I thought over all this and saw quite plainly that if truth was really so far above everything else, it must be much more valuable than soup from a sausage skewer. So I hastened to get away, that I might be in time and bring what was highest and best and above everything—namely, the truth.

"The mice are enlightened people, and the mouse-king is above them all. He is therefore capable of making me queen for the sake of truth."

"Your truth is a falsehood," said the mouse who had not yet spoken. "I can prepare the soup, and I mean to do so."

HOW IT WAS PREPARED

"I did not travel," said the third mouse, "I stayed in this country; that was the right way. One gains nothing by traveling. Everything can be acquired here quite as easily, so I stayed at home. I have not obtained what I know from supernatural beings; I have neither swallowed it nor learned it from conversing with owls. I have gained it all from my own reflections and thoughts. Will you now set the kettle on the fire—so? Now pour the water in, quite full up to the brim; place it on the fire; make up a good blaze; keep it burning, that the water may boil, for it must boil over and over. There, now I throw in the skewer. Will the mouse-king be pleased now to dip his tail into the boiling water and stir it round with the tail? The longer the king stirs it the stronger the soup will become. Nothing more is necessary, only to stir it."

"Can no one else do this?" asked the king.

"No," said the mouse; "only in the tail of the mouse-king is this power contained."

And the water boiled and bubbled, as the mouse-king stood close beside the kettle. It seemed rather a dangerous performance, but he turned round and put out his tail, as mice do in a dairy when they wish to skim the cream from a pan of milk with their tails and afterwards lick it off. But the mouse-king's tail had only just touched the hot steam when he sprang away from the chimney in a great hurry, exclaiming:

"Oh, certainly, by all means, you must be my queen. We will let the soup question rest till our golden wedding, fifty years hence, so that the poor in my kingdom who are then to have plenty of food will have something to look forward to for a long time, with great joy."

And very soon the wedding took place. Many of the mice, however, as they were returning home, said that the soup could not be properly called "soup from a sausage skewer," but "soup from a mouse's tail." They acknowledged that some of the stories were very well told, but thought that the whole might have been managed differently.

WHAT THE GOODMAN DOES IS ALWAYS RIGHT

I WILL tell you a story that was told to me when I was a little boy. Every time I think of this story it seems to me more and more charming; for it is with stories as it is with many people—they become better as they grow older.

I have no doubt that you have been in the country and seen a very old farmhouse, with thatched roof, and mosses and small plants growing wild upon it. There is a stork's nest on the ridge of the gable, for we cannot do without the stork. The walls of the house are sloping, and the windows are low, and only one of the latter is made to open. The baking oven sticks out of the wall like a great knob. An elder tree hangs over the palings, and beneath its branches, at the foot of the paling, is a pool of water in which a few ducks are sporting. There is a yard dog, too, that barks at all comers.

Just such a farmhouse as this stood in a country lane, and in it dwelt an old couple, a peasant and his wife. Small as their possessions were, they had one thing they could not do without, and that was a horse, which contrived to live upon the grass found by the side of the highroad. The old peasant rode into the town upon this horse, and his neighbors often borrowed it of him and paid for the loan of it by rendering some service to the old couple. Yet after a time the old people thought it would be as well to sell the horse or exchange it for something which might be more useful to them. But what should this *something* be?

And then our peasant ... continued his way.

"You will know best, old man," said the wife. "It is fair day to-day; so ride into town and get rid of the horse for money or make a good exchange. Whichever you do will please me; so ride to the fair."

She fastened his neckerchief for him, for she could do that better than he could and she could also tie it very prettily in a double bow. She also smoothed his hat round and round with the palm of her hand and gave him a kiss. Then he rode away upon the horse that was to be sold, or bartered for something else. Yes, the goodman knew what he was about. The sun shone with great heat, and not a cloud was to be seen in the sky. The road was very dusty, for many people, all going to the fair, were driving, riding, or walking up-on it. There was no shelter anywhere from the hot sun. Among the crowd a man came trudging along, driving a cow to the fair. The cow was as beautiful a creature as any cow could be.

"She gives good milk, I am certain," said the peasant to himself. "That would be a very good exchange: the cow for the horse. Halloo there! you with the cow," he said. "I tell you what, I dare say a horse is of more value than a cow; but I don't care for that. A cow will be more useful to me, so if you like we'll exchange."

"To be sure I will," said the man.

Accordingly the exchange was made. When the matter was settled the peasant might have turned back, for he had done the business he came to do. But having made up his mind to go to the fair, he determined to do so, if only to have a look at it. So on he went to the town with his cow. Leading the animal, he strode on sturdily, and, after a short time, overtook a man who was driving a sheep. It was a good fat sheep, with a fine fleece on its back.

"I should like to have that fellow," said the peasant to himself. "There is plenty of grass for him by our palings, and in the winter we could keep him in the room with us. Perhaps it would be more profitable to have a sheep than a cow. Shall I exchange?"

The man with the sheep was quite ready, and the bargain was quickly made. And then our peasant continued his way on the highroad with his sheep. Soon after this, he over-took another man, who had come into the road from a field, and was carrying a large goose under his arm.

"What a heavy creature you have there!" said the peasant. "It has plenty of feathers and plenty of fat, and would look well tied to a string, or paddling in the water at our place. That would be very useful to my old woman; she could make all sorts of profit out of it. How often she has said, 'If we only had a goose!' Now here is an opportunity, and, if possible, I will get it for her. Shall we exchange? I will give you my sheep for your goose, and thanks into the bargain."

The other had not the least objection, and accordingly the exchange was made, and our peasant became possessor of the goose. By this time he had arrived very near the town. The crowd on the highroad had been gradually increasing, and there was quite a rush of men and cattle. The cattle walked on the path and by the palings, and at the turn-pike gate they even walked into the toll keeper's potato field, where one fowl was strutting about with a string tied to its leg, lest it should take fright at the crowd and run away and get lost. The tail feathers of this fowl were very short, and it winked with both its eyes, and looked very cunning as it said, "Cluck, cluck." What were the thoughts of the fowl as it said this I cannot tell you, but as soon as our good man saw it, he thought, "Why, that's the finest fowl I ever saw in my life; it's finer than our parson's brood hen, upon my word. I should like to have that fowl. Fowls can always pick up a few grains that lie about, and almost keep themselves. I think it would be a good exchange if I could get it for my goose. Shall we exchange?" he asked the toll keeper.

"Exchange?" repeated the man. "Well, it would not be a bad thing."

So they made an exchange; the toll keeper at the turnpike gate kept the goose, and the peasant carried off the fowl. Now he really had done a great deal of business on his way to the fair, and he was hot and tired. He wanted something to eat, and a glass of ale to refresh himself; so he turned his steps to an inn. He was just about to enter, when the ostler came out, and they met at the door. The ostler was carrying a sack. "What have you in that sack?" asked the peasant.

"Rotten apples," answered the ostler; "a whole sackful of them. They will do to feed the pigs with."

"Why, that will be terrible waste," the peasant replied. "I should like to take them home to my old woman. Last year the old apple tree by the grassplot bore only one apple, and we kept it in the cupboard till it was quite withered and rotten. It was property, my old woman said. Here she would see a great deal of property—a whole sackful. I should like to show them to her."

"What will you give me for the sackful?" asked the ostler.

"What will I give? Well, I will give you my fowl in exchange."

So he gave up the fowl and received the apples, which he carried into the inn parlor. He leaned the sack carefully against the stove, and then went to the table. But the stove was hot, and he had not thought of that. Many guests were present—horse-dealers, cattle-drovers, and two Englishmen. The Englishmen were so rich that their pockets bulged and seemed ready to burst; and they could bet too, as you shall hear. Hiss—s—s, hiss—s—s. What could that be by the stove? The apples were beginning to roast. "What is that?" asked one.

"Why, do you know—" said our peasant, and then he told them the whole story of the horse, which he had exchanged for a cow, and all the rest of it, down to the apples.

"Well, your old woman will give it to you when you get home," said one of the Englishmen. "Won't there be a noise?"

"What! Give me what?" said the peasant. "Why, she will kiss me, and say, 'What the goodman does is always right.'"

"Let us lay a wager on it," said the Englishman. "We'll wager you a ton of coined gold, a hundred pounds to the hundredweight."

"No, a bushel will be enough," replied the peasant. "I can only set a bushel of apples against it, and I'll throw myself and my old woman into the bargain. That will pile up the measure, I fancy."

"Done! taken!" and so the bet was made.

Then the landlord's coach came to the door, and the two Englishmen and the peasant got in, and away they drove. Soon they had stopped at the peasant's hut. "Good evening, old woman."

"Good evening, old man."

"I've made the exchange."

"Ah, well, you understand what you're about," said the woman. Then she embraced him, and paid no attention to the strangers, nor did she notice the sack.

"I got a cow in exchange for the horse."

"Oh, how delightful!" said she. "Now we shall have plenty of milk, and butter, and cheese on the table. That was a capital exchange."

"Yes, but I changed the cow for a sheep."

"Ah, better still!" cried the wife. "You always think of everything; we have just enough pasture for a sheep. Ewe's milk and cheese, woolen jackets and stockings! The cow could not give all these, and her hairs only fall off. How you think of everything!"

"But I changed away the sheep for a goose."

"Then we shall have roast goose to eat this year. You dear old man, you are always thinking of something to please me. This is delightful. We can let the goose walk about with a string tied to her leg, so that she will get fatter still before we roast her."

"But I gave away the goose for a fowl."

"A fowl! Well, that was a good exchange," replied the woman. "The fowl will lay eggs and hatch them, and we shall have chickens. We shall soon have a poultry yard. Oh, this is just what I was wishing for!"

"Yes, but I exchanged the fowl for a sack of shriveled apples."

"What! I must really give you a kiss for that!" exclaimed the wife. "My dear, good husband, now I'll tell you something. Do you know, almost as soon as you left me this morning, I began thinking of what I could give you nice for supper this evening, and then I thought of fried eggs and bacon, with sweet herbs. I had eggs and bacon but lacked the herbs, so I went over to the schoolmaster's. I knew they had plenty of herbs, but the schoolmistress is very mean, although she can smile so sweetly. I begged her to lend me a handful of herbs. 'Lend!' she exclaimed, 'I have nothing to lend. I could not even lend you a shriveled apple, my dear woman.' But now I can lend her ten, or a whole sackful, for which I'm very glad. It makes me laugh to think of it." Then she gave him a hearty kiss.

"Well, I like all this," said both the Englishmen; "always going down the hill and yet always merry. It's worth the money to see it." So they paid a hundredweight of gold to the peasant who, whatever he did, was not scolded but kissed.

Yes, it always pays best when the wife sees and maintains that her husband knows best and that whatever he does is right.

This is a story which I heard when I was a child. And now you have heard it, too, and know that "What the goodman does is always right."

THE OLD STREET LAMP

ID you ever hear the story of the old street lamp? It is not remarkably interesting, but for once you may as well listen to it.

It was a most respectable old lamp, which had seen many, many years of service and now was to retire with a pension. It was this very evening at its post for the last time, giving light to the street. Its feelings were something like those of an old dancer at the theater who is dancing for the last time and knows that on the morrow she will be in her garret, alone and forgotten.

The lamp had very great anxiety about the next day, for it knew that it had to appear for the first time at the town hall to be inspected by the mayor and the council, who were to decide whether it was fit for further service; whether it was good enough to be used to light the inhabitants of one of the suburbs, or in the country, at some factory. If the lamp could not be used for one of these purposes, it would be sent at once to an iron foundry to be melted down. In this latter case it might be turned into anything, and it wondered very much whether it would then be able to remember that it had once been a street lamp. This troubled it exceedingly.

Whatever might happen, it seemed certain that the lamp would be separated from the watchman and his wife, whose family it looked upon as its own. The lamp had first been hung up on the very evening that the watchman, then a robust young man, had entered upon the duties of his office. Ah, well! it was a very long time since one became a lamp and the other a watchman. His wife had some little pride in those days; she condescended to glance at the lamp only when she passed by in the evening—never in the daytime. But in later years, when all of them—the watchman, the wife, and the lamp—had grown old, she had attended to it, cleaning it and keeping it supplied with oil. The old people were thoroughly honest; they had never cheated the lamp of a single drop of the oil provided for it.

This was the lamp's last night in the street, and to-morrow it must go to the town hall—two very dark things to think of. No wonder it did not burn brightly. How many persons it had lighted on their way, and how much it had seen! As much, very likely, as the mayor and corporation themselves! None of these thoughts were uttered aloud, however, for the lamp was good and honorable and would not willingly do harm to any one, especially to those in authority. As one thing after another was recalled to its mind, the light would flash up with sudden brightness. At such moments the lamp had a conviction that it would be remembered.

"There was a handsome young man, once," thought the lamp; "it is certainly a long while ago, but I remember that he had a little note, written on pink paper with a gold edge. The writing was elegant, evidently a lady's. Twice he read it through, and kissed it, and then looked up at me with eyes that said quite plainly, 'I am the happiest of men!' Only he and I know what was written on this, his first letter from his lady-love. Ah, yes, and there was another pair of eyes that I remember; it is really wonderful how the thoughts jump from one thing to another! A funeral passed through the street. A young and beautiful woman lay on a bier decked with garlands of flowers, and attended by torches which quite overpowered my light. All along the street stood the people from the houses, in crowds, ready to join the procession. But when the torches had passed from before me and I could look around, I saw one person standing alone, leaning against my post and weeping. Never shall I forget the sorrowful eyes that looked up at me."

These and similar reflections occupied the old street lamp on this the last time that its light would shine. The sentry, when he is relieved from his post, knows, at least, who will be his successor, and may whisper a few words to him. But the lamp did not know its successor, or it might have given him a few hints respecting rain or mist and might have informed him how far the moon's rays would reach, and from which side the wind generally blew, and so on.

On the bridge over the canal stood three persons who wished to recommend themselves to the lamp, for they thought it could give the office to whomsoever it chose. The first was a herring's head, which could emit light in the darkness. He remarked that it would be a great saving of oil if they placed him on the lamp-post. Number two was a piece of rotten wood, which also shines in the dark. He considered himself descended from an old stem, once the pride of the forest. The third was a glowworm, and how he found his way there the lamp could not imagine; yet there he was, and could really give light as well as the others. But the rotten wood and the herring's head declared most solemnly, by all they held sacred, that the glowworm only gave light at certain times and must not be allowed to compete with them. The old lamp assured them that not one of them could give sufficient light to fill the position of a street lamp, but they would believe nothing that it said. When they discovered that it had not the power of naming its successor, they said they were very glad to hear it, for the lamp was too old and worn out to make a proper choice.

At this moment the wind came rushing round the corner of the street and through the air-holes of the old lamp. "What is this I hear?" it asked. "Are you going away to-morrow? Is this evening the last time we shall meet? Then I must present you with a farewell gift. I will blow into your brain, so that in future not only shall you be able to remember all that you have seen or heard in the past, but your light within shall be so bright that you will be able to understand all that is said or done in your presence."

"Oh, that is really a very, very great gift," said the old lamp. "I thank you most heartily. I only hope I shall not be melted down."

"That is not likely to happen yet," said the wind. "I will also blow a memory into you, so that, should you receive other similar presents, your old age will pass very pleasantly."

"That is, if I am not melted down," said the lamp. "But should I, in that case, still retain my memory?"

"Do be reasonable, old lamp," said the wind, puffing away.

At this moment the moon burst forth from the clouds. "What will you give the old lamp?" asked the wind.

"I can give nothing," she replied. "I am on the wane, and no lamps have ever given me light, while I have frequently shone upon them." With these words the moon hid herself again behind the clouds, that she might be saved from further importunities. Just then a drop fell upon the lamp from the roof of the house, but the drop explained that it was a gift from those gray clouds and perhaps the best of all gifts. "I shall penetrate you so thoroughly," it said, "that you will have the power of becoming rusty, and, if you wish it, can crumble into dust in one night."

But this seemed to the lamp a very shabby present, and the wind thought so, too. "Does no one give any more? Will no one give any more?" shouted the breath of the wind, as loud as it could. Then a bright, falling star came down, leaving a broad, luminous streak behind it.

"What was that?" cried the herring's head. "Did not a star fall? I really believe it went into the lamp. Certainly, when such high-born personages try for the office we may as well go home."

And so they did, all three, while the old lamp threw a wonderfully strong light all around.

"This is a glorious gift," it said. "The bright stars have always been a joy to me and have always shone more brilliantly than I ever could shine, though I have tried with my whole might. Now they have noticed me, a poor old lamp, and have sent me a gift that will enable me to see clearly everything that I remember, as if it still stood before me, and to let it be seen by all those who love me. And herein lies the truest happiness, for pleasures which we cannot share with others are only half enjoyed."

"That sentiment does you honor," said the wind; "but for this purpose wax lights will be necessary. If these are not lighted in you, your peculiar faculties will not benefit others in the least. The stars have not thought of this. They suppose that you and every other light must be a wax taper. But I must go down now." So it laid itself to rest.

"Wax tapers, indeed!" said the lamp; "I have never yet had these, nor is it likely I ever shall. If I could only be sure of not being melted down!"

The next day—well, perhaps we had better pass over the next day. The evening had come, and the lamp was resting in a grandfather's chair; and guess where! Why, at the old watchman's house. He had begged as a favor that the mayor and corporation would allow him to keep the street lamp in consideration of his long and faithful service, as he had himself hung it up and lighted it on the day he first commenced his duties, four and twenty years ago. He looked upon it almost as his own child. He had no children, so the lamp was given to him.

There lay the lamp in the great armchair near the warm stove. It seemed almost to have grown larger, for it appeared quite to fill the chair. The old people sat at their supper, casting friendly glances at it, and would willingly have admitted it to a place at the table. It is quite true that they dwelt in a cellar two yards below ground, and had to cross a stone passage to get to their room. But within, it was warm and comfortable, and strips of list had been nailed round the door. The bed and the little window had curtains, and everything looked clean and neat. On the window seat stood two curious flowerpots, which a sailor named Christian had brought from the East or West Indies. They were of clay, and in the form of two elephants with open backs; they were filled with earth, and through the open space flowers bloomed. In one grew some very fine chives or leeks; this was the kitchen garden. The other, which contained a beautiful geranium, they called their flower garden. On the wall hung a large colored print, representing the Congress of Vienna and all the kings and emperors. A clock with heavy weights hung on the wall and went "tick, tick," steadily enough; yet it was always rather too fast, which, however, the old people said was better than being too slow. They were now eating their supper, while the old street lamp, as we have heard, lay in the grandfather's armchair near the stove.

It seemed to the lamp as if the whole world had turned round. But after a while the old watchman looked at the lamp and spoke of what they had both gone through together—in rain and in fog, during the short, bright nights of summer or in the long winter nights, through the drifting snowstorms when he longed to be at home in the cellar. Then the lamp felt that all was well again. It saw everything that had happened quite clearly, as if the events were passing before it. Surely the wind had given it an excellent gift!

The old people were very active and industrious; they were never idle for even a single hour. On Sunday afternoons they would bring out some books, generally a book of travels which they greatly liked. The old man would read aloud about Africa, with its great forests and the wild elephants, while his wife would listen attentively, stealing a glance now and then at the clay elephants which served as flowerpots. "I can almost imagine I am seeing it all," she said.

Ah! how the lamp wished for a wax taper to be lighted in it, for then the old woman would have seen the smallest detail as clearly as it did itself; the lofty trees, with their thickly entwined branches, the naked negroes on horseback, and whole herds of elephants treading down bamboo thickets with their broad, heavy feet.

"What is the use of all my capabilities," sighed the old lamp, "when I cannot obtain any wax lights? They have only oil and tallow here, and these will not do." One day a great heap of wax-candle ends found their way into the cellar. The larger pieces were burned, and the smaller ones the old woman kept for waxing her thread. So there were now candles enough, but it never occurred to any one to put a little piece in the lamp.

"Here I am now, with my rare powers," thought the lamp. "I have faculties within me, but I cannot share them. They do not know that I could cover these white walls with beautiful tapestry, or change them into noble forests or, indeed, to anything else they might wish."

The lamp, however, was always kept clean and shining in a corner, where it attracted all eyes. Strangers looked upon it as lumber, but the old people did not care for that; they loved it. One day—it was the watchman's birthday—the old woman approached the lamp, smiling to herself, and said, "I will have an illumination to-day, in honor of my old man." The lamp rattled in its metal frame, for it thought, "Now at last I shall have a light within me." But, after all, no wax light was placed in the lamp—only oil, as usual.

The lamp burned through the whole evening and began to perceive too clearly that the gift of the stars would remain a hidden treasure all its life. Then it had a dream; for to one with its faculties, dreaming was not difficult. It dreamed that the old people were dead and that it had been taken to the iron foundry to be melted down. This caused the lamp quite as much anxiety as on the day when it had been called upon to appear before the mayor and the council at the town hall. But though it had been endowed with the power of falling into decay from rust when it pleased, it did not make use of this power. It was therefore put into the melting furnace and changed into as elegant an iron candle-stick as you could wish to see—one intended to hold a wax taper. The candlestick was in the form of an angel holding a nosegay, in the center of which the wax taper was to be placed. It was to stand on a green writing table in a very pleasant room, where there were many books scattered about and splendid paintings on the walls.

The owner of the room was a poet and a man of intellect. Everything he thought or wrote was pictured around him. Nature showed herself to him sometimes in the dark forests, sometimes in cheerful meadows where the storks were strutting about, or on the deck of a ship sailing across the foaming sea, with the clear, blue sky above, or at night in the glittering stars.

"What powers I possess!" said the lamp, awaking from its dream. "I could almost wish to be melted down; but no, that must not be while the old people live. They love me for myself alone; they keep me bright and supply me with oil. I am as well off as the picture of the Congress, in which they take so much pleasure." And from that time it felt at rest in itself, and not more so than such an honorable old lamp really deserved to be.

THE SHEPHERDESS AND THE CHIMNEY SWEEP

HAVE you ever seen an old wooden cabinet, quite worn black with age, and ornamented with all sorts of carved figures and flourishes?

Just such a one stood in a certain parlor. It was a legacy from the great-grandmother, and was covered from top to bottom with carved roses and tulips. The most curious flourishes were on it, too; and between them peered forth little stags' heads, with their zigzag antlers. On the door panel had been carved the entire figure of a man, a most ridiculous man to look at, for he grinned—you could not call it smiling or laughing—in the drollest way. Moreover, he had crooked legs, little horns upon his forehead, and a long beard.

The children used to call him the "crooked-legged field-marshal-major-general-corporal-sergeant," which was a long, hard name to pronounce. Very few there are, whether in wood or in stone, who could get such a title. Surely to have cut him out in wood was no trifling task. However, there he was. His eyes were always fixed upon the table below, and toward the mirror, for upon this table stood a charming little porcelain shepherdess, her mantle gathered gracefully about her and fastened with a red rose. Her shoes and hat were gilded, and her hand held a shepherd's crook; she was very lovely. Close by her stood a little chimney sweep, also of porcelain. He was as clean and neat as any other figure. Indeed, he might as well have been made a prince as a sweep, since he was only make-believe; for though everywhere else he was as black as a coal, his round, bright face was as fresh and rosy as a girl's. This was certainly a mistake—it ought to have been black.

There he stood so prettily, with his ladder in his hand, quite close to the shepherdess. From the first he had been placed there, and he always remained on the same spot; for they had promised to be true to each other. They suited each other exactly—they were both young, both of the same kind of porcelain, and both equally fragile.

Close to them stood another figure three times as large as themselves. It was an old Chinaman, a mandarin, who could nod his head. He was of porcelain, too, and he said he was the grandfather of the shepherdess; but this he could not prove. He insisted that he had authority over her, and so when the crooked-legged field-marshal-major-general-corporal-sergeant made proposals to the little shepherdess, he nodded his head, in token of his consent.

"You will have a husband," said the old mandarin to her, "a husband who, I verily believe, is of mahogany wood. You will be the wife of a field-marshal-major-general-corporal-sergeant, of a man who has a whole cabinet full of silver plate, besides a store of no one knows what in the secret drawers."

"I will never go into that dismal cabinet," declared the little shepherdess. "I have heard it said that there are eleven porcelain ladies already imprisoned there."

"Then," rejoined the mandarin, "you will be the twelfth, and you will be in good company. This very night, when the old cabinet creaks, we shall keep the wedding, as surely as I am a Chinese mandarin." And upon this he nodded his head and fell asleep.

But the little shepherdess wept, and turned to the beloved of her heart, the porcelain chimney sweep.

"I believe I must ask you," she said, "to go out with me into the wide world, for here it is not possible for us to stay."

"I will do in everything as you wish," replied the little chimney sweep. "Let us go at once. I am sure I can support you by my trade."

"If we were only down from the table," said she. "I shall not feel safe till we are far away out in the wide world and free."

The little chimney sweep comforted her, and showed her how to set her little foot on the carved edges, and on the gilded foliage twining round the leg of the table, till at last they both reached the floor. But, turning for a last look at the old cabinet, they saw that everything was in commotion. All the carved stags stretched their heads farther out than before, raised their antlers, and moved their throats, while the crooked-legged field-marshal-major-general-corporal-sergeant sprang up and shouted to the old Chinese mandarin, "Look! they are eloping! they are eloping!"

They were not a little frightened at this, and jumped quickly into an open drawer in the window seat.

Here lay three or four packs of cards that were not quite complete, and a little doll's theater, which had been set up as nicely as could be. A play was going on, and all the queens sat in the front row, and fanned themselves with the flowers which they held in their hands, while behind them stood the knaves, each with two heads, one above and one below, as playing cards have. The play was about two persons who were not allowed to marry, and the shepherdess cried, for it seemed so like her own story.

"I cannot bear this!" she said. "Let us leave the drawer."

But when she had again reached the floor she looked up at the table and saw that the old Chinese mandarin was awake, and that he was rocking his whole body to and fro with rage.

"The old mandarin is coming!" cried she, and down she fell on her porcelain knees, so frightened was she.

"I have thought of a plan," said the chimney sweep. "Suppose we creep into the jar of perfumes, the potpourri vase which stands in the corner. There we can rest upon roses and lavender, and throw salt in his eyes if he comes near."

"That will not do at all," she said. "Besides, I know that the old mandarin and the potpourri vase were once betrothed; and no doubt some slight friendship still exists between them. No, there is no help for it; we must wander forth together into the wide world."

"Have you really the courage to go out into the wide world with me?" asked the chimney sweep. "Have you considered how large it is, and that if we go, we can never come back?"

"I have," replied she.

And the chimney sweep looked earnestly at her and said, "My way lies through the chimney. Have you really the courage to go with me through the stove, and creep through the flues and the tunnel? Well do I know the way! we shall come out by the chimney, and then I shall know how to manage. We shall mount so high that they can never reach us, and at the top there is an opening that leads out into the wide world."

And he led her to the door of the stove.

"Oh, how black it looks!" she said. Still she went on with him, through the stove, the flues, and the tunnel, where it was as dark as pitch.

"Now we are in the chimney," said he; "and see what a lovely star shines above us."

There actually was a star in the sky, that was shining right down upon them, as if to show them the way. Now they climbed and crept—a frightful way it was, so steep and high! But he went first to guide, and to smooth the way as much as he could. He showed her the best places on which to set her little china foot, till at last they came to the edge of the chimney and sat down to rest, for they were very tired, as may well be supposed.

The sky and all its stars were above them, and below lay all the roofs of the town. They saw all around them the great, wide world. It was not like what the poor little shepherdess had fancied it, and she leaned her little head upon her chimney sweep's shoulder and wept so bitterly that the gilding was washed from her golden sash.

"This is too much," said she; "it is more than I can bear. The world is too large! I wish I were safe back again upon the little table under the mirror. I shall never be happy till I am there once more. I have followed you out into the wide world. Surely, if you really love me, you will follow me back."

The chimney sweep tried to reason with her. He reminded her of the old mandarin, and the crooked-legged field-marshal-major-general-corporal-sergeant, but she wept so bitterly, and kissed her little chimney sweep so fondly, that he could not do otherwise than as she wished, foolish as it was.

So they climbed down the chimney, though with the greatest difficulty, crept through the flues, and into the stove, where they paused to listen behind the door, to discover what might be going on in the room.

All was quiet, and they peeped out. Alas! there on the floor lay the old mandarin. He had fallen from the table in his attempt to follow the runaways, and had broken into three pieces. His whole back had come off in a single piece, and his head had rolled into a corner. The crooked-legged field-marshal-major-general-corporal-sergeant stood where he had always stood, reflecting upon what had happened.

"This is shocking!" said the little shepherdess. "My old grandfather is broken in pieces, and we are the cause of it," and she wrung her little hands.

"He can be riveted," said the chimney sweep; "he can certainly be riveted. Do not grieve so! If they cement his back and put a rivet through his neck, he will be just as good as new, and will be able to say as many disagreeable things to us as ever."

"Do you really think so?" asked she. Then they climbed again up to the place where they had stood before.

"How far we have been," observed the chimney sweep, "and since we have got no farther than this, we might have saved ourselves all the trouble."

"I wish grandfather were mended," said the shepherdess; "I wonder if it will cost very much."

Mended he was. The family had his back cemented and his neck riveted, so that he was as good as new, only he could not nod.

"You have become proud since you were broken to shivers," observed the crooked-legged field-marshal-major-general-corporal-sergeant, "but I must say, for my part, I don't see much to be proud of. Am I to have her, or am I not? Just answer me that."

The chimney sweep and the shepherdess looked most piteously at the old mandarin. They were so afraid that he would nod his head. But he could not, and it would have been beneath his dignity to have confessed to having a rivet in his neck. So the young porcelain people always remained together, and they blessed the grandfather's rivet and loved each other till they were broken in pieces.

THE DROP OF WATER

OU know, surely, what the microscope is—that wonderful little glass which makes everything appear a hundred times larger than it really is.

If you look through a microscope at a single drop of ditch water, you will see a thousand odd-looking creatures, such as you never could imagine dwelled in water. They do not look unlike a whole plateful of shrimps, all jumping and crowding upon each other. So fierce are these little creatures that they will tear off each other's arms and legs without the least mercy, and yet after their fashion they look merry and happy.

Now there was once an old man, whom his neighbors called Cribbley Crabbley—a curious name, to be sure, which meant something like "creep-and-crawl." He always liked to make the most of everything, and when he could not manage it in the ordinary way, he tried magic.

One day he sat looking through his microscope at a drop of water that had been brought from a neighboring ditch. What a scene of scrambling and swarming it was, to be sure! All the thousands of little imps in the water jumped and sprang about, devouring each other, or tearing each other to bits.

"Upon my word this is really shocking. There must surely be some way to make them live in peace and quiet, so that each attends only to his own concerns." And he thought and thought, but still could not hit upon any plan, so he must needs have recourse to conjuring.

"I must give them color so that they may be seen more plainly," said he. Accordingly he poured something that looked like a drop of red wine—but which in reality was witch's blood—upon the drop of water. Immediately all the strange little creatures became red all over, and looked for all the world like a whole town full of naked red Indi-Indians.

"Why, what have you here?" asked another old magician, who had no name at all, which made him even more remarkable than Cribbley Crabbley.

"If you can find out what it is," replied Cribbley Crabbley, "I will give it you; but I warn you you'll not do so easily."

The conjurer without a name looked through the microscope, and it seemed to him that the scene before him was a whole town, in which the people ran about naked in the wildest way. It was quite shocking! Still more horrible was it to see how they kicked and cuffed, struggled and fought, pecked, bit, tore, and swallowed, each his neighbor. Those that were under wanted to be at the top, while those that chanced to be at the top must needs thrust themselves underneath.

"And now look, his leg is longer than mine, so off with it!" one seemed to be saying. Another had a little lump behind his ear,—an innocent little lump enough,—but it seemed to pain him, and therefore the others seemed determined that it should pain him more. So they hacked at it, and dragged the poor thing about, and at last ate him up, all on account of the little lump. One only of the creatures was quiet, a modest little maid, who sat by herself evidently wishing for nothing but peace and quietness. The others would not have it so, however. They soon pulled the little damsel forward, cuffed and tore her, and then ate her up.

"This is uncommonly droll and amusing!" said the nameless magician.

"Yes. But what do you think it is?" asked Cribbley Crabbley. "Can you make it out?"

"It is easy enough to guess, to be sure," was the reply of the nameless magician; "easy enough. It is either Paris or Copenhagen, or some other great city; I don't know which, for they are all alike. It is some great city, of course."

"It is a drop of ditch-water," said Cribbley Crabbley.

THE SWINEHERD

THERE was once a poor prince who had a kingdom, but it was a very small one. Still it was quite large enough to admit of his marrying, and he wished to marry.

It was certainly rather bold of him to say, as he did, to the emperor's daughter, "Will you have me?" But he was renowned far and wide, and there were a hundred princesses who would have answered, "Yes," and, "Thank you kindly." We shall see what this princess said. Listen!

It happened that where the prince's father lay buried there grew a rose tree, a most beautiful rose tree, which blossomed only once in five years, and even then bore only one flower. Ah, but that was a rose! It smelled so sweet that all cares and sorrows were forgotten by those who inhaled its fragrance!

Moreover, the prince had a nightingale that could sing in such a manner that it seemed as if all sweet melodies dwelt in her little throat. Now the princess was to have the rose and the nightingale; and they were accordingly put into large silver caskets and sent to her.

The emperor had them brought into a large hall, where the princess and the ladies of the court were playing at "Visiting." When she saw the caskets with the presents, the princess clapped her hands for joy.

"Ah, if it should be a little pussy cat," exclaimed she. Instead, the rose tree, with its beautiful rose, came to view.

"Oh, how prettily it is made!" said all the court ladies.

"It is more than pretty," said the emperor; "it is charming."

The princess touched it and was ready to cry. "Fie, papa," said she, "it is not made at all. It is natural!"

"Fie," said all the court ladies; "it is natural!"

"Let us see what the other casket contains before we get into bad humor," proposed the emperor. So the nightingale came forth, and sang so delightfully that at first no one could say anything ill-humored of her.

"*Superbe! charmant!*" exclaimed the ladies, for they all used to chatter French, and each worse than her neighbor.

"How much the bird reminds me of the musical box that belonged to our blessed empress!" remarked an old knight. "Oh! yes, these are the same tunes, the same execution."

"Yes, yes!" said the emperor, and at the remembrance he wept like a child.

"I still hope it is not a real bird," said the princess.

"Yes, it is a real bird," said those who had brought it.

"Well, then, let the bird fly," returned the princess. And she positively refused to see the prince.

However, he was not to be discouraged. He stained his face brown and black, pulled his cap over his ears, and knocked at the door of the castle.

"Good day to my lord the emperor," said he. "Can I have employment here at the palace?"

"Why, yes," said the emperor. "It just occurs to me that I want some one to take care of the pigs, there are so many of them."

So the prince came to be the imperial swineherd.

He had a miserable little room, close by the pigsty, and here he was obliged to stay; and he sat the whole day long and worked. By evening he had made a pretty little saucepan. Little bells were hung all around it; and when the pot was boiling, the bells tinkled in the most charming manner, and played the old melody,

"Ach, du lieber Augustin,
Alles ist weg, weg, weg."

But what was still more curious, whoever held his finger in the smoke of this saucepan, at once smelled all the dishes that were cooking on every hearth of the city. This, you see, was something quite different from the rose.

Now the princess happened to walk that way with her court ladies, and when she heard the tune she stood quite still and seemed pleased, for she could play "Dearest Augustine." It was the only piece she knew, and she played it with one finger.

"Why, that is the piece that I play on the piano!" said the princess. "That swineherd must certainly have been well educated. Go in and ask him the price of the instrument."

So one of the court ladies had to go in, but she drew on wooden slippers first.

"What will you take for the saucepan?" inquired the lady.

"I must have ten kisses from the princess," said the swineherd.

"Heaven preserve us!" exclaimed the maid of honor.

"I cannot sell it for less," answered the swineherd.

"Well, what does he say?" asked the princess.

"I cannot tell you, really," replied the lady. "It is too dreadful."

"Then you may whisper it." So the lady whispered it.

"He is an impudent fellow," said the princess, and she walked on. But when she had gone a little way, the bells again tinkled prettily,

"Ah! thou dearest Augustine,
All is gone, gone, gone."

"Stay!" said the princess. "Ask him if he will have ten kisses from the ladies of my court."

"No, thank you!" answered the swineherd. "Ten kisses from the princess, or I keep the saucepan myself."

"How tiresome! That must not be either!" said the princess; "but do you all stand before me, that no one may see us."

The court ladies placed themselves in front of her, and spread out their dresses. So the swineherd got ten kisses, and the princess got the saucepan.

That was delightful! The saucepan was kept boiling all the evening and the whole of the following day. They knew perfectly well what was cooking on every hearth in the city, from the chamberlain's to the cobbler's. The court ladies danced and clapped their hands.

"We know who has soup, and who has pancakes for dinner to-day; who has cutlets, and who has eggs. How interesting!"

"Yes, but keep my secret, for I am an emperor's daughter."

The prince—that is, the swineherd, for no one knew that he was other than an ill-favored swineherd—let not a day pass without working at something. At last he constructed a rattle, which, when it was swung round and round, played all the waltzes and jig tunes which have been heard since the creation of the world.

"Ah, that is *superbe!*" said the princess, when she passed by. "I have never heard prettier compositions. Go in and ask him the price of the instrument. But mind, he shall have no more kisses."

"He will have a hundred kisses from the princess," said the lady who had been to ask.

"He is not in his right senses," said the princess, and walked on. But when she had gone a little way she stopped again. "One must encourage art," said she; "I am the emperor's daughter. Tell him he shall, as on yesterday, have ten kisses from me, and may take the rest from the ladies of the court."

"Oh, but we should not like that at all," said the ladies.

"What are you muttering?" asked the princess. "If I can kiss him, surely you can! Remember I give you food and wages."

"A hundred kisses from the princess," said he, "or else let every one keep his own."

"Stand round," said she, and all the ladies stood round as before.

"What can be the reason for such a crowd close by the pigsty?" asked the emperor, who happened just then to step out on the balcony. He rubbed his eyes and put on his spectacles.

"They are the ladies of the court. I must go and see what they are about." So he pulled up his slippers at the heel, for he had trodden them down.

As soon as he had got into the courtyard he moved very softly, and the ladies were so much engrossed with counting the kisses that they did not perceive the emperor. He rose on his tiptoes.

"What is all this?" said he, when he saw what was going on, and he boxed the princess's ear with his slipper, just as the swineherd was taking the eighty-sixth kiss.

"Be off with you! March out!" cried the emperor, for he was very angry. Both princess and swineherd were thrust out of the city, and the princess stood and wept, while the swineherd scolded, and the rain poured down.

"Alas, unhappy creature that I am!" said the princess. "If I had but married the handsome young prince! Ah, how unfortunate I am!"

The swineherd went behind a tree, washed the black and brown from his face, threw off his dirty clothing, and stepped forth in his princely robes. He looked so noble that the princess could not help bowing before him.

"I have come to despise thee," said he. "Thou wouldst not have an honorable prince! Thou couldst not prize the rose and the nightingale, but thou wast ready to kiss the swineherd for the sake of a trumpery plaything. Thou art rightly served."

He then went back to his own little kingdom, where he shut the door of his palace before her very eyes. Now she might well sing,

"Ah! thou dearest Augustine,
All is gone, gone, gone."

THE METAL PIG

I N THE city of Florence, not far from the Piazza del Granduca, runs a little cross street called Porta Rosa. In this street, just in front of the market place where vegetables are sold, stands a pig, made of brass and curiously formed. The color has been changed by age to dark green, but clear, fresh water pours from the snout, which shines as if it had been polished—and so indeed it has, for hundreds of poor people and children seize it in their hands as they place their mouths close to the mouth of the animal to drink. It is quite a picture to see a half-naked boy clasping the well-formed creature by the head as he presses his rosy lips against its jaws. Every one who visits Florence can very quickly find the place; he has only to ask the first beggar he meets for the Metal Pig, and he will be told where it is.

It was late on a winter evening. The mountains were covered with snow, but the moon shone brightly, and moonlight in Italy is as good as the light of gray winter's day in the north. Indeed, it is better, for the clear air seems to raise us above the earth; while in the north a cold, gray, leaden sky appears to press us down to earth, even as the cold, damp earth shall one day press on us in the grave.

In the garden of the grand duke's palace, under the roof of one of the wings, where a thousand roses bloom in winter, a little ragged boy had been sitting the whole day long. The boy might serve as a type of Italy: lovely and smiling, and yet suffering. He was hungry and thirsty, but no one gave him anything; and when it became dark and they were about to close the gardens, the porter turned him out. A long time he stood musing on the bridge which crosses the Arno and looking at the glittering stars that were reflected in the water which flowed between him and the wonderful marble bridge Delia Trinità. He then walked away towards the Metal Pig, half knelt down, clasped it with his arms, and, putting his mouth to the shining snout, drank deep draughts of the fresh water. Close by lay a few salad leaves and two chestnuts, which were to serve for his supper. No one was in the street but himself. It belonged only to him. He boldly seated himself on the pig's back, leaned forward so that his curly head could rest on the head of the animal, and, before he was aware, fell asleep.

It was midnight. The Metal Pig raised himself gently, and the boy heard him say quite distinctly, "Hold tight, little boy, for I am going to run"; and away he started for a most wonderful ride. First they arrived at the Piazza del Granduca, and the metal horse which bears the duke's statue neighed aloud. The painted coats of arms on the old council house shone like transparent pictures, and Michelangelo's "David" swung his sling. It was as if everything had life. The metallic groups of figures, among which were "Perseus" and "The Rape of the Sabines," looked like living persons, and cries of terror sounded from them all across the noble square. By the Palazzo degli Uffizi, in the arcade where the nobility assembled for the carnival, the Metal Pig stopped. "Hold fast," said the animal, "hold fast, for I am going upstairs."

The little boy said not a word. He was half pleased and half afraid. They entered a long gallery, where the boy had been before. The walls were resplendent with paintings, and here and there stood statues and busts, all in a clear light as if it were day. The grandest sight appeared when the door of a side room opened. The little boy could remember what beautiful things he had seen there, but to-night everything shone in its brightest colors. Here stood the figure of a beautiful woman, as radiantly beautiful as nature and the art of one of the great masters could make her. Her graceful limbs appeared to move; dolphins sprang at her feet, and immortality shone from her eyes. The world called her the "Venus de' Medici." By her side were statues of stone, in which the spirit of life breathed; figures of men, one of whom whetted his sword and was named "The Grinder"; fighting gladiators, for whom the sword had been sharpened, and who strove for the goddess of beauty. The boy was dazzled by so much glitter, for the walls were gleaming with bright colors. Life and movement were in everything.

As they passed from hall to hall, beauty showed itself in whatever they saw; and, as the Metal Pig went step by step from one picture to another, the little boy could see it all plainly. One glory eclipsed another; yet there was one picture that fixed itself on the little boy's memory more especially, because of the happy children it represented; for these the little boy had seen in daylight. Many pass this picture with indifference, and yet it contains a treasure of poetic feeling. It represents Christ descending into Hades. It is not those who are lost that one sees, but the heathen of olden times.

The Florentine, Angiolo Bronzino, painted this picture. Most beautiful is the expression on the faces of two children who appear to have full confidence that they shall reach heaven at last. They are embracing each other, and one little one stretches out his hand towards another who stands below them, and points to himself as if he were saying, "I am going to heaven." The older people stand as if uncertain yet hopeful, and bow in humble adoration to the Lord Jesus. On this picture the boy's eyes rested longer than on any other, and the Metal Pig stood still before it. A low sigh was heard. Did it come from the picture or from the animal? The boy raised his hands toward the smiling children, and then the pig ran off with him through the open vestibule.

"Thank you, thank you, you beautiful animal," said the little boy, caressing the Metal Pig as it ran down the steps.

"Thanks to yourself also," replied the Metal Pig. "I have helped you and you have helped me, for it is only when I have an innocent child on my back that I receive the power to run. Yes, as you see, I can even venture under the rays of the lamp in front of the picture of the Madonna, but I must not enter the church. Still, from without, and while you are upon my back, I may look in through the open door. Do not get down yet, for if you do, then I shall be lifeless, as you have seen me in the daytime in the Porta Rosa."

"I will stay with you, my dear creature," said the little boy. So they went on at a rapid pace through the streets of Florence, till they came to the square before the church of Santa Croce. The folding doors flew open, and lights streamed from the altar, through the church, into the deserted square. A wonderful blaze of light streamed from one of the monuments in the left aisle, and a thousand moving stars formed a kind of glory round it. Even the coat of arms on the tombstone shone, and a red ladder on a blue field gleamed like fire. It was the grave of Galileo. The monument is unadorned, but the red ladder is an emblem of art—signifying that the way to glory leads up a shining ladder, on which the great prophets rise to heaven like Elijah of old. In the right aisle of the church every statue on the richly carved sarcophagi seemed endowed with life. Here stood Michelangelo; there Dante, with the laurel wreath around his brow; Alfieri and Machiavelli; for here, side by side, rest the great men, the pride of Italy.

The church itself is very beautiful, even more beautiful than the marble cathedral at Florence, though not so large. It seemed as if the carved vestments stirred, and as if the marble figures which they covered raised their heads higher to gaze upon the brightly colored, glowing altar, where the white-robed boys swung the golden censers amid music and song; and the strong fragrance of incense filled the church and streamed forth into the square. The boy stretched out his hands toward the light, and at the same moment the Metal Pig started again, so rapidly that he was obliged to cling tightly to him. The wind whistled in his ears. He heard the church door creak on its hinges as it closed, and it seemed to him as if he had lost his senses; then a cold shudder passed over him, and he awoke.

It was morning. The Metal Pig stood in its old place on the Porta Rosa, and the boy found that he had nearly slipped off its back. Fear and trembling came upon him as he thought of his mother. She had sent him out the day before to get some money, but he had not been able to get any, and now he was hungry and thirsty. Once more he clasped the neck of his metal steed, kissed its nose, and nodded farewell to it. Then he wandered away into one of the narrowest streets, where there was scarcely room for a loaded donkey to pass. A great iron-bound door stood ajar; and, passing through, he climbed a brick staircase with dirty walls, and a rope for balustrade, till he came to an open gallery hung with rags. From here a flight of steps led down to a court, where from a fountain water was drawn up by iron rollers to the different stories of the house. Many water buckets hung side by side. Sometimes the roller and the bucket danced in the air, splashing the water all over the court. Another broken-down staircase led from the gallery, and two Russian sailors running down it almost upset the poor boy. They were coming from their nightly carousal. A woman, not very young, with an unpleasant face and a quantity of black hair, followed them. "What have you brought home?" she asked when she saw the boy.

"Don't be angry," he pleaded. "I received nothing, I have nothing at all"; and he seized his mother's dress and would have kissed it. Then they went into a little room. I need not describe it, but only say that there stood in it an earthen pot with handles, made for holding fire, which in Italy is called a *marito*. This pot she took in her lap, warmed her fingers, and pushed the boy with her elbow.

"Certainly you must have some money," she said. The boy began to cry, and then she struck him till he cried aloud.

"Be quiet, or I'll break your screaming head." She swung about the fire pot which she held in her hand, while the boy crouched to the earth and screamed. Then a neighbor came in, who also had a *marito* under her arm. "Felicita," she said, "what are you doing to the child?"

"The child is mine," she answered; "I can murder him if I like, and you too, Giannina."

Then again she swung the fire pot about. The other woman lifted hers up to defend herself, and the two pots clashed so violently that they were dashed to pieces and fire and ashes flew about the room.

The boy rushed out at the sight, sped across the courtyard, and fled from the house. The poor child ran till he was quite out of breath. At last he stopped at the church the doors of which were opened to him the night before, and went in. Here everything was bright, and the boy knelt down by the first tomb on his right hand, the grave of Michelangelo, and sobbed as if his heart would break. People came and went; the service went on, but no one noticed the boy except an elderly citizen, who stood still and looked at him for a moment and then went away like the rest. Hunger and thirst overpowered the child, and he became quite faint and ill. At last he crept into a corner behind the marble monuments and went to sleep. Towards evening he was awakened by a pull at his sleeve. He started up, and the same old citizen stood before him.

"Are you ill? Where do you live? Have you been here all day?" were some of the questions asked by the old man. After hearing his answers, the old man took him to a small house in a back street close by. They entered a glovemaker's shop, where a woman sat sewing busily. A little white poodle, so closely shaved that his pink skin could plainly be seen, frisked about the room and gamboled over the boy.

"Innocent souls are soon intimate," said the woman, as she caressed both the boy and the dog.

These good people gave the child food and drink, and said he should stay with them all night, and that the next day the old man, who was called Giuseppe, would go and speak to his mother. A simple little bed was prepared for him, but to him who had so often slept on the hard stones it was a royal couch, and he slept sweetly and dreamed of the splendid pictures, and of the Metal Pig. Giuseppe went out the next morning, and the poor child was not glad to see him go, for he knew that the old man had gone to his mother, and that perhaps he would have to return. He wept at the thought, and then played with the lively little dog and kissed it, while the old woman looked kindly at him to encourage him.

What news did Giuseppe bring back? At first the boy could not find out, for the old man talked to his wife, and she nodded and stroked the boy's cheek. Then she said, "He is a good lad, he shall stay with us. He may become a clever glovemaker, like you. Look what delicate fingers he has. Madonna intended him for a glovemaker."

So the boy stayed with them, and the woman herself taught him to sew. He ate well, and slept well, and became very merry. But at last he began to tease Bellissima, as the little dog was called. This made the woman angry, and she scolded him and threatened him, which made him unhappy, and he went and sat in his own room, full of sad thoughts. This chamber looked out upon the street, in which hung skins to dry, and there were thick iron bars across his window. That night he lay awake, thinking of the Metal Pig. Indeed, it was always in his thoughts. Suddenly he fancied he heard feet outside going pitapat. He sprang out of bed and went to the window. Could it be the Metal Pig? But there was nothing to be seen. Whatever he had heard had passed already.

"Go help the gentleman to carry his box of colors," said the woman the next morning when their neighbor, the artist, passed by, carrying a paint box and a large roll of canvas. The boy instantly took the box and followed the painter. They walked on till they reached the picture gallery, and mounted the same staircase up which he had ridden that night on the Metal Pig. He remembered all the pictures and statues, especially the marble Venus, and again he looked at the Madonna with the Saviour and St. John. They stopped before the picture by Il Bronzino, in which Christ is represented as standing in the lower world, with the children smiling before him in the sweet expectation of entering heaven. The poor boy smiled, too, for here was his heaven.

"You may go home now," said the painter, while the boy stood watching him till he had set up his easel.

"May I see you paint?" asked the boy. "May I see you put the picture on this white canvas?"

"I am not going to paint," replied the artist, bringing out a piece of chalk. His hand moved quickly, and his eye measured the great picture, and though nothing appeared but a faint line, the figure of the Saviour was as clearly visible as in the colored picture.

"Why don't you go?" said the painter. Then the boy wandered home silently, and seated himself on the table, and learned to sew gloves. But all day long his thoughts were in the picture gallery, and so he pricked his fingers and was awkward. But he did not tease Bellissima. When evening came, and the house door stood open, he slipped out. It was a bright, beautiful, starlight evening, but rather cold. Away he went through the already deserted streets, and soon came to the Metal Pig. He stooped down and kissed its shining nose, and then seated himself on its back.

"You happy creature," he said; "how I have longed for you! We must take a ride to-night."

But the Metal Pig lay motionless, while the fresh stream gushed forth from its mouth. The little boy still sat astride its back, when he felt something pulling at his clothes. He looked down, and there was Bellissima, little smooth-shaven Bellissima, barking as if she would have said, "Here I am, too. Why are you sitting there?"

A fiery dragon could not have frightened the little boy so much as did the little dog in this place. Bellissima in the street and not dressed! as the old lady called it. What would be the end of this? The dog never went out in winter, unless she was attired in a little lambskin coat, which had been made for her. It was fastened round the little dog's neck and body with red ribbons, and decorated with rosettes and little bells. The dog looked almost like a little kid when she was allowed to go out in winter and trot after her mistress. Now, here she was in the cold, and not dressed. Oh, how would it end? All his fancies were quickly put to flight; yet he kissed the Metal Pig once more, and then took Bellissima in his arms. The poor little thing trembled so with cold that the boy ran homeward as fast as he could.

"What are you running away with there?" asked two of the police whom he met, and at whom the dog barked. "Where have you stolen that pretty dog?" they asked, and took it away from him.

"Oh, I have not stolen it. Do give it back to me," cried the boy, despairingly.

"If you have not stolen it, you may say at home that they can send to the watch-house for the dog." Then they told him where the watch-house was, and went away with Bellissima.

Here was trouble indeed. The boy did not know whether he had better jump into the Arno or go home and confess everything. They would certainly kill him, he thought.

"Well, I would gladly be killed," he reasoned; "for then I should die and go to heaven." And so he went home, almost hoping for death.

The door was locked, and he could not reach the knocker. No one was in the street, so he took up a stone and with it made a tremendous noise at the door.

"Who is there?" asked somebody from within.

"It is I," said he. "Bellissima is gone. Open the door, and then kill me."

Then, indeed, there was a great panic, for madam was so very fond of Bellissima. She immediately looked at the wall where the dog's dress usually hung; and there was the little lambskin.

"Bellissima in the watch-house!" she cried. "You bad boy! How did you entice her out? Poor little delicate thing, with those rough policemen! And she'll be frozen with cold."

Giuseppe went off at once, while his wife lamented and the boy wept. Several of the neighbors came in, and among them the painter. He took the boy between his knees and questioned him. Soon he heard the whole story, told in broken sentences, and also about the Metal Pig and the wonderful ride to the picture gallery, which was certainly rather incomprehensible. The painter, however, consoled the little fellow, and tried to soften the woman's anger, but she would not be pacified till her husband returned from the police with Bellissima. Then there was great rejoicing, and the painter caressed the boy and gave him a number of pictures.

Oh, what beautiful pictures those were—figures with funny heads! And, best of all, the Metal Pig was there, too. Nothing could be more delightful! By means of a few strokes it was made to appear on the paper; and even the house that stood behind it had been sketched. Oh, if he could only draw and paint! He who could do this could conjure all the world before him. The first leisure moment during the next day the boy got a pencil, and on the back of one of the other drawings he attempted to copy the drawing of the Metal Pig, and he succeeded. Certainly it was rather crooked, rather up and down, one leg thick, and another thin. Still it was like the copy, and he was overjoyed at what he had done. The pencil would not go quite as it ought, he had found, but the next day he tried again. A second pig was drawn by the side of the first, and this looked a hundred times better. The third attempt was so good that everybody could see what it was meant to represent.

And now the glovemaking went on but slowly. The orders given by the shops in the town were not finished quickly; for the Metal Pig had taught the boy that all objects may be drawn upon paper, and Florence is a picture book in itself for any one who chooses to turn over its pages. On the Piazza della Trinità stands a slender pillar, and upon it is the goddess of justice blindfolded, with her scales in her hand. She was soon represented on paper, and it was the glovemaker's boy who placed her there. His collection of pictures increased, but as yet they were only copies of lifeless objects, when one day Bellissima came gamboling before him. "Stand still," cried he, "and I will draw you beautifully, to put in my collection."

Bellissima would not stand still, so she must be bound fast in one position. He tied her head and tail, but she barked and jumped and so pulled and tightened the string that she was nearly strangled. And just then her mistress walked in.

"You wicked boy! The poor little creature!" was all she could utter.

She pushed the boy from her, thrust him away with her foot, called him a most ungrateful, good-for-nothing, wicked boy, and forbade him to enter her house again. Then she wept, and kissed her little half-strangled Bellissima. At this moment the painter entered the room—and here is the turning point of the story.

In the year 1834 there was an exhibition in the Academy of Arts at Florence. Two pictures, placed side by side, attracted many people. The smaller of the two represented a little boy sitting at a table drawing. Before him was a little white poodle, curiously shaven, but as the animal would not stand still, its head and tail had been fastened with a string, to keep it in one position. The truthfulness and life in this picture interested every one. The painter was said to be a young Florentine, who had been found in the streets when a child by an old glovemaker, who had brought him up. The boy had taught himself to draw. It was also said that a young artist, now famous, had discovered this talent in the child just as he was about to be sent away for having tied up madam's favorite little dog to use as a model.

The glovemaker's boy had become a really great painter, as the picture proved; but the larger picture by its side was a still greater proof of his talent. It represented a handsome boy asleep, clothed in rags and leaning against the Metal Pig, in the street of the Porta Rosa. All the spectators knew the spot well. The child's arms were round the neck of the Pig, and he was in a deep sleep. The lamp before the picture of the Madonna threw a strong light on the pale, delicate face of the child. It was a beautiful picture. A large gilt frame surrounded it, and on one corner of the frame a laurel wreath had been hung. But a black band, twined unseen among the green leaves, and a streamer of crape hung down from it; for within the last few days the young artist had—died.

THE FLYING TRUNK

THERE was once a merchant who was so rich that he could have paved a whole street with gold, and would even then have had enough left for a small alley. He did not do so; he knew the value of money better than to use it in this way. So clever was he that every shilling he put out brought him a crown, and so it continued as long as he lived.

His son inherited his wealth, and lived a merry life with it. He went to a masquerade every night, made kites out of five-pound notes, and threw pieces of gold into the sea instead of stones, making ducks and drakes of them.

In this manner he soon lost all his money. At last he had nothing left but a pair of slippers, an old dressing gown, and four shillings. And now all his companions deserted him. They would not walk with him in the streets, but one of them, who was very good-natured, sent him an old trunk with this message, "Pack up!"

"Yes," he said, "it is all very well to say 'pack up.'" But he had nothing left to pack, therefore he seated himself in the trunk.

It was a very wonderful trunk, for no sooner did any one press on the lock than the trunk could fly. He shut the lid and pressed the lock, when away flew the trunk up the chimney, with him in it, right up into the clouds. Whenever the bottom of the trunk cracked he was in a great fright, for if the trunk had fallen to pieces, he would have turned a tremendous somersault over the trees. However, he arrived safely in Turkey. He hid the trunk in a wood under some dry leaves and then went into the town. This he could do very well, for among the Turks people always go about in dressing gowns and slippers, just as he was.

He happened to meet a nurse with a little child. "I say, you Turkish nurse," cried he, "what castle is that near the town, with the windows placed so high?"

"The Sultan's daughter lives there," she replied. "It has been prophesied that she will be very unhappy about a lover, and therefore no one is allowed to visit her unless the king and queen are present."

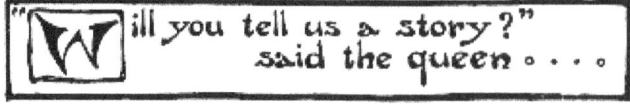

"Will you tell us a story?" said the queen . . .

"Thank you," said the merchant's son. So he went back to the wood, seated himself in his trunk, flew up to the roof of the castle, and crept through the window into the room where the princess lay asleep on the sofa. She awoke and was very much frightened, but he told her he was a Turkish angel who had come down through the air to see her. This pleased her very much. He sat down by her side and talked to her, telling her that her eyes were like beautiful dark lakes, in which the thoughts swam about like little mermaids; and that her forehead was a snowy mountain which contained splendid halls full of pictures. He related to her the story about the stork, who brings the beautiful children from the rivers. These stories delighted the princess, and when he asked her if she would marry him, she consented immediately.

"But you must come on Saturday," she said, "for then my parents will take tea with me. They will be very proud when they find that I am going to marry a Turkish angel. But you must think of some very pretty stories to tell them, for they like to hear stories better than anything. My mother prefers one that is deep and moral, but my father likes something funny, to make him laugh."

"Very well," he replied, "I shall bring you no other marriage portion than a story"; and so they parted. But the princess gave him a sword studded with gold coins, and these he could make useful.

He flew away to the town and bought a new dressing gown, and afterwards returned to the wood, where he composed a story so as to be ready by Saturday; and that was no easy matter. It was ready, however, when he went to see the princess on Saturday. The king and queen and the whole court were at tea with the princess, and he was received with great politeness.

"Will you tell us a story?" said the queen; "one that is instructive and full of learning."

"Yes, but with something in it to laugh at," said the king.

"Certainly," he replied, and commenced at once, asking them to listen attentively.

"There was once a bundle of matches that were exceedingly proud of their high descent. Their genealogical tree—that is, a great pine tree from which they had been cut—was at one time a large old tree in the wood. The matches now lay between a tinder box and an old iron saucepan and were talking about their youthful days. 'Ah! then we grew on the green boughs,' said they, 'and every morning and evening we were fed with diamond drops of dew. Whenever the sun shone we felt his warm rays, and the little birds would relate stories to us in their songs. We knew that we were rich, for the other trees only wore their green dresses in summer, while our family were able to array themselves in green, summer and winter. But the woodcutter came like a great disaster, and our family fell under the ax. The head of the house obtained a situation as mainmast in a very fine ship and can sail round the world whenever he will. Other branches of the family were taken to different places, and our own office now is to kindle a light for common people. This is how such highborn people as we came to be in a kitchen.'

"'Mine has been a very different fate,' said the iron pot, which stood by the matches. 'From my first entrance into the world I have been used to cooking and scouring. I am the first in this house when anything solid or useful is required. My only pleasure is to be made clean and shining after dinner and to sit in my place and have a little sensible conversation with my neighbors. All of us excepting the water bucket, which is sometimes taken into the courtyard, live here together within these four walls. We get our news from the market basket, but it sometimes tells us very unpleasant things about the people and the government. Yes, and one day an old pot was so alarmed that it fell down and was broken in pieces.'

"'You are talking too much,' said the tinder box; and the steel struck against the flint till some sparks flew out, crying, 'We want a merry evening, don't we?'

"'Yes, of course,' said the matches. 'Let us talk about those who are the highest born.'

"'No, I don't like to be always talking of what we are,' remarked the saucepan. 'Let us think of some other amusement; I will begin. We will tell something that has happened to ourselves; that will be very easy, and interesting as well. On the Baltic Sea, near the Danish shore—'

"'What a pretty commencement!' said the plates. 'We shall all like that story, I am sure.'

"'Yes. Well, in my youth I lived in a quiet family where the furniture was polished, the floors scoured, and clean curtains put up, every fortnight.'

"'What an interesting way you have of relating a story,' said the carpet broom. 'It is easy to perceive that you have been a great deal in society, something so pure runs through what you say.'

"'That is quite true,' said the water bucket; and it made a spring with joy and splashed some water on the floor.

"Then the saucepan went on with its story, and the end was as good as the beginning.

"The plates rattled with pleasure, and the carpet broom brought some green parsley out of the dust hole and crowned the saucepan. It knew this would vex the others, but it thought, 'If I crown him to-day, he will crown me to-morrow.'

"'Now let us have a dance,' said the fire tongs. Then how they danced and stuck one leg in the air! The chair cushion in the corner burst with laughter at the sight.

"'Shall I be crowned now?' asked the fire tongs. So the broom found another wreath for the tongs.

"'They are only common people after all,' thought the matches. The tea urn was now asked to sing, but she said she had a cold and could not sing unless she felt boiling heat within. They all thought this was affectation; they also considered it affectation that she did not wish to sing except in the parlor, when on the table with the grand people.

"In the window sat an old quill pen, with which the maid generally wrote. There was nothing remarkable about the pen, except that it had been dipped too deeply in the ink; but it was proud of that.

"'If the tea urn won't sing,' said the pen, 'she needn't. There's a nightingale in a cage outside, that can sing. She has not been taught much, certainly, but we need not say anything this evening about that.'

"'I think it highly improper,' said the teakettle, who was kitchen singer and half brother to the tea urn, 'that a rich foreign bird should be listened to here. Is it patriotic? Let the market basket decide what is right.'

"'I certainly am vexed,' said the basket, 'inwardly vexed, more than any one can imagine. Are we spending the evening properly? Would it not be more sensible to put the house in order? If each were in his own place, I would lead a game. This would be quite another thing.'

"'Let us act a play,' said they all. At the same moment the door opened and the maid came in. Then not one stirred; they remained quite still, although there was not a single pot among them that had not a high opinion of himself and of what he could do if he chose.

"'Yes, if we had chosen,' each of them thought, 'we might have spent a very pleasant evening.'

"The maid took the matches and lighted them, and dear me, how they spluttered and blazed up!

"'Now then,' they thought, 'every one will see that we are the first. How we shine! What a light we give!' But even while they spoke their lights went out."

"What a capital story!" said the queen. "I feel as if I were really in the kitchen and could see the matches. Yes, you shall marry our daughter."

"Certainly," said the king, "thou shalt have our daughter." The king said "thou" to him because he was going to be one of the family. The wedding day was fixed, and on the evening before, the whole city was illuminated. Cakes and sweetmeats were thrown among the people. The street boys stood on tiptoe and shouted "Hurrah," and whistled between their fingers. Altogether it was a very splendid affair.

"I will give them another treat," said the merchant's son. So he went and bought rockets and crackers and every kind of fireworks that could be thought of, packed them in his trunk, and flew up with it into the air. What a whizzing and popping they made as they went off! The Turks, when they saw the sight, jumped so high that their slippers flew about their ears. It was easy to believe after this that the princess was really going to marry a Turkish angel.

As soon as the merchant's son had come down to the wood after the fireworks, he thought, "I will go back into the town now and hear what they think of the entertainment." It was very natural that he should wish to know. And what strange things people did say, to be sure! Every one whom he questioned had a different tale to tell, though they all thought it very beautiful.

"I saw the Turkish angel myself," said one. "He had eyes like glittering stars and a head like foaming water."

"He flew in a mantle of fire," said another, "and lovely little cherubs peeped out from the folds."

He heard many more fine things about himself and that the next day he was to be married. After this he went back to the forest to rest himself in his trunk. It had disappeared! A spark from the fireworks which remained had set it on fire. It was burned to ashes. So the merchant's son could not fly any more, nor go to meet his bride. She stood all day on the roof, waiting for him, and most likely she is waiting there still, while he wanders through the world telling fairy tales—but none of them so amusing as the one he related about the matches.

THE BUTTERFLY

THERE was once a butterfly who wished for a bride; and, as may be supposed, he wanted to choose a very pretty one from among the flowers. He glanced with a very critical eye at all the flower beds and found that the flowers were seated quietly and demurely on their stalks, just as maidens should sit. But there was a great number of them, and it appeared as if making his choice would become very wearisome. The butterfly did not like to take too much trouble, so he flew off on a visit to the daisies.

The French call this flower Marguerite and say that it can prophesy. Lovers pluck off the leaves, and as they pluck each leaf they ask a question about their sweethearts, thus: "Does he or she love me? Dearly? Distractedly? Very much? A little? Not at all?" and so on. Each one speaks these words in his own language.

The butterfly came, also, to Marguerite to inquire, but he did not pluck off her leaves; he pressed a kiss on each of them, for he thought there was always more to be done by kindness.

"Darling Marguerite daisy," he said to her, "you are the wisest woman of them all. Pray tell me which of the flowers I shall choose for my wife. Which will be my bride? When I know, I will fly directly to her and propose."

But Marguerite did not answer him. She was offended that he should call her a woman when she was only a girl; there is a great difference. He asked her a second time, and then a third, but she remained dumb, answering him not at all. Then he would wait no longer, but flew away to commence his wooing at once. It was in the early spring, when the crocus and the snowdrop were in full bloom.

"They are very pretty," thought the butterfly; "charming little lasses, but they are rather stiff and formal."

Then, as young lads often do, he looked out for the older girls. He next flew to the anemones, but these were rather sour to his taste. The violet was a little too sentimental; the lime blossoms were too small—and, besides, there was such a large family of them. The apple blossoms, though they looked like roses, bloomed to-day, but might fall off to-morrow with the first wind that blew; and he thought a marriage with one of them might last too short a time. The pea blossom pleased him most of all. She was white and red, graceful and slender, and belonged to those domestic maidens who have a pretty appearance, yet can be useful in the kitchen. He was just about to make her an offer when, close by her, he saw a pod, with a withered flower hanging at the end.

"Who is that?" he asked.

"That is my sister," replied the pea blossom.

"Oh, indeed! and you will be like her some day," said he. And at once he flew away, for he felt quite shocked.

A honeysuckle hung forth from the hedge, in full bloom; but there were so many girls like her, with long faces and sallow complexions! No, he did not like her. But which one did he like?

Spring went by, and summer drew toward its close. Autumn came, but he had not decided. The flowers now appeared in their most gorgeous robes, but all in vain—they had not the fresh, fragrant air of youth. The heart asks for fragrance even when it is no longer young, and there is very little of that to be found in the dahlias or the dry chrysanthemums. Therefore the butterfly turned to the mint on the ground. This plant, you know, has no blossom, but is sweetness all over; it is full of fragrance from head to foot, with the scent of a flower in every leaf.

"I will take her," said the butterfly; and he made her an offer. But the mint stood silent and stiff as she listened to him. At last she said:

"I can give you friendship if you like, nothing more. I am old, and you are old, but we may live for each other just the same. As to marrying, however, no! that would appear ridiculous at our age."

And so it happened that the butterfly got no wife at all. He had been too long choosing, which is always a bad plan, and became what is called an old bachelor.

It was late in the autumn, with rainy and cloudy weather. The cold wind blew over the bowed backs of the willows, so that they creaked again. It was not the weather for flying about in summer clothes, but fortunately the butterfly was not out in it. By a happy chance he had got a shelter. It was in a room heated by a stove and as warm as summer. He could live here, he said, well enough.

"But it is not enough merely to exist," said he. "I need freedom, sunshine, and a little flower for a companion."

So he flew against the window-pane and was seen and admired by those in the room, who caught him and stuck him on a pin in a box of curiosities. They could not do more for him.

"Now I am perched on a stalk like the flowers," said the butterfly. "It is not very pleasant, certainly. I imagine it is something like being married, for here I am stuck fast." And with this thought he consoled himself a little.

"That seems very poor consolation," said one of the plants in the room, that grew in a pot.

"Ah," thought the butterfly, "one can't very well trust these plants in pots; they have had too much to do with human beings."

THE GOBLIN AND THE HUCKSTER

T HERE was once a regular student, who lived in a garret and had no possessions. And there was also a regular huckster, to whom the house belonged, and who occupied the ground floor. A goblin lived with the huckster because at Christmas he always had a large dishful of jam, with a great piece of butter in the middle. The huckster could afford this, and therefore the goblin remained with him—which was very shrewd of the goblin.

One evening the student came into the shop through the back door to buy candles and cheese for himself; he had no one to send, and therefore he came himself. He obtained what he wished, and then the huckster and his wife nodded good evening to him. The huckster's wife was a woman who could do more than merely nod, for she usually had plenty to say for herself. The student nodded also, as he turned to leave, then suddenly stopped and began reading the piece of paper in which the cheese was wrapped. It was a leaf torn out of an old book; a book that ought not to have been torn up, for it was full of poetry.

"Yonder lies some more of the same sort," said the huckster. "I gave an old woman a few coffee berries for it; you shall have the rest for sixpence if you will."

"Indeed I will," said the student. "Give me the book instead of the cheese; I can eat my bread and butter without cheese. It would be a sin to tear up a book like this. You are a clever man and a practical man, but you understand no more about poetry than that cask yonder."

This was a very rude speech, especially against the cask, but the huckster and the student both laughed, for it was only said in fun. The goblin, however, felt very angry that any man should venture to say such things to a huckster who was a householder and sold the best butter. As soon as it was night, the shop closed, and every one in bed except the student, the goblin stepped softly into the bedroom where the huckster's wife slept, and took away her tongue, which of course she did not then want. Whatever object in the room he placed this tongue upon, immediately received voice and speech and was able to express its thoughts and feelings as readily as the lady herself could do. It could only be used by one object at a time, which was a good thing, as a number speaking at once would have caused great confusion. The goblin laid the tongue upon the cask, in which lay a quantity of old newspapers.

"Is it really true," he asked, "that you do not know what poetry is?"

"Of course I know," replied the cask. "Poetry is something that always stands in the corner of a newspaper and is sometimes cut out. And I may venture to affirm that I have more of it in me than the student has, even if I am only a poor tub of the huckster's."

Then the goblin placed the tongue on the coffee mill, and how it did go, to be sure! Then he put it on the butter-tub, and the cash-box, and they all expressed the same opinion as the waste-paper tub. A majority must always be respected.

"Now I shall go and tell the student," said the goblin. With these words he went quietly up the back stairs to the garret, where the student lived. The student's candle was burning still, and the goblin peeped through the keyhole and saw that he was reading in the torn book which he had bought out of the shop. But how light the room was! From the book shot forth a ray of light which grew broad and full like the stem of a tree, from which bright rays spread upward and over the student's head. Each leaf was fresh, and each flower was like a beautiful female head—some with dark and sparkling eyes and others with eyes that were wonderfully blue and clear. The fruit gleamed like stars, and the room was filled with sounds of beautiful music. The little goblin had never imagined, much less seen or heard of, any sight so glorious as this. He stood still on tiptoe, peeping in, till the light went out. The student no doubt had blown out his candle and gone to bed, but the little goblin remained standing there, listening to the music which still sounded, soft and beautiful—a sweet cradle song for the student who had lain down to rest.

"This is a wonderful place," said the goblin; "I never expected such a thing. I should like to stay here with the student." Then the little man thought it over, for he was a sensible sprite. At last he sighed, "But the student has no jam!" So he went downstairs again to the huckster's shop, and it was a good thing he got back when he did, for the cask had almost worn out the lady's tongue. He had given a description of all that he contained on one side, and was just about to turn himself over to the other side to describe what was there, when the goblin entered and restored the tongue to the lady. From that time forward, the whole shop, from the cash-box down to the pine-wood logs, formed their opinions from that of the cask. They all had such confidence in him and treated him with so much respect that when, in the evening, the huckster read the criticisms on theatricals and art, they fancied it must all come from the cask.

After what he had seen, the goblin could no longer sit and listen quietly to the wisdom and understanding downstairs. As soon as the evening light glimmered in the garret, he took courage, for it seemed to him that the rays of light were strong cables, drawing him up and obliging him to go and peep through the keyhole. While there, a feeling of vastness came over him, such as we experience by the ever-moving sea when the storm breaks forth, and it brought tears into his eyes. He did not himself know why he wept, yet a kind of pleasant feeling mingled with his tears. "How wonderfully glorious it would be to sit with the student under such a tree!" But that was out of the question; he must be content to look through the keyhole and be thankful for even that.

There he stood on the cold landing, with the autumn wind blowing down upon him through the trapdoor. It was very cold, but the little creature did not really feel it till the light in the garret went out and the tones of music died away. Then how he shivered and crept downstairs again to his warm corner, where he felt at home and comfortable! And when Christmas came again and brought the dish of jam and the great lump of butter, he liked the huckster best of all.

Soon after, the goblin was waked in the middle of the night by a terrible noise and knocking against the window shutters and the house doors and by the sound of the watchman's horn. A great fire had broken out, and the whole street seemed full of flames. Was it in their house or a neighbor's? No one could tell, for terror had seized upon all. The huckster's wife was so bewildered that she took her gold earrings out of her ears and put them in her pocket, that she might save something at least. The huckster ran to get his business papers, and the servant resolved to save her black silk mantle, which she had managed to buy. All wished to keep the best things they had. The goblin had the same wish, for with one spring he was upstairs in the student's room. He found him standing by the open window and looking quite calmly at the fire, which was raging in the house of a neighbor opposite.

The goblin caught up the wonderful book, which lay on the table, and popped it into his red cap, which he held tightly with both hands. The greatest treasure in the house was saved, and he ran away with it to the roof and seated himself on the chimney. The flames of the burning house opposite illuminated him as he sat with both hands pressed tightly over his cap, in which the treasure lay. It was then that he understood what feelings were really strongest in his heart and knew exactly which way they tended. Yet, when the fire was extinguished and the goblin again began to reflect, he hesitated, and said at last, "I must divide myself between the two; I cannot quite give up the huckster, because of the jam."

This is a representation of human nature. We are like the goblin; we all go to visit the huckster, "because of the jam."

EVERYTHING IN ITS RIGHT PLACE

ORE than a hundred years ago, behind the wood and by a deep lake, stood an old baronial mansion. Round it lay a deep moat, in which grew reeds and rushes, and close by the bridge, near the entrance gate, stood an old willow that bent itself over the moat.

From a narrow lane one day sounded the clang of horns and the trampling of horses. The little girl who kept the geese hastened to drive them away from the bridge before the hunting party came galloping up to it. They came, however, with such haste that the girl was obliged to climb up and seat herself on the parapet of the bridge, lest they should ride over her. She was scarcely more than a child, with a pretty, delicate figure, a gentle expression of face, and two bright blue eyes—all of which the baron took no note of; but as he galloped past, he reversed the whip held in his hand, and in rough play gave the little goose-watcher such a push with the butt end that she fell backward into the ditch.

"Everything in its right place," cried he. "Into the puddle with you!" and then he laughed aloud at what he called his own wit, and the rest joined with him. The whole party shouted and screamed, and the dogs barked loudly.

Fortunately for herself, the poor girl in falling caught hold of one of the overhanging branches of the willow tree, by which she was able to keep herself from falling into the muddy pool. As soon as the baron, with his company and his dogs, had disappeared through the castle gate, she tried to raise herself by her own exertions; but the bough broke off at the top, and she would have fallen backwards among the reeds if a strong hand had not at that moment seized her from above. It was the hand of a peddler, who, at a short distance, had witnessed the whole affair and hastened up to give assistance.

"Everything in its right place," he said, imitating the noble baron, as he drew the little maiden up on dry ground. He would have restored the bough to the place from which it had been broken off, but "everything in its right place" is not always so easy to arrange, so he stuck the bough in the soft earth. "Grow and prosper as much as you can," said he, "till you produce a good flute for some of them over there. With the permission of the noble baron and his family, I should like them to hear my challenge."

So he betook himself to the castle, but not into the noble hall; he was too humble for that. He went to the servants' apartments, and the men and maids examined and turned over his stock of goods, while from above, where the company were at table, came sounds of screaming and shouting which they called singing—and indeed they did their best. Loud laughter, mingled with the howling of dogs, sounded through the open windows. All were feasting and carousing. Wine and strong ale foamed in the jugs and glasses; even the dogs ate and drank with their masters. The peddler was sent for, but only to make fun for them. The wine had mounted to their heads, and the sense had flown out. They poured wine into a stocking for him to drink with them—quickly, of course—and this was considered a rare jest and occasioned fresh bursts of laughter. At cards, whole farms, with their stock of peasants and cattle, were staked on a card and lost.

"Everything in its right place," said the peddler, when he at last escaped from what he called the Sodom and Gomorrah up there. "The open highroad is my right place; that house did not suit me at all." As he stepped along, he saw the little maiden keeping watch over the geese, and she nodded to him in a friendly way.

Days and weeks passed, and it soon became evident that the willow branch which had been stuck in the ground by the peddler, near to the castle moat, had taken root, for it remained fresh and green and put forth new twigs.

The little girl saw that the branch must have taken root, and she was quite joyful about it. "This tree," she said, "must be my tree now."

The tree certainly flourished, but at the castle, what with feasting and gambling, everything went to ruin; for these two things are like rollers, upon which no man can possibly stand securely. Six years had not passed away before the noble baron wandered out of the castle gate a poor man, and the mansion was bought by a rich dealer. This dealer was no other than the man of whom he had made fun and for whom he had poured wine into a stocking to drink. But honesty and industry are like favorable winds to a ship, and they had brought the peddler to be master of the baron's estates. From that hour no more card playing was permitted there.

The new proprietor took to himself a wife, and who should it be but the little goose-watcher, who had always remained faithful and good, and who looked as beautiful and fine in her new clothes as if she had been a highly born lady. It would be too long a story in these busy times to explain how all this came about, but it really did happen, and the most important part is to come.

It was pleasant to live in the old court now. The mistress herself managed the house-keeping within, and the master superintended the estate. Their home overflowed with blessings, for where rectitude leads the way, prosperity is sure to follow. The old house was cleaned and painted, the moat dried up, and fruit trees planted in it. The floors of the house were polished as smoothly as a draftboard, and everything looked bright and cheerful.

During the long winter evenings the lady of the house sat with her maidens at the spinning wheel in the great hall. Her husband, in his old age, had been made a magistrate. Every Sunday evening he read the Bible with his family, for children had come to him and were all instructed in the best manner, although they were not all equally clever—as is the case in all families. In the meantime, the willow branch at the castle gate had grown into a splendid tree and stood free and unrestrained.

"That is our genealogical tree," said the old people, "and the tree must therefore be honored and esteemed, even by those who are not very wise."

A hundred years passed away, and the place presented a much-changed aspect. The lake had been converted into moorland, and the old baronial castle had almost disappeared. A pool of water, the deep moat, and the ruins of some of the walls were all that remained. Close by grew a magnificent willow tree, with overhanging branches—the same genealogical tree of former times. Here it still stood, showing to what beauty a willow can attain when left to itself. To be sure, the trunk was split through, from the root to the top, and the storm had slightly bent it; but it stood firm through all, and from every crevice and opening into which earth had been carried by the wind, shot forth blossoms and flowers. Near the top, where the large boughs parted, the wild raspberry twined its branches and looked like a hanging garden. Even the little mistletoe had here struck root, and flourished, graceful and delicate, among the branches of the willow, which were reflected in the dark waters beneath it. Sometimes the wind from the sea scattered the willow leaves. A path led through the field, close by the tree.

On the top of a hill, near the forest, with a splendid prospect before it, stood the new baronial hall, with panes of such transparent glass in the windows that there appeared to be none. The grand flight of steps leading to the entrance looked like a bower of roses and broad-leaved plants. The lawn was as fresh and green as if each separate blade of grass were cleaned morning and evening. In the hall hung costly pictures. The chairs and sofas were of silk and velvet and looked almost as if they could move of themselves. There were tables with white marble tops, and books bound in velvet and gold. Here, indeed, resided wealthy people, people of rank—the new baron and his family.

Each article was made to harmonize with the other furnishings. The family motto still was, "Everything in its right place." Therefore the pictures which were once the honor and glory of the old house now hung in the passage leading to the servants' hall. They were considered mere lumber; especially two old portraits, one of a man in a wig and a rose-colored coat, the other of a lady with frizzed and powdered hair, holding a rose in her hand, each surrounded by a wreath of willow leaves. Both the pictures had many holes in them, for the little barons always set up the two old people as targets for their bows and arrows; and yet these were pictures of the magistrate and his lady, from whom the present family were descended. "But they did not properly belong to our family," said one of the little barons; "he was a peddler, and she kept the geese. They were not like pa-pa and mamma." So the pictures, being old, were considered worthless; and the motto being "Each in its right place," the great-grandfather and the great-grandmother of the family were sent into the passage leading to the servants' hall.

The son of the clergyman of the place was tutor at the great house. One day he was out walking with his pupils—the little barons—and their eldest sister, who had just been confirmed. They took the path through the fields, which led past the old willow tree. While they walked, the young lady made a wreath of hedge blossoms and wild flowers, "each in its right place," and the wreath was, as a whole, very pretty. At the same time she heard every word uttered by the son of the clergyman. She liked very much to hear him talk of the wonders of nature and of the great men and women of history. She had a healthy mind, with nobility of thought and feeling, and a heart full of love for all God's creation.

The walking party halted at the old willow tree; the youngest of the barons wanted a branch from it to make a flute, as he had already made them from other willows. The tutor broke off a branch. "Oh, don't do that," exclaimed the young baroness; but it was already done. "I am so sorry," she continued; "that is our famous old tree, and I love it very much. They laugh at me for it at home, but I don't mind. There is a story told about that tree."

Then she told him what we already know: about the old castle, and about the peddler and the girl with the geese, who had met at this spot for the first time and were the ancestors of the noble family to which the young baroness belonged. "The good old folks would not be ennobled," said she. "Their motto was 'Everything in its right place,' and they thought it would not be right for them to purchase a title with money. My grandfather, the first baron, was their son. He was a very learned man, known and appreciated by princes and princesses, and was present at all the festivals at court. At home, they all love him best, but I scarcely know why. There seems to me something in the first old pair that draws my heart towards them. How sociable, how patriarchal, it must have been in the old house, where the mistress sat at the spinning wheel with her maids while her husband read aloud to them from the Bible!"

"They must have been charming, sensible people," said the tutor, and then the conversation turned upon nobles and commoners. It was almost as if the tutor did not belong to an inferior class, he spoke so wisely upon the purpose and intention of nobility.

"It is certainly good fortune to belong to a family that has distinguished itself in the world, and to inherit the energy which spurs us on to progress in everything noble and useful. It is pleasant to bear a family name that is like a card of admission to the highest circles. True nobility is always great and honorable. It is a coin which has received the impression of its own value. It is a mistake of the present day, into which many poets have fallen, to affirm that all who are noble by birth must therefore be wicked or foolish, and that the lower we descend in society the oftener we find great and shining characters. I feel that this is quite false. In all classes can be found men and women possessing kindly and beautiful traits.

"My mother told me of one, and I could tell you of many more. She was once on a visit to a nobleman's house in the town; my grandmother, I believe, had been brought up in the family. One day, when my mother and the nobleman happened to be alone, an old woman came limping into the court on crutches. She was accustomed to come every Sunday and always carried away a gift with her. 'Ah, there is the poor old woman,' said the nobleman; 'what pain it is for her to walk!' And before my mother understood what he said, he had left the room and run downstairs to the old woman. Though seventy years old himself, the old nobleman carried to the woman the gift she had come to receive, to spare her the pain of walking any farther. This is only a trifling circumstance, but, like the two mites given by the widow in the Bible, it wakes an echo in the heart.

"These are subjects of which poets should write and sing, for they soften and unite mankind into one brotherhood. But when a mere sprig of humanity, because it has noble ancestors of good blood, rears up and prances like an Arabian horse in the street or speaks contemptuously of common people, then it is nobility in danger of decay—a mere pretense, like the mask which Thespis invented. People are glad to see such persons turned into objects of satire."

This was the tutor's speech—certainly rather a long one, but he had been busily engaged in cutting the flute while he talked.

There was a large party at the Hall that evening. The grand salon was crowded with guests—some from the neighborhood, some from the capital. There was a bevy of ladies richly dressed with, and without, taste; a group of the clergy from the adjoining parishes, in a corner together, as grave as though met for a funeral. A funeral party it certainly was not, however; it was meant for a party of pleasure, but the pleasure was yet to come. Music and song filled the rooms, first one of the party volunteering, then another. The little baron brought out his flute, but neither he nor his father, who tried it after him, could make anything of it. It was pronounced a failure.

"But you are a performer, too, surely," said a witty gentleman, addressing the tutor. "You are of course a flute player as well as a flute maker. You are a universal genius, I hear, and genius is quite the rage nowadays—nothing like genius. Come now; I am sure you will be so good as to enchant us by playing on this little instrument." He handed it over, announcing in a loud voice that the tutor was going to favor the company with a solo on the flute.

It was easy to see that these people wanted to make fun of him, and he refused to play. But they pressed him so long and so urgently that at last, in very weariness, he took the flute and raised it to his lips.

It was a strange flute! A sound issued from it, loud, shrill, and vibrating, like that sent forth by a steam engine—nay, far louder. It thrilled through the house, through garden and woodland, miles out into the country; and with the sound came also a strong, rushing wind, its stormy breath clearly uttering the words, "Everything in its right place!"

Forthwith the baron, the master of the Hall, was caught up by the wind, carried out at the window, and was shut up in the porter's lodge in a trice. The porter himself was borne up, not into the drawing room—no, for that he was not fit—but into the servants' hall, where the proud lackeys in their silk stockings shook with horror to see so low a person sit at table with them.

But in the grand salon the young baroness was wafted to the seat of honor, where she was worthy to sit, and the tutor's place was by her side. There they sat together, for all the world like bride and bridegroom. An old count, descended from one of the noblest houses in the land, retained his seat, not so much as a breath of air disturbing him, for the flute was strictly just. The witty young gentleman, who had been the occasion of all this tumult, was whirled out headforemost to join geese and ganders in the poultry yard.

Half a mile out in the country the flute wrought wonders. The family of a rich merchant, who drove with four horses, were all precipitated from the carriage window. Two farmers, who had of late grown too wealthy to know their nearest relations, were puffed into a ditch. It was a dangerous flute. Luckily, at the first sound it uttered, it burst and was then put safely away in the tutor's pocket. "Everything in its right place!"

Next day no more was said about the adventure than as if it had never happened. The affair was hushed up, and all things were the same as before, except that the two old portraits of the peddler and the goose girl continued to hang on the walls of the salon,

303

whither the wind had blown them. Here some connoisseur chanced to see them, and because he pronounced them to be painted by a master hand, they were cleaned and restored and ever after held in honor. Their value had not been known before.

"Everything in its right place!" So shall it be, all in good time, never fear. Not in this world, perhaps. That would be expecting rather too much.

THE REAL PRINCESS

T HERE was once a prince who wanted to marry a princess. But she must be a real princess, mind you. So he traveled all round the world, seeking such a one, but everywhere something was in the way. Not that there was any lack of princesses, but he could not seem to make out whether they were real princesses; there was always something not quite satisfactory. Therefore, home he came again, quite out of spirits, for he wished so much to marry a real princess.

One evening a terrible storm came on. It thundered and lightened, and the rain poured down; indeed, it was quite fearful. In the midst of it there came a knock at the town gate, and the old king went out to open it.

It was a princess who stood outside. But O dear, what a state she was in from the rain and bad weather! The water dropped from her hair and clothes, it ran in at the tips of her shoes and out at the heels; yet she insisted she was a real princess.

"Very well," thought the old queen; "that we shall presently see." She said nothing, but went into the bedchamber and took off all the bedding, then laid a pea on the sacking of the bedstead. Having done this, she took twenty mattresses and laid them upon the pea and placed twenty eider-down beds on top of the mattresses.

The princess lay upon this bed all the night. In the morning she was asked how she had slept.

"Oh, most miserably!" she said. "I scarcely closed my eyes the whole night through. I cannot think what there could have been in the bed. I lay upon something so hard that I am quite black and blue all over. It is dreadful!"

It was now quite evident that she was a real princess, since through twenty mattresses and twenty eider-down beds she had felt the pea. None but a real princess could have such delicate feeling.

So the prince took her for his wife, for he knew that in her he had found a true princess. And the pea was preserved in the cabinet of curiosities, where it is still to be seen unless some one has stolen it.

And this, mind you, is a real story.

THE EMPEROR'S NEW CLOTHES

MANY years ago there was an emperor who was so fond of new clothes that he spent all his money on them. He did not give himself any concern about his army; he cared nothing about the theater or for driving about in the woods, except for the sake of showing himself off in new clothes. He had a costume for every hour in the day, and just as they say of a king or emperor, "He is in his council chamber," they said of him, "The emperor is in his dressing room."

Life was merry and gay in the town where the emperor lived, and numbers of strangers came to it every day. Among them there came one day two rascals, who gave themselves out as weavers and said that they knew how to weave the most exquisite stuff imaginable. Not only were the colors and patterns uncommonly beautiful, but the clothes that were made of the stuff had the peculiar property of becoming invisible to every person who was unfit for the office he held or who was exceptionally stupid.

"Those must be valuable clothes," thought the emperor. "By wearing them I should be able to discover which of the men in my empire are not fit for their posts. I should distinguish wise men from fools. Yes, I must order some of the stuff to be woven for me directly." And he paid the swindlers a handsome sum of money in advance, as they required.

As for them, they put up two looms and pretended to be weaving, though there was nothing whatever on their shuttles. They called for a quantity of the finest silks and of the purest gold thread, all of which went into their own bags, while they worked at their empty looms till late into the night.

"I should like to know how those weavers are getting on with the stuff," thought the emperor. But he felt a little queer when he reflected that those who were stupid or unfit for their office would not be able to see the material. He believed, indeed, that he had nothing to fear for himself, but still he thought it better to send some one else first, to see how the work was coming on. All the people in the town had heard of the peculiar property of the stuff, and every one was curious to see how stupid his neighbor might be.

"I will send my faithful old prime minister to the weavers," thought the emperor. "He will be best capable of judging of this stuff, for he is a man of sense and nobody is more fit for his office than he."

So the worthy old minister went into the room where the two swindlers sat working the empty looms. "Heaven save us!" thought the old man, opening his eyes wide. "Why, I can't see anything at all!" But he took care not to say so aloud.

Both the rogues begged him to step a little nearer and asked him if he did not think the patterns very pretty and the coloring fine. They pointed to the empty loom as they did so, and the poor old minister kept staring as hard as he could—but without being able to see anything on it, for of course there was nothing there to see.

"Heaven save us!" thought the old man. "Is it possible that I am a fool? I have never thought it, and nobody must know it. Is it true that I am not fit for my office? It will never do for me to say that I cannot see the stuffs."

"Well, sir, do you say nothing about the cloth?" asked the one who was pretending to go on with his work.

"Oh, it is most elegant, most beautiful!" said the dazed old man, as he peered again through his spectacles. "What a fine pattern, and what fine colors! I will certainly tell the emperor how pleased I am with the stuff."

"We are glad of that," said both the weavers; and then they named the colors and pointed out the special features of the pattern. To all of this the minister paid great attention, so that he might be able to repeat it to the emperor when he went back to him.

And now the cheats called for more money, more silk, and more gold thread, to be able to proceed with the weaving, but they put it all into their own pockets, and not a thread went into the stuff, though they went on as before, weaving at the empty looms.

After a little time the emperor sent another honest statesman to see how the weaving was progressing, and if the stuff would soon be ready. The same thing happened with him as with the minister. He gazed and gazed, but as there was nothing but empty looms, he could see nothing else.

"Is not this an exquisite piece of stuff?" asked the weavers, pointing to one of the looms and explaining the beautiful pattern and the colors which were not there to be seen.

"I am not stupid, I know I am not!" thought the man, "so it must be that I am not fit for my good office. It is very strange, but I must not let it be noticed." So he praised the cloth he did not see and assured the weavers of his delight in the lovely colors and the exquisite pattern. "It is perfectly charming," he reported to the emperor.

Everybody in the town was talking of the splendid cloth. The emperor thought he should like to see it himself while it was still on the loom. With a company of carefully selected men, among whom were the two worthy officials who had been there before, he went to visit the crafty impostors, who were working as hard as ever at the empty looms.

"Is it not magnificent?" said both the honest statesmen. "See, your Majesty, what splendid colors, and what a pattern!" And they pointed to the looms, for they believed that others, no doubt, could see what they did not.

"What!" thought the emperor. "I see nothing at all. This is terrible! Am I a fool? Am I not fit to be emperor? Why nothing more dreadful could happen to me!"

"Oh, it is very pretty! it has my highest approval," the emperor said aloud. He nodded with satisfaction as he gazed at the empty looms, for he would not betray that he could see nothing.

His whole suite gazed and gazed, each seeing no more than the others; but, like the emperor, they all exclaimed, "Oh, it is beautiful!" They even suggested to the emperor that he wear the splendid new clothes for the first time on the occasion of a great procession which was soon to take place.

"Splendid! Gorgeous! Magnificent!" went from mouth to mouth. All were equally delighted with the weavers' workmanship. The emperor gave each of the impostors an order of knighthood to be worn in their buttonholes, and the title Gentleman Weaver of the Imperial Court.

Before the day on which the procession was to take place, the weavers sat up the whole night, burning sixteen candles, so that people might see how anxious they were to get the emperor's new clothes ready. They pretended to take the stuff from the loom, they cut it out in the air with huge scissors, and they stitched away with needles which had no thread in them. At last they said, "Now the clothes are finished."

The emperor came to them himself with his grandest courtiers, and each of the rogues lifted his arm as if he held something, saying, "See! here are the trousers! here is the coat! here is the cloak," and so on. "It is as light as a spider's web. One would almost feel as if one had nothing on, but that is the beauty of it!"

"Yes," said all the courtiers, but they saw nothing, for there was nothing to see.

"Will your Majesty be graciously pleased to take off your clothes so that we may put on the new clothes here, before the great mirror?"

The emperor took off his clothes, and the rogues pretended to put on first one garment and then another of the new ones they had pretended to make. They pretended to fasten something round his waist and to tie on something. This they said was the train, and the emperor turned round and round before the mirror.

"How well his Majesty looks in the new clothes! How becoming they are!" cried all the courtiers in turn. "That is a splendid costume!"

"The canopy that is to be carried over your Majesty in the procession is waiting outside," said the master of ceremonies.

"Well, I am ready," replied the emperor. "Don't the clothes look well?" and he turned round and round again before the mirror, to appear as if he were admiring his new costume.

The chamberlains, who were to carry the train, stooped and put their hands near the floor as if they were lifting it; then they pretended to be holding something in the air. They would not let it be noticed that they could see and feel nothing.

So the emperor went along in the procession, under the splendid canopy, and every one in the streets said: "How beautiful the emperor's new clothes are! What a splendid train! And how well they fit!"

No one wanted to let it appear that he could see nothing, for that would prove him not fit for his post. None of the emperor's clothes had been so great a success before.

"But he has nothing on!" said a little child.

"Just listen to the innocent," said its father; and one person whispered to another what the child had said. "He has nothing on; a child says he has nothing on!"

"But he has nothing on," cried all the people. The emperor was startled by this, for he had a suspicion that they were right. But he thought, "I must face this out to the end and go on with the procession." So he held himself more stiffly than ever, and the chamber-lains held up the train that was not there at all.

GREAT CLAUS AND LITTLE CLAUS

IN A VILLAGE there once lived two men of the same name. Both of them were called Claus. But because one of them owned four horses while the other had but one, people called the one who had the four horses Big, or Great, Claus and the one who owned but a single horse Little Claus. Now I shall tell you what happened to each of them, for this is a true story.

All the days of the week Little Claus was obliged to plow for Great Claus and to lend him his one horse; then once a week, on Sunday, Great Claus helped Little Claus with his four horses, but always on a holiday.

"Hurrah!" How Little Claus would crack his whip over the five, for they were as good as his own on that one day.

The sun shone brightly, and the church bells rang merrily as the people passed by. The people were dressed in their best, with their prayer books under their arms, for they were going to church to hear the clergyman preach. They looked at Little Claus plowing with five horses, and he was so proud and merry that he cracked his whip and cried, "Gee-up, my fine horses."

"You mustn't say that," said Great Claus, "for only one of them is yours."

But Little Claus soon forgot what it was that he ought not to say, and when any one went by he would call out, "Gee-up, my fine horses."

"I must really beg you not to say that again," said Great Claus as he passed; "for if you do, I shall hit your horse on the head so that he will drop down dead on the spot, and then it will be all over with him."

"I will certainly not say it again, I promise you," said Little Claus. But as soon as any one came by, nodding good day to him, he was so pleased, and felt so grand at having five horses plowing his field, that again he cried out, "Gee-up, all my horses."

"I'll gee-up your horses for you," said Great Claus, and he caught up the tethering mallet and struck Little Claus's one horse on the head, so that it fell down dead.

"Oh, now I haven't any horse at all!" cried Little Claus, and he began to weep. But after a while he flayed the horse and hung up the skin to dry in the wind.

Then he put the dried skin into a bag, and hanging it over his shoulder, went off to the next town to sell it. He had a very long way to go and was obliged to pass through a great, gloomy wood. A dreadful storm came up. He lost his way, and before he found it again, evening was drawing on. It was too late to get to the town, and too late to get home before nightfall.

Near the road stood a large farmhouse. The shutters outside the windows were closed, but lights shone through the crevices and at the top. "They might let me stay here for the night," thought Little Claus. So he went up to the door and knocked. The door was opened by the farmer's wife, but when he explained what it was that he wanted, she told him to go away; her husband, she said, was not at home, and she could not let any strangers in.

"Then I shall have to lie out here," said Little Claus to himself, as the farmer's wife shut the door in his face.

Close to the farmhouse stood a tall haystack, and between it and the house was a small shed with a thatched roof. "I can lie up there," said Little Claus, when he saw the roof. "It will make a capital bed, but I hope the stork won't fly down and bite my legs." A stork was just then standing near his nest on the house roof.

So Little Claus climbed onto the roof of the shed and proceeded to make himself comfortable. As he turned round to settle himself, he discovered that the wooden shutters did not reach to the tops of the windows. He could look over them straight into the room, in which a large table was laid with wine, roast meat, and a fine, great fish. The farmer's wife and the sexton were sitting at the table all by themselves, and she was pouring out wine for him, while his fork was in the fish, which he seemed to like the best.

"If I could only get some too," thought Little Claus, and as he stretched his neck toward the window he spied a large, beautiful cake. Goodness! what a glorious feast they had before them.

At that moment some one came riding down the road towards the farm. It was the farmer himself, returning. He was a good man enough, but he had one very singular prejudice—he could not bear the sight of a sexton, and if he came on one he fell into a terrible rage. This was the reason that the sexton had gone to visit the farmer's wife during his absence from home and that the good wife had put before him the best she had.

When they heard the farmer they were frightened, and the woman begged the sexton to creep into a large empty chest which stood in a corner. He did so with all haste, for he well knew how the farmer felt toward a sexton. The woman hid the wine and all the good things in the oven, for if her husband were to see them, he would certainly ask why they had been provided.

"O dear!" sighed Little Claus, on the shed roof, as he saw the good things disappear.

"Is any one up there?" asked the farmer, looking up where Little Claus was. "What are you doing up there? You had better come with me into the house."

Then Little Claus told him how he had lost his way, and asked if he might have shelter for the night.

"Certainly," replied the farmer; "but the first thing is to have something to eat."

The wife received them both in a friendly way, and laid the table, bringing to it a large bowl of porridge. The farmer was hungry and ate with a good appetite. But Little Claus could not help thinking of the capital roast meat, fish, and cake, which he knew were hidden in the oven.

He had put his sack with the hide in it under the table by his feet, for, we must remember, he was on his way to the town to sell it. He did not relish the porridge, so he trod on the sack and made the dried skin squeak quite loudly.

"Hush!" said Little Claus to his bag, at the same time treading upon it again, to make it squeak much louder than before.

"Hollo! what's that you've got in your bag?" asked the farmer.

"Oh, it's a magician," said Little Claus, "and he says we needn't eat the porridge, for he has charmed the oven full of roast meat, fish, and cake."

"What?" cried the farmer, and he opened the oven with all speed and saw all the nice things the woman had hidden, but which he believed the magician had conjured up for their special benefit.

The farmer's wife did not say a word, but set the food before them; and they both made a hearty meal of the fish, the meat, and the cake. Little Claus now trod again upon his sack and made the skin squeak.

"What does he say now?" inquired the farmer.

"He says," promptly answered Little Claus, "that he has conjured up three bottles of wine, which are standing in the corner near the stove." So the woman was obliged to bring the wine which she had hidden, and the farmer and Little Claus became right merry. Would not the farmer like to have such a conjurer as Little Claus carried about in his sack?

"Can he conjure up the Evil One?" inquired the farmer. "I shouldn't mind seeing him now, when I'm in such a merry mood."

"Yes," said Little Claus, "he will do anything that I please"; and he trod on the bag till it squeaked. "You hear him answer, 'Yes, only the Evil One is so ugly that you had better not see him.'"

"Oh, I'm not afraid. What will he look like?"

"Well, he will show himself to you in the image of a sexton."

"Nay, that's bad indeed. You must know that I can't abide a sexton. However, it doesn't matter, for I know he's a demon, and I shan't mind so much. Now my courage is up! Only he mustn't come too close."

"I'll ask him about it," said Little Claus, putting his ear down as he trod close to the bag.

"What does he say?"

"He says you can go along and open the chest in the corner, and there you'll see him cowering in the dark. But hold the lid tight, so that he doesn't get out."

"Will you help me to hold the lid," asked the farmer, going along to the chest in which his wife had hidden the sexton, who was shivering with fright.

The farmer opened the lid a wee little way and peeped in. "Ha!" he cried, springing backward. "I saw him, and he looks exactly like our sexton. It was a shocking sight!"

They must needs drink after this, and there they sat till far into the night.

315

"You must sell me your conjurer," said the farmer. "Ask anything you like for him. Nay, I'll give you a bushel of money for him."

"No, I can't do that," said Little Claus. "You must remember how much benefit I can get from such a conjurer."

"Oh, but I should so like to have him!" said the farmer, and he went on begging for him.

"Well," said Little Claus at last, "since you have been so kind as to give me a night's shelter, I won't say nay. You must give me a bushel of money, only I must have it full to the brim."

"You shall have it," said the farmer; "but you must take that chest away with you. I won't have it in the house an hour longer. You could never know that he might not still be inside."

So Little Claus gave his sack with the dried hide of the horse in it and received a full bushel of money in return, and the measure was full to the brim. The farmer also gave him a large wheelbarrow, with which to take away the chest and the bushel of money.

"Good-by," said Little Claus, and off he went with his money and the chest with the sexton in it.

On the other side of the forest was a wide, deep river, whose current was so strong that it was almost impossible to swim against it. A large, new bridge had just been built over it, and when they came to the middle of the bridge Little Claus said in a voice loud enough to be heard by the sexton: "What shall I do with this stupid old chest? It might be full of paving stones, it is so heavy. I am tired of wheeling it. I'll just throw it into the river. If it floats down to my home, well and good; if not, I don't care. It will be no great matter." And he took hold of the chest and lifted it a little, as if he were going to throw it into the river.

"No, no! let be!" shouted the sexton. "Let me get out."

"Ho!" said Little Claus, pretending to be frightened. "Why, he is still inside. Then I must heave it into the river to drown him."

"Oh, no, no, no!" shouted the sexton; "I'll give you a whole bushelful of money if you'll let me out."

"Oh, that's another matter," said Little Claus, opening the chest. He pushed the empty chest into the river and then went home with the sexton to get his bushelful of money. He had already had one from the farmer, you know, so now his wheelbarrow was quite full of money.

"I got a pretty fair price for that horse, I must admit," said he to himself, when he got home and turned the money out of the wheelbarrow into a heap in the middle of the floor. "What a rage Great Claus will be in when he discovers how rich I am become through my one horse. But I won't tell him just how it happened." So he sent a boy to Great Claus to borrow a bushel measure.

"What can he want with it?" thought Great Claus, and he rubbed some tallow on the bottom so that some part of whatever was measured might stick to it. And so it did, for when the measure came back, three new silver threepenny bits were sticking to it.

"What's this!" said Great Claus, and he ran off at once to Little Claus. "Where on earth did you get all this money?" he asked.

"Oh, that's for my horse's skin. I sold it yesterday morning."

"That was well paid for, indeed," said Great Claus. He ran home, took an ax, and hit all his four horses on the head; then he flayed them and carried their skins off to the town.

"Hides! hides! who'll buy my hides?" he cried through the streets.

All the shoemakers and tanners in the town came running up and asked him how much he wanted for his hides.

"A bushel of money for each," said Great Claus.

"Are you mad?" they all said. "Do you think we have money by the bushel?"

"Skins! skins! who'll buy them?" he shouted again, and the shoemakers took up their straps, and the tanners their leather aprons, and began to beat Great Claus.

"Hides! hides!" they called after him. "Yes, we'll hide you and tan you. Out of the town with him," they shouted. And Great Claus made the best haste he could to get out of the town, for he had never yet been thrashed as he was being thrashed now.

"Little Claus shall pay for this," he said, when he got home. "I'll kill him for it."

Little Claus's old grandmother had just died in his house. She had often been harsh and unkind to him, but now that she was dead he felt quite grieved. He took the dead woman and laid her in his warm bed to see if she would not come to life again. He himself intended to sit in a corner all night. He had slept that way before.

As he sat there in the night, the door opened and in came Great Claus with his ax. He knew where Little Claus's bed stood, and he went straight to it and hit the dead grandmother a blow on the forehead, thinking it was Little Claus.

"Just see if you'll make a fool of me again," said he, and then he went home.

"What a bad, wicked man he is!" said Little Claus. "He was going to kill me. What a good thing that poor grandmother was dead already! He would have taken her life."

He now dressed his grandmother in her best Sunday clothes, borrowed a horse of his neighbor, harnessed it to a cart, and set his grandmother on the back seat, so that she could not fall when the cart moved. Then he started off through the woods. When the sun rose, he was just outside a big inn, and he drew up his horse and went in to get something to eat.

The landlord was a very rich man and a very good man, but he was hot-tempered, as if he were made of pepper and snuff. "Good morning!" said he to Little Claus; "you have your best clothes on very early this morning."

"Yes," said Little Claus, "I'm going to town with my old grandmother. She's sitting out there in the cart; I can't get her to come in. Won't you take her out a glass of beer? You'll have to shout at her, she's very hard of hearing."

"Yes, that I'll do," said the host, and he poured a glass and went out with it to the dead grandmother, who had been placed upright in the cart.

"Here is a glass of beer your son has sent," said the landlord but she sat quite still and said not a word.

"Don't you hear?" cried he as loud as he could. "Here is a glass of beer from your son."

But the dead woman replied not a word, and at last he became quite angry and threw the beer in her face—and at that moment she fell backwards out of the cart, for she was only set upright and not bound fast.

"Now!" shouted Little Claus, as he rushed out of the inn and seized the landlord by the neck, "you have killed my grandmother! Just look at the big hole in her forehead!"

"Oh! what a misfortune!" cried the man, "and all because of my quick temper. Good Little Claus, I will pay you a bushel of money, and I will have your poor grandmother buried as if she were my own, if only you will say nothing about it. Otherwise I shall have my head cut off—and that is so dreadful."

So Little Claus again received a whole bushel of money, and the landlord buried the old grandmother as if she had been his own.

When Little Claus got home again with all his money, he immediately sent his boy to Great Claus to ask to borrow his bushel measure.

"What!" said Great Claus, "is he not dead? I must go and see about this myself." So he took the measure over to Little Claus himself.

"I say, where did you get all that money?" asked he, his eyes big and round with amazement at what he saw.

"It was grandmother you killed instead of me," said Little Claus. "I have sold her and got a bushel of money for her."

"That's being well paid, indeed," said Great Claus, and he hurried home, took an ax and killed his own old grandmother.

He then put her in a carriage and drove off to the town where the apothecary lived, and asked him if he would buy a dead person.

"Who is it and where did you get him?" asked the apothecary.

"It is my grandmother, and I have killed her so as to sell her for a bushel of money."

"Heaven preserve us!" cried the apothecary. "You talk like a madman. Pray don't say such things, you may lose your head." And he told him earnestly what a horribly wicked thing he had done, and that he deserved punishment. Great Claus was so frightened that he rushed out of the shop, jumped into his cart, whipped up his horse, and galloped home through the wood. The apothecary and all the people who saw him thought he was mad, and so they let him drive away.

"You shall be paid for this!" said Great Claus, when he got out on the highroad. "You shall be paid for this, Little Claus!"

Directly after he got home, Great Claus took the biggest sack he could find and went over to Little Claus.

"You have deceived me again," he said. "First I killed my horses, and then my old grandmother. That is all your fault; but you shall never have the chance to trick me again." And he seized Little Claus around the body and thrust him into the sack; then he threw the sack over his back, calling out to Little Claus, "Now I'm going to the river to drown you."

It was a long way that he had to travel before he came to the river, and Little Claus was not light to carry. The road came close to the church, and the people within were singing beautifully. Great Claus put down his sack, with Little Claus in it, at the church door. He thought it would be a very good thing to go in and hear a psalm before he went further, for Little Claus could not get out. So he went in.

"O dear! O dear!" moaned Little Claus in the sack, and he turned and twisted, but found it impossible to loosen the cord. Then there came by an old drover with snow-white hair and a great staff in his hand. He was driving a whole herd of cows and oxen before him, and they jostled against the sack in which Little Claus was confined, so that it was upset.

"O dear," again sighed Little Claus, "I'm so young to be going directly to the kingdom of heaven!"

"And I, poor fellow," said the drover, "am so old already, and cannot get there yet."

"Open the sack," cried Little Claus, "and creep into it in my place, and you'll be there directly."

"With all my heart," said the drover, and he untied the sack for Little Claus, who crept out at once. "You must look out for the cattle now," said the old man, as he crept in. Then Little Claus tied it up and went his way, driving the cows and the oxen.

In a little while Great Claus came out of the church. He took the sack upon his shoulders and thought as he did so that it had certainly grown lighter since he had put it down, for the old cattle-drover was not more than half as heavy as Little Claus.

"How light he is to carry now! That must be because I have heard a psalm in the church."

He went on to the river, which was both deep and broad, threw the sack containing the old drover into the water, and called after him, thinking it was Little Claus, "Now lie there! You won't trick me again!"

He turned to go home, but when he came to the place where there was a crossroad he met Little Claus driving his cattle.

"What's this?" cried he. "Haven't I drowned you?"

"Yes," said Little Claus, "you threw me into the river, half an hour ago."

"But where did you get all those fine cattle?" asked Great Claus.

"These beasts are sea cattle," said Little Claus, "and I thank you heartily for drowning me, for now I'm at the top of the tree. I'm a very rich man, I can tell you. But I was frightened when you threw me into the water huddled up in the sack. I sank to the bottom immediately, but I did not hurt myself, for the grass is beautifully soft down there. I fell upon it, and the sack was opened, and the most beautiful maiden in snow-white garments and a green wreath upon her hair took me by the hand, and said to me, 'Have you come, Little Claus? Here are cattle for you, and a mile further up the road there is another herd!'

"Then I saw that she meant the river and that it was the highway for the sea folk. Down at the bottom of it they walk directly from the sea, straight into the land where the river ends. Lovely flowers and beautiful fresh grass were there. The fishes which swam there glided about me like birds in the air. How nice the people were, and what fine herds of cattle there were, pasturing on the mounds and about the ditches!"

"But why did you come up so quickly then?" asked Great Claus. "I shouldn't have done that if it was so fine down there."

"Why, that was just my cunning. You know, I told you that the mermaid said there was a whole herd of cattle for me a mile further up the stream. Well, you see, I know how the river bends this way and that, and how long a distance it would have been to go that way. If you can come up on the land and take the short cuts, driving across fields and down to the river again, you save almost half a mile and get the cattle much sooner."

"Oh, you are a fortunate man!" cried Great Claus. "Do you think I could get some sea cattle if I were to go down to the bottom of the river?"

"I'm sure you would," said Little Claus. "But I cannot carry you. If you will walk to the river and creep into a sack yourself, I will help you into the water with a great deal of pleasure."

"Thanks!" said Great Claus. "But if I do not find sea cattle there, I shall beat you soundly, you may be sure."

"Oh! do not be so hard on me."

And so they went together to the river. When the cows and oxen saw the water, they ran to it as fast as they could. "See how they hurry!" cried Little Claus. "They want to get back to the bottom again."

"Yes, but help me first or I'll thrash you," said Great Claus. He then crept into a big sack, which had been lying across the back of one of the cows. "Put a big stone in or I'm afraid I shan't sink."

"Oh, that'll be all right," said Little Claus, but he put a big stone into the sack and gave it a push. Plump! and there lay Great Claus in the river. He sank at once to the bottom.

"I'm afraid he won't find the cattle," said Little Claus. Then he drove homeward with his herd.

Also from Benediction Books ...
Wandering Between Two Worlds: Essays on Faith and Art
Anita Mathias
Benediction Books, 2007
152 pages
ISBN: 0955373700

Available from www.amazon.com, www.amazon.co.uk

In these wide-ranging lyrical essays, Anita Mathias writes, in lush, lovely prose, of her naughty Catholic childhood in Jamshedpur, India; her large, eccentric family in Mangalore, a sea-coast town converted by the Portuguese in the sixteenth century; her rebellion and atheism as a teenager in her Himalayan boarding school, run by German missionary nuns, St. Mary's Convent, Nainital; and her abrupt religious conversion after which she entered Mother Teresa's convent in Calcutta as a novice. Later rich, elegant essays explore the dualities of her life as a writer, mother, and Christian in the United States-- Domesticity and Art, Writing and Prayer, and the experience of being "an alien and stranger" as an immigrant in America, sensing the need for roots.

About the Author

Anita Mathias is the author of *Wandering Between Two Worlds: Essays on Faith and Art.* She has a B.A. and M.A. in English from Somerville College, Oxford University, and an M.A. in Creative Writing from the Ohio State University, USA. Anita won a National Endowment of the Arts fellowship in Creative Nonfiction in 1997. She lives in Oxford, England with her husband, Roy, and her daughters, Zoe and Irene.

Visit Anita at http://www.anitamathias.com.

The Church Thad Had Too Much
Anita Mathias
Benediction Books, 2010
52 pages
ISBN: 9781849026567

Available from www.amazon.com, www.amazon.co.uk

The Church That Had Too Much was very well-intentioned. She wanted to love God, she wanted to love people, but she was both hampered by her muchness and the abundance of her possessions, and beset by ambition, power struggles and snobbery. Read about the surprising way The Church That Had Too Much began to resolve her problems in this deceptively simple and enchanting fable.

About the Author

Anita Mathias is the author of *Wandering Between Two Worlds: Essays on Faith and Art.* She has a B.A. and M.A. in English from Somerville College, Oxford University, and an M.A. in Creative Writing from the Ohio State University, USA. Anita won a National Endowment of the Arts fellowship in Creative Nonfiction in 1997. She lives in Oxford, England with her husband, Roy, and her daughters, Zoe and Irene.

Visit Anita at http://www.anitamathias.com

Francesco, Artist of Florence: The Man Who Gave Too Much
Anita Mathias
Benediction Books, 2014
52 pages (full colour)
ISBN: 978-1781394175

In this lavishly illustrated book by Anita Mathias, Francesco, artist of Florence, creates magic in pietre dure, inlaying precious stones in marble in life-like "paintings." While he works, placing lapis lazuli birds on clocks, and jade dragonflies on vases, he is purely happy. However, he must sell his art to support his family. Francesco, who is incorrigibly soft-hearted, cannot stand up to his haggling customers. He ends up almost giving away an exquisite jewellery box to Signora Farnese's bambina, who stands, captivated, gazing at a jade parrot nibbling a cherry. Signora Stallardi uses her daughter's wedding to cajole him into discounting his rainbowed marriage chest. His old friend Girolamo bullies him into letting him have the opulent table he hoped to sell to the Medici almost at cost. Carrara is raising the price of marble; the price of gems keeps rising. His wife is in despair. Francesco fears ruin.

* * *

Sitting in the church of Santa Maria Novella at Mass, very worried, Francesco hears the words of Christ. The lilies of the field and the birds of the air do not worry, yet their Heavenly Father looks after them. As He will look after us. He resolves not to worry. And as he repeats the prayer the Saviour taught us, Francesco resolves to forgive the friends and neighbours who repeatedly put their own interests above his. But can he forgive himself for his own weakness, as he waits for the eternal city of gold whose walls are made of jasper, whose gates are made of pearls, and whose foundations are sapphire, emerald, ruby and amethyst? There time and money shall be no more, the lion shall live with the lamb, and we shall dwell trustfully together. Francesco leaves Santa Maria Novella, resolving to trust the One who told him to live like the lilies and the birds, deciding to forgive those who haggled him into bad bargains--while making a little resolution for the future

www.ingramcontent.com/pod-product-compliance
Lightning Source LLC
Chambersburg PA
CBHW080731250626
47170CB00010B/2795